North America

This edition published 2025
by Living Book Press
Copyright © Living Book Press, 2025

ISBN: 978-1-76153-808-7 (hardcover)
       978-1-76153-794-3 (softcover)

First published in 1922.

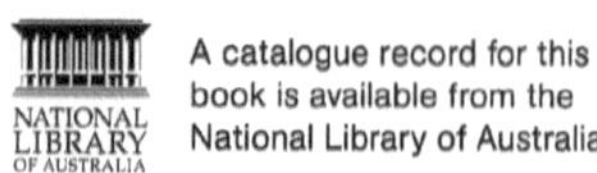

North America

by

NELLIE BURNHAM ALLEN

FOR BEAUTY OF SCENERY, FOR ENJOYMENT OF NATURE, NO CONTINENT
EXCELS OUR OWN

Contents

PREFACE

The socialized recitation, with its projects and problems, is doubtless the most democratic form of classwork that has ever been practiced in our schools. Geography lends itself more readily, perhaps, than any other subject to this method of teaching. In these pages, many problems are brought up, many subjects for class debate suggested, and many opportunities given for independent work on the part of the pupils. It is through such activities that self-reliance is developed and real strength and knowledge are gained.

In former days, people were accustomed to think of schools as places where children were prepared for real life. We know today that life and activities in a classroom are just as real to the child as any which will come to him later. With this thought in mind, the author has made many suggestions for doing real things, writing real letters, making real comparisons, building up a real reference library, using public-library facilities and reference books, and learning firsthand many of the lines of work of the various departments of government.

The people in the different countries of North America are our nearest world neighbors. We should know as intimately as possible their life and activities and the provisions of nature which govern them. There is a mutual dependence between people of different localities for many materials and products. If troubles and misunderstandings arise, the interchange of commodities is retarded, and inconvenience or suffering results. One of the best ways of preventing such troubles is by increasing our knowledge of peoples in other countries. The study of our

North American neighbors may well result in a greater confidence and a more intimate relationship between them and us.

The effect of environment on the life and occupations of a people and the gifts of nature in soil, climate, minerals, power, and other resources should be emphasized as the underlying foundation of human activities. Therefore, regional geography has been made the basis of the various chapters in this book.

The value of locational geography is well known, and exercises for the location of places, sketching and filling in of maps, and other forms of handwork are included in the topics at the end of the chapters. From the names of places mentioned in the text of each chapter, the most important should be selected, and their locations and the most essential facts concerning them should be thoroughly mastered.

The subject of geography affords an opportunity for the teacher to stimulate the reasoning power of his pupils, broaden their outlook, develop their knowledge of and sympathy for other peoples of the world, create respect for our government among our girls and boys, and cultivate a love for our country, along with a sense of responsibility for its future growth and prosperity.

The author hopes that the teachers and pupils who use this book may find therein material that will help in accomplishing these ends.

NELLIE B. ALLEN

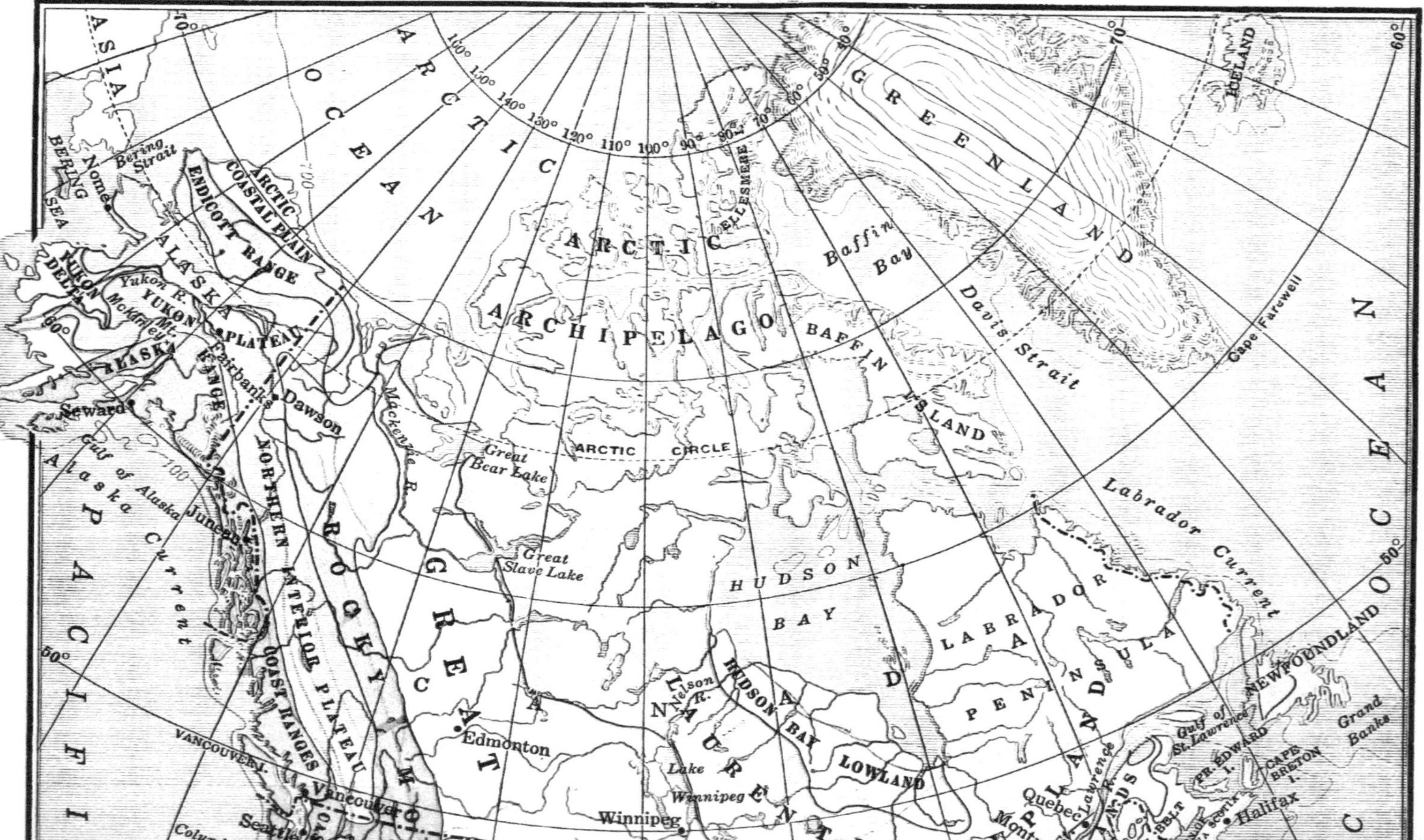
ASIA
ARCTIC OCEAN
BERING SEA
Nome
Bering Strait
YUKON DELTA
Yukon R.
Mt. McKinley
YUKON PLATEAU
ALASKA
ALASKA RANGE
Fairbanks
Dawson
Seward
Gulf of Alaska
Juneau
Alaska Current
ARCTIC COASTAL PLAIN
ENDICOTT RANGE
ROCKY MTS.
NORTHERN INTERIOR PLATEAU
COAST RANGES
VANCOUVER I.
Vancouver I.
Seattle
Columbia R.
PACIFIC
GREENLAND
ICELAND
Cape Farewell
Davis Strait
Baffin Bay
ELLESMERE
ARCTIC ARCHIPELAGO
BAFFIN ISLAND
ARCTIC CIRCLE
Mackenzie R.
Great Bear Lake
Great Slave Lake
GREAT
HUDSON BAY
Nelson R.
HUDSON BAY LOWLAND
LAURENTIA
Edmonton
Lake Winnipeg
Winnipeg
Labrador Current
LABRADOR PENINSULA
OCEAN
NEWFOUNDLAND
Grand Banks
Gulf of St. Lawrence
St. Lawrence
PR. EDWARD I.
CAPE BRETON I.
N. S.
Quebec
Montreal
Halifax

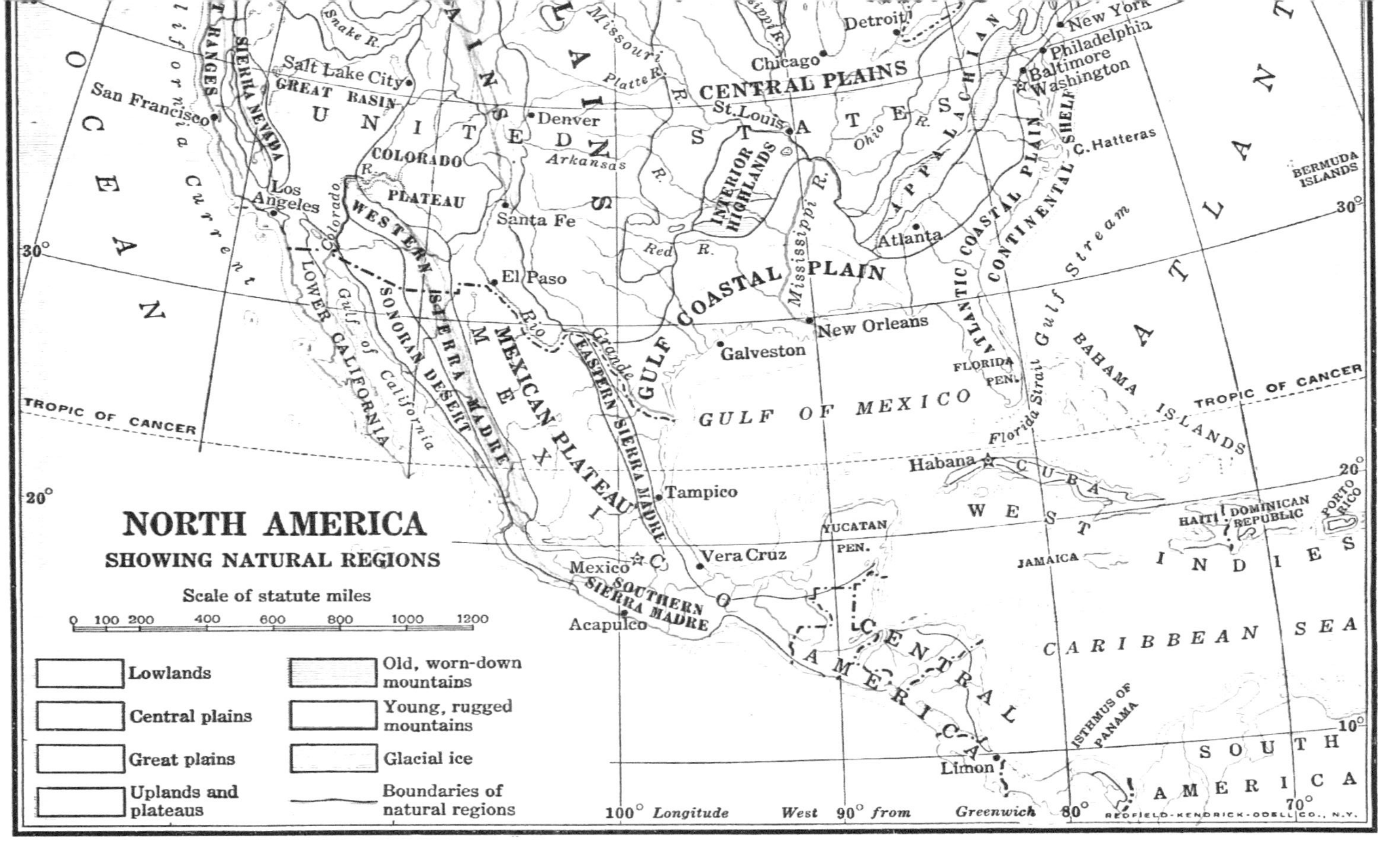

NORTH AMERICA
SHOWING NATURAL REGIONS
Scale of statute miles
0 100 200 400 600 800 1000 1200
Lowlands
Central plains
Great plains
Uplands and plateaus
Old, worn-down mountains
Young, rugged mountains
Glacial ice
Boundaries of natural regions
OCEAN
San Francisco
SIERRA NEVADA
T RANGES
California Current
Salt Lake City
GREAT BASIN
Snake R.
Los Angeles
COLORADO PLATEAU
WESTERN SIERRA MADRE
LOWER CALIFORNIA
Gulf of California
SONORAN DESERT
Colorado R.
UNITED
Denver
Santa Fe
El Paso
Arkansas
Platte R.
Missouri
Red R.
Rio Grande
EASTERN SIERRA MADRE
MEXICAN PLATEAU
M E X I C O
Mexico
SOUTHERN SIERRA MADRE
Acapulco
Tampico
Vera Cruz
CENTRAL PLAINS
Chicago
St. Louis
Detroit
Mississippi R.
Ohio R.
INTERIOR HIGHLANDS
GULF COASTAL PLAIN
Galveston
New Orleans
GULF OF MEXICO
APPALACHIAN
Atlanta
ATLANTIC COASTAL PLAIN
CONTINENTAL SHELF
C. Hatteras
New York
Philadelphia
Baltimore
Washington
BERMUDA ISLANDS
ATLANTIC
Gulf Stream
Florida Strait
FLORIDA PEN.
BAHAMA ISLANDS
TROPIC OF CANCER
Habana
CUBA
WEST INDIES
HAITI
DOMINICAN REPUBLIC
PORTO RICO
JAMAICA
YUCATAN PEN.
CARIBBEAN SEA
CENTRAL AMERICA
Limon
ISTHMUS OF PANAMA
SOUTH AMERICA
100° Longitude   West   90° from   Greenwich   80°   70°
REDFIELD-KENDRICK-ODELL CO., N.Y.
30°   20°   10°

ACKNOWLEDGMENTS

In the preparation of this book, thanks are due to the following people and institutions whose help, in the shape of suggestions, criticisms, photographs, and other material, has been most valuable to the author: Akron Chamber of Commerce; American Woolen Company; Asbestos Corporation of Canada, Ltd.; Dr. Wallace W. Atwood, Clark University; boards of trade in many Canadian cities; Boston, Cape Cod, and New York Canal Company; Canadian Pacific Railroad; E. R. Brow, Charlottetown, P.E.I.; De Laval Separator Company; Denver and Rio Grande Railroad; departments of government of the Canadian provinces; departments of the federal and state governments of the United States; Fitchburg Public Library; Ford Motor Company; members of the staff of Ginn and Company; International Harvester Company; Lothrop, Lee & Shepard, for permission to use a quotation from one of their publications; Mexican Embassy, Washington, D.C.; Mississippi River Power Company; Mond Nickel Company, Ltd.; New York Central Railroad; Omaha Chamber of Commerce; Pan-American Union; Royal Geographical Society, London; Miss Corina Rodriguez y Lopez, North Western College, Naperville, Illinois; Seattle Chamber of Commerce; Waltham Watch Company; G. R. Weeks, editor of the *Mexican Review,* Washington, D.C.

CHAPTER I

INTRODUCTION

We live in North America; that is one reason why we should know a great deal about this continent. It is one of the most important land masses on the earth. The countries of which it is composed supply many products and manufactured goods to other countries; their people are found in every country in the world; the influence of their schools, hospitals, churches, government, and other institutions has spread into every continent, country, and island on the face of the earth, - these are other reasons why we should know a great deal about the countries, people, and occupations of the continent on which we live.

Some of the countries of North America are much richer and more prosperous than others, and it is well for us to know the reasons for this. Our own country is rich and powerful. This is a fine thing, and we are glad that it is true; but this is not enough — we should know the reasons why it is so. We should know also how we are using our riches and strength. So, you see, this great wealth and power of our own United States become a responsibility which every man and woman and every boy and girl in the

FIG 1. This is one of our Canadian neighbors. His father owns a fox farm.

country must share. We must always uphold the best things, or we shall put our country to shame.

In the chapters which follow, we shall see the people of the United States, Alaska, Canada, Mexico, Central America, and the neighboring islands at work and at play. We shall visit their farms, their factories, and their homes. We shall learn that the kind of region where they make their homes determines to a large extent what they shall do and how they shall live.

In the western part of North America, stretching from Alaska in the north to Panama in the south, lies the lofty Rocky Mountain Highland. To the west of it are great plateaus made dry and barren by the wall of mountains on either side: the Rockies on the east and the Sierra Nevada and Cascade Mountains on the west. All through these western highlands, nature has stored treasures of gold, silver, and copper.

Still nearer the Pacific lie those wonderfully fertile valleys of California, Oregon, Washington, and British Columbia. Here

FIG 2. These Indian neighbors live in northern Canada, on the plains near the great Mackenzie River. Describe their home.

are raised delicious fruits which make one's mouth water to think of. In these regions, also, are vast stretches of deep forests wherein grow the largest trees on the continent.

East of the Rocky Mountain Highland are high, dry, treeless plains where cattle and sheep feed. Most of the rain that might be brought to these plains by the westerly winds is shut out by the Rocky Mountain wall. Here, as in the regions farther west, people have done wonderful work in irrigating some of these dry lands and transforming them into fertile farms.

To the east of the Great Plains lie the marvelous Central Plains of North America — fertile, level, rich beyond measure in their farms, pastures, minerals, and cities. Deprived of this region, we would suffer hunger, our factories would have little or no coal, our mills would lie idle, our railroads would lack freight, and our exports to other countries would cease.

Still traveling eastward, we should next climb the Appalachian Highlands, or, if in Canada, the lower hills of the ancient Laurentian Upland. How different these mountain regions

FIG 3. Here is a nestful of our Indian neighbors in the West. (Courtesy of the Department of the Interior)

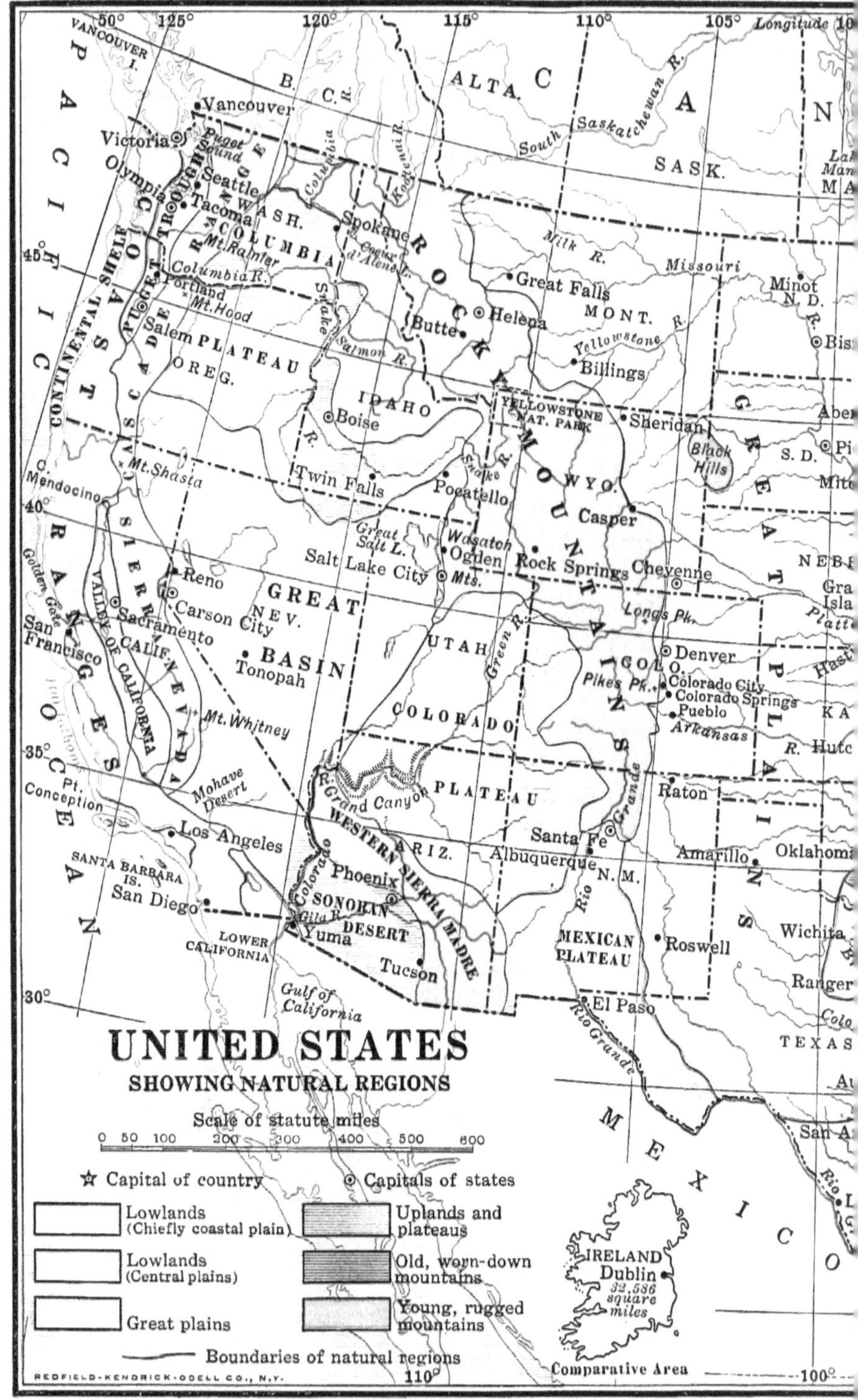

PACIFIC OCEAN
VANCOUVER I.
Vancouver
Victoria
Puget Sound
Olympia
Seattle
Tacoma
WASH.
Mt. Rainier
COLUMBIA
Columbia R.
Portland
Mt. Hood
Salem
OREG.
PLATEAU
CASCADE RANGE
PUGET TROUGH
CONTINENTAL SHELF
Mt. Shasta
C. Mendocino
SIERRA NEVADA
VALLEY OF CALIFORNIA
San Francisco
Golden Gate
Sacramento
Carson City
Reno
CALIF.
NEV.
Tonopah
Mt. Whitney
Pt. Conception
SANTA BARBARA IS.
Los Angeles
Mohave Desert
San Diego
LOWER CALIFORNIA
Gulf of California
Colorado R.
Yuma
Gila R.
Phoenix
SONORAN DESERT
Tucson
WESTERN SIERRA MADRE
ARIZ.
Grand Canyon
PLATEAU
Great Salt L.
Salt Lake City
GREAT
BASIN
NEV.
UTAH
COLORADO
Spokane
Coeur d'Alene
ROCKY
IDAHO
Boise
Snake R.
Salmon R.
Twin Falls
Pocatello
Snake R.
YELLOWSTONE NAT. PARK
MOUNTAINS
WYO.
Wasatch Mts.
Ogden
Rock Springs
Green R.
Casper
ALTA.
CANADA
South Saskatchewan R.
Saskatchewan R.
SASK.
Milk R.
Great Falls
MONT.
Helena
Butte
Billings
Yellowstone R.
Missouri R.
Sheridan
Black Hills
S. D.
Longs Pk.
Cheyenne
COLO.
Denver
Pikes Pk.
Colorado City
Colorado Springs
Pueblo
Arkansas
Longitude
N. D.
Minot
Bis
La Man
MA
Aber
Pi
Mitc
NEBR.
Gra
Isla
Platt
KA
R. Hutc
GREAT PLAINS
Raton
Santa Fe
N. M.
Albuquerque
Amarillo
Oklahoma
MEXICAN PLATEAU
Roswell
Wichita
Ranger
Colo
El Paso
Rio Grande
Rio Grande
TEXAS
Au
San A
Rio
MEXICO
IRELAND
Dublin
32,586 square miles
UNITED STATES
SHOWING NATURAL REGIONS
Scale of statute miles
0 50 100 200 300 400 500 600
Capital of country
Capitals of states
Lowlands (Chiefly coastal plain)
Uplands and plateaus
Lowlands (Central plains)
Old, worn-down mountains
Great plains
Young, rugged mountains
Boundaries of natural regions
Comparative Area
REDFIELD-KENDRICK-ODELL CO., N.Y.
110
100°

© Ginn and Company

FIG 4. These are some of our little Chinese neighbors who live
in the largest city of the world. Where is this city located?

are, with their low, rounded peaks and gentle slopes, from the
younger, higher mountains in the West, with their sharp, jagged
summits and precipitous sides.

In these eastern highlands, valuable minerals are found —
not as much gold, silver, and copper as in the West, but coal,
iron, nickel, and asbestos.

Beyond the eastern slopes of the Appalachians, the level
Coastal Plain, with its clay beds, fruit and vegetable farms, pine
woods, and drowned valleys, stretches down to the Atlantic
Ocean. Here are situated great seaports, to which come all manner of necessities and luxuries from countries across the water.
From these ports, and from those on the western and southern
coasts, go the meat, grain, cotton, oil, furs, and lumber, as well

as flour, cloth, shoes, machinery, and hundreds of other things which the people of North America have worked to produce.

We must not forget that nature has had a great deal to do with filling our factories and stores and our ships. Her rich gifts make possible our products and manufactures, and therefore our exports to other countries. Her agents have accomplished wonderful things in building up, wearing down, and changing the face of this old earth of ours. Her book is an interesting one. She has written her stories in the soil, the rock, and the rivers, and anyone with sharp eyes, keen ears, and an alert mind may read and profit thereby.

The author wonders as she writes these pages what work in the world the boys and girls who read them will do. Some of them will doubtless be factory workers, helping to feed or clothe or make more comfortable, in some way, the lives of their world neighbors. Some will work in the great outdoors — in forests or fields — and their work will help in supplying materials which others must use. Some will help sail the great ships over the ocean, build bridges, dig tunnels, work in mines, in crowded cities with thousands of others, or alone on grassy plains or lonely mountains. Wherever you are, remember that your work always counts for something, that you are helping to make the world better or worse according to how well or ill your work is done. Neglect or failure to do your best hurts not only yourself but also others whom you may never have seen.

TOPICS FOR STUDY

1. Name the countries of North America. Which is the largest? the smallest? the most northern? the most southern? How many of them touch two oceans? Does any one touch more than two oceans?
2. Name all the reasons you can think of that have caused the United States to become rich and powerful. Name some of her riches. Why does she excel Canada and Mexico in these respects?
3. What have you done or what has your school done to make your hometown or city a better place to live? Can you think of any other things worth doing?

CHAPTER II

A TRIP THROUGH NEW ENGLAND

New England is an interesting section of our country — interesting in its formation, its industries, its history, and in the spirit of its people. Here in 1620, the Pilgrims first set foot. Here our earliest industries — fishing, farming, lumbering, and manufacturing — developed, and from here pioneers have traveled to all parts of the United States and to Canada and Alaska, settling new regions, building new towns, and developing new industries.

The six states in the northeastern corner of the country comprise only one forty-fifth of the entire area of the United States, yet they contain one fourteenth of its population. Nowhere else in the country are there so many cities and towns so closely clustered together. Nowhere else is there such a large proportion of the people living in mill towns and manufacturing centers, and nowhere else is there such an amount and so great a variety of goods manufactured in so small an area.

New England produces no coal for its furnaces, no gold and silver or iron and copper for its metal manufactures, no cotton and but little wool for its textile mills. Why is it, then, that New England has become so thickly populated and so important in manufacturing? Let us keep this problem in mind and see if we can find at least a part of the answer as we read of the position, surface, rivers, coastline, climate, and other factors on which the life and occupations of a people depend.

Look at the map and notice that New England lies nearer to European countries than any other part of the United States. This fact alone has tended to stimulate commerce between the lands on either side of the ocean. Here, then, is the first part of the answer to our problem.

Look again at the map. Notice how many bays and inlets there are in New England. Can you find a coast as irregular as that of Maine? The sheltered inlets make excellent harbors. These are necessary before any region can develop to any great extent. Here is another part of the answer to our problem.

Perhaps you are wondering why it is that New England has such an irregular coastline while the South Atlantic coast and most of the Pacific is so much more even. We shall find the answer to this question in Mother Nature's storybook. Let us see what she has to tell us.

Ages and ages ago, this earth on which we live was an intensely heated ball. Through a longer period of time than you can imagine — even for millions of years — it has gradually been growing cooler. The outside, the part on which we live, has become cold and hard. This cooled and hardened crust is many miles thick. The hot water from geysers, the melted rock from erupting volcanoes, the heat in deep mines, tell us that the interior of the earth is still very hot. It is slowly cooling, however, and shrinking as it cools. The crust is constantly trying to adjust itself to the shrinking interior much as the skin of a baked apple wrinkles as it cools. In places, the earth's crust has been pushed up into huge wrinkles which we call mountains. In some places, the crust is slowly rising; in others, it is as gradually sinking.

These movements take place very, very slowly indeed, perhaps at the rate of only a few inches a year, but as the long centuries go by, great changes are wrought. The sinking of the crust is more noticeable along the shorelines, for there the ocean waters push up farther into the land, fill the river valleys, and change them into deep bays. Narragansett Bay, Buzzards Bay, and Penobscot Bay are drowned valleys made in this way.

In Maine, the hilly region came close to the shore. With the sinking of the land, the valleys were filled with water, and in many cases, the mountain tops appear as islands. The deep bays make excellent harbors, but many lighthouses are needed

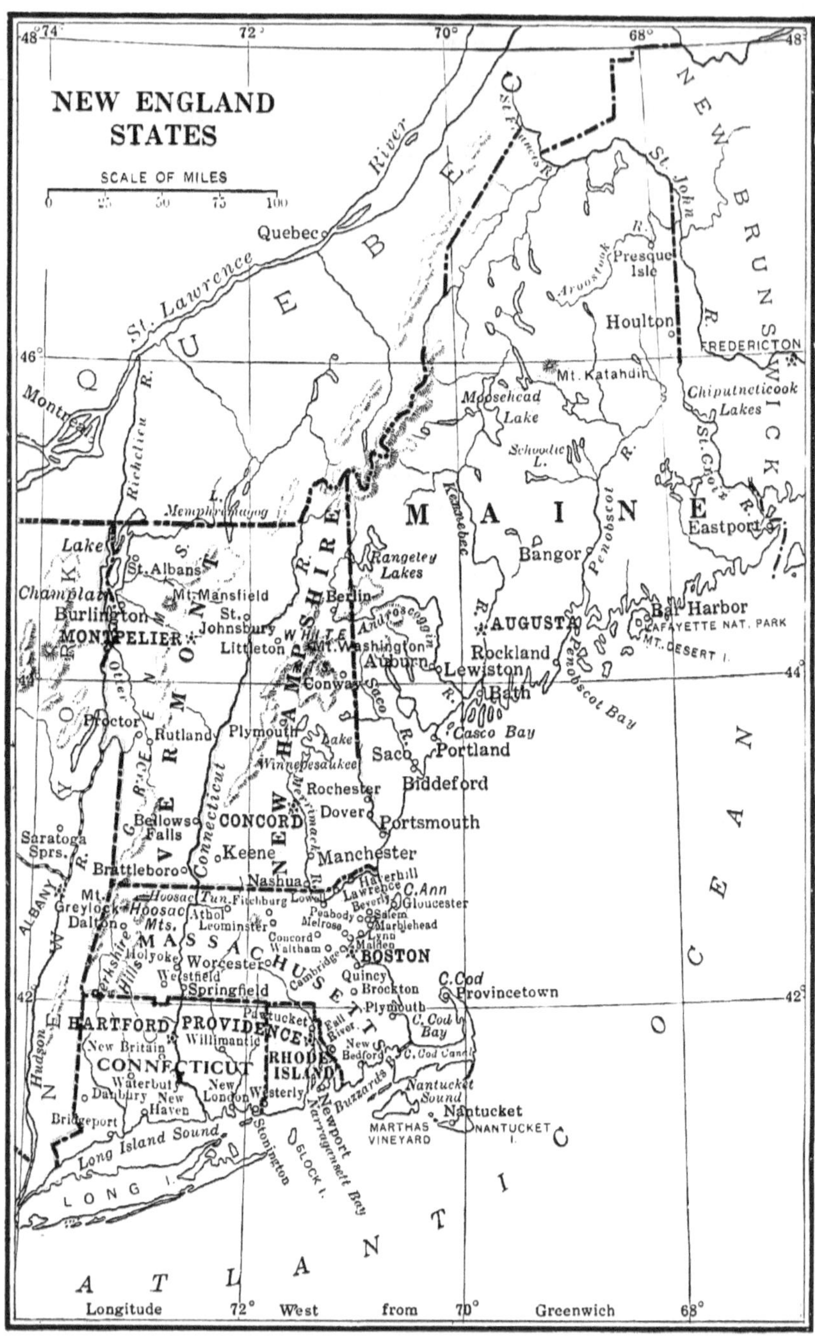

NEW ENGLAND STATES
SCALE OF MILES
0 25 50 75 100
QUEBEC
Quebec
St. Lawrence River
Richelieu R.
Montreal
L. Memphremagog
Lake Champlain
St. Albans
Mt. Mansfield
Burlington
MONTPELIER
St. Johnsbury
Littleton
Otter
Proctor
Rutland
Bellows Falls
Brattleboro
Saratoga Sprs.
ALBANY
Mt. Greylock
Hoosac Mts.
Dalton
Hoosac Tun.
Berkshire Hills
MASSACHUSETTS
Holyoke
Westfield
Springfield
Worcester
HARTFORD
New Britain
CONNECTICUT
Waterbury
Danbury
New Haven
Bridgeport
Hudson R.
Long Island Sound
LONG I.
VERMONT
Green Mts.
Connecticut R.
NEW HAMPSHIRE
WHITE MTS.
Berlin
Mt. Washington
Conway
Plymouth
Lake Winnepesaukee
CONCORD
Keene
Nashua
Fitchburg
Athol
Leominster
Concord
Waltham
Cambridge
Lowell
Lawrence
Haverhill
Peabody
Melrose
Salem
Marblehead
Lynn
Malden
BOSTON
Quincy
Brockton
Plymouth
Pawtucket
PROVIDENCE
Willimantic
RHODE ISLAND
New London
Westerly
Stonington
Narragansett Bay
Newport
BLOCK I.
Fall River
New Bedford
Buzzards Bay
Beverly
C. Ann
Gloucester
Merrimack R.
Rochester
Dover
Portsmouth
Manchester
Androscoggin R.
Rangeley Lakes
Kennebec R.
MAINE
AUGUSTA
Auburn
Lewiston
Bath
Saco R.
Saco
Biddeford
Casco Bay
Portland
Rockland
Penobscot Bay
Bangor
Penobscot R.
Mt. Katahdin
Moosehead Lake
Schoodic L.
Aroostook R.
Presque Isle
Houlton
NEW BRUNSWICK
FREDERICTON
St. John R.
St. Croix R.
Chiputneticook Lakes
Eastport
Bar Harbor
LAFAYETTE NAT. PARK
MT. DESERT I.
St. Francis R.
C. Cod
Provincetown
C. Cod Bay
C. Cod Canal
Nantucket Sound
Nantucket
NANTUCKET I.
MARTHAS VINEYARD
ATLANTIC OCEAN
Longitude   72°   West   from   70°   Greenwich   68°
48° 74° 72° 70° 68° 48°
46°
44°
42°

FIG 5. This is a picture of a drowned valley. See how the ocean has
filled the lowlands. Why do drowned valleys make good harbors?
If the land along this coast should rise, how would the length of
the inlet compare with the length as shown in the picture?

to warn vessels of the rocky isles. On the peninsulas, fishermen
live, and on the islands and the mainland, there are pleasant
summer resorts.

The larger part of New England is made up of a hilly belt
which extends from the interior nearly or quite to the shore. It
is a pleasant region of green, rounded hills and broad valleys,
winding rivers, and sparkling lakes.

North of Cape Cod, the hilly region extends nearly or quite
down to the water. Along the shores of Connecticut, Rhode
Island, and southeastern Massachusetts, there is a narrow
coastal lowland. In Rhode Island, this lowland region and the
drowned valley of Narragansett Bay occupy the greater part of
the state, and more than seven-eighths of the people live in
this lowland area.

The Green Mountains of Vermont and the White Mountains
of New Hampshire make up the chief mountain region of New
England. The Green Mountain belt extends southward through
Massachusetts, where the range is known as the Berkshire Hills,
into northwestern Connecticut. Through the Hoosac Mountains

FIG 6. This is a scene on the Maine coast. Why is this coast so irregular? Why are many lighthouses needed ?

in northwestern Massachusetts, the Hoosac Tunnel has been cut. This tunnel, the first of any great length to be built in the country, is about five miles long. It gives Boston direct connection across northern Massachusetts with Albany and the rich plains of the Middle West. The White Mountain belt extends in lower hills into Maine and southward through Massachusetts into northern Connecticut. Between the two mountain belts is the rich valley of the Connecticut River, and west of the Green Mountain belt, the land slopes down to the Hudson-Champlain Lowland. All these natural regions — the low coastal plain, the hilly belt, the mountain areas, and the river and lake lowlands — are important and have determined to a large extent the occupations of the people who live in them.

New England is a very old region. Its hills and mountains were once much higher than at present. Through long ages, the rains, the frosts, the streams, and the great glacier have been slowly wearing away the rock and soil and washing it into the valleys and the ocean. Therefore, the mountains of New England are not very high and the scenery is not so wild and grand as it is in some parts of the country, but it is restful and

FIG 7. This is a view of the White Mountains. How do
they differ in appearance from those in the West?

beautiful. Mt. Washington, the highest peak, is six thousand two hundred and ninety-three feet high. A railroad and an automobile road lead to the summit. Should you like to ride to the top in a train or automobile, or should you prefer to take your time and "hike" through the wooded trail?

Most of the rivers in New England have falls and rapids which furnish valuable power. This is one of the chief reasons why manufacturing developed so early in this section. Mills for grinding grain, for sawing lumber, and later for manufacturing cotton and woolen goods were located on the streams near the early settlements, and many of these places have since grown into important manufacturing centers.

In Rhode Island and southeastern Massachusetts, the falls in the streams are near the coast. The cities situated at these power sites have a double advantage. They have become important not only in manufacturing but in commerce as well. They can easily bring their raw material and send away many of their manufactures by water. Can you explain now why Fall River has grown to be a large, important city and why more than half of

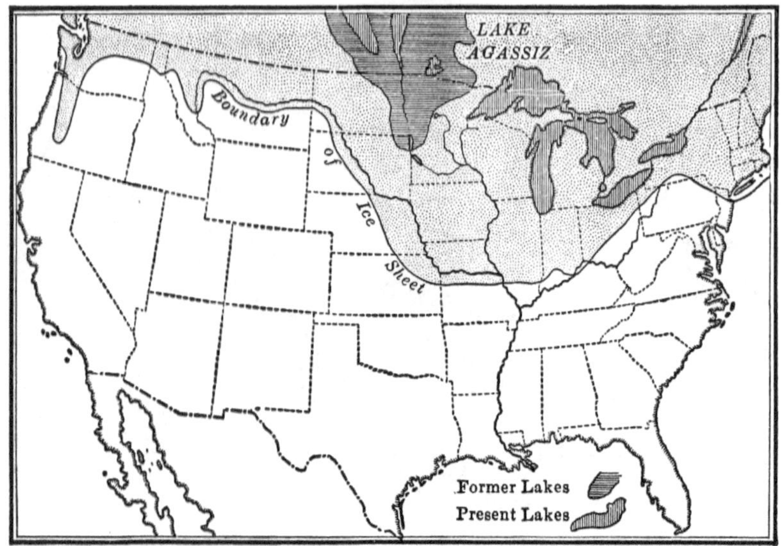

FIG 8. This map shows the part of the United States once covered by glaciers. Name the states which lay under its southern edge. What states were wholly covered by the glacier?

the people in Rhode Island live in the cities of Providence and Pawtucket?

The rivers of New England have been important lumber highways, and millions of logs from the forests of Maine, New Hampshire, and Vermont have come down the streams to the sawmills. Many of the rivers, as well as many lakes in New England, also yield a winter harvest of ice.

If you would like to know why it is that New England has so many falls in its rivers, so many lovely lakes and ponds, and such rounded hilltops, you must read another story in Mother Nature's book. Long, long ages ago, the climate of North America was much colder than it is at present, and all of Canada and the northern United States were covered with a great ice sheet hundreds of feet thick, just as Greenland is today.

The ice filled the valleys and rose higher than the tops of the highest mountains. Very slowly, it crept along from its home in the colder regions of the north, rounding the hilltops as it passed, scraping the rock waste from the land, carrying many great boulders and much gravel and fine sand embedded in its mass, digging the beds for hundreds of lakes, and scouring out the valleys.

The New England rivers, clogged and dammed by the material brought by the glacier, were turned into new courses. Here they encountered rocks of varying hardness. The softer ones were, of course, worn away first. Where the stream leaped from the harder rock bed to the lower one worn in the softer material, falls occurred. Ever since the early settlers made use of this water power to grind their grain, it has been of tremendous value to the people of this section.

The Connecticut is the longest and most important river of New England. Not only the river itself but many of its branches have falls and rapids on which manufacturing towns and cities are situated. In several places, the falling water is used to generate electricity, which is carried on wires to cities many miles away. Some of the largest cities in western Massachusetts are located on the Connecticut River, and about half of the people in Connecticut live in its valley. Can you tell why this is so?

Besides the manufacturing cities, there are many fine farms in the Connecticut valley where tobacco is cultivated and dairy cattle are raised.

The Merrimack River turns more spindles in textile manufacturing than any river in the world. What important cities are located on it? In New Hampshire, nearly half of the people in the state live in or near its valley. The little Blackstone River is one of the best-harnessed streams in the country, and mill towns and manufacturing cities are located all along its banks.

On the map of New England, find the largest rivers of Maine and New Hampshire. These furnish power for the many manufacturing centers situated on them. They are the means, also, by which lumber is floated down from the forests to the sawmills, the paper and pulp mills, and other establishments.

The early settlers of New England were much influenced by the surface and the rivers of the region. Their first settlements were on the shore, where good harbors made landing easy and commerce with the homeland possible. Some of their

FIG 9. Nature's agents are skillful sculptors. They have carved the face of the "Old Man of the Mountains" from the solid rock. Have you ever read the story of "The Great Stone Face" by Nathaniel Hawthorne?

towns were founded near river mouths, and the colonists followed the streams inland to build new homes. The first English settlements in Vermont were made by colonists who followed the Connecticut River northward. Before this time, however, the Frenchman Samuel de Champlain had entered the state by way of Lake Champlain. The early Maine settlements were near the mouths of the rivers and spread northward along the river valleys. The rivers were the first highways of the colonists, just as they had been of the Indians.

The position and climate of a region also have a large influence on the lives of the people who live there. Can you prove by studying a map that New England lies almost exactly halfway between the equator and the North Pole? This is a very favorable position, for the climate is neither too hot nor too cold. The winters are seldom severe enough to fill the harbors with ice and thus check commerce. The heat of the summers is good for growing crops. There is plenty of rainfall for agriculture, and the moisture in the air is favorable for textile manufactures. In a very dry air, the threads break much more quickly. The hot waves and the cold waves, which chase one another from west to east over the country, tend to develop in the people of any region over which they pass a strength and energy which affect their work and their lives. Now that we have read about the ways in which Nature has favored this

FIG 10. This picture shows a part of the largest watch factory in the world as it looks at night across the river. What are the two cities in New England which are noted for the manufacture of watches? (Courtesy of the Waltham Watch Company)

part of the United States, we are more ready to understand the reasons for its development into an important manufacturing and commercial section. Its water power, its fine harbors, its favorable position for commerce with Europe, its stimulating climate, its energetic, inventive people, and its highly skilled workmen all help to offset the fact that nearly all its fuel and its raw materials for manufacture — its cotton, wool, hides, and iron — must be brought from other sections.

Because the raw material must be brought from a distance, many of the articles made in New England are small, specialized goods requiring not so much a vast amount of material as highly skilled workmen. For example, Athol, Massachusetts, contains the largest concern in the world for making fine tools, Waltham the largest watch factory, and Plymouth the largest cordage company. Hartford, Connecticut, has the largest typewriter company. Worcester, Massachusetts, makes more wire and wire goods than any other city; New Britain, Connecticut, more builders' hardware. Leominster, Massachusetts, makes two-thirds of our combs and hairpins; Holyoke more than half of our fine writing paper, and Dalton the paper for our government

FIG 11. This is a spinning-room in one of the mills of the largest cotton-manufacturing company in the world. Along what rivers in New England shall we find textile manufactories?

banknotes. Westfield is the whip city of the world; Providence, Rhode Island, is the jewelry city; Danbury, Connecticut, is the hat city; and Waterbury is the brass city.

The textile manufactures — cotton, wool, and silk — are the most important industries in New England. The preparation of the raw material, the spinning and weaving, and the dyeing and finishing of the goods use more capital and engage more workmen than are employed in any other occupation in this section. New England also leads all other parts of the country in its output of sewing silk.

Between fifteen and twenty miles of cotton cloth are made each minute in New England factories. Nearly half of all the woolen mills in the entire country are in New England. One mill in Lawrence, Massachusetts, uses daily the fleece of twenty-five thousand sheep. One company in Willimantic, Connecticut,

FIG 12. The picture shows a part of a great manufacturing plant on the Merrimack River in Manchester, New Hampshire. Why is so much manufacturing carried on along the Merrimack? Name the important manufacturing cities on this river.

makes more than a million miles of thread per week. The largest cotton-manufacturing establishment in the world is located in Manchester, New Hampshire, and the largest woolen-manu-facturing company in the world has more than thirty different mills in New England cities. Manchester, in the state of New Hampshire; Lowell, Lawrence, Fall River, and New Bedford in Massachusetts; and Providence in Rhode Island are textile centers of worldwide reputation.

The variety of metal manufactures made in New England seems almost endless. It includes all kinds of articles, from bridges and automobiles to the tiny hairspring of a wristwatch. If you would like to weigh either a locomotive or a postage stamp, go to St. Johnsbury and Rutland, Vermont, where more scales for weighing are made than anywhere in the world. Millions of watches are made each year in Waterbury, Connecticut, and Waltham, Massachusetts. Connecticut ranks first in the country in a great variety of metal products, such as edge tools, silver-plated ware, brass, bronze, and copper articles, clocks and watches, needles and pins, and hooks and eyes.

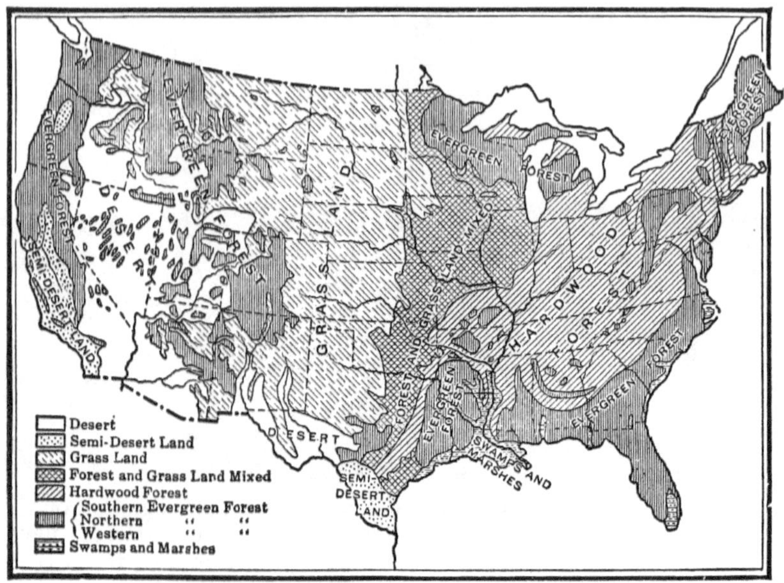

FIG 13. Map of the forest areas of the United States. Make a list of the states included in the hardwood area. What natural regions are wholly or partly included in the grassland area? How many regions of evergreen forests do you see? (Courtesy of the American Geographical Society of New York)

An important class of metal manufactures is machinery, especially the machinery needed in shoe factories and in textile and paper mills. Beverly, Massachusetts, supplies the shoe factories of the world with machinery. New England leads the world in the manufacture of boots and shoes. So much leather for this industry is needed in its many large shoe factories that Boston has become the greatest leather market, and Peabody, Massachusetts, the greatest sheepskin-tanning center, of the world.

Now let us see something of another important New England industry. If you will look at the map above, you will see that there are several large forested areas in the United States. One of these lies in New England, and lumbering has been carried on here longer than anywhere else in the country. Maine is often called the Pine Tree State. Enormous numbers of trees have been cut there, but large areas are still covered with pine and spruce forests. Many streams flow southward from its forested areas.

On these, where falls furnish power, there are great sawmills and mills for making pulp and paper. These manufactures of Maine exceed all others in value. Many of the cities and towns of the state are connected in some way with the lumber industry and make an enormous variety of wooden articles, such as shingles, lathes, sleds, toys, spools, clothespins, matches, snowshoes, toothpicks, boxes, and furniture. Bangor is one of the most important lumber markets of the country. Portland and other Maine cities have a large lumber trade, while Burlington, Vermont, receives and ships away large quantities of lumber.

The forests of New England yield other products besides lumber. One of these is maple sugar. This is made from the sap of the sugar-maple tree. Thirteen states furnish our supply of maple sugar. Vermont is perhaps the most famous for its maple products, but New Hampshire and Massachusetts, in New England, and New York, Pennsylvania, Ohio, Michigan, Wisconsin, and Indiana make quantities of both sugar and syrup. In the

FIG 14. This is a logging camp in the Maine woods. What season of the year is it? Why is lumbering in New England usually carried on during this season?

spring, when the sap begins to flow, the men tap the sugar-maple trees and hang buckets to catch the liquid, which slowly runs through the little tubes that have been inserted. The sap is collected in barrels and drawn to the sugarhouse, where it is boiled down into syrup and made into sugar.

Ever since the settlement of New England, the fishing industry has been of great importance there. The fish not only furnished food for the settlers but were also an important article of commerce. The necessity for boats and ships stimulated shipbuilding, which soon became an important New England industry. The dangers and hardships of fishing voyages developed expert sailors. They went on long trips carrying New England exports — fish, lumber, and farm products — to the West Indies, England, and southern European countries. Later,

FIG 15. The picture shows a part of a maple-sugar orchard in Vermont. What other states help to furnish our maple sugar and syrup supply? From the sap of what other trees are useful products made?

after the Revolutionary War, their voyages were extended even to China and the East Indies. In those days, Salem was one of the most important commercial cities of the New World, and the city of Providence carried on at one time more commerce than New York.

In those early days, nearly every coastal town was engaged in fishing, and Marblehead, New Bedford, and Gloucester were important centers. Some of the fishermen, especially those from Nantucket and New Bedford in Massachusetts, and New London and Stonington in Connecticut, went on long voyages to northern seas in search of whales and seals. It was a hard, adventurous life, and the stories told by some of these old seafaring men of their exciting experiences — when the whale dove or lashed the water into fury in his struggle to free himself from the harpoon — are as interesting as the scenes in Stevenson's Treasure Island.

Much of the whaling and sealing at the present time is carried on from the Pacific ports, and New England's share in this industry is comparatively small. Fishing is still very important. Many vessels sail from Gloucester, and two-thirds of the world's supply of salted codfish is prepared in that city. The fishing schooners of today are fine, large vessels fitted with all conveniences for handling the fish. Ice and salt for packing and curing are taken on the long voyages to the banks of Newfoundland, where much of the fishing is carried on. Boston is one of the largest fish markets in the world, and its great Fish Pier is considered finer than any similar structure at any other port.

Formerly, those parts of the fish not used for food were thrown away. Now, every part yields some useful product — oil, glue, gelatin, or fertilizer.

The shore fisheries of Maine are important. Many men are employed in catching and canning lobsters. Millions of boxes of sardines also come from Maine; in fact, the larger part of our domestic supply is prepared in this state. Along the shores of southern New England, we should find fishermen dredging for oysters. Because of the oyster industry, the ocean bottom under Long Island Sound is said to be more valuable than

FIG 16. This picture shows large quantities of codfish drying on the frames in Gloucester. In what other places in New England might you see similar sights? Where was this fish probably caught? (Courtesy of the Detroit Publishing Company)

some of the land on its shores. We shall learn more about the oyster industry when we visit the states farther south, for Chesapeake Bay is more famous for oysters than any other place in the country.

What are the principal occupations around your home? Have you ever stopped to think that, of all the different kinds of work people do, farming is more important than any other? The whole world depends on the farmer. Without him, the world would starve. For two hundred years, farming was the most important occupation in New England. Now, as you have already read, more of the people are employed in manufacturing. Farming, however, is still very important. The people in the many cities of this section have little or no land to cultivate. They need fruits, vegetables, milk, and eggs. These are produced on nearly all New England farms. Most farmers raise hay for their cattle and have orchards of apples, pears, and, in the three southern states, peaches. Near the large cities, there are truck farms, often with great hothouses, where many vegetables and small fruits are raised.

The tobacco fields of the Connecticut Valley are an interesting sight. Do you know of any other plant which has leaves a yard or more long? Many acres in the tobacco area are overspread with white cloth, making the region resemble an immense camp. This shade-grown tobacco is considered of excellent quality. The long leaves are cured for market in open sheds in the fields.

To see the splendid farms which produce the famous Aroostook County potatoes, we must go to the fertile valley of the Aroostook River in northern Maine. The soil here is well adapted to the growing of potatoes. The finest ones are sold in the spring to farmers all over the country for planting. Many are used for food. Starch factories have been built in which the smaller potatoes are used for the starch they contain.

On the Cape Cod peninsula, many cranberries are raised. Wisconsin, New Jersey, and Massachusetts produce nearly all the country's supply. On the large farms in Massachusetts, the berries are picked, cleaned, and sorted by machines. Several million quarts have been picked here in a single season. What immense quantities of sugar it must take to sweeten such an amount of cranberry sauce!

Nature was generous in her gifts to New England. The forests, the fish, the good harbors, and the swift rivers have all been of great value to the people of this section. Even the rock found here has made New England famous, and quarrying has become an important industry. Marble, granite, and slate are quarried in immense quantities, and other stones are also worked. Some of the government buildings in Washington, the public library in New York City, some of the state capitols, and many other buildings are made of Vermont marble. The Green Mountain Belt is the greatest marble region in the world. In a ride through this section, you would know that you were in a marble area, for the foundations of the houses, the steps, and even the stone fences and hitching posts are made of marble.

Granite is more widely distributed than marble and is

FIG 17. This is the training ship *Newport* passing through Cape Cod Canal. Where is this canal? What route is shortened by it? What dangers are avoided?

quarried in all the New England states. More granite for monuments is sold in Vermont than in all the other states of the country, and more granite for building purposes than in any other one state. Granite is quarried also near the coast in Maine, Massachusetts, and Connecticut, where it can be easily shipped away. Both granite and marble are quarried in other sections of the country. What is there in your town or city made of either kind of stone? Can you find out where it was quarried?

In Vermont, there is also a belt of fine slate rocks useful for roofing and other purposes. These are quarried in such quantities that, next to Pennsylvania, Vermont produces more slate than any other state.

New England has many noted summer resorts. Bar Harbor, on Mount Desert Island, is one of the most famous of these. About eight square miles of the island are now included in Lafayette National Park. Rhode Island owes not only its important commerce and industry but much of its popularity in summer as well to the deep indentation of Narragansett

FIG 18. A granite quarry in New England. Which of the New England States is most noted for granite? Explain the use of the derricks in the picture.

Bay. Newport, situated near the southern end of the largest island in the bay, is one of the most fashionable resorts in the United States.

There are many other places in New England which we would like to visit. One of these is the old city of Portsmouth, the only seaport of New Hampshire, where, in 1905, at the invitation of President Roosevelt, the delegates from the warring countries came to sign the peace treaty which closed the Russo-Japanese War.

We should not wish to leave New England without a glimpse of the historic gates and old dormitories of Harvard University in Cambridge or the elm-shaded buildings of Yale at New Haven. We must be sure to go to the bridge in Concord, where, in 1775, was fired "the shot heard 'round the world." We must follow the roads on which Paul Revere rode when he went to warn the villagers that the British were coming, and where, a few hours later, as the British soldiers marched along,

FIG 19. This is one of many beautiful boulevards in Newport. Behind the walls and trees on either side are lovely estates. What advantages does Newport have which make it a summer resort?

the farmers gave them ball for ball,
From behind each fence and farmyard wall.

At Plymouth, you must surely see the famous rock on which the Pilgrims landed "on a stern and rock-bound coast." In Memorial Hall is the cradle in which Peregrine White was rocked, the sword with which Miles Standish fought the Indians, and many other interesting relics of Pilgrim days.

Our visit to New England would be very incomplete without a visit to Boston.

If you are interested in history, we can go to the belfry of the church where the lanterns were hung as a signal to Paul Revere of the approach of the British troops. We can visit Faneuil Hall, the birthplace of liberty, or climb to the top of Bunker Hill Monument.

If you wish to see some of the big things people are doing, we can go to the building where a hundred million pounds of wool can be stored. Boston is the greatest wool market in the country and handles enough wool each year to make an all-wool suit for every man, woman, and child in the country. We can visit the offices, headquarters, or factories of more than a thousand firms engaged in the manufacture or sale of leather, hides, footwear, and shoe machinery. We can go down to the waterside and see the largest dry dock in the world, watch the vessels discharging their slippery cargoes on Fish Pier — the largest in the world — and visit Commonwealth Pier, one of the largest freight and passenger piers of any country.

Boston is as important in manufacturing as it is in commerce. We shall find in the city great sugar refineries, establishments where quantities of men's and women's clothing are made, factories for making rubber boots and shoes, the largest shoe factory in the world, many printing and publishing houses, and the largest cocoa and chocolate manufacturing plant of any country.

SUGGESTIONS FOR STUDY

I

1. Size and population of New England.
2. The coastline and drowned valleys.
3. Surface and drainage.
4. The great glacier and its work.
5. Influence of physical features on history.
6. The New England climate.
7. Manufacturing in New England.
8. Forest and forest products.
9. Fishing and farming.
10. Marble, granite, and slate.
11. New England scenery and summer resorts.
12. Some New England cities.

II

1. Name the New England States. Which is the largest? the smallest? the most western? the most eastern? the most southern? Which one has no seacoast? Which ones border on another group of states? Which ones have rivers for boundaries? Which

one borders on a lake? Which one has the highest mountains? the deepest bays?

2. Why do so many people in New England live in cities?

3. On what waters must Champlain have sailed to get from the ocean to Lake Champlain?

4. Who was Lafayette? Why should one of our national parks be named for him?

5. Write to the National Park Service, Department of the Interior, Washington, D.C., and ask for pamphlets describing our national parks. State in your letter that they are for use in your geography classes.

6. Name the capital of each New England state; the largest city; the longest river; the chief manufactures.

7. On page 8 the following problem is suggested: Why has New England become so thickly populated and so important in manufacturing? What reasons have you found, in reading the chapter, which will help you in solving the problem?

III

Make a list of all the places mentioned in this chapter. Arrange them by countries, cities, mountains, rivers, etc. Be able to locate each place and tell what was said about it in the chapter.

CHAPTER III

IN AND AROUND THE APPALACHIAN HIGHLANDS

The New England area of which you have just read includes the northern part of the Appalachian Highlands. From here they stretch southward through several states into northern Alabama. To the east is the low, level Coastal Plain, while stretching away to the west lie the fertile lands of the Central Plains.

The Appalachian Highland region is one of the most important industrial areas of the United States. The swift rivers and deep forests and the coal, iron, petroleum, and natural gas have made possible many busy cities, with their furnaces, foundries, and factories. Before we visit these cities, let us hear Nature's story about the materials which she has so generously supplied here.

This area is a very ancient one. For many, many centuries, the frosts, the rains, and the streams have been busy wearing down the mountains and carrying the material into the sea, just as they are doing all around us today. The mountains are therefore much lower than the younger ranges in the West, their tops are smoother and rounder, and the valleys between them are wider. The highest mountain peak east of the Rockies is Mt. Mitchell in North Carolina — six thousand seven hundred and eleven feet high. This is only a baby in size compared with some of the Western giants.

Some of the mountains in this region are much more ancient than others. Those on the eastern border of the area are so old that they have been worn down into hills. This older region is called the Piedmont Belt — a very appropriate name, meaning "foot of the mountains."

When studying the map of this region, perhaps you have noticed that many of the rivers rise west of the mountains, and you may have wondered how it was possible for them to flow across the highland.

These rivers are older than the mountains and wore down their valleys faster than the great mountain wrinkles were pushed up. Thus, they were able to keep their eastward courses. The Delaware at the Delaware Water Gap and the Potomac at Harpers Ferry are good examples of the work of rivers in cutting passes through the mountains. The Cumberland, flowing west into the Ohio, has also cut a pass in the mountains at Cumberland Gap.

The cutting of the river valleys through the mountain wall was of great benefit to the early colonists along the coast. Because of the rich mineral deposits, we think of the Appalachian Highlands today as a source of great wealth, but in the days of the early settlements, when roads were unknown, we cannot imagine a greater barrier to westward expansion. The parallel ranges, about three hundred miles wide and thirteen hundred miles long, were covered with dense forests. Wild beasts lurked in the undergrowth, and Indians skulked in ambush there. In order to cross to the western side of the highlands, the colonists followed a river valley into the mountains and made their way along some valley between the ranges until they came to a place where a westward-flowing stream began. This they followed down to the Central Plains. It was in this way that the early pioneers first reached the fertile lands of these great plains.

Daniel Boone, that brave old pioneer, was one of the first to make his way across the mountains. From his home on the Yadkin River in North Carolina, he followed up the stream and its branches into a long valley between the ranges. Here he found the headwaters of the Cumberland River, which he followed through Cumberland Gap into the rich lands of Kentucky.

The river valleys not only furnished highways for the Indians and the early colonists but they have determined the routes of

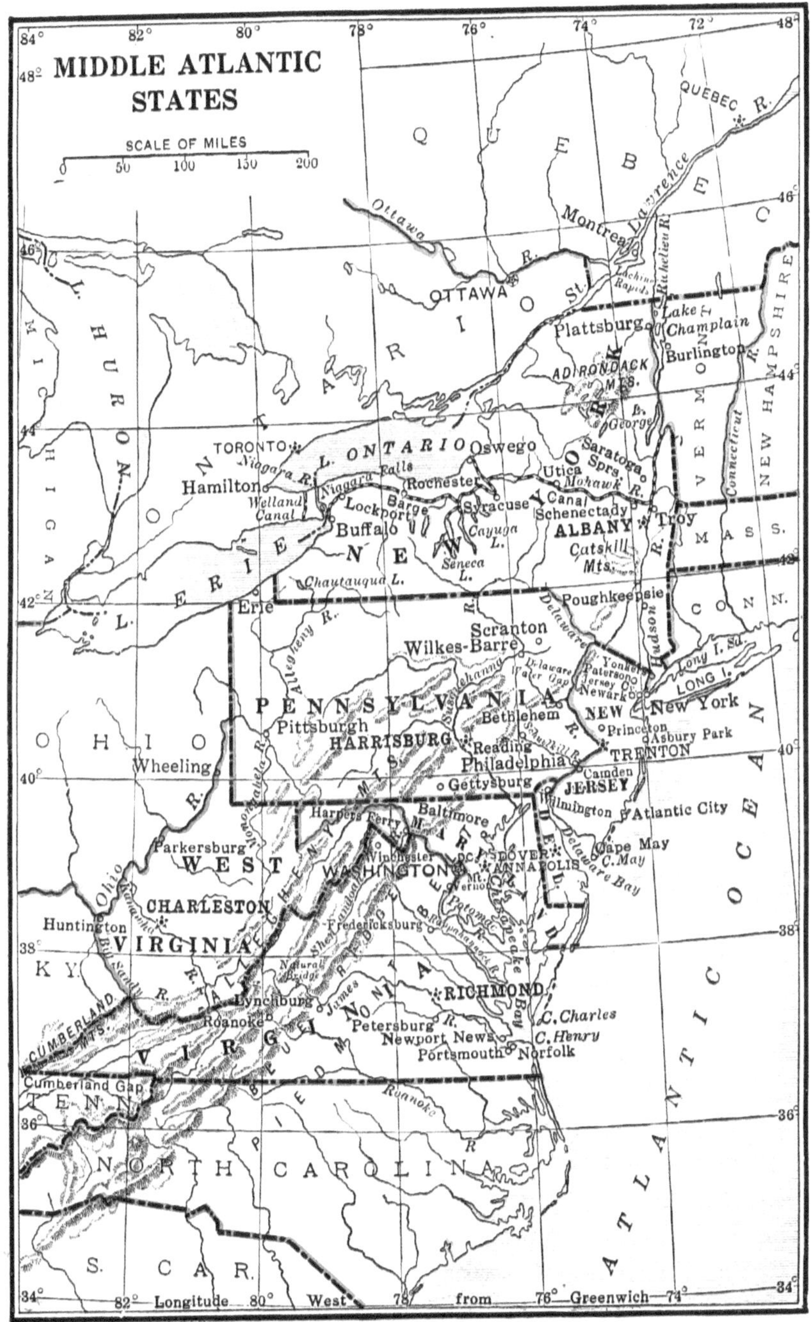

MAP II
MIDDLE ATLANTIC STATES
SCALE OF MILES
0 50 100 150 200
84° 82° 80° 78° 76° 74° 72° 48°
48°
46°
44°
42°
40°
38°
36°
34°
QUEBEC
Ottawa R.
Montreal
St. Lawrence R.
Lachine Rapids
Richelieu R.
OTTAWA
Plattsburg
Lake Champlain
Burlington
ADIRONDACK MTS.
L. George
L. ONTARIO
TORONTO
Niagara R.
Hamilton
Niagara Falls
Welland Canal
Lockport
Buffalo
L. ERIE
Erie
Chautauqua L.
Allegheny R.
Oswego
Rochester
Barge Canal
Syracuse
Cayuga L.
Seneca L.
NEW YORK
Saratoga Sprs.
Utica
Mohawk R.
Canal
Schenectady
ALBANY
Troy
Catskill Mts.
VERMONT
Connecticut R.
NEW HAMPSHIRE
MASS.
Hudson R.
Poughkeepsie
CONN.
N.
Long I. Sd.
LONG I.
Delaware R.
Scranton
Wilkes-Barre
Susquehanna R.
Delaware Water Gap
Yonkers
Paterson
Jersey City
Newark
NEW York
PENNSYLVANIA
Pittsburgh
HARRISBURG
Bethlehem
Reading
Schuylkill R.
Princeton
Asbury Park
NEW JERSEY
TRENTON
Camden
OHIO
Monongahela R.
Wheeling
Philadelphia
Gettysburg
Wilmington
Atlantic City
DELAWARE
DOVER
Delaware Bay
Cape May
C. May
ATLANTIC OCEAN
Harpers Ferry
Baltimore
MARYLAND
WASHINGTON
D.C.
ANNAPOLIS
Chesapeake Bay
Parkersburg
WEST
Winchester
Mt. Vernon
Potomac R.
WEST VIRGINIA
Ohio R.
Kanawha R.
CHARLESTON
Huntington
Big Sandy R.
VIRGINIA
Natural Bridge
Fredericksburg
Rappahannock R.
KY.
CUMBERLAND MTS.
Lynchburg
Roanoke
James R.
VIRGINIA
RICHMOND
Petersburg
Newport News
Portsmouth
Norfolk
C. Charles
C. Henry
BLUE RIDGE MTS.
Shenandoah R.
Cumberland Gap
TENN.
Roanoke R.
PIEDMONT
NORTH CAROLINA
S. CAR.
82° Longitude 80° West 78° from 76° Greenwich 74°

FIG 20. Do you see in the background of the picture the gap which the Cumberland River has cut through the mountains? Can you imagine how different this region looked at the time when Daniel Boone and the colonists who followed him passed through this gap?

most of the railroads which connect the cities of the Atlantic coast with those of the Mississippi Valley. You will read later what an influence the Hudson-Mohawk Valley and the railroads which follow it have had on the growth of New York City.

Coal is one of the very valuable products of the Appalachian Highlands, and Pennsylvania is our most important coal state. No other equal area in the world has such rich deposits of the hard, or anthracite, coal. Pennsylvania also mines much more than any other one state of the soft, or bituminous, coal, such as is used in engines and manufacturing plants. What other states in the Appalachian area produce large amounts of coal?

Perhaps you have already read Nature's story about coal. If so, you know that coal is made from vegetable matter, for in it have been found impressions of leaves, twigs, and roots. You read in the story of the great glacier that the climate of North America was once much colder than it is today. That was many

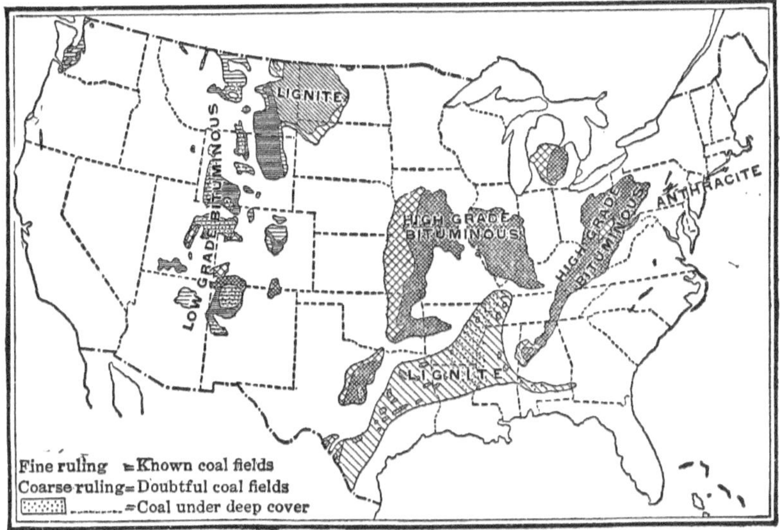

FIG 21. This map shows the chief coal fields of the country. Make a list of the states where bituminous coal is found; another list of those containing lignite. What is the difference between these two kinds of coal?

centuries ago. Ages and ages before that, in what scientists call the Carboniferous Period, the climate was much warmer than it is at present. Tropical trees and plants of immense size grew far beyond the torrid zone. These great forests of giant ferns and trees grew and died for many long ages until their decaying leaves, trunks, and twigs formed a thick mat of vegetation. With the sinking of the land, the sea came in, covering everything with water. Through long centuries, the rivers and streams brought sand and gravel and clay and deposited them over the old forests, making the vegetation more and more compact as the accumulation grew deeper. Then came another movement of the earth's crust, this time an upward one, and the land gradually rose until it appeared above the old sea. Forests grew again and made the thick carpet of vegetation at their feet. Their growth was again checked by the water which covered the area when the land sank once more. This happened several times, so that various layers, or seams, of vegetable matter were formed. Shut off from the air by the covering of soils, and subjected to heat and pressure, this buried vegetable matter changed slowly into

FIG 22. These tanks for the storage of petroleum are located near the oil wells. The dark smoke cloud comes from one of the tanks which has been set on fire by lightning. (Courtesy of the Department of the Interior)

coal. Since the old Carboniferous Age, when the coal beds were formed, the busy agents of Nature have been wearing away the overlying rock and soil. Thus, the layers of coal have been brought nearer the surface, and man has been able to make use of them.

Should you like to go down in a mine? In some, you would descend in an elevator through a deep shaft. In others, you could ride in on a car through a sloping tunnel. What a queer world it is here beneath the surface of the ground, where thousands of men spend their days! The long gangways are lighted with electricity and made safe by props of heavy timbers. The miners blast out the coal from the walls, and laborers break it up and load it on the waiting cars. In some mines, these are lifted up on elevators; in others, they are run out through tunnels.

The hard anthracite coal has to go through more processes than the softer bituminous kind. These processes are carried

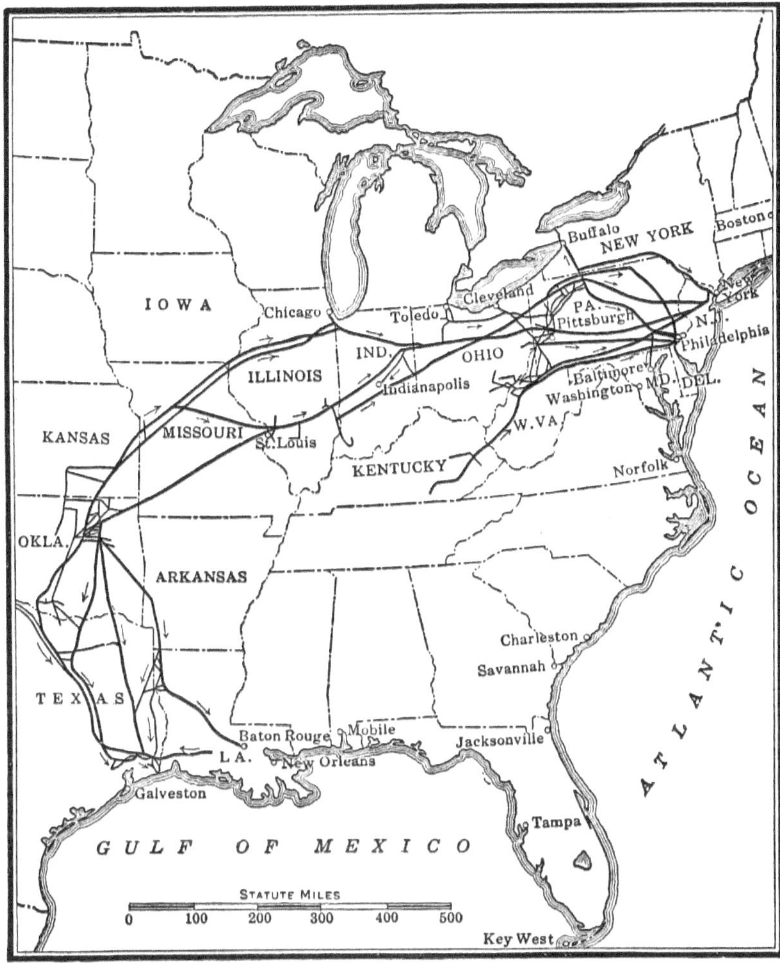

FIG 23. Some petroleum is shipped in tank cars and boats, but much the greater part goes in underground pipes. This map shows the pipe-line system of the eastern United States. There are enough miles of these pipe lines in the United States to girdle the earth at the equator and still have five thousand miles to spare.

on in big buildings called breakers. Here the coal is broken into smaller pieces, sorted according to size, and separated from the slate which it contains. It is then loaded on cars which carry it to the seaports or to cities in the interior. Thus, you see that the labor of many different workers is necessary before your

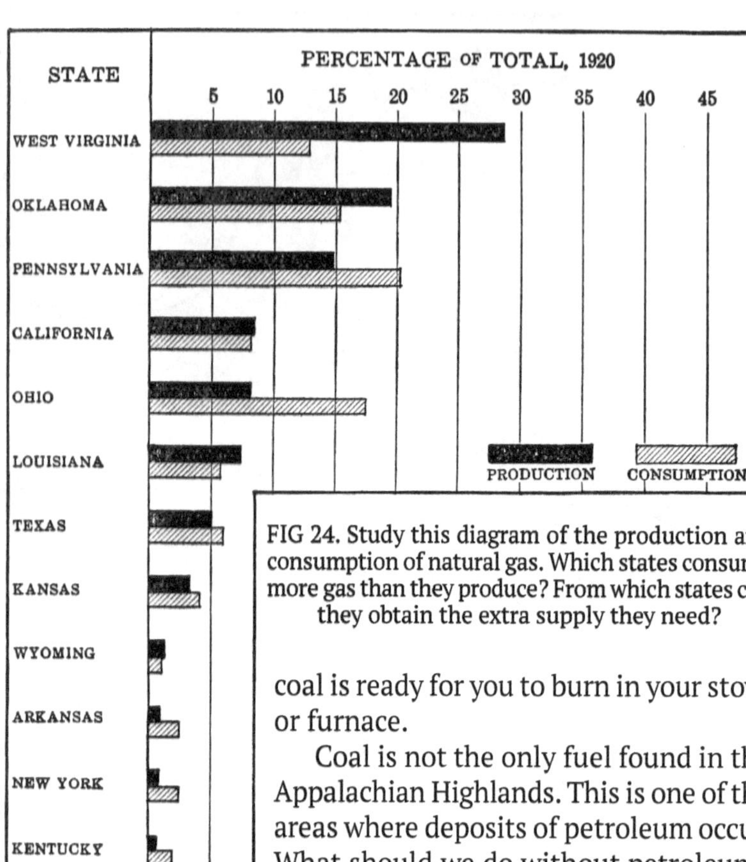

FIG 24. Study this diagram of the production and consumption of natural gas. Which states consume more gas than they produce? From which states can they obtain the extra supply they need?

coal is ready for you to burn in your stove or furnace.

Coal is not the only fuel found in the Appalachian Highlands. This is one of the areas where deposits of petroleum occur. What should we do without petroleum? It runs locomotives and automobiles, propels aircraft and seacraft, and moves machinery in mills, factories, and power plants. From it are obtained naphtha, gasoline, kerosene, vaseline, benzine, and paraffin.

To reach the petroleum deposits, pipes are sunk to great depths — sometimes, though rarely, more than a mile — before reaching the oil-bearing rock. A well often yields thousands of barrels a day, and the value of the product pays for the enormous expense of getting it.

Natural gas is often found in connection with petroleum. It is a valuable fuel and, in cities near the source of supply, is used in industrial establishments and in houses for both heating and lighting. In the Pittsburgh district, enormous quantities are used in the blast furnaces, foundries, and rolling mills. West Virginia produces about twice as much natural gas as any other state, but it uses much less than either Pennsylvania or Ohio. Both of these states rank high in the production of gas, but they use so much more than they produce that they import large quantities from West Virginia. The supply of natural gas is limited. When the present deposits are gone, there will be no more. Such enormous quantities have been used and have been allowed to escape that it is feared that the supply will soon be exhausted.

We have already learned of three kinds of fuel which Nature has provided in the Appalachian Highlands. The white coal, as water power is often called, which is found in this region, is also very important. The river which furnishes more power than any other in the country is the Niagara, which leaps in one great fall more than a hundred and sixty feet. This falling water has been harnessed and is working for man — lighting his cities, running his cars, and moving machinery in his mills and factories.

The Coastal Plain to the east of the highland is composed of looser material and softer rocks than those of the ancient mountain region. The rivers which flow from the mountains to the sea cross both areas. They can wear away the softer material in the Coastal Plain much more quickly than they can the harder rocks of the Piedmont Belt. Therefore, at the place in the rivers where the two regions meet, there are falls and rapids.

In early days, the Indians, and later the white men, sailed up these rivers in their canoes. Arriving at the falls, they were obliged to leave the streams and carry their canoes to the smooth waters above. Therefore, it was natural that settlements should spring up at the places where navigation was blocked. Many of these early towns, situated at the head of navigation on the streams and with water power for manufacturing, have since grown into important industrial centers. The line between the Piedmont Belt and the Coastal Plain where falls and rapids occur in the streams is called the fall line. On the map on page 40,

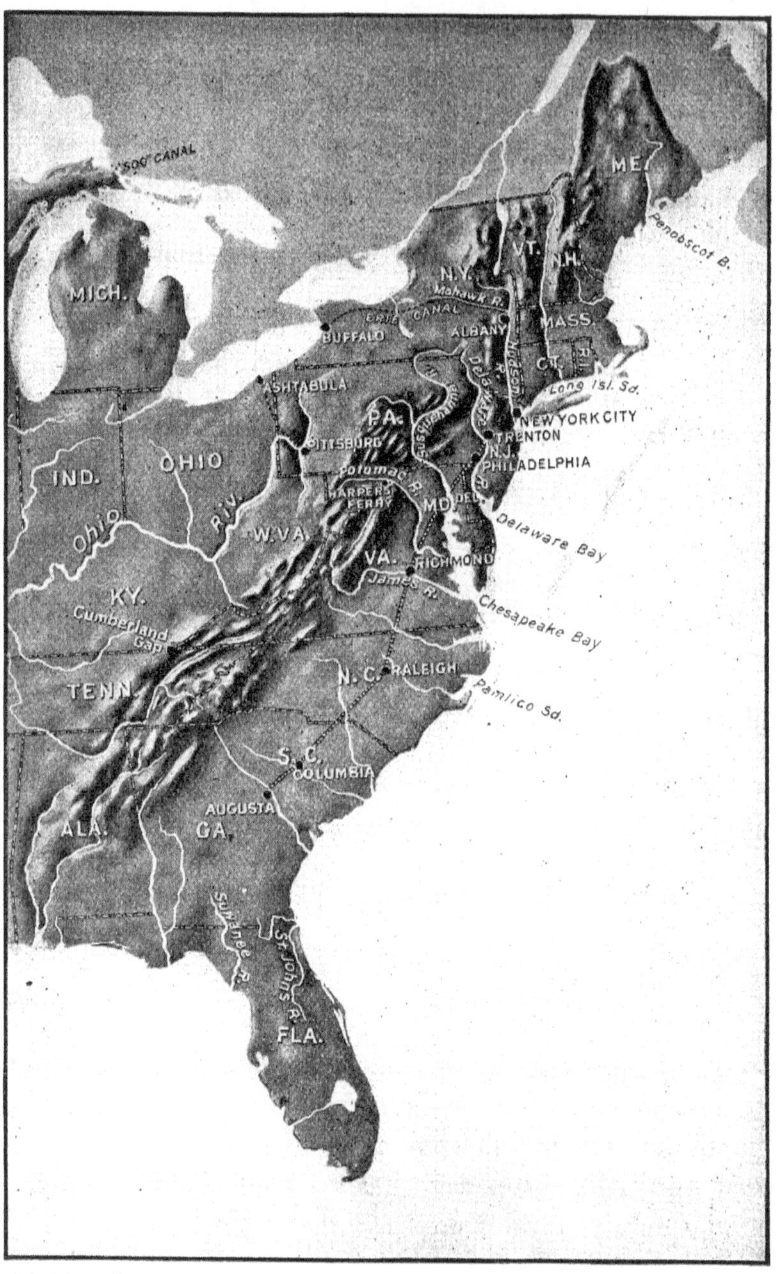

FIG 25. Follow the course of the fall line on this map. Between what two natural regions does it lie? Why are there falls in the rivers here? How has the fall line helped in the growth of cities on it?

FIG 26. Making steel by the Bessemer process. Find out from an encyclopedia what causes the shower of sparks. Find out also by what other process steel is made.

trace this line and see what cities are located on it.

There seems to be plenty of both fuel and power in the Appalachian Highlands. Now let us see what materials Nature has supplied for manufactures. Iron is the most important of such materials. It is impossible to think of any industry in which some iron or steel tool or machine is not used. The first step in providing these is to get the ore from the earth. In mountainous regions, this work is carried on much as coal mining is. When we visit regions farther west, we shall see iron mined in a very different way.

After the iron is mined, it must be separated from the rock which contains it. This is done in blast furnaces — tall, round structures, sometimes a hundred feet high. There are many blast furnaces at Pittsburgh, Birmingham, and other manufacturing cities. What an enormous amount of material it must take to fill them! First, a quantity of ore is poured in, then some coke, and then limestone. Coke is coal which has had some of its gases burned out. It makes a hotter fire than coal. But even this great heat is not enough to melt the iron, so a strong blast of air is forced in to make the fire burn even more fiercely. In the fierce heat, the iron melts, and on account of its weight, it sinks to the bottom of the furnace. The impurities in the ore combine with the limestone and form a lighter material called slag.

When an opening is made in the lower part of the furnace,

the molten iron starts out, making a shower of bright sparks which look like a display of Fourth of July fireworks. The iron flows freely like a stream of liquid fire and is so bright that it dazzles one's eyes to watch it. It is run into molds, where it grows darker and blackens as it hardens. In this form, it is known as pig iron. Pig iron is too brittle to work easily and must be still further purified and made into wrought iron and steel.

Can you think of any industry which can be carried on without the use of steel? We need such enormous quantities of articles made of it that the manufacture of steel is a most important occupation and is carried on in many cities in the eastern highland, where coal can be easily obtained. There are many important steel-manufacturing cities on and near the Great Lakes to which both coal and iron can be easily brought. We shall read about some of these in later chapters.

In the western part of Pennsylvania, you will find two rivers, the Allegheny and the Monongahela, which unite to form the Ohio. Pittsburgh is located at the junction of these rivers. The Monongahela River valley connects the city with the coal fields of West Virginia, and the Allegheny River links it with the coal and oil regions of western Pennsylvania. The Ohio River leads west and south to the Mississippi River and the Gulf of Mexico. Through the Great Lake route, iron is brought from the rich mines west of Lake Superior. Many railroads enter the city, bringing materials and carrying away its manufactured products. With all these advantages, it is no wonder that Pittsburgh has become a great steel-manufacturing center. There are establishments for making steel for building, steel rails, wire, nails, boilers, armor plate, projectiles for great guns, agricultural implements, stoves, engines, and other articles too numerous to mention. Later, you will read about Birmingham, another very important steel-manufacturing city, situated near the southern end of the Appalachian Highlands.

There are many other products besides those of steel manufactured in Pittsburgh. The largest cork factory in the world is located here. Sandstone, useful in glass-making, is found in the Ohio Valley, and Pittsburgh has become famous also for its glass manufactures.

Philadelphia is greatly influenced by the coal deposits of the state. Her position on the Delaware River is favorable both for her manufacturing and for her commerce. Many raw materials needed in her manufactures can be brought by water. The river is deep enough for large ocean vessels, and her commerce has become of great importance. More locomotives are made in Philadelphia than in any other city of the United States. There are shipyards also, where we can see great ships in all stages of completion, from the barest skeletons to the finished product. The woolen industry is important, too. Yonkers, near New York City, and Philadelphia are famous for the manufacture of carpets.

Instead of inspecting these or any of the other industrial plants of Philadelphia, perhaps you would prefer to go to the old mint, the first one to be established in the United States, where in 1793 the first copper cents were coined. This mint is a very important one. More money is coined here today than in any other mint in the world. Among your trips to places of historical interest, you will enjoy a visit to Independence Hall, from whose belfry, on July 4, 1776, pealed out the joyful news that the Declaration of Independence was signed and that our country was no longer a colony of England but a free and independent nation.

That old bell now is silent and hushed its iron tongue,
But the spirit it awakened still lives forever young.
And when we greet the sunlight on the Fourth of each July,
We'll ne'er forget the bellman, who, 'twixt the earth and
    sky,
Rang out our independence, which, please God, shall never
    die.

Around Trenton, the capital of New Jersey, there are deposits of clay useful for making porcelain, chinaware, bricks, and tiles. In Trenton, there are between forty and fifty establishments engaged in clay manufacture. In the year 1918, one of these establishments made a beautiful china dinner set for the use of the president of the United States. This service was the first White House china designed by an American citizen, made from American clays at an American pottery, decorated by American artists, and fired in American kilns. There are about seventeen hundred pieces in the complete set, and each piece is decorated in gold with the Stars and Stripes and the president's seal.

The Appalachian Highlands extend into Alabama, and the richest mineral deposits of the South are located there. Near these deposits, the city of Birmingham has grown up and become one of our most important steel-manufacturing centers. Iron and steel are not its only manufactures. It has great cotton factories, cottonseed-oil mills, lumber mills, and woodworking establishments. Can you tell why such industries should prosper in Birmingham?

In other cities and towns of northern Alabama and in the mountainous districts of eastern Kentucky and Tennessee, the tall chimneys of blast furnaces, foundries, and factories may be seen, and important manufactures are carried on.

Coal and iron are the most important minerals of the Appalachian Highlands, but there are others born in the waters of the old sea which once covered much of this region. Then, as now, the streams collected mineral matter from the soils and deposited it in the water into which they flowed. Among these minerals, salt is important. Like the other deposits, it was deeply covered by sands and gravels, until today some of the beds are more than two thousand feet underground. In the salt works in the state of New York, wells are drilled by sinking an iron pipe down to the salt rock. Water is forced into the pipe to dissolve the salt, and the brine is then pumped out through another pipe. The water is evaporated by heating, and the salt that is left is refined and made ready to use. There are different methods of obtaining salt in other states, one of which you will read about on page 65. New York, however, is second only to Michigan in its production.

Beautiful marble is found in the southern part of the Appalachian Highlands as well as in the northern part, and large quantities are quarried in both Tennessee and Georgia. The highland regions of Maryland, Alabama, and some other states also have marble quarries.

What articles have you ever seen that are made of aluminum? Most of the bauxite from which aluminum is made comes from Alabama, Georgia, and Tennessee in the Appalachian Highlands, and especially from the interior highlands of Arkansas farther west.

There are many places in this highland region that we wish we had time to visit before leaving for other parts of the country. In the forested Adirondacks, we could watch the lumbermen at work, visit paper and pulp mills, or join summer campers beneath the green trees on the bank of some stream or lake.

We could visit Albany, the capital of New York, climb the hill, and see its lovely capitol building. We could sail southward on the beautiful Hudson to New York City and see on our way the buildings of the famous Military Academy at West Point. We could follow the Barge Canal northward to Lake Champlain or westward from the Hudson River along the valley of the Mohawk to Buffalo. On these trips, we would learn a great deal about the state of New York, for four-fifths of its people and nine-tenths of

FIG 27. This is a scene on the New York Barge Canal. Why is this canal important? What waters does it connect?

FIG 28. The tallest building in the picture is the Woolworth Building in New York City. What does the text tell you about it?

its wealth are found along the Hudson River and the Barge Canal. The canal trip would take us to the largest cities of the state — Schenectady, Utica, Oswego, Syracuse, Rochester, and Buffalo. Can you find out from an encyclopedia what the people in these cities are doing?

New York, the largest city in the world, has twice the population of any other American city and contains more people than live in the ten states of Idaho, Montana, Wyoming, Colorado, Utah, Nevada, New Mexico, Oregon, North Dakota, and South Dakota. An average of fifteen thousand people live on each square mile of its area. Because of this dense population, the buildings of the city have grown higher and higher, until today the tallest skyscrapers in the world are located in New York. Dozens, scores, and in some cases even hundreds of families live in one apartment house, and hundreds of offices are located under one roof. The southern end of the city is its busiest part. Here, the streets seem narrower than they really are because the buildings are so high. Here stands the famous Woolworth Building, fifty-five stories (almost eight hundred feet) high. The Metropolitan Life Insurance Building has fifty stories. On this building, nearly three hundred and fifty feet above the sidewalk, is an immense clock, the largest four-faced timekeeper in the world. Each face is twenty-six and one-half feet in diameter, the figures that mark the hours are four feet high, and

FIG 29. This is a view of Fifth Avenue in New York City. This avenue does not look wide because the buildings are high, but how many auto-mobiles will it accommodate side by side.

the minute hand is seventeen feet long. Compare the size of the face of this wonderful clock with the floor of your schoolroom. Which has the greater diameter?

Let us take a seat on the top of a motorbus and ride up the beautiful Riverside Drive. On our left, we see the Hudson River with all its boats, while on our right are many magnificent residences. On a commanding height where there is a splendid view of the river, the Palisades, and the country beyond, stands the massive granite tomb of General Grant.

The Statue of Liberty stands on an island in the harbor. It was designed by a French artist and was given to the United States by the people of France as a token of their friendship. The statue is so beautifully proportioned that it is hard for one looking at it to realize its immense size. From its heels to the top of its head, it is one hundred and eleven feet high. The right arm, which holds aloft the flaming torch, is forty-two feet long, and the forefinger is eight feet in length.

To the right of this magnificent statue is Ellis Island, where the large buildings of the Immigration Station stand. Here, all immigrants to the United States who arrive at the port of New York must go for examination before they are allowed to enter the country. The industries of New York are extremely important. The city has become the leading financial center of the world. It is without a rival in the wholesale dry-goods and grocery business. It ranks far ahead of any other city in making clothing for men and women and in printing and publishing books, magazines, and papers. Enormous quantities of sugar to be refined, coffee to be roasted, and spices to be ground are brought from foreign lands to the piers of New York. Of course, these are only a few of the many industries that are carried on in this big city.

Clustered around New York are large, important cities. Many of these are on the New Jersey side of the river and are connected with New York by ferries and tunnels. Among these places is Jersey City, with its splendid docks and wharves. Newark, New Jersey's largest city, and Paterson, the silk city of America, lie only a short distance away.

In earlier periods of our history, both Philadelphia and Baltimore were larger than New York, but as years went by, they were left behind in the race. Why was this so?

One of the reasons that New York has grown to be the largest city in the world is because it is nearer to Europe than are the ports farther south. Another important reason is that it has an excellent harbor, where vessels from all countries of the world may come and from which great quantities of freight may be shipped away. The city is situated at the mouth of a river leading into the country. The sinking of the land deepened the Hudson and made it navigable as far as Albany. Here it is joined by the Mohawk River, whose valley leads westward to the Great Lakes. Along this valley, the Erie Canal and, more recently, the Barge Canal have been built to Buffalo, the doorway of the Great Lake route into the Central Plains. It was the Erie Canal which gave the first great impetus to New York's growth. The Hudson-Mohawk Valley route and the Great Lakes beyond furnish a splendid highway between New York City and the grain, cattle, and mineral area of the Middle West. Farther south, there is no such easy route between either Philadelphia or Baltimore and the rich plains to the west, for the Appalachian ranges bar the way.

Had we time to linger, we should find as many interesting

places to visit in the South as in the North. At Annapolis, the capital of Maryland, we might see the students at the United States Naval Academy going through their drills. Sailing from here down Chesapeake Bay, we could visit Norfolk and Newport News and see the wharves and the vessels loading with coal at these Virginia seaports. We should realize that we were in the part of the country where peanuts are grown when we saw the large quantities that are shipped away.

Baltimore is the largest city on Chesapeake Bay. It is an important manufacturing center, while its position on the bay makes it a busy commercial port as well. Virginia is one of our tobacco-growing states, and large quantities are sent to Baltimore to be manufactured.

If you lived near the shores of Chesapeake Bay or its inlets, you would see in the early morning scores of men putting out in their small boats to gather oysters. Chesapeake Bay has the largest oyster beds in the United States. Many people who live in Baltimore and other places around the bay earn their living by removing the oysters from the shells, packing them for market, or canning them. So many oysters are shipped from Baltimore that it has become the largest oyster port in the world.

We should like to visit the famous marble quarries in Tennessee and other states and compare the colors of the stone and the methods of quarrying with those in Vermont. We would go also to Atlanta, the Gate City, at the base of the Blue Ridge, and follow the long trainloads of cotton, tobacco, grain, and mules "from Atlanta to the sea."

The most interesting city in this section is Washington, the capital of the United States. It is the only city in the entire country not located in any state. It is in the District of Columbia, an area of sixty square miles lying between Maryland and Virginia.

Washington is located near the falls of the Potomac River, but, unlike the other cities on the fall line, it is not an industrial center. It is one of the most beautiful cities in the world, with its broad avenues, magnificent public buildings, splendid hotels, and luxurious homes. To many people who visit the city, the Capitol is the center of interest. It contains the Senate Chamber, the Hall of Representatives, and the Supreme Court Room. The building is seven hundred and fifty feet long and three hundred and fifty feet wide. How does it compare with the size of your schoolhouse?

The White House, the home of the president of the United States, is about a mile from the Capitol. It was the first public building to be erected in Washington and is an object of interest to all sightseers. You will wish to visit the buildings where the various departments of government carry on their work. Can you name these different departments? You will wish to see also the National Museum, the Library of Congress, the home of the Red Cross, the headquarters of the National Geographic Society, and, newest of all, the lovely Lincoln Memorial, finished in 1920. The Pan-American Building is one of the most beautiful in the world. It was built in 1910 by the Pan-American Union, an organization made up of all the republics in the Western Hemisphere. How many of these can you name?

Of course, you will wish to go to the top of the Washington Monument, the tallest stone column in the world. It is five hundred and fifty-five feet high, and an elevator runs to the top to carry those who wish to enjoy the beautiful view. Most visitors to Washington take a trip to Mount Vernon, the home of George Washington, our first president. It is a fine old mansion overlooking the blue waters of the Potomac.

SUGGESTIONS FOR STUDY

I

1. Nature's story of this mountain region.
2. Influence of mountains and rivers on early settlements.
3. The formation and mining of coal.
4. Petroleum and natural gas.
5. Water power in the Appalachian Highlands.
6. The fall line.
7. Iron and steel.
8. Pittsburgh and Birmingham.

9. The old city of Philadelphia.
10. Trenton and its clay industry.
11. Manufacturing in the southern Appalachians.
12. The salt industry.
13. Some trips through New York State.
14. New York, the largest city in the world.
15. Baltimore and the oyster industry.
16. Side trips in other states.
17. Our capital city, Washington.

II

1. Name the states which are included in the Appalachian Highland region.
2. Sketch Lake Erie and Lake Ontario, the Niagara River, and the Welland Canal. In what direction does the Niagara River flow? Make an arrow beside the river to show this on the map which you have drawn. The water in the Falls is constantly wearing away the cliff over which it flows. As this work goes on, in which direction are the Falls moving? Nearer which lake were they formerly? How has the position of the Falls affected the size of the city of Buffalo?
3. Find in an encyclopedia the larger cities mentioned in this chapter. What facts are given which are not mentioned here?
4. The natural supply of oysters long since failed to fill the demand for this seafood. Find out if you can how man has met this problem and tell the class about it.
5. Study the map of the coal areas on page 35 and make a list of the states where coal is mined.
6. Write to the Geological Survey, Washington, D.C., and ask for a pamphlet giving the names of the states in the order of their coal production. Perhaps you would like similar information on iron, petroleum, and natural gas. You can start a valuable reference library for your school in this way. Can you plan a card catalog for it? The librarian in the public library will help you to do this.

III

Make a list of the places mentioned in this chapter. Arrange them by countries, cities, mountains, rivers, etc. Be able to locate each place and tell what was said about it in the chapter.

CHAPTER IV

A VISIT TO OUR COASTAL PLAIN

Our next trip will take us into the great lowland belt of the United States. This stretches nearly the entire length of the Atlantic coast and along the Gulf of Mexico. On this great plain, we can see cotton, sugar, rice, and tobacco plantations and groves of oranges and grapefruit. We can wander through forests of tall pine trees, visit oil fields where derricks dot the land far and near, go out with the sponge gatherers as they gather their harvests from the ocean waters, or enjoy a bath with the crowds on one of the splendid beaches on the coast. You can travel for miles without seeing a hill or finding a large stone. In this great lowland, we find no evidences of the old glacier, no boulders which the farmers must remove from their fields, no hills of glacial waste, no hollows scraped out for glacial lakes, and no rivers turned out of their courses by the material piled up by the ice sheet.

All this region was once covered by the ocean, which extended to the edge of the mountain belt. In that period, long, long ages ago, the United States must have been narrower from east to west than it is now. The rivers brought down from the mountains great quantities of soil, just as they are doing today, and deposited it near their mouths, thus building up, very gradually indeed, the land under the shallow water. We call this the submarine plain or continental shelf. In time, the materials which the rivers carried, together with the rising of the land, brought some of this plain above the water. Thus, very, very gradually, the United States was made wider, and the lengthened rivers cut their courses across the young Coastal Plain to the ocean. Later, a sinking of the land, of which you read in the chapter on New England, drowned the mouths of the rivers and thus made excellent harbors along the coast. Many of the important commercial cities of this section, such as Charleston, Savannah, Jacksonville, Mobile, and Galveston, have grown up near such drowned river mouths. Most of the states which lie along the Atlantic coast stretch back into the Piedmont Belt, or hilly region. You remember that the fall line lies between these two areas and that some of our important cities lie along this line. Florida, Mississippi, and Louisiana lie wholly within the Coastal Plain.

The story of the Mississippi River is one of the most interesting in Nature's book. Look at the map opposite this page; notice how the coast bends southward at the mouth of the Mississippi. That is due to the work of the river. The great stream and its branches bring from the mountains and spread out over its flood plains and around its mouth an enormous amount of soil. If we should dig five hundred, a thousand, and in some places fifteen hundred and two thousand feet deep, we should find the same fine soil.

Near the mouth of the river, the current was so slow that the soil which was carried was laid down in the channels and at the mouths of the passes through which the river reached the Gulf. This checked the flow of the water even more, and the silt was therefore dropped farther and farther up the channels. Thus, you see, if nothing were done to prevent it, the passes would gradually fill up and vessels would be hindered in their passage to and from New Orleans. The water would become too shallow for large vessels, and the commerce of the city would be checked. Accordingly, embankments, called jetties, were built which confined the water in a narrow channel and thus increased its speed. After the jetties were built, the current became fast enough to carry the silt farther out into the open water of the Gulf of Mexico, and the mouth of the river was thus made navigable for large vessels.

We have read some of the stories which nature has written about the Coastal Plain; now let us see what the people here have to tell us about their lives and work.

MAP III
SOUTHERN STATES
EASTERN SECTION
SCALE OF MILES
0 50 100 150 200 250
Longitude
West
from Greenwich
KAN.
OKLA.
MISSOURI
KENTUCKY
VIRGINIA
TENNESSEE
NORTH CAROLINA
SOUTH CAROLINA
ARKANSAS
TEXAS
LOUISIANA
MISSISSIPPI
ALABAMA
GEORGIA
FLORIDA
ILL.
NASHVILLE
RALEIGH
ATLANTA
COLUMBIA
MONTGOMERY
JACKSON
TALLAHASSEE
Norfolk
Elizabeth City
Albemarle Sd.
Roanoke R.
Clarksville
Cumberland Gap
Cumberland Mts.
Cumberland R.
Winston
Durham
Greensboro
Mt. Salem
Mitchell
Knoxville
Gt. Smoky Mts.
Charlotte
Pamlico
C. Hatteras
New Bern
Neuse R.
Beaufort
C. Lookout
Fayetteville
Fear R.
Wilmington
Columbia
Asheville
Spartanburg
Greenville
Florence
C. Fear
Jackson
Memphis
Arkansas R.
LITTLE ROCK
Fayetteville
Chattanooga
Florence
Chickamauga Park
Lookout Mt.
Tennessee R.
Decatur
Huntsville
Gadsden
Koine
Gainesville
Anderson
Athens
Augusta
Sumter
Red R.
Sabine R.
Aberdeen
Columbus
Greenville
Birmingham
Anniston
Bessemer
Tuscaloosa
Atlanta
Columbia
Charleston
Savannah R.
Santee R.
Beaufort
Meridian
Selma
Tuskegee
Columbus
Macon
Savannah
Jackson
Vicksburg
Hattiesburg
Natchez
Montgomery
Eufaula
Americus
Albany
Altamaha R.
Brunswick
Pearl R.
Tombigbee R.
Alabama R.
Chattahoochee R.
Flint R.
Thomasville
Valdosta
Baton Rouge
Pontchartrain L.
Biloxi
Mobile
New Orleans
Gulfport
Mobile Bay
Pensacola
Apalachicola R.
Apalachee Bay
Jacksonville
St. Augustine
Daytona
Delta of the Mississippi R.
Orlando
C. Canaveral
Indian R.
St. Johns R.
Tarpon Springs
St. Petersburg
Tampa
Tampa Bay
L. Okeechobee
Ft. Myers
Palm Beach
The Everglades
C. Sable
Key West
Miami
Florida Strait
PLORIDA KEYS
BAHAMA ISLANDS
GULF OF MEXICO
ATLANTIC OCEAN
Mississippi R.
Ohio R.

FIG 30. This is a part of the bathing beach at Coney Island. There are many fine beaches along the shores of the Atlantic Plain. Do you know the names of any others?

If someone were to ask you to name the three greatest needs of your life, you would probably tell them your food, clothing, and shelter. The cotton plant supplies clothing for most of the people on earth. No other plant that grows is so important, for none can take its place.

The farmers of our southern states raise more cotton than those of all other lands of the world put together. It would take nearly all the gold mined in every mine on earth in the last five years to pay for one crop of cotton fiber and seed. The cotton crop of the South is of more value to the people there than all the other crops combined.

Imagine a line drawn on your map of the United States from Norfolk, Virginia, westward through Memphis, Tennessee, and Little Rock, Arkansas, to Dallas, Texas. The cotton belt of the country lies chiefly south of this line. In the planting

FIG 31. "We's done all dis s'mornin'"
(Courtesy of the Keystone View Co.)

season, the plows travel back and forth over the fields, open the furrow, and drop the seed and fertilizer. Some months later, the cotton fields appear as if a curious snowstorm had showered the plants with fluffy snowballs instead of snowflakes. These white balls are the opened pods of fiber. After the flower petals have dropped from the plant, a small pod, or "boll," forms in their place. This soon grows to a size somewhat smaller than a hen's egg; then it bursts open and shows the white, fluffy cotton within.

This is the busiest time of the year for the cotton planters, and the fields are dotted with people, each laden with a bag to hold the fiber.

If you were to examine a cotton boll, you would find in it a number of small seeds. Formerly, these had to be picked out by hand, and it was slow, tiresome work. A man could clean only a pound or two of fiber in a day. This made cotton expensive, and garments made from it were a luxury which only the rich could afford.

In 1793, Eli Whitney invented the cotton gin. This machine can clean the seeds from more cotton in a day than can a hundred people working by hand. Farmers soon began planting more and more cotton, and so the industry grew.

Formerly, the cotton seeds were a waste product; today they are of great value, and the products made from them are worth millions of dollars. The seeds are crushed by machinery and the oil extracted. This is used by many housewives instead of lard or olive oil. The poorer grades are utilized in the making of soap. After the oil is extracted, the crushed seeds are made into

FIG 32. These farmers have brought their loads of cotton to the gin. What will be done to it there? (Courtesy of the Keystone View Co.)

meal. Many southern farmers now feed their cattle on the product of their cotton fields. The hulls which were removed before the oil was extracted are also used as a cattle food.

By looking at a map, you can tell at what cities you would be likely to find large quantities of cotton and cotton products ready for shipping. The farmers in the states on either side of the Mississippi River, northern Mississippi, Arkansas, and Tennessee, send their cotton to Memphis. This city has grown to be the largest inland market in the world for cotton and cottonseed products. From Memphis, the cotton is sent to New Orleans. Texas produces more cotton than any other state. This is sent away largely through Galveston. These two cities, New Orleans and Galveston, are the largest cotton ports in the world. Mobile, on the Gulf coast, and Savannah and Charleston, on the Atlantic, also ship much cotton. Large quantities are sent to European countries from Norfolk and New York City.

More than half of all our cotton is sent abroad to be manufactured in foreign cities, but enormous quantities are spun and woven in the United States. You read on page 18 how important the industry is in New England. A great many cotton mills are running also in the southern states, and more and more cotton is being manufactured every year in the states which produce it.

While we are in this section, we shall wish to visit a sugar plantation. Later, we shall see many acres on the Central Plains planted with the sugar beet, but sugar cane grows only in the southern states. A field of cane looks much like a cornfield except that the cane is taller. To see the largest sugar plantations in the country, we will go to Louisiana, for that state produces nearly all our cane sugar. The best time for a visit is during the harvesting. The workers cut the tall stalks, load them on cars on the large plantations and on mule teams on the smaller ones, and take them to the mills. Here they are placed on long carriers, which feed them to heavy rollers that crush the stalks, while the juice drips down into receptacles beneath. How dark the juice is! It hardly seems possible that fine white sugar can ever be made from it. But we watch it as it is boiled down in great vats until it is a thick brown syrup. Then we see this syrup put into great cylinders with walls like sieves. The cylinders revolve so fast that the liquid part, the molasses, oozes out through the holes in the sides, and crystals of sugar coat the inner walls.

This sugar is not yet ready for your sugar bowls. It must be refined—that is, put through processes which will remove the impurities and make it fine-grained and white. The machinery for refining sugar is so expensive that the work is done in a few immense refineries. These are situated in some of our large seaports, to which the imported sugar can be easily brought. Near the city of New Orleans is the largest sugar refinery in the world. We produce in the United States much less sugar than we use, and billions of pounds are brought from the Hawaiian and Philippine Islands, from Cuba, Puerto Rico, and other islands of the West Indies, and from South American countries.

Another important food crop is rice. It is the principal food of more than half the people on earth. Enormous quantities are produced, chiefly in the countries of southeastern Asia. The people there live on it and also export large amounts.

In former days, rice was raised only along the lowlands of North Carolina, South Carolina, and Georgia. With the development of the country, many industries have moved farther west, rice-growing among the number. Today, most of our rice is raised in Louisiana and Texas. Arkansas raises a considerable amount, and California has added this industry to her many others and is increasing her crop each year.

FIG 33. These people in Japan are transplanting the rice plants one by one. They will reap the grain by hand with sickles. How does their work differ from methods used in this country?

Rice needs great quantities of water during its growth. Fields on which it is raised must be so arranged that they can be flooded and drained from time to time. On the large plantations in the United States, powerful pumps raise the water from wells or rivers and distribute it over the level fields. The seed is sown by machines, and at harvest time, the grain is reaped by great harvesters. These great machines can do the work of so many men that, although the laborers in the East are paid only a few cents a day, we can raise rice more cheaply in the United States than Eastern countries can produce it. One man with his machine can do as much work as fifty laborers can, working only with their hands.

The Atlantic Plain has become a very important area for truck farmers, who supply garden truck to the large cities — New York, Philadelphia, Baltimore, and others. Vegetables and fruits are produced on the more southerly parts of the Coastal Plain early in the season, and in the spring and early summer are sent by fast freights to the states farther north. Many of these products are also canned, and the city of Baltimore, on the edge of the plain, has become an important canning center.

The long growing season and the mild winters have caused many farmers to specialize in fruit-growing. Have you ever eaten Georgia peaches or Delaware grapes? In Florida, there are large groves of oranges and grapefruit. Pineapples are also

FIG 34. Why are we able to produce rice more cheaply than people in Eastern countries can? (Courtesy of the Department of Agriculture)

raised here, but most of our canned pineapples come from the Hawaiian Islands.

Do nuts of any kind grow in the part of the country where you live? Pecans, walnuts, almonds, and other varieties are produced in large quantities in some states. Most of the walnuts and almonds come from California and the pecans from the Southern states. There are thousands of wild pecan trees in this section, and many groves have been planted, from which thousands of bushels of nuts are gathered each year.

When you ask your mother for a peanut butter sandwich, you probably do not think of the importance of our peanut crop. Peanut oil is one of the commercial food oils of the world, and millions of bushels of the nuts are raised in the Southern states, from which large quantities of oil are made. The plant has other uses. The dried vines, the meal made from the crushed nuts after the oil is extracted, the hulls, and the waste from the peanut butter factories are all used as cattle food. Animals like peanuts as well as people do, and in some places, hogs are turned into the peanut fields to harvest the crop.

Peanuts are grown on a large scale in many other warm parts of the world — in Central and South America, Africa, India, and China. The plant is a cousin of the bean and pea. It differs from its relations, however, in that its fruit ripens underground rather than in the air. One of its common names is the groundnut.

All plants must have air, sunshine, and water. Besides these, they need foods with which you may not be so familiar, such as potassium, nitrogen, and phosphorus. Most of the phosphorus, in the form that can be used in fertilizers, comes from rock found in several states — Florida, Tennessee, Kentucky, and South Carolina. Florida has the largest phosphate mines in the world and yields most of the phosphate produced in our country.

The workmen scrape off the overlying rock and soil, dig out the phosphate rock, and load it on cars. These take it to the crushers, where it is ground to powder. In this form, it is shipped away.

In the last chapter, you read about the rich iron and coal

FIG 35. The picture shows a part of a field of peanuts in Virginia. On what part of the plant do the nuts grow? (Courtesy of the Department of Agriculture)

beds in the southern part of the Appalachian Highlands. Besides these, there are other valuable minerals in the South. Sulfur is one of these. This is used in the manufacture of drugs and chemicals, paper, and steel, and in the refining of oil. During the World War, our production was doubled because of the large quantities needed in making explosives and fertilizers. Nearly all the sulfur produced in the United States comes from Louisiana and Texas. The sulfur is usually found several hundred feet below the surface of the ground. Powerful machines bore holes down to the sulfur beds. Pipes are run down the holes; water, intensely hot, is forced down the pipes and melts the sulfur; the liquid sulfur is then driven up to the surface by compressed air and piped to great bins. Here it cools and becomes solid. The workmen break it up by blasting, and big steam shovels scoop it up and drop it into cars. These take it to different states or to the seaports for shipment abroad. Some of our richest petroleum deposits lie along the Gulf of Mexico. Louisiana ranks high in its production, and even more is obtained in Texas. Some

FIG 36. This well produced 55,000 barrels of petroleum a day for a long period. Its total production is estimated at 6,000,000 barrels. (Courtesy of the Department of the Interior)

wells yield for years immense quantities of oil; others flow only for a few months; and still others, after all the expense of drilling, do not yield at all. What is said about the uses of petroleum on page 38?

Louisiana and Texas contain also great salt deposits. We could go down to these salt beds in an elevator and walk through long, glittering tunnels lighted by electricity. We

FIG 37. This is a forest of long-leaf Southern pine. Notice how tall and straight the trees are. What products are obtained from these trees?

could see miners blasting out the salt rock and shoveling it onto cars, which run to the shaft where they are lifted out. In what other way have you read of salt being obtained (see page 44)?

Much kaolin, the purest form of clay and useful in the manufacture of fine china, is found in the South, especially in North Carolina. Another variety, used in paper-making, comes from South Carolina and Georgia. What did you read about the clay industry on page 43?

Look at the map on page 20, which shows you the large forest areas of the United States. Of which one of the areas shown here have you already read? Here on the Coastal Plain is another wooded area, one of the most important in the country. Lumbering in these forests of yellow pine is a leading industry of the plain, and immense quantities of valuable lumber are produced. The trees are useful not only for their wood but also for their sap, from which turpentine and rosin are made. In the earlier days of this industry, tar and pitch were the chief products made from the sap. They were called naval stores because they were necessary in the building and repairing of the wooden ships then in common use. Today, turpentine and rosin are far more important products. If you consult an encyclopedia, you will find the uses of these products. The United States pro-

FIG 38. This man is cleaning the gutter so that the sticky sap will flow more freely. What use will be made of the sap? (Courtesy of the Department of Agriculture)

Map IV

SOUTHERN STATES
WESTERN SECTION
SCALE OF MILES
0 50 100 150 200 250
Longitude West from Greenwich
COLORADO
KANSAS
NEW MEXICO
TEXAS
OKLAHOMA
ARKANSAS
LOUISIANA
MISSISSIPPI
ALABAMA
TENNESSEE
KENTUCKY
MISSOURI
ILL.
FLA.
GULF OF MEXICO
Rio Grande
Pecos
Canadian
Cimarron
Arkansas R.
Red R.
Colorado
Brazos
Trinity
Nueces
Sabine
Ouachita R.
White R.
Black R.
Yazoo R.
Pearl R.
Mississippi R.
Pontchartrain
Ozark Plateau
Guadalupe Mts.
Wichita Mts.
Ouachita Mts.
Boston Mts.
El Paso
Pecos
Laredo
Eagle Pass
Brownsville
San Antonio
Corpus Christi
AUSTIN
Brenham
Houston
Galveston
Galveston Bay
Beaumont
Waco
Fort Worth
Corsicana
Palestine
Tyler
Dallas
Sherman
Denison
Paris
Texarkana
Marshall
Shreveport
Alexandria
Lake Charles
New Iberia
Donaldsonville
New Orleans
BATON ROUGE
Natchez
Vicksburg
JACKSON
Meridian
Monroe
MONTGOMERY
NASHVILLE
Memphis
Cairo
Helena
Pine Bluff
N. Little Rock
LITTLE ROCK
HOT SPRINGS NAT. PARK
Eureka Sprs.
Jonesboro
F. Smith
McAlester
Tahlequah
Muskogee
OKLAHOMA CITY
Guthrie
Tulsa
Enid
PLATT NAT. PARK
108° 104° 100° 96° 92° 88°
34° 30° 26°

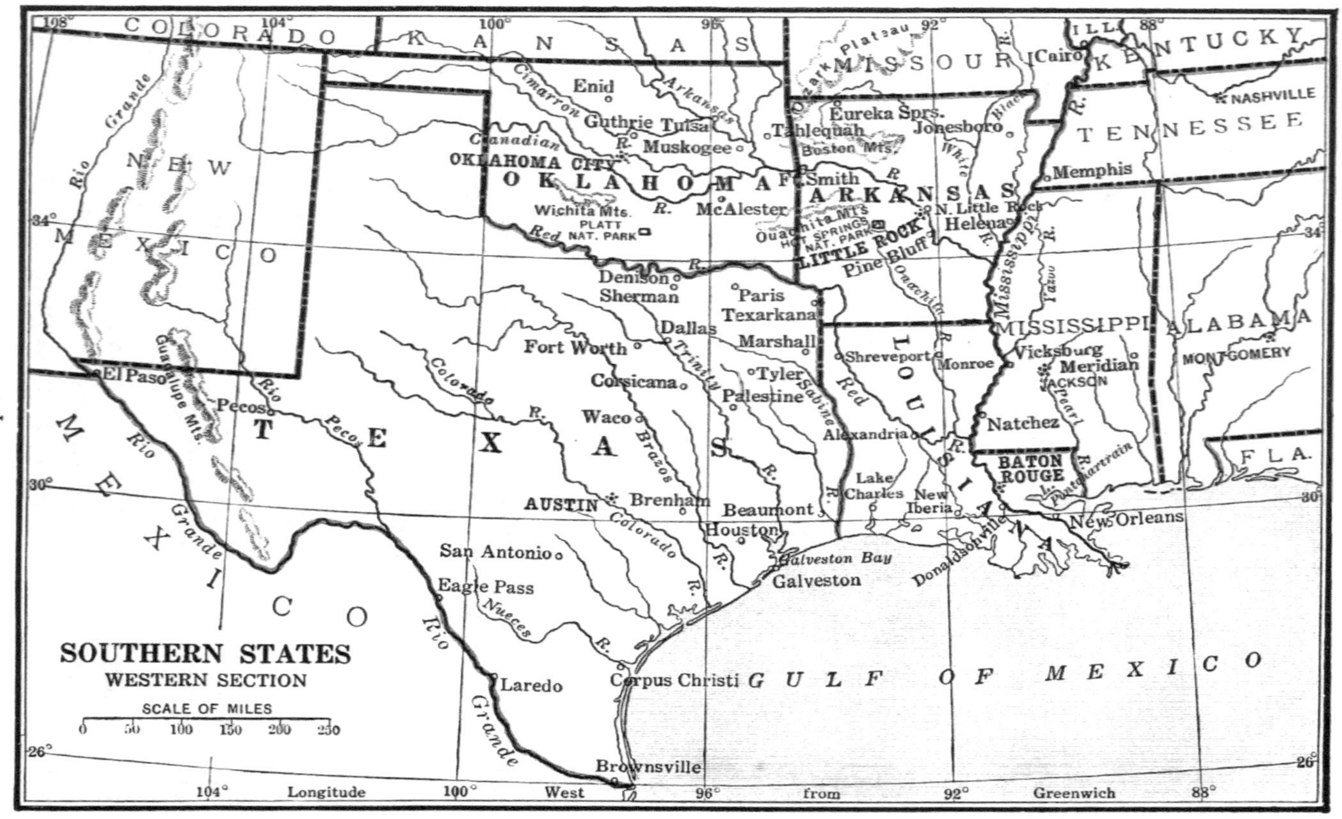

duces much larger quantities of naval stores than any other country, and more are shipped from Savannah than from any other city in the world.

When you use your sponge for your bath or see sponges displayed in stores, do you ever wonder where they come from? The industry is an important one in the United States, and millions are gathered each year. Most of these are secured from the Caribbean Sea and the Gulf of Mexico. They are made by great numbers of tiny, jelly-like creatures, which are protected by a skeleton framework. It is this skeleton which is the sponge of commerce.

In the early days of the industry, the sponge gatherers waded into the water and tore the sponges from the rocks to which they were attached. Today, the men go out into the deeper water and make use of a heavy hook attached to the end of a long pole. In order to look down far enough through the water, a water telescope is used. This is a sort of bucket with a glass bottom. By placing this in the water and looking through it,

FIG 39. This is a lumber mill on the lower Mississippi. Where else in the country could you see similar sights?

FIG 40. These are sponges for sale on the wharf at Key West. How are sponges obtained? (Courtesy of the Keystone View Co.)

the sponge gatherer can see, when the ocean is not too rough, for forty or fifty feet and can thus easily locate the sponges. In some places, it is the custom for men to dive for sponges. The divers can get them from deeper, rougher waters, where the hook would not be successful.

After the sponges are brought to shore, they are washed, cleaned, dried, and sorted. Some of them are bleached also. They are then tied up in bales and shipped away.

We shall not wish to leave this southernmost part of the country without seeing something of the state of Florida, for there is much to interest us there. St. Augustine is the oldest permanent settlement in the United States.

The modern hotels, with their courtyards and gardens, beautiful with tropical plants and flowers and cool, splashing fountains, are a great contrast to the old Spanish buildings with their barred windows and latticed balconies.

Jacksonville, on the St. Johns River, is Florida's largest city and

FIG 41. This is a tower in which a man is stationed to watch for forest fires. The Forest Service has built many of these towers in wooded areas of the country. (Courtesy of the Department of Agriculture)

its chief commercial and railroad center. Our visit would not be complete without a sail up the St. Johns, the largest river of Florida. Around this stream, the scenery is so lovely that thousands of visitors make the interesting trip every year. The waving shadows of the live oak, the magnolia, the cypress, the palmetto, the gum tree, gleam along the water. The dogwood with its white star flowers, the orchids of delicate tints, the dainty, perfumed jasmine, and festoons of gray moss hanging from the trees make a picture of indescribable charm.

Of all the winter resorts in Florida, Palm Beach is the most famous. It has the largest hotels, the most fashionable visitors, and the gayest season of any winter resort in America. Its immense hotels fitted with every convenience and many luxuries, its gardens a riot of color, its palm-shaded walks thronged with richly dressed ladies, and its gleaming white beach dotted with hundreds of bathers make it seem almost like fairyland. Miami, also, is a very popular resort and has thousands of winter visitors. There are many other places in Florida whose population in summer is much smaller than in winter.

In the south of Florida are large swampy areas which are

called the Everglades. Here, as someone has remarked, "there is too much water for farming and not enough for swimming." Large projects are now underway for draining this region and so changing the swamps to good farming lands. The draining of some of the cypress swamps of Louisiana has furnished much rich land, where farmers today are raising cotton, rice, and sugar cane. Wet lands in other places have been drained with good results.

Southern Florida is made of coral formation. Millions and millions of the tiny coral polyps, living, growing, and dying, leave behind their skeletons, which in time decay and powder into soil. From the mainland, we can go by train out along the low coral islands, or keys, and over long bridges between them to Key West. This city is only sixty miles from the torrid zone, yet, because of the ocean breezes, it is cooler than some places farther north. Some people here earn their living by making cigars from tobacco imported from Cuba. Others are sponge gatherers.

The situation of the cities on the Coastal Plain makes an interesting study and well illustrates the fact that it is usually Nature rather than man who decides where our cities shall be built.

In looking at your maps, you will notice that there are few large cities between the fall line on the inner edge of the Coastal Plain and its outer border. Except in rare cases, there is no reason for building cities there. Such a situation would be unfavorable either for manufacturing or for the carrying on of commerce. Can you tell why?

You have read about the fall-line cities, and you know why they grew up at the inner margin of the Coastal Plain. Some of the manufacturing plants in these cities, like the pottery establishments in Trenton, use materials from the Coastal Plain; others, like the locomotive works in Philadelphia, use products of the highland region.

Many cities are situated along the coast and inlets where there are good harbors, and others are near the deep mouths of rivers whose valleys lead into the country. From studying the map, can you tell how the position of Norfolk, Wilmington, Charleston, Savannah, Pensacola, Mobile, New Orleans, Houston, and Galveston has helped these cities to grow?

Perhaps of all Southern cities, New Orleans, the largest in that section, is the most interesting to visitors. It is situated one hundred miles from the mouth of the Mississippi River. How do you account for the fact that, in its younger days, New Orleans was nearer the mouth of the river than it is today? The great seaport is located just where the Mississippi makes a sharp curve, and for this reason, it was often called the Crescent City. It is no longer embraced by the crescent-shaped bend in the river but stretches away in all directions.

Some of the land on which New Orleans is built is lower than the great river which flows through the city, and banks, called levees, have been built on either side of the channel to prevent the river from overflowing. Many of the houses have no cellars, for before the city was as well-drained as it is today, one could not dig far before striking wet and porous soil. In some of the cemeteries, the graves are above the ground. The region has now been drained much more thoroughly than formerly; deeper foundations can be laid, and taller buildings can be erected in the city.

On the wharves, we see bales upon bales of cotton, which are to be loaded on vessels that will take them to European countries and to the manufacturing cities of the North. Many barrels of sugar are here also, for you remember that Louisiana raises more sugar than all the rest of the Southern states put together. Wheat, flour, lumber, and rice are also exported in large quantities.

If you were to visit the manufacturing part of the city, you would see great sugar refineries, buildings where rice is milled, cigar and tobacco factories, and the signs of many other industries.

The foreign commerce of New Orleans has increased greatly in recent years. The building of the Panama Canal has had a great influence on her commerce with South American lands. Many of the products shipped away from the Crescent City come from the great areas included in the Central Plains, which stretch away to the north for hundreds of miles. New Orleans is really the doorway to the heart of these rich plains, which we are to see in our next visit. We will leave the rice and cane fields, the cotton plantations, and the deep forests of the South and sail northward on the great Mississippi. On such a trip, we shall see many other farms, other cities, and other industries just as interesting as those of our Coastal Plain.

SUGGESTIONS FOR STUDY

I.

1. Surface and industries of the Coastal Plain.
2. Formation of the lowland.
3. The delta and jetties of the Mississippi River.
4. The cotton industry.
5. Sugar cane and sugar refineries.
6. Rice production.
7. Truck farming and fruit growing.
8. Pecans and peanuts.
9. Mineral productions of the South.
10. Forests and forest products.
11. The sponge industry.
12. Interesting places in Florida.
13. New Orleans and other cities.

II.

1. Be able to name the states which are included in the Atlantic Coastal Plain; in the Gulf Plain.
2. After a heavy rain, find a stream by the roadside building its delta. Try to draw the shape of the delta. Where, besides at its mouth, was the stream leaving some of the soil which it carried?
3. Using the diagram given on page 75, and an outline map of the United States, shade the petroleum-producing states. Number each according to rank. While the class does this, two pupils

may put a stencil map of the United States on the blackboard. Color the petroleum-producing states with green chalk. Fill with diagonal lines of blue chalk the coal-producing states; with lines of red chalk running in the other direction the states where iron is mined.

4. Write a letter to the Department of Agriculture at Washington asking for pamphlets describing rice cultivation in the United States also for a description of the peanut industry.

III.

Make a list of the places mentioned in this chapter. Arrange them by cities, mountains, rivers, etc. Be able to spell, pronounce, and locate all the names in your list, and tell what was said in the chapter about each one.

CHAPTER V

UP THE MISSISSIPPI INTO THE CENTRAL PLAINS

Our trip over the Central Plains will be a most interesting one. Agriculture, manufacturing, and commerce have increased so rapidly that we shall find here, in the heart of the country, some of the finest farms, the greatest and most important industries, and the largest cities of the United States.

If we would learn some of the reasons for the remarkable growth of this section of the country, we must look first for the resources with which Nature has supplied this great area. Of all these, the soil is the most important. The Central Plains contain no deserts and no high mountains. In all the world, there is no equally large area that is so uniformly fertile. Such great crops are raised here that the region is often called the Bread Basket of the United States.

Beneath the soil, also, great resources are hidden. Immense beds of coal covering thousands of acres are found here. Look at the map on page 35 and see which states contain these deposits. Besides coal, Nature has provided other fuels. Natural gas is found, and some of our greatest petroleum-producing states lie in this region. Oklahoma alone produces each year many million barrels. Kansas, its neighbor on the north, and Ohio, Indiana, Illinois, Tennessee, and Kentucky, across the great river, all produce large quantities. Of what other petroleum-producing states have you already read?

The Central Plains supply enormous quantities of coal, oil, and gas, and furnish plenty of "white coal," as water power is often called. In the old highland regions of this part of the country, many materials for manufacturing are found. The richest iron beds in the world lie in an ancient upland near Lake Superior, and valuable copper mines are found south of the lake. In the highland regions of Missouri, Oklahoma, Wisconsin, Kansas, and other states, zinc and lead are mined.

Among the resources that have helped in the building of the West are the evergreen forests of Minnesota, Michigan, and Wisconsin, along with the hardwood forests of the Ohio Valley. Farmers of the treeless plains needed lumber for their houses and barns, furniture for their homes, and wagons and tools to help them in their work; the deep forests supplied the materials for these and other uses. Perhaps the desks and chairs in your schoolroom were made in Grand Rapids, Chicago, or another city of the Central Plains. Some firms that began by making small wooden tools now manufacture, from wood and steel, giant reapers and harvesters, essential for the people of the United States and other countries to harvest their vast grain crops. The forests also made possible the manufacture of wooden carriages and cars; later, the plentiful supply of iron helped establish the cities of the lake region as the center of the world's automobile industry.

You have already read about the rich salt deposits in New York. Salt is found also in large quantities in the Central Plains, especially in Michigan. This state ranks first in the country in its production. Later you will read about Great Salt Lake in Utah and of the

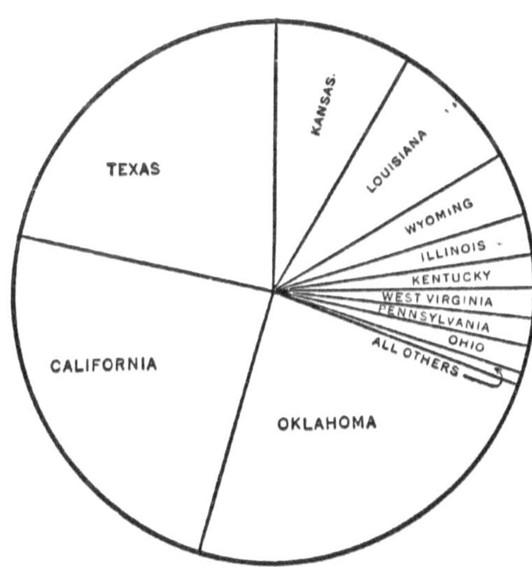

FIG 42. This diagram shows the production of petroleum by states. Make a list of these states, arranging them in the order of production.

Map V
CENTRAL STATES
EASTERN SECTION
SCALE OF MILES
0   50   100   150   200
L. Nipigon
ONTARIO
QUEBEC
ISLE ROYAL
LAKE SUPERIOR
Port Arthur
Calumet
Houghton Hancock
Mineral Range
Superior
Ashland
Marquette
Ironwood
Ishpeming
Escanaba
Sault Ste. Marie
Soo Canals
St. Marys R.
Sault Ste. Marie
Penokee Iron Range
MICHIGAN
St. Croix R.
Menominee R.
Str. Mackinac
Cheboygan
Georgian Bay
Wausau
Menominee
Marinette
Alpena
LAKE HURON
MINNESOTA
Chippewa R.
Eau Claire
Green Bay
WISCONSIN
Manistee
Muskegon R.
Toronto
L. Ontario
Hamilton
Mississippi
Black R.
Appleton
Oshkosh
La Crosse
L. Winnebago
Green Bay
Saginaw Bay
Saginaw
Bay City
Fond du Lac
Sheboygan
Grand
Muskegon R.
Flint Port
Huron
Wisconsin R.
Watertown
Waukesha
Milwaukee
Saginaw
Muskegon
MADISON
Janesville
Racine
Grand Rapids
LANSING
St. Clair R.
IOWA
Beloit
Kenosha
Battle Creek
Detroit
Ann Arbor
L. St. Clair
ERIE
Erie
Freeport
Waukegan
Elgin
Evanston
Kalamazoo
Jackson
Detroit R.
Ashtabula Conneaut
Davenport
Rockford
Oak Park
Chicago
Adrian
L. ERIE
Cleveland
Lorain
Youngstown
Rock R.
Aurora
Ill. & Mich.
South Bend
Elkhart
Goshen
Toledo
Maumee R.
Sandusky
Akron
Alliance
Moline
Rock Island
Canal Joliet
Gary
Hammond
Michigan City
Wabash & Erie Canal
Findlay
Massillon
Canton
PA.
Des Moines R.
La Salle
Ottawa
Kankakee
Ft. Wayne
Maumee R.
Mansfield
E. Liverpool
Galesburg
Streator
Logansport
Lima
Marion
Steubenville
Pittsburg
Keokuk
Peoria
Bloomington
Marion
OHIO
Newark
Wheeling
ILLINOIS
Danville
Lafayette
Muncie
Piqua
Zanesville
Quincy
Decatur
INDIANA
Anderson
Richmond
Dayton
COLUMBUS
Springfield
Marietta
MISSOURI
SPRINGFIELD
Jacksonville
INDIANAPOLIS
Terre Haute
Hamilton
Cincinnati
Chillicothe
Scioto R.
Mississippi R.
Illinois R.
Kaskaskia R.
Newport
Portsmouth
Ironton
W. VA.
Alton
Wabash R.
Jeffersonville
New Albany
Covington
Licking R.
Ohio R.
Big Sandy R.
CHARLESTON
Missouri R.
E. St. Louis
Evansville
Louisville
Kentucky R.
FRANKFORT
Lexington
St. Louis
Belleville
Owensboro
Green R.
KENTUCKY
Henderson
Cairo
Ohio R.
CUMBERLAND MTS.
VIRGINIA
Paducah
Tennessee R.
Bowling Green
Mammoth Cave
Middlesboro
Cumberland Gap
ARK.
TENNESSEE
Cumberland R.
NASHVILLE
N. CAR.
Longitude 90° West from 85° Greenwich
50°
45°
40°
90°
85°
80°

great amount of salt in its waters. Ohio, Kansas, Louisiana, California, and Texas also produce large quantities. Indeed, salt is obtained in nearly half of the states in the country.

Still another abundant mineral product found in the Central Plains is clay, which has numerous uses, though its primary use is in making bricks. Millions of bricks are produced in nearly every state - including common building bricks, paving bricks, fancy and ornamental bricks, and fire bricks for furnaces. Think also of the many tiles used in building houses, for floors and walls in bathrooms, and around fireplaces. There are also miles of water pipes, drainage pipes, and sewer pipes needed throughout the country each year, along with stove linings, bathroom fixtures, clay pipes for smoking, flowerpots, door knobs, doll heads, and marbles for play.

The Mississippi River, which has greatly contributed to the formation of the Central Plains, is as remarkable as the plains themselves. With its largest branch, the Missouri, the Mississippi forms the longest river in the world - stretching forty-two hundred miles in length. It receives the waters of numerous navigable rivers and hundreds of others that are not.

Our trip up the Mississippi first takes us through a section of the Coastal Plain, with forests of live oak hung with long, trailing gray moss, and shadowy cypress swamps with impenetrable undergrowth of vines and shrubs. In his poem "Evangeline," Longfellow offers a beautiful description of this part

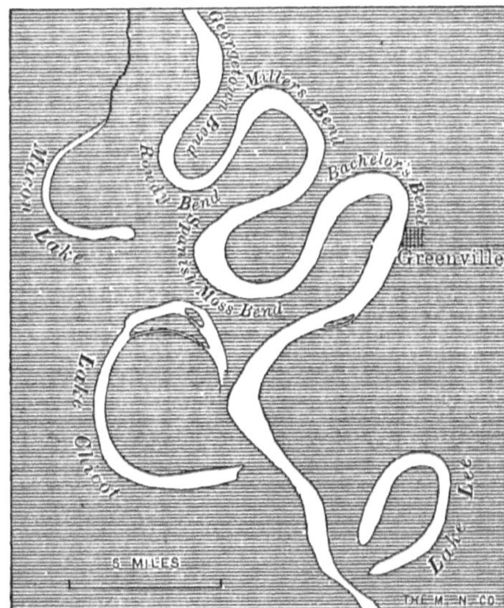

FIG 43. This illustration shows you some of the crooks in the Mississippi River. Can you explain how the lakes shown, which were once a part of the river, have been cut off?

FIG 44. This picture shows a levee on the bank of the Mississippi River. Can you tell why many miles of such levees have been built? (Courtesy of the Weather Bureau)

of the river. Choose someone from the class to read it to you while you close your eyes and try to picture the scene.

Here on the Coastal Plain, we see everywhere the presence of the cotton industry. Large plantations line the river, and steamers loaded with cotton make their way down to New Orleans. Cotton fills the wharves at Natchez and Vicksburg. Memphis, Tennessee, is the largest city on the river between St. Louis and New Orleans. This city lies between the hardwood area of the Ohio Valley and the pine-forest belt of the Southern states. It is in the cotton belt and near the tobacco lands. From these facts, what industries do you think are important in Memphis? Look it up in an encyclopedia to check if you are correct.

As we observe the countryside on each side of the river, we notice that it is lower than the river's surface. This seems unusual, doesn't it? The land is so level that the river flows more slowly as it nears the Gulf, unable to carry all its load of silt and constantly dropping some of it. Thus, the great Mississippi continually builds up its channel until it eventually becomes higher than the land on either side.

When rains fall and snows melt in the mountains where the river's tributaries originate, the river's water level rises dramatically. If not for the dikes, or levees, along the riverbanks, these waters would often overflow, flooding the low-lying plains on each side. Hundreds of miles of levees protect the farms in these flood plains.

Most people are not familiar with the brief weather forecast issued by the Weather Bureau at Washington, except the short paragraph in the daily paper telling the people of a small area what to expect for the next day's weather. This is only a very small part of the valuable work which the Bureau is doing and which saves the country millions of dollars and hundreds of lives each year. The sea captains who do not leave port when the Bureau issues storm warnings along the coast, the owners of cranberry bogs who flood their fields when a freeze is pre-

FIG 45. The picture here shows some of the effects of a flood on the Mississippi River. What causes such floods? (Courtesy of the Department of Agriculture)

dicted, the fruit growers who are saved thousands of dollars by a timely warning of a cold snap, all these and others will testify to the value of the work which the Weather Bureau is doing for the people of the United States.

The people living in the Mississippi Valley's lowlands also rely on the Bureau for flood warnings, which allow them to strengthen levees, appoint guards to watch for weak points, and move property and livestock to higher ground.

The Ohio River, the largest eastern tributary of the Mississippi, has a series of dams and locks to regulate its water level, ensuring navigability. In Figure 46, you can see coal barges being towed by small tugboats. This coal, mined from the Appalachian Highlands, is destined for manufacturing towns and cities along or near the Ohio River, perhaps to Cincinnati or Louisville. Vast amounts of coal, coke, and iron are transported from Pittsburgh to these cities, fueling industries or being distributed to other bustling industrial centers.

FIG 46. These are coal barges on the Ohio River. How are they being moved? Do you think they are going up or down the river? Give the reason for your answer. (Courtesy of the Cincinnati Industrial Bureau)

We wish that we had time for a trip up the Ohio River with stop-off privileges so that we could visit the states in this region and see what the people are doing. We should visit some of the famous tobacco farms in Kentucky, measure some of the longest leaves, and see the crop hanging in the drying sheds. We should go into the forests and see if we could name the hardwood trees which grow there. Of course you know the oak and the maple, but can you recognize a chestnut, a walnut, a hickory, or an ash? We should visit the Blue Grass region of Kentucky, where splendid horses are raised, beautiful, swift, and strong. We should explore Mammoth Cave, see the rooms which the water has made in the limestone, and admire the objects, the altars and pillars and statues, carved from the rock.

One of the things we shall see in the Central Plains are the great cornfields. Corn has always been an important crop in the United States. The Indians raised it long before the white man ever visited America. When starvation threatened the early colonists, the red men showed them how to raise corn. But all the cornfields of the Indians and the early settlers, put together, would not equal those in one county of our great corn-producing states.

You will be as interested in the hogs and cattle in this section of the country as in the cornfields. We do not export much of our great corn crop, but use it instead to feed the animals which we raise. The hogs eat a third of the crop. Many cattle are raised in the corn belt, and many are shipped there from ranches farther west to be fattened for market. They eat nearly as much as the hogs do, while horses and mules eat even more. Not only the kernels, but the stalks and leaves of the corn make good cattle food. On many farms, these are cut and fed when green. Sometimes they are chopped up and put into silos and fed to the animals during the winter months. Notice the large round silos in the picture on page 231.

Nature has stored away a great deal of starch in the kernels of corn. The cornstarch which your mother uses for her puddings, and the starch which stiffens your clothes, are made from this grain. She may use corn oil for salads and cooking. This oil

FIG 47. This beautiful creature is a Morgan horse. Kentucky has long been famous for her Morgan horses. Because of their fine qualities for cavalry uses the government maintains a farm in Vermont where horses of this breed are raised. (Courtesy of the Department of Agriculture)

is also used for making soap, lubricating machinery, and other purposes. In times of sugar shortage, people use corn syrup. Mattresses are made from corn husks, pipes from the cobs, and filters from the silk.

We raise each year more than three billion bushels of corn. Some of this immense crop is raised in every one of our forty-eight states. The most important area, however, lies in the Central Plains, north of the cotton belt. The chief corn-producing area does not extend as far north as the wheat belt does, because in the northern part of the United States, the summers are not long enough and hot enough to produce good corn crops. Neither does corn grow well on the Great Plains to the west, where, because of the altitude, the summers are cooler than in the Central Plains. The rainfall also is less on the Great Plains, and corn does not grow well in dry regions. If the heat and rainfall of our corn belt were lessened, the industry would soon disappear. The farmers could no longer raise the hogs which depend on the corn for food. The ranchmen of the West could no longer send their cattle to be fattened in the corn belt. Many of the big packing companies, which kill and prepare the hogs and cattle for market, would go out of business. Some of the railroad lines, which carry tons of animal products daily, would not have freight enough to pay them to run their trains. The stopping of all these activities would throw many, many men out of work, and they would have little money to spend. Thus, the merchants who sell to them would suffer. All these and many other misfortunes would happen because of the lack of raindrops and a little heat from the sun's rays. It is well, once in a while, to stop and think how dependent we are on Nature and the conditions which she provides, and on the farmer who makes use of these conditions.

When we interrupted our sail up the Mississippi to find out more about the work of the people in the Central Plains, we had just passed the mouth of the Ohio River. In the region to the west, occupying a part of Missouri and Arkansas and extending a little way into Oklahoma, there is an area of hills and low mountains known as the Interior Highlands. This area was once a plateau region, in which the rivers cut their valleys, leaving between them the rounded ridges as hills and mountains. A large part of these Interior Highlands is known as the Ozark Plateau. Between two low mountain ranges in the highland, the Arkansas River has cut a beautiful valley.

This highland area does not cover all, or even the larger part of the three states mentioned above, and in the valleys and on the plains, there are fine farms. Horses, mules, and cattle are raised in large numbers in the Central States, and we should find some exceptionally good ones on the farms of the Ozark Plateau.

Some of the mountains are covered with deep forests, and here lumbering is carried on. The wearing down of the old plateau by the rivers has brought nearer the surface the mineral treasures which Nature had stored away in the rocks. Among these are coal, iron, petroleum, gas, and manganese (useful in the making of steel). Here also, in Arkansas, is produced much of the bauxite of the country, from which aluminum is made. Marble, limestone, granite, cement rocks, and clay beds are found here also, as well as excellent sand for glass-making.

Lead and zinc are the most important minerals found in the Interior Highlands. The workmen mine the lead ore, bring it to the surface, and crush it in the ore mills. Here, much of the waste rock is washed away. The crushed ore is smelted to remove the impurities, and the melted lead, called pig lead, is run into molds much as pig iron is. Missouri mines more lead than any other state.

Zinc and lead often occur together in the earth, and they are found also with other minerals. Zinc is mined in the highland regions of Oklahoma, New Jersey, Montana, Kansas, Missouri, and other states.

A little farther up the Mississippi is St. Louis, one of the largest cities in the United States. Why has it grown so? Look at the map and you will find many of the reasons. It lies nearer the center of the Mississippi Valley than any other city. It is situated on the great river between the mouths of its two largest branches — the Ohio, leading to the Eastern states, and the Missouri, opening up a route to the West. It lies near the corn and wheat regions. It is connected with both the hardwood area of the Ohio Valley and the softwood belt of the Northern states by waterways down which the lumber can be floated. Rivers connect it also with coal and iron areas and with the tobacco fields of Kentucky and neighboring states. A wide grazing area lies all around it, and it is far enough south to be in easy communication with the cotton and sugar-cane states. Because of these facts, what industries should you expect to find in the city?

In former days, when St. Louis was only a frontier trading post, large quantities of furs were brought here by trappers who came over the trails leading from the north and west. St. Louis has retained and increased her great fur market, and sales are held here each year to which buyers come from all over the world.

North of St. Louis, the Missouri, hurrying from its home in the mountains nearly three thousand miles away, pours its muddy water into the blue Mississippi. In a trip on the "Big Muddy," we should see many interesting sights — great fields of corn, wheat, flax, oats, barley, and other grains, cattle and sheep ranches, and large, important cities.

There are several pairs of twins in the Central Plains (twin cities, not twin children). One pair is located on the Missouri, where the Kansas River enters it from the west. Their names are Kansas City. One of them is in Missouri and the other in Kansas. As is often the case with twin children, one of them has grown much larger than the other. The one in Missouri is three times as large as its twin in Kansas. These cities lie in the center of the country, with connections by rail and water leading in all directions. Can you explain why they should have become an important market for farm implements, automobiles, hay, and lumber?

FIG 48. Notice how long the leaves are on these tobacco plants. Of what use is the cloth which is stretched over the field? (Courtesy of the Department of Agriculture)

FIG 49. These are the stockyards at Omaha, Nebraska. Notice how far they extend. What other cities have large stockyards?

Why they should rank next to Chicago as a live-stock market and meat-packing center, and why they should have grown to be one of the greatest oil-refining centers in all the United States and one of its largest horse and mule markets?

Farther up the Missouri is another pair of twin cities. These are Omaha, Nebraska, and Council Bluffs, Iowa. As in the case of the other twins, one, Omaha, is much larger than the other. Also, as in the twin cities farther down the river, meat-packing is an important industry. Omaha is not only one of the most important live-stock centers in the country, it is also a great grain market.

In its upper course, especially, the Missouri has many rapids and falls, which will, in the future, move the machinery, light the streets, and run the cars in many cities in the northwest. At Great Falls, located farther west in the Great Plains, and at some other places, the river has already been harnessed. The electricity generated in the power plants near Great Falls is used not only in that city but is carried on wires to the copper-mining centers of Butte and Anaconda in Montana.

On the Mississippi, five miles above the mouth of the Des Moines River, is the largest hydroelectric plant in the world. What is the meaning of "hydroelectric"? The dam built here is one of the largest in the world. It is nearly a mile long and fifty feet high. What is there near your school with which you can compare it? It spans the Mississippi below the rapids near the

FIG 50. This picture shows the power house and the dam across the river at Keokuk, Iowa. What is the use of the lock of which you get a glimpse on this side of the river?

mouth of the branch stream and extends from Keokuk, Iowa, to Hamilton on the Illinois shore. Vessels on the river avoid the dam by means of a lock. The powerhouse, as planned, will be 1,800 feet long, and its electric generators will develop as much power as three hundred thousand horses could, all pulling together. This power, in the form of electricity, is carried on wires to many cities and towns. The people in the city of St. Louis ride in electric cars run by the power of the falling water in the Mississippi River, about one hundred and thirty-five miles away. It is a wonderful world in which we live, is it not, when men can compel Nature to do such marvelous things?

On Rock Island in the Mississippi, opposite the busy city of Davenport, Iowa, is the government's largest manufacturing plant. In the arsenal here are made rifles, swords, bayonets, armored cars, tanks, and tractors.

In the northern half of the Mississippi Valley, the cornfields grow fewer, and larger areas are covered with wheat. We shall see great wheatfields also as we go westward into the Great Plains, and we can ride for hours within sight of fields where the grain is rising and falling in the breeze, like a green or yellow sea. Everywhere, from middle Canada nearly to the Gulf of Mexico and from the Appalachians to the Rockies and even beyond, we shall

FIG 51. These wires carry electricity from the power plant to cities many miles away. What use are you told in the text is made of this power in St. Louis?

find large wheat-fields. We raise immense quantities of wheat, more than any other nation in the world. It takes a great deal to supply us all with flour and breakfast foods, but our great crop gives us enough to use at home and to ship abroad to foreign countries.

The national government and the individual states have done a great deal to aid in the development of our wheat industry. They have helped to rid our fields of pests and have bred new kinds of seed suited to different conditions of soil and climate. Among these is a variety which requires a comparatively small amount of heat but which does well in long days of moderate sunshine. This variety has made possible the raising of wheat farther north. Other kinds have been developed which need little moisture. This has caused the industry to extend into the drier regions of the West.

In the southern part of the wheat belt, the grain is planted in the fall and grows a few inches before frost comes. The winter is not cold enough to kill it, and it is reaped in the early summer. This variety is called winter wheat. Farther north, the planting is done in the spring, and the grain is harvested in the fall. This is known as spring wheat.

The harvest time begins in June in Texas and occurs later as

FIG 52. Notice how far in the distance you can see the sheaves of wheat. In what natural region of the country do we find many such fields? (Courtesy of the International Harvester Company)

one goes north. Numbers of workmen follow the harvest from one ranch to another and from one state to another, gradually moving northward across the country. The machines which are used in the harvesting are even more wonderful than those which plow the land and sow the grain. Some are drawn by from two to thirty horses, while more are drawn by tractors. Picture the great reapers moving back and forth over the field, cutting the wheat, gathering it into bundles, and tying them up. Steam threshers separate the seed, bag it, and blow the straw into great piles. The most wonderful machines do all of this work — reaping, threshing, and bagging. One of these machines, with four or five men, will do the work of dozens laboring by hand. Without this harvesting machinery, our great wheat crops of nearly a billion bushels would be impossible. We could not help each year to feed a hungry world, nor would it have been possible for us, in the food crisis of the World War, to supply the starving peoples of Europe.

Suppose you try to count the number of machines which have helped in preparing your food and clothing. The labor of men's hands is extremely useful. We could not do without it. But the work of men's brains has been of much greater use in the development of our industrial world. If you would be of the very greatest value to the world about you, you must fit your brains as well as your hands for doing something worthwhile.

Before we finish our study of wheat, we shall surely wish to visit Minneapolis and St. Paul, the Twin Cities of the North. More wheat is ground into flour in Minneapolis than in any other city in the world. Some of the flour mills here are immense. All together, they can turn out about a hundred thousand barrels a day. There are many flour mills in other cities in and near the wheat region. Think of the enormous amount which must be made in all of them. Think, too, of the miles of railroads and the hundreds of freight cars which are necessary to carry away all the flour and bring in the fresh supplies of wheat.

The early mills for grinding grain into flour were built where water would furnish power to run them. The Falls of St. Anthony on the Mississippi thus determined the position of Minneapolis. The great plains to the west and south of Minnesota were treeless and furnished no lumber for the settlers who wished to make their homes there. Minnesota, you remember, has large forests. The sawmills of Minneapolis supplied the lumber for houses, barns, and furniture. The settlers of the treeless plains around were glad to get the lumber and to pay for it with the wheat which they raised on their farms.

The grain elevators in Minneapolis, Chicago, Duluth, and other cities on and near the Great Lakes are among the largest

FIG 53. This machine is threshing out the grains of wheat and blowing the straw into piles. Can you see the belt which connects the threshing machine with the engine which runs it?

in the world. They are so situated that cars and boats can be filled through long chutes, direct from the great bins. We ship large quantities of wheat abroad, and we find elevators also in New York, Boston, Philadelphia, Baltimore, and other cities. The freight boats on the Great Lakes carry immense quantities of wheat to Buffalo, where it is transferred to canal barges and cars. Long trains carry the wheat also to the Pacific coast, to the cities on Puget Sound, and to San Francisco. From these busy ports on our Western shores, it is sent across the wide ocean to the crowded lands of the Far East.

While we are in the Central Plains, we shall wish to visit some of the farms where sugar beets are raised. Thousands of tons of beet sugar are produced annually in this section and in areas farther west.

In the fall, the farmers plow the beets loose, pull them up, cut off the tops, and carry them to the factories. Here, they are washed, sliced, and soaked in hot water, which gradually

FIG 54. On some of our large dairy farms milking is now done by machinery run by electricity.

absorbs the sugar. The liquid is put through several processes which remove the impurities and cause the water to evaporate, leaving the grains of sugar.

Among other important farms on the Central Plains are those where cattle are raised. The cattle of the states farther west are valuable chiefly for their flesh. Many also are raised for this purpose here in the Central Plains, but many more are kept for the milk which they give. Immense quantities are sent daily by special trains to all the large cities. In some areas, it is carried to cheese factories and creameries and is sent to market in the shape of butter and cheese.

Having seen something of the farms of the Central Plains and their products, let us now visit some different industries. We shall find coal mines in many of the states of this section. Look again at the map on page 35 and name these coal-producing states. Is it not wonderful to think of the deep shafts, the long tunnels, the telephones, the electric lights and cars, and the many workmen, hundreds of feet deep in the earth beneath us? The black rock itself, with its story of ancient forests, is equally wonderful. What should we do without coal? How many occupations do you think would cease, and how many workmen would be thrown out of work if your home city were suddenly deprived of this fuel?

The occupations in the cities and towns on the shores of the Mississippi, as well as the logs floating in the upper river and its branches, remind us that we are near a great lumber region. Thousands of logs are floated on the waters of the main river and its branches down to the sawmills located in the cities. Here we find various manufactures of wood, such as carriages, furniture, matches, farm implements, and many other articles, both large and small.

By looking at the map on pages 4 and 5, you will see that the Laurentian Upland, an ancient worn-down mountain region, extends into the United States, south and west of Lake Superior. It is in the low hills and mountains of this upland that we shall find some of the most wonderful iron mines in the world. These mines are very different from the deep mines in the Appalachian

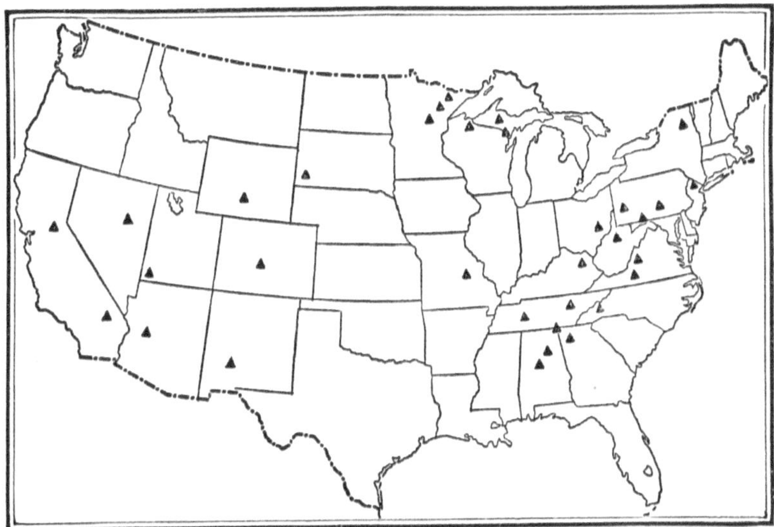

FIG 55. The map shows you the chief iron areas of the country. Make a list of the states containing these deposits. In which of these areas are the richest deposits?

Highlands, where the ore is mined in much the same way as coal is. It is brought up to the surface through a shaft. Here, in many of the Superior mines, the iron is mixed with loose soil so near the surface that the work is carried on in a very different manner. Powerful steam shovels bite out several tons of the reddish-colored gravel at a single mouthful. The long steel arm, which holds the great shovel, swings around, the giant jaws open, and the load falls into the waiting cars. The long trains run to Duluth and Superior, where great ore docks, the largest in the world, reach out hundreds of feet into the lake. The trains run out on the docks, the bottoms of the cars drop, and the ore falls into great pockets. These pockets are opened, long chutes are placed in position, and the ore slides down into the steamers, which are always waiting for cargoes. These ships then head to Milwaukee, Chicago, and Gary on Lake Michigan, Detroit on the Detroit River, and Toledo, Cleveland, Ashtabula, Erie, and Buffalo on Lake Erie. In these and other ports, the iron is manufactured into a thousand articles or distributed to other manufacturing centers.

Because of the vast forests in the vicinity, the manufacture of wooden articles early became an important industry in many cities along the Great Lakes and the rivers of the region. Since the discovery of the rich iron deposits around Lake Superior, a great increase in manufactures in which iron and steel are used has taken place in many cities. The manufacture of steel plows in South Bend and the automobile industry in Detroit and some other cities are good examples of the influence of these mines.

Detroit has become the greatest automobile manufacturing city in the world, and the growth of this industry has affected the industries of other cities. Lansing, Michigan, is one of the most important centers in the world for the manufacture of gasoline engines. If Detroit is known as "auto town," then Akron, Ohio, can be referred to as "tire town." In just ten years, Akron has grown to be three times its former size, with many people flocking there to work in the tire factories. One tire company in the city employs nearly thirty thousand men. This great corporation

FIG 56. These men work in a great automobile plant in Detroit, Michigan. Some, not all, of the buildings of the plant are shown in the background. Make a list of the kinds of automobiles that you know. Try to find out where they are manufactured.

owns its rubber plantation in Sumatra, its cotton plantation in Arizona, and its cotton factories in Connecticut and California. Besides manufacturing automobile tires, this firm also produces millions of rubber heels and soles and miles of rubber belting and hose each year.

South of Lake Superior is one of the important copper areas of the United States. From its early use in spearheads and cooking utensils copper has grown to be one of the most important commercial minerals on earth. This has come about with the increased use of electricity. Think of the thousands of miles of telegraph and telephone wires in our country alone, to say nothing of those of other nations, and of the great cables which stretch under the ocean waters and link the continents together. Copper wires carry the electricity from the power houses, where it is generated to cities and towns miles away. More and more copper is needed each year for those railroads which are using electricity instead of steam to operate their locomotives. There are copper eyelets in your shoes. Even in the pins we use, thousands of pounds of copper are consumed annually.

The World War could hardly have been carried on without copper. It was needed for telephone wires and for the cases of shells and cartridges. It was used in every big gun, in every airplane, and on every motor car. So great was the demand for copper dur-

FIG 57. This is a part of the great rubber factory in Akron, Ohio, which is spoken of in the text. What materials are used in such a factory? Where are they obtained?

ing the war that millions of pounds more than were ever before mined were taken from the earth. Later we shall read more about copper, for more is mined in the West than in any other section of the country.

You have read of so many important products that come from the states near the Great Lakes, and you now realize that enormous quantities of freight must be carried on their waters. But freight boats are not the only vessels that sail on the Great Lakes. At Duluth, we can take a fine passenger steamer for a trip through this most wonderful inland waterway, which links the great farms, the iron and copper mines, the flour mills, and the meat-packing centers of the Central Plains with the coal mines, the shipping ports, and the manufacturing cities of the East. This great water highway has helped make Pittsburgh the great steel-manufacturing city that it is, Chicago the second-largest city in the country, and more than doubled the population of Detroit in just ten years.

We might start our trip through the Lakes from Chicago at

FIG 58. This is one of the busy commercial streets of Chicago. How many reasons can you give for the growth of this city?

the southern end of Lake Michigan. This great city is surpassed in size by only three other cities in the world. Although it ranks fourth in population, it holds the first position in several industries — the packing of meat, the building of cars, the manufacture of machinery, and the manufacture and shipping of lumber and furniture. A fourth of all the animals used annually for meat in the United States are slaughtered in Chicago. The great stockyards, with their miles of food and watering troughs and their hundreds of pens where the animals are kept until they are slaughtered or sold, are the largest in the world.

Think of the advantages of the position of this great city. Rich coal fields lie all around it. Lumber, iron, and copper can be brought by water from the forests and mines to the north. Stretching for miles in every direction are the great wheatlands and cornfields. Farms where hundreds of sheep and cattle graze are not far away. Its advantages for commerce are as great as those which help in its industrial life. It lies at one end of the greatest inland transportation route in the world. It is situated at the most northern point where railroads can cross the country without being blocked by the Great Lakes. It is connected with the Mississippi and Gulf of Mexico and lies in nearly a straight line between our two greatest Atlantic and Pacific ports.

Whether you visit steel foundries, lumber mills, furniture factories, car shops, grain elevators, flour mills, or stockyards, you will be astonished at the size and importance of this great city and its industries.

Eighty-five miles north of Chicago, on the western shore of Lake Michigan, is Milwaukee, which has a population of half a million people. It is not hard to tell in what occupations many of them are engaged. The city is connected by the great waterway with the iron and copper regions to the north, and thousands of her people work in machine shops and foundries. Since Milwaukee is located near the cattle-producing areas of the plains and near the northern forests, many workers are employed in the tanneries where hides are made into leather, and many others in the lumber yards, sawmills, and woodworking factories.

Whether we start our trip from Duluth or Chicago, the sail

through the Lakes will seem like an ocean voyage, for we are out of sight of land much of the time. The waters narrow, and the scenery becomes very beautiful in the Strait of Mackinac, which lies between Lake Michigan and Lake Huron. In the trip from Duluth, we should pass through the Soo Canal, one of the most important canals in the world. It was built to avoid the rapids in St. Mary's River, which connects Lake Superior and Lake Huron. Great locks on both the Canadian and the United States sides lift the vessels or lower them from the level of one lake to the other. Lines of vessels are usually waiting their turn to go through the locks, for enormous quantities of freight pass through the Soo Canal, more, in fact, than through any other canal in the world except that at Panama. Millions of bushels of wheat and other grains, barrels and bags of flour, tons of iron ore and copper, and large quantities of lumber are carried eastward during the eight months that the canal is open to traffic. Westward-bound vessels are loaded with coal and salt and manufactured goods either imported or made in Eastern cities.

After sailing southward through Lake Huron, we find the waters narrowing again into two small rivers and a small lake.

FIG 59. The vessels at the left are in a lock on the Soo Canal and are being lowered to another level. Notice the closed gates at the further end of the lock. Explain how vessels are raised and lowered in locks.

Can you find on the map on page 76 the names of these bodies and the large city which is located on one of them? Passing through these small bodies of water, we come to Lake Erie. Here our voyage will be interrupted, for there are several cities on this lake which we wish to see. What ones can you find on the map?

Cleveland is one of the chief ports on Lake Erie. Situated as it is on the Great Lake route between the largest coal fields and the richest iron mines of the world, you can easily understand why this city has become one of the great steel-manufacturing centers of the country. Ships, wire and wire nails, and bolts and nuts are included in its manufactures. It ranks next to Detroit in the manufacture of automobiles, and next to New York in the making of clothing.

In Toledo, at the end of Lake Erie, there are large automobile factories. Many other articles of iron and steel, of glass, and of wood are made here. Splendid farms lie all around the city. In connection with these, Toledo has

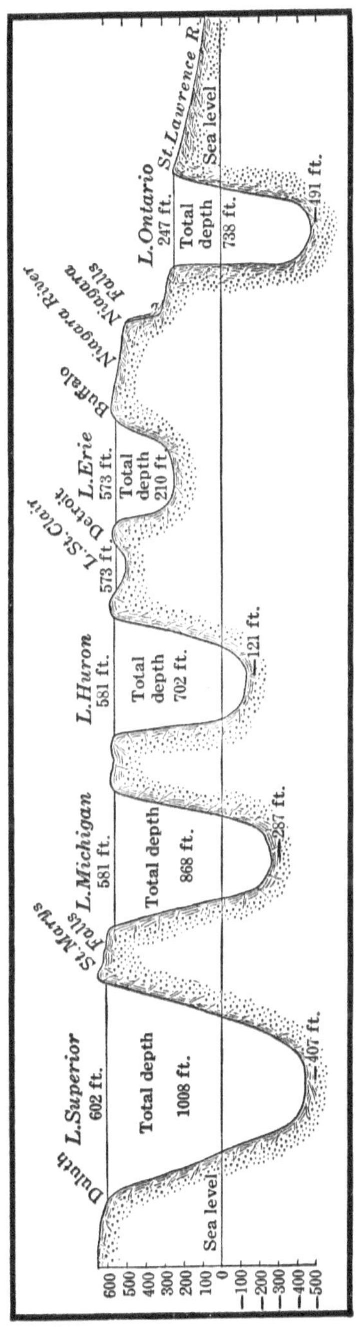

FIG 60. Studying this diagram of the Great Lakes, find out which is the shallowest; the deepest. Prove from the figure that the water flows from Lake Superior toward Lake Ontario rather than in the opposite direction.

the largest vegetable-forcing greenhouse in the country and has become the greatest clover-seed market in the world.

Along the southern shores of Lake Erie and Lake Ontario, there are many fine farms, where grapes, peaches, apples, and other fruits are raised. The lake breezes temper the climate of the surrounding regions, and heavy frosts are unusual during the growing season. For this reason, the fruit industry has become of great importance here. New York is a notable fruit-growing area, and more apples are raised here than in any other state.

At Buffalo, at the eastern end of Lake Erie, freight intended for New York City must be unloaded and sent by rail or by canal and river. Between Lake Erie and Lake Ontario are the Niagara River and Falls. Ships go through the Welland Canal into Lake Ontario, thence into the St. Lawrence River, and so out of the country through Canadian ports. Buffalo, located at this break in transportation routes, has grown to be a large, important city. Our sail through the Lakes has taken us back into the part of the United States which we have already visited. So we must turn our faces westward toward the Great Plains, where other interesting sights and scenes await us.

SUGGESTIONS FOR STUDY

I

1. Some of the resources of the Central Plains.
2. The Missouri-Mississippi.
3. River floods and the Weather Bureau.
4. In the Ohio Valley.
5. Our great corn crop.
6. The Interior Highlands and their resources.
7. The great city of St. Louis.
8. Three pairs of twin cities.
9. The great hydroelectric plant at Keokuk.
10. Davenport and the government arsenal at Rock Island.
11. The wheat industry.
12. Beet farms and beet sugar.

13. Cattle of the Central Plains.
14. Coal, iron, and copper.
15. Lumber and lumber products.
16. Detroit and automobiles.
17. The Great Lakes and their traffic.
18. The city of Chicago.
19. Other cities of the Central Plains.

II

1. What states are included in the Central Plains? What natural region bounds it on the east? on the west? on the south? on the north?
2. Learn the capitals of the states in this region.
3. Sketch a map of the Great Lakes and show on it the most important lake ports.
4. Name the mineral products of the Central Plains, the vegetable products, the animal products.
5. From an encyclopedia, find out how coal is made into coke.
6. How much shorter than the Missouri-Mississippi is the Amazon River? the Nile? Locate these two rivers.
7. In the chapter on New England, you read about the starch factories in the Aroostook Valley of Maine. Find the uses of potato starch. For what is cornstarch used?
8. Material on the crops of the Central Plains may be obtained from the Department of Agriculture at Washington. In your letter, state very definitely what you desire, and do not ask for too many things in one note.

III

Make a list of the places mentioned in this chapter. Arrange them by countries, cities, mountains, rivers, etc. Be able to locate each place and tell what was said about it in the chapter.

CHAPTER VI

WESTWARD TO THE GREAT PLAINS

The Mississippi River lies in the lowest part of its broad valley. As we travel westward from the river, the land becomes higher, but so gradually does it rise that one scarcely notices the difference. This higher, drier area lying just east of the Rocky Mountains is known as the Great Plains. The land here is many hundred feet, and in places several thousand feet, higher than it is in the low Mississippi Valley.

West of the Great Plains, the high Rocky Mountain wall stretches from north to south across the country. If these mountains and the Sierra Nevada system farther west extended from east to west instead of from north to south, the Great Plains would be very different from what they are. The winds which blow against the western slopes of the mountains are carrying moisture which they obtained from the Pacific Ocean. The tops of the mountains are always cold, and the winds become chilled as they blow over them. Cold air cannot hold as much moisture as warmer air. Try an experiment and prove this. Have some boiling water in your teakettle. When the air, full of moisture, comes out of the nose of the kettle, hold a cold plate against it. You will find drops of water on the plate. That water came from the hot air coming out of the kettle. When the cold plate chilled the hot air, it could no longer hold the moisture which it was carrying and so dropped it on the plate.

The cold top of the mountain wall acts like the cold plate and chills the wind as it blows up the slopes, so that it has to drop much of its moisture on the western side. Thus, the winds have little or no moisture left in them to give to the thirsty lands on the eastern slopes. The low Coast Mountains near the Pacific are not high enough to squeeze much moisture from the winds, but the high Sierra Nevadas do it very thoroughly, and the winds are very dry as they cross the plateaus between the Sierras and Rockies. The little moisture which remains falls on the high western slopes of the Rockies. Were it not for the moisture which comes from the Gulf of Mexico, the Great Plains would be even drier than they are.

You see what Nature has done to the Great Plains by stretching these mountain systems across the country in the path of the westerly winds. Now let us see what man has done to conquer Nature and to raise fine crops here where she decreed that little should grow.

Look at the map of the United States on page 4 and find the hundredth meridian. Through what states does it pass? Except near the Pacific coast and in a few other small areas, the annual rainfall west of this meridian is less than twenty inches. This amount of moisture is not enough to make farming a success, and yet thousands of acres here are dotted with prosperous farms green with growing crops of grain, vegetables, and fruits. It seems like a miracle, doesn't it? Let us see how it was done.

There are many rivers flowing through the Great Plains, which are fed by the snows on the mountain tops. In the spring, when the snows melt, a great deal of water runs to waste. By saving this water and storing it in reservoirs, there is enough to water a great many acres of land.

Study the map on the next page and name the states in which water has been stored. In these places, immense dams have been built across some river, perhaps at the mouth of some mountain valley, and the water has piled up behind it until large reservoirs, like lakes, have been formed. Canals, sometimes many miles long, lead to the district to be irrigated. Even mountains have been tunneled in order to carry the water to the farms. Smaller canals lead off from the main one, and ditches branch from these to the fields where the crops are growing.

In the parts of the country where there is very little or no rainfall, irrigation is a necessity. In other regions, where the amount of moisture is uncertain, where it may not come at the right time, or where an unexpected dry spell may injure the crops, irrigation is a protection.

Not all water for irrigation comes from that stored in reservoirs. In many areas, even where little or no rain falls, there is plenty of water under the ground. Farmers in such localities drill wells and, with wind or electricity, pump the water to the surface and use it as needed. In still other parts of the West the farmers practice what is called dry farming. The amount of rain that falls is not sufficient to water the crops unless it can all be kept in the soil and little or none be allowed to evaporate.

FIG 61. This map shows some of the largest irrigation projects which our government has undertaken. Make a list of the states which contain them. In what part of the country are these projects? Explain the reason for this location.

MAP VI

CENTRAL STATES
WESTERN SECTION
SCALE OF MILES
0 50 100 150 200 250
SASK.
Assiniboine
MANITOBA
Lake Manitoba
Lake Winnipeg
Lake
R.
R.
50
Red
Turtle Mts.
Souris
Mouse
Williston
Cando
Grafton
Devils Lake
Minot or
Devils L.
PARK
Grand Forks
SULLYS HILL NAT.
Sheyenne
Hillsboro
Red L.
Rainy L.
Lake of the Woods
ONTARIO
L. Nipigon
Rainy R.
Vermilion L.
Masaba Heights
Pigeon R.
L. SUPERIOR
NORTH DAKOTA
Dickinson
Valley City
Jamestown
BISMARCK
Mandan
Missouri
Little Missouri
Lisbon
Fargo
Wahpeton
Oakes
James
R.
Height
of
Land
Itasca
MINNESOTA
Virginia
Chisholm
Hibbing
Two Harbors
Duluth
MICH.
Brainerd
Mille Lacs
Fergus Falls
Little Falls
St. Cloud
St. Croix R.
Stillwater
WISCONSIN
45
Grand R.
Aberdeen
Redfield
Webster
Falls of St. Anthony
Minnesota
Minneapolis
ST. PAUL
Mississippi
45
Deadwood
Lead
Cheyenne
SOUTH
PIERRE
Watertown
Brookings
Huron
Red Wing
Faribault
Mankato
Winona
Rapid City
Black Hills
DAKOTA
WIND CAVE NAT. PARK
Bad Lands
White
R.
Mitchell
Madison
Sioux Falls
Canton
Yankton
Mason City
Dubuque
Chadron
Niobrara
R.
Vermilion
Wayne
Norfolk
Sioux City
Des Moines R.
Waterloo
Marshalltown
Cedar R.
Cedar Rapids
Clinton
Alliance
Loup
Boone
Iowa City
Muscatine
IOWA
NEBRASKA
N. Platte R.
North Platte
Grand Island
Kearney
Platte R.
Fremont
Blair
Omaha
S. Omaha
Plattsmouth
York
Hastings
LINCOLN
DES MOINES
Council Bluffs
Ottumwa
Burlington
Davenport
Missouri R.
Nebraska City
Keokuk
ILLINOIS
Republican
Red Cloud
Beatrice
40
Grand R.
Chillicothe
Hannibal
Moberly
40
COLORADO
Solomon R.
R.
Atchison
Leavenworth
St. Joseph
Columbia
St. Charles
Smoky Hill
Beloit
Junction City
Salina
Lawrence
Kansas R.
TOPEKA
Kansas City
Kansas City
Sedalia
JEFFERSON CITY
St. Louis
KANSAS
Great Bend
Garden City
Dodge City
Arkansas
Emporia
Hutchinson
Wichita
Independence
Arkansas City
Ottawa
Ft. Scott
Pittsburg
Parsons
Coffeyville
Osage
Neosho R.
Webb City
Joplin
Springfield
OZARK PLATEAU
White R.
MISSOURI
Pilot Knob
35
N. MEX.
TEXAS
OKLAHOMA
Arkansas
ARKANSAS
TENN. KY.
Mississippi R.
35
Longitude
100
West
from
95
Greenwich
90
105
100
95
90
50
MONTANA

FIG 62. Small canals or ditches carry the water to the fields where it is needed. Explain why the climate in the West is so dry that irrigation is used over large areas, while in the Eastern states the rainfall is sufficiently large so that irrigation is seldom used.

So the farmers cultivate and stir up the ground in order that the rains may sink in well. The newly stirred soil acts also as a blanket to keep the moisture from escaping into the air. By practicing dry farming and by using seed which requires little moisture fine crops are raised.

Most of our reclaimed dry area, however, is watered from great reservoirs by systems of canals. On such irrigated farms in the once barren areas of Arizona, some of the finest quality of Egyptian cotton is now raised; great sugar-beet farms are prospering on the deserts of Utah; peaches, melons, and other fruits are growing in Colorado, New Mexico, and other states on areas which were once covered with cactus and sagebrush.

The great reservoirs are useful for another purpose besides irrigation. The force of the water confined in them is tremendous. In powerhouses, this force can be transformed into electricity, as it is in areas of which we have read. Already in some places in

FIG 63. You will read on page 137 of the Strawberry Valley Irrigation Project in Utah. This picture shows some of the valley before irrigation. Only coarse grass and some useless desert shrubs grew here. (Courtesy ofthe Department of the Interior)

the western part of the United States, the electricity generated in this way is furnishing light and power for the neighboring towns.

Nature had furnished conditions in many parts of our Western states which made life impossible there, but man, through his knowledge, has conquered Nature. Ignorance never conquered anything. That is the difference between ignorance and knowledge. Ignorance is weak; knowledge is powerful. Because they have studied, men have conquered the oceans and are now able to enjoy the products of every country on earth. Because they have gained knowledge, men have overcome the unhealthfulness of hot climates and live comfortably there, producing foods and other supplies for the welfare of the world. And so, because they have studied and worked on the problem of irrigation until they have conquered it, men have changed deserts into fertile

FIG 64. This is a picture of the same part of the Strawberry Valley shown in FIG 63, after irrigation was practiced. (Courtesy of the Department of the Interior)

farms. They have captured rivers and stored their waters in huge reservoirs. They have built the biggest dams in the world. They have cut canals even through mountains. It has all meant hard, exhausting, dangerous work. Men have risked their lives to scale slippery cliffs, to explore deep canyons, to sail swift rivers, to measure high waterfalls, to climb unexplored mountains. The work of these engineers has been as splendid a thing, as heroic a task, as any ever done by our brave soldiers; and their object was not to tear down industries but to build them up, not to kill people but to help them to live.

When you look at the map on page 104 and see the irrigation projects which dot the western part of our country, remember that this great work would not have been possible without the help of our government at Washington. If you would know more about irrigation and see pictures of dams that have been built, farms that have been made possible, and the splendid crops raised on them, write a letter to the Reclamation Service in Washington and ask for material on this subject to help you in your schoolwork.

Let us go next to the part of the plains covered with the brown bunch grass and visit some of the great cattle ranches which are located there.

In large areas on the Great Plains, the grass starts up in the spring, but in the hot, dry summer, it withers and turns brown. Some grasses, when they dry up, contain little or no nourishment, but the bunch grass in this region, as it dries, retains its nourishing qualities. This fact has made possible the ranching industry in the dry areas. The grass is scanty, however, and the cattle need to roam over many, many acres if they are to find all their food in the open. As irrigation makes farming possible in larger and larger areas, the unfenced, open range is growing smaller each year. Many ranches today are enclosed with miles of wire fence, within which there must be somewhere an unfailing supply of water.

The rough, open life on the plains, caring for the cattle in all kinds of weather and facing dangers of many kinds, developed the wild cowboy life of which you like to read. With the fencing of the ranches and the winter feeding with alfalfa, a kind of clover, the life in many cases has become much easier. The cowboys of today, however, are splendid riders and are more skilled than many circus performers in the use of their horses. It is hard work to rope out an animal from a restless herd of hundreds, and it requires much knowledge and skill on the part of both the horse and its rider.

The bunch grass which grows in the grazing areas serves the cattle well, and they thrive on it, though it does not give them much fat. Many are sent, therefore, to the corn belt farther east to be fattened for market. They remain here for several months and are then shipped to the stockyards in the great packing centers. As you already know, there are several cities in the Middle West where cattle trains, stockyards, slaughterhouses, and cold-storage plants are familiar sights. Among the most

FIG 65. These cattle belong to a ranch on the Great Plains. Why are there many cattle ranches in this natural region? What has caused the increase in the number of farms where fruit, vegetables, and grain are raised? (Courtesy of the Publishers' Photo Service, Inc.)

important are Chicago, Omaha, East St. Louis, Kansas City, St. Joseph, St. Paul, and Fort Worth.

Our cattle products are many and varied. Of course, there are meats of various kinds — fresh, canned, and dried. Besides these, there are also beef extracts, leather, soap, gelatin, fertilizers, candles, glue, buttons, hairpins, combs, toothbrush handles, and lubricating oil.

Not only cattle but sheep and hogs as well are sent to the stockyard centers. The old story of using all of the hog but its squeal and all of the sheep but its bleat seems true when you read the long list of products which are obtained from these animals. Besides the meat and the wool, there are bristles for brushes, skins for riding saddles and saddlebags, strings for musical instruments, surgeons' thread for sewing up wounds, tallow, medicines, and cases for sausages.

Should you like to be a shepherd and live alone with your dog for weeks at a time out on the silent plains? You would have to take care of the little lambs, see that the animals were getting plenty of good food and water, drive them to new pastures when the supply of either gave out, and guard them against wolves and mountain lions.

Sheep are raised in every state of the Union, but the greatest ranches, where many thousands are owned, are for the most part in the dry regions. As in the case of cattle, the sheep are raised here not because it is the best place in the country for this industry but because the region is not suited for agriculture. Many thousand sheep are raised also in the states of the Central Plains. The sheep industry of New England was once more important than it is today, and efforts are being made to increase the number of animals in that section of the country.

The millions of pounds of wool which the sheep in the United States yield every year is an immense quantity, but we need so much for clothing, blankets, carpets, and other articles that we import very large amounts. Most of this comes from Australia, New Zealand, and Argentina, three of the world's great wool-exporting countries.

Most of the sheep are sheared in the spring. Their coats are cut off by shears which are operated by power, instead of being clipped by hand as in earlier days. The wool is packed in bags or bales and sent to manufacturing centers. More woolen cloth is woven in New England than in any other section of the country. Therefore, much of this wool, and most of that which is imported from other countries, is sent to

FIG 66. Explain how the old-time method of sheep-shearing differed from the method shown in the picture. (Courtesy of the Department of Agriculture)

Boston and thence distributed to the manufacturing cities. What was said on page 28 about Boston and her wool market?

Another animal which wears a valuable coat of wool and which is being raised in increasing numbers in the United States is the Angora goat. Its wool is longer than that of the sheep and is more valuable for certain kinds of manufactures. The next time that you ride in a railroad car, or in an electric car that has upholstered seats, remember as you lean back on the soft cushion that the plush with which it is covered was probably woven from Angora wool.

A large part of the wheat area of the country is located on the Great Plains. Because of the greater rainfall, more is raised toward its eastern border than in the western part. The seed sown in the drier parts of the wheat belt has been produced

© Underwood & Underwood

FIG 67. The picture shows a flock of Angora goats in the province of Angora. Try to locate this region in the Asiatic peninsula which stretches westward between the Black and the Mediterranean Sea. Of what country is it a part? (Courtesy of the Underwood & Underwood)

through long years of careful breeding, and the grain which grows from it requires little moisture. This is another benefit which has come to the people from the help of the national and state governments. At different experiment stations, the work of breeding drought-resisting seeds has been going on for years. Large areas which were formerly considered too dry for agriculture are now owned by farmers who, by using seed which has been produced for use in just such regions, raise fine fields of grain.

Not all the grainfields which we see are devoted to wheat. You will find, both in the Central Plains and in the Great Plains, as well as in states still farther west, fields of barley, oats, and rye. None of these, however, compares in importance with wheat.

Another crop raised in the northern states of the country is flax. Strange to say, though we devote more than two million acres to flax, we produce very little of the flax fiber from which linen cloth is made. Most of the linen we use is imported from European countries. We raise flax not for its fiber but for its seeds. These are crushed for the oil which they contain, much the same as the seeds of the cotton plant are. This is called linseed oil. Can you find out its uses?

The part of our country occupied by the Great Plains is not as thickly settled as are the regions farther east. Most of the cities and larger towns are situated in the river valleys. On the uplands between the valleys, one can travel long distances without coming to a city. Most of the railroads follow the river valleys. Some of these routes are the very ones along which the early pioneers first found their way to the Far West. Two of the earliest explorers were Lewis and Clark. They followed the valley of the Missouri River through the Northwest. Others went by what is known as the Oregon Trail along the North Platte River across the mountains into the valley of the Snake River. Some, following the course of the Humboldt River, took the California Trail across what was then the Great Desert into central California. The Santa Fe route led to the south by means of the Arkansas valley and thence along the eastern edge of the mountains into northern New Mexico, while the upper Rio

FIG 68. The wagon in this picture is similar to the "prairie schooners" in which the pioneers crossed the country. What caused so many to undergo the hardships of such a journey?

Grande and Gila River valleys brought the brave pioneers to the southern boundary of California. Along these old trails, where once sunburned men trudged wearily beside the heavily loaded "prairie schooners," we can go today in swift, comfortable trains.

Many of the pioneers who followed the trails westward saw signs of mineral deposits in the Great Plains and the foothills of the mountains. Such mineral wealth in the form of coal and oil is causing today a growth of the towns and cities in eastern Wyoming. In the foothills and in the mountains to the west, there are beds of rock, called shale, which will yield quantities of oil. In the next chapter, we shall read of many other minerals found in the mountains west of the Great Plains.

Denver, the largest city of the Great Plains, is situated at the edge of the Rocky Mountain Highland and is often called the "Gateway to the Mountains." Built on a plateau nearly as high as the top of Mt. Washington, the city has a background of lofty mountains cutting the blue sky. From Colorado Springs, a famous resort for tourists, an even better view of the mountains may be obtained. As you ride through the broad streets of Denver, you will notice that few buildings are made of wood. Why is this so?

Though Denver owes its birth to the minerals in the mountains, many other things have caused it to grow into the beautiful city that it is today. The climate is dry and remarkably healthful. The scenery is beautiful and attracts many people. The grazing lands, the irrigated farms and gardens, and the position of the city at the gateway to the great highland have all aided its growth. Denver is located on the South Platte River. In this region, it is too dry to raise crops without irrigation, and the water of the river is used for this purpose. The fruits and vegetables raised on the farms around are not only sold in the markets of Denver and other cities and towns in Colorado, but are sent to other parts of the country.

The great smelters in Denver telling their stories of rich mines and busy miners, the beautiful mountains rising against the blue sky, the mountain parks where one may enjoy many kinds of outdoor sports, all invite us farther west into the great Rocky Mountain Highland. So we will leave the Great Plains with their ranches and wheatfields, and start on our westward journey.

SUGGESTIONS FOR STUDY

I

1. Position and elevation of the Great Plains.
2. Cause of the light rainfall in this area.
3. Methods and value of irrigation.
4. Ranching on the Great Plains.
5. Wheat and other grains.
6. Pioneer routes over the plains.
7. The city of Denver.

II

1. Make a simple sketch of the United States. Show the natural regions into which the country is divided.
2. Write a description of the natural region where you live. What are the chief occupations in which the people are engaged? What resources of the region make these occupations possible?
3. Why are there fewer large cities on the Great Plains than in some other natural regions?
4. Of how many departments of government have you read thus far in this book? In what ways have they helped the people of the country? What service which the government has rendered is spoken of in this chapter?
5. On an outline map of the United States, show as well as you can the pioneer routes to the West. Show the rivers which the explorers followed.
6. Of what city of the Great Plains did you read on page 86?

III

Make a list of the places mentioned in this chapter. Arrange them by cities, mountains, rivers, etc. Be able to spell and pronounce the names and locate the places in your list. Tell what was said in the chapter about each one.

CHAPTER VII

THE WONDERS OF OUR ROCKY MOUNTAIN HIGHLAND

The high mountain wall which bounds the Great Plains on the west is made up for the most part of parallel ranges running from north to south. Here and there it is crossed by ranges extending from east to west. Inclosed by these ranges, there are large, high valleys, called parks, some of them larger than our largest states. Covered with fine soil washed from the mountains around, they are valuable as pasture lands, and some of our best ranches and farms are located on them. Each park contains streams which are the sources of large rivers.

It is in vain that we search in the United States for the ends of the great Rocky Mountain Highland. This highland is the longest in the world and extends through North and South America from the Arctic Ocean on the north to the Antarctic on the south. In South America, the mountains are called the Andes and in North America, the Rockies, but both systems are parts of the same great highland. It was through the lowest part of these mountains, at the Isthmus of Panama, that the Panama Canal was cut.

Pikes Peak, though not the highest, is one of our noted mountains. It is situated on a spur of the Rocky Mountain system which extends to the east and was the first peak to greet the eyes of the early emigrants after their long journey over the plains. The mountain is named for Zebulon Pike, who was one of the first men to try to climb it. He was forced to give it up, being sure, as he said, that "nothing but a bird could ever succeed in reaching the top." But both man and burro have succeeded not only in getting to the top but in carrying up material for a railroad. A smooth, winding road for carriages and automobiles has also been built.

Colorado is fortunate in her playgrounds. She has two large ones — the Mesa Verde National Park in the southwest, of which you will read later, and the Rocky Mountain National Park in the north. Besides these, she has several smaller ones. The Rocky Mountain National Park is only fifty miles from Denver. No other national park is so near to a large city; no other park is so high. People who camp at the base of the great mountains are eight thousand feet above sea level. Towering into the blue sky, a mile above them in the air, are the lofty peaks of the Rockies. Longs Peak, the highest in the park, is more than fourteen thousand feet above the ocean level, and several others are more than twelve thousand feet high. Beds of wild flowers grow in the green valleys. Cold streams from the snows and glaciers above tumble down the steep slopes and water the glens. The leaves of the silver-stemmed aspens rustle in the silence, and the pine forests whisper to the brooks at their feet.

In other parts of Colorado, we can find equally beautiful scenery, for this state contains forty-one mountain peaks which are more than fourteen thousand feet high and a hundred and forty-one peaks more than thirteen thousand feet in height. It has many lovely green valleys, sparkling lakes, and swift rivers. On the mountain slopes in the Colorado National Forest, glaciers have been found. Add to these attractions the clear, cool air and the healthful climate, and we do not wonder at the thousands of people who visit this state every year.

Of all the agents of Nature which are continually changing the face of this great world of ours, the rivers, perhaps, have done the most wonderful work. Waterfalls, cascades, canyons, valleys, plains and deltas, and winding channels all testify to the tremendous power of running water. To realize something of the work that water does, it is not necessary to take long journeys or to explore some mighty waterfall. Right at your feet in the little brook made by the rain, you can see the work going on. Rushing down the steep hillside, the little stream digs its chan-

FIG 69. This is the Royal Gorge of the Arkansas River. Rivers have done a tremendous work in changing the surface of our earth. Why is this gorge so narrow? (Courtesy of the Denver and Rio Grande Railroad)

nel deeper and deeper until it lies embedded in its steep-walled, narrow gorge, a miniature of the wonderful canyons of our great Western rivers.

In Colorado are the sources of many long rivers which flow through other states on their way to their ocean home. Some of these, as they pushed their way through the highlands, have cut deep canyons. One of the greatest of these has been made by the Arkansas. From its source in the mountains, ten thousand feet above sea level, the river makes its way to the plains by means of its canyon, a gigantic gash which it has cut in the mountains to their very foundations. In the deepest, narrowest portion of the canyon is the part called the Royal Gorge. Here the rock walls, in places only thirty feet apart, rise perpendicularly for nearly half a mile above the turbulent river below.

By making use of the wonderful canyon which the river has worn, the Denver and Rio Grande Railroad cuts through the mountains to the Western Plateau, thus shortening the route and avoiding a climb of three thousand feet to the lowest pass over the mountains. In the narrowest part of the gorge, the engineers could find no safe foothold for the track. Here they built the famous hanging bridge. Steel supports extend from one side of the canyon to the other, and on these, the bridge is hung.

When we think of the wonderful work that is done by the

FIG 70. This is the Black Canyon of the Gunnison River. Notice how high and how vertical its walls are. Do you think you could climb out of the canyon? What led to its exploration? (Courtesy of the Department of the Interior)

railroads in transporting goods, carrying passengers, and feeding and clothing the world, we appreciate the feeling of a famous man who said, "I never see a locomotive without wanting to take off my hat to it." To this we might well add, "and to the men who have made them and their work for humanity possible." More marvelous than the country through which they travel, and greater than the power of the locomotives that draw the long trains, is the human brain which devised the engine and built the railroads. I wonder if any of the boys who read this book will fit themselves to survey routes, build railroads or bridges, or in any way help in the work of bringing the peoples of the world nearer together.

It was the minerals in the mountains which first brought people to Colorado. In many cases, it has been the fine pastures and the fertile soil which have kept them there and brought others to this part of the country. Among the farms of Colorado and other mountain states, we shall find many where sugar beets, alfalfa, vegetables, grains, and fruits are raised. Do you like cantaloupes and melons? These are produced in great quantities in the Arkansas Valley and are shipped all over the country.

Most of these crops depend on irrigation for the water necessary for their growth. One of the irrigation projects in Colorado is that in the Un-com-pah-gre Valley. The story of the planning of this project is wonderfully interesting, and some of the engineers who were engaged in it were as brave as soldiers on a battlefield.

It was desired to reclaim the valley of the Uncompahgre River, but the amount of water in this river was not sufficient for the purpose. The Gunnison River had plenty of water, but it lay on the other side of the mountains. More than this, it flowed for miles in a gorge three thousand feet deep and called, from the color of its walls, the Black Canyon. No one had ever explored this canyon. The cliffs were too high and steep, and the river too swift. In order to make use of the water for irrigating the Uncompahgre Valley, someone must survey this awful gorge and plan a tunnel six miles long through the mountains to connect with the Uncompahgre River. Five brave men undertook the task. With boats, food, and other necessities, they descended into the deep, black-walled gorge. In the angry river, they lost all but their lives. Their food gave out, and they traveled for two weeks with scarcely any. Finally, they came to a place where they could hear just beyond them the roar of a waterfall. To go on was sure death. Just here, in the canyon wall half a mile high,

FIG 71. No engine could pull a train directly up the side of this mountain. The track has to twist and turn to find the easiest grades. How much longer than the vertical distance do the loops make the railroad?

was a place which gave them a possible chance of climbing out. They started early in the morning, and at nine o'clock at night, they stepped out onto the plateau. They were nearly exhausted but succeeded in getting to a ranch house fifteen miles away, where they all collapsed.

What they had learned about the river was of great value, but it was not enough. The stream must be explored to its end. The next year two men, one of whom had been a member of the first party, volunteered to finish the task. In their exploration, they came to the same falls which had blocked the path of the first surveyors. They heard its sullen roar; they looked into the seething, swirling current; and yet they went on! At the head of the falls, they shook hands and plunged in. Aided by their rubber rafts, they succeeded in landing below the falls, bruised and exhausted, but alive. The dangers were not yet over. Their food gave out, and they faced starvation, but finally succeeded in killing a mountain sheep in the canyon. In their trip, they swam across the river seventy times. The information they had gained and the measurements they had taken enabled the government to undertake the work. The six-mile tunnel which brings the water from the Gunnison River to the Uncompahgre was dug two thousand feet below the summit of a mountain, and today happy families are living in the Uncompahgre Valley and farmers are raising fruits, vegetables, and grains on a hundred thousand acres of rich soil. All this was made possible by the courage and perseverance of two men. Wouldn't you like to be one of them?

The United States is the greatest mineral-producing country in the world. We produce more silver, iron, coal, copper, lead, zinc, sulfur, and petroleum than any other nation. The Rocky Mountains, the high plateaus west of that great system, and the mountains along the Pacific coast are stored with mineral wealth.

The story of these mineral deposits is another interesting chapter in Nature's book. This story tells of the work which underground waters have done. Often intensely hot, they have flowed for ages in their dark channels gathering the mineral matter from the rocks and soil. As the waters cool, these minerals are deposited in cracks in the earth. These are the veins which are worked in our mines. As age after age has passed, the mountains have been slowly uplifted. Then those tireless workers of Nature, the wind, the rain, and the frost, have slowly, very slowly, worn down the mountains and carried away much of the rock surface into the valleys and oceans. This work has not only made the valleys more fertile but has brought the mineral deposits nearer to the surface, where they could be more easily obtained.

Colorado is one of our important mining states. Almost every known mineral is found there. Gold, silver, copper, lead, iron, coal, zinc, and others which are not so well known, are taken from its mountains.

One of the most important minerals of the West is gold. In 1849, it was the gold of California that lured the pioneers across the plains, the mountain passes, and the dreary deserts. The discovery of gold did more in a few years to people the West than would have been done under ordinary circumstances in a much longer time.

Some of the gold mines of Colorado are very deep. Think of a mine having twenty-five stories, or levels, as they are called. As you go down in the elevator, or cage, you may stop at any one of the levels, follow long passages leading out into the darkness, find more lumber used to support the ceilings, or roofs, than is needed for building purposes in many a city, and see miners drilling holes for blasting and laborers loading the ore.

Cripple Creek is one of the important mining towns in Colorado. It is almost ten thousand feet above the level of the sea. Before the discovery of the minerals in the mountains, Cripple Creek was a cattle range. The gold for which it has since become so famous was first found by a ranchman whose cattle fed on the brown grass. Today, it is one of the great mineral districts of the world, producing millions of dollars' worth each year.

Most silver mined today is found in combination with other minerals. In some regions, it is combined with copper; in others, with lead or gold. There are mines which are worked for silver alone, but these are comparatively few. There are many processes through which both gold and silver must be put before they are ready to be sent to the mints to be made into money or to the factories to be fashioned into jewelry and other articles. The rocks which contain them must be broken up into small pieces and then crushed into powder. This is done in stamp mills. A stamp is a heavy hammer weighing half a ton or more. Can you imagine the clatter and bang and jar of a stamp mill when hundreds of these huge mallets are all pounding at once?

After the ore is crushed, the gold and silver must be separated from the rock. This is done by the use of mercury and cyanide of potassium. These substances seem almost like fairies in their ability to attract the precious metals and remove them from the powdered rock.

Other impurities are removed in the smelters. This is done in furnaces, from which the molten metal is finally drawn and cooled in molds. Still other refining processes are necessary before the metal bricks are sent to the mints.

Not all the states producing gold and silver are in the Rocky Mountain area. Some of them are in the natural regions which lie farther west. Indeed, these metals are produced to some extent in all our Western states.

Copper is one of the most valuable minerals which the earth contains. You have already read about the deposits of nearly pure copper which are mined near Lake Superior. Our other great copper-producing states lie in the West. These are Arizona, Montana, and Utah. Copper is found to some extent in nearly all our states, and our deposits are the largest and richest in the world. Yet we use so much copper in our great manufactories that we import large quantities from other countries.

Butte, Montana, is the greatest copper-mining center in the world. In this region, you would miss the green grass, the shade of tall trees, and gardens and flowers. Grass, trees, and flowers do not thrive well in the sulphurous smoke of the big smelters.

Many processes are necessary to separate the copper from the other materials with which it is found. It is most unusual to mine nearly pure copper, as is done in the Michigan district. When copper is smelted, sulphur is usually one of the impuri-

FIG 72. This is a picture of Anaconda Hill near Butte. Notice the chimneys of the smelters. What is done to the copper in these smelters? (Photograph by N. A. Forsyth)

ties to be driven off. The sulphur fumes from the chimneys of the smelters have killed the vegetation for miles around. Today, in many large smelting plants, the sulphur is not set free to destroy the vegetation around but is saved and used in the making of sulphuric acid.

Many of the copper mines in the West are deep mines reached by a vertical shaft, an incline, or a tunnel. Others, like the mines in Utah, are worked from the surface. In Utah, a mountain of copper is slowly disappearing as the steam shovels bite into it, deeper and deeper, for their great mouthfuls.

Not all the Rocky Mountain region is bare and brown and disfigured by unsightly heaps of rock waste or the effects of sulphur fumes. There are some regions so lovely and their wonders so marvelous that our government has made them national parks.

We have in the United States nineteen national parks and more than this number of other interesting areas called national monuments. One of the most beautiful of these pleasure resorts is Glacier National Park in Montana. This park is larger than the state of Rhode Island and contains more than sixty glaciers, which creep down the steep mountain slopes. From the lower edges of the glaciers, where the ice melts as fast as it advances, swift, cold rivers flow into clear, blue valley lakes. In the park, there is some of the most beautiful mountain scenery in America.

Hundreds and even thousands of feet above your heads, there are wonderfully colored rocks, like beds of flowers in bloom. Through the park runs the crest of the Rocky Mountains, known as the Continental Divide. This separates the rivers which flow to the Pacific from those which find their homes in the Gulf of Mexico.

The Yellowstone National Park is the largest in the country. In all the world, there is no wonderland like it. It is situated principally in the northwestern part of Wyoming and is more than two and a half times as large as Rhode Island. It is a mile and a half above sea level and is enclosed by mountain ranges half a mile higher. It contains a greater collection of wonders than can be seen in any other similar area. There are geysers, hot springs, colored terraces, deep canyons, high waterfalls, mountains of glass, and forests changed to stone.

The park is the largest game preserve in the world. Its thirty-three hundred square miles of mountain and valley and forest remain nearly as Nature made them, and no rifle is ever fired within its boundaries except by permission of Uncle Sam. The lakes and streams are a fisherman's paradise, and there are many varieties of birds and fowl. There are bears — big griz-

FIG 73. These are some terraces in Yellowstone Park. The water of hot springs becomes cooler as it reaches the surface of the ground. It then cannot hold all the mineral matter which it has been carrying. The material which it deposits often builds up mounds and terraces.

zlies, brown, cinnamon, and black. Elk, moose, deer, antelope, mountain sheep, and bison also roam there in large numbers.

Among the sights in the park are the Mammoth Hot Springs and the Terraces. The water of these springs contains much mineral matter in solution, such as sulphur, iron, lime, and salt. On reaching the surface of the ground, the water becomes cooled and can no longer carry its load and so deposits it in formations of various colors. One spring has built up a hill, all gleaming, glistening white, nearly two hundred feet high; others have made terraces of blue, green, red, and yellow. Over the edges of these carved basins pours the hot water.

The chief attractions in the park are the geysers of all ages, from the Baby Geyser, only a few years old, to the Castle Geyser, probably one of the oldest in the region. The eruption of a geyser is a wonderful sight. Think of seeing a million and a half gallons of water spout into the air to the height of a hundred

FIG 74. Here is another example of the work of water. This is the canyon of the Yellowstone River. The rocks are tinted in yellow, red, green, and violet. Try to imagine how beautiful it must be.

and eighty feet, day and night, winter and summer, at intervals of about an hour. Yet this is the record of Old Faithful, one of the most noted geysers in the park.

Geysers are, roughly speaking, water volcanoes. The hot water which is forced upward in an eruption is only the surface of a tall column which reaches down to the volcanic furnace beneath in the intensely heated portion of the earth. The underground water, furnished by the rains and snows, percolates deeper and deeper until, reaching the heated rock, it is turned to steam. This seeks a vent, and the results are seen in geysers and hot springs such as are found in the Yellowstone National Park, Alaska, New Zealand, and Iceland.

Yellowstone Lake, the source of Yellowstone River, is the highest large body of water in the United States. Its area is about three hundred square miles, and its surface is considerably higher than the top of Mt. Washington. It is well supplied with fish. The far-famed story of catching a fish in this lake and, without moving from the spot, cooking it in a boiling spring is really true.

The canyon and falls of the Yellowstone River are among the greatest scenic wonders of our country. Over some hard ledges not far from the lake, the river falls in two great leaps. The Upper (or lesser) Falls are more than a hundred feet, and the Lower or Great Falls are more than three times as high.

Below the falls is the canyon, from a thousand to fifteen hundred feet deep, which the river has carved in the softer rock. Its most beautiful part lies near the falls. Other canyons are as deep and narrow, but the Yellowstone exceeds all others in the beauty of its coloring.

In the mountains of Wyoming is the burial place of some of those monsters which, long ages before man appeared upon the earth, roamed over its surface. Their fossil skeletons, found here and in other places in the rocks, have been chiseled out and mounted in museums. Some of these creatures were immense. If any were living today, what a wonderful circus procession they would make! Imagine several dinosaurs, each from sixty to eighty feet long, marching along the street. How would their length compare with that of the largest elephant which you have ever seen? If one of these great creatures managed to escape from its keeper, what a commotion there would be in the crowd! Even the people in the buildings might not be safe, for if the dinosaur raised himself on his hind legs, he could easily put his ugly head into a fourth-story window.

SUGGESTIONS FOR STUDY

I

1. The Rocky Mountain Highland.
2. Pikes Peak.
3. Colorado's playgrounds.
4. The Royal Gorge of the Arkansas River.
5. Story of the Uncompahgre Irrigation Project.
6. Minerals in the Rocky Mountain Highland.
7. Cripple Creek.
8. Gold, silver, and copper.
9. Glacier National Park.
10. Yellowstone National Park.
11. One of Nature's cemeteries.

II

1. Name the states of the Rocky Mountain Highland. From the appendix in your textbook in geography, find which is the largest one. How many states the size of Massachusetts could be made out of it?
2. Which of the Rocky Mountain states do you think is the most important? Give the reasons for your choice. From the figures given in the appendix of your textbook in geography, find out if this state is the most densely peopled of those in this section.
3. Make a list of the national parks in the country (see page 30, suggestion 5). Opposite each one, write the name of the state in which it is situated. In a third column, write the name of the feature in each park which you would best like to see.

4. Imagine yourself one of the engineers who explored the Black Canyon and write the story of your adventures.

III

Make a list of the places mentioned in this chapter. Arrange them by countries, cities, mountains, rivers, etc. Be able to locate the places and tell what was said in the chapter about each one.

CHAPTER VIII

OVER THE MOUNTAINS TO THE WESTERN PLATEAUS

Beyond the Rocky Mountain Highland, an area of high plateaus stretches westward to the Sierra Nevada and Cascade Mountains. The Mexican Plateau, of which you will read in later chapters, is a continuation of the plateau region of the United States and is very similar to it in appearance, climate, and resources.

When a region is wholly or nearly surrounded by mountains, it is likely to be dry. In the chapter on the Great Plains, you read the reasons for this. Rain falls plentifully on the wooded western sides of the Sierra Nevada Mountains, but the eastern slopes of the mountains, where little or no rain falls, are bare and brown. The sunshine in the high, dry air of the plateau is very hot. Rocks may become too heated to make comfortable seats. If left for some time in the sunshine, a knife or tin plate may become hot enough to burn your fingers. On the other hand, after the sun has set, the nights are always cool, and one can enjoy refreshing sleep.

Perhaps you are thinking that this high, dry region, shut in by mountain walls, may not be a very interesting place to visit. It contains, however, some of the most wonderful things in our country — trees turned to stone, a lake in whose waters you could not possibly sink, natural bridges carved from rock, and the widest, deepest river canyon to be found in the whole world.

The northern part of this region is known as the Columbia Plateau. Ages and ages ago, through cracks and fissures in the earth's crust, there flowed from time to time enormous quantities of lava. This filled the deep valleys and entirely covered some of the mountains. The greater parts of Washington, Idaho, and Oregon were buried hundreds or even thousands of feet deep beneath these lava deposits.

Through these beds of volcanic rock, the Columbia River and its largest tributary, the Snake River, have cut their way to the ocean in deep canyon beds. In cutting their channels, these rivers, like those of New England, found rocks of varying hardness. The softer rock was more quickly worn away than the harder strata, and consequently, falls and rapids were formed. The beautiful Shoshone Falls on the Snake River were made in this way. The falls on the Spokane River furnish much valuable water power. This is used to generate electricity for lighting the city of Spokane and running its streetcars. The electricity is also carried to Coeur d'Alene in Idaho and used in the famous lead mines there.

These lava beds in the Northwest are the largest in the world. During the long centuries, the surface lava has crumbled to a fine soil which, with the moist winds from the Pacific, make possible the great wheat and fruit farms of these states and their forests of tall trees.

In the eastern part of the Columbia Plateau, little rain falls, and few crops could be raised there were

FIG 75. Find the Shoshone Project on the map on page 104. The dam at the opening of this mountain valley is 328 feet high, 200 feet long at the top, and 108 feet thick at the bottom. How does your schoolhouse compare in height? (Courtesy of the Department of the Interior)

it not for irrigation. Some of the finest apples in the country come from these lava beds of the Northwest. Other fruits are raised here, also, and many vegetables. As in the Great Plains and the Central Plains, we shall see here large fields of grain stretching away for many miles.

South of the Columbia Plateau is a region known as the Great Basin. This name is given to it not because it is low, for parts of it are thousands of feet high, but because it is bordered by a rim of mountains. Its history is more interesting than the wonderful sights which it contains. Here is the story as Nature has written it.

Once upon a time, ages and ages ago, when the Sierra Nevada Mountains were much, very much, younger and consequently a great deal smaller than they are at present, the Great Basin was not the dry place that it is today. It was then very well watered. The mountains at that time were not high enough to shut out the moist westerly winds, and the rainfall was greater than the amount of water that evaporated in the sunshine. Because of

FIG 76. There are six million feet of lumber in this seagoing raft on the Columbia River. Of what kind of wood do you think it is made? (Courtesy of the Department of Agriculture)

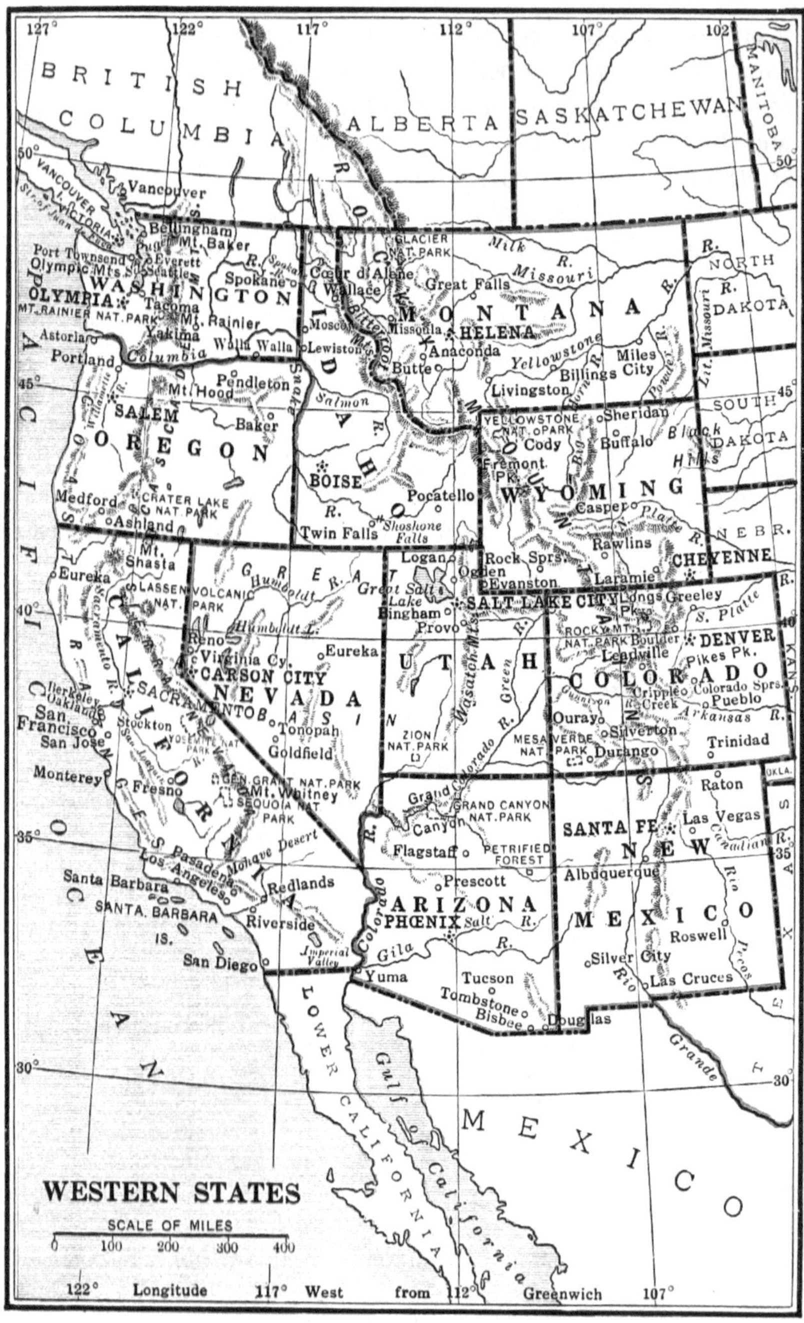
BRITISH COLUMBIA
ALBERTA
SASKATCHEWAN
MANITOBA
127° 122° 117° 112° 107° 102°
50° 50°
Vancouver
VANCOUVER I.
VICTORIA
Str. of Juan de Fuca
Port Townsend
Olympic Mts.
Bellingham
Mt. Baker
Puget Sd.
Everett
Seattle
WASHINGTON
OLYMPIA
Tacoma
MT. RAINIER NAT. PARK
Mt. Rainier
Yakima
Astoria
Portland
Columbia
Spokane
Spokane R.
Coeur d'Alene
Wallace
Moscow
Lewiston
Bitterroot Mts.
GLACIER NAT. PARK
Milk R.
Missouri
Great Falls
MONTANA
HELENA
Missoula
Anaconda
Butte
Livingston
Yellowstone R.
Billings
Miles City
NORTH DAKOTA
Lit. Missouri R.
Missouri R.
SOUTH DAKOTA
Walla Walla
Snake R.
Salmon R.
Pendleton
Mt. Hood
SALEM
OREGON
Baker
Willamette R.
Mt. Shasta
CRATER LAKE NAT. PARK
Medford
Ashland
BOISE
IDAHO
Twin Falls
Pocatello
Shoshone Falls
Logan
Ogden
Great Salt Lake
SALT LAKE CITY
Evanston
Bingham
Provo
YELLOWSTONE NAT. PARK
Cody
Fremont Pk.
WYOMING
Casper
Rawlins
Laramie
CHEYENNE
Sheridan
Buffalo
Black Hills
Big Horn R.
Powder R.
N. Platte R.
NEBR.
45° 45°
40° 40°
35° 35°
30° 30°
Eureka
LASSEN VOLCANIC NAT. PARK
Sacramento R.
Reno
Virginia Cy.
CARSON CITY
NEVADA
SACRAMENTO
Eureka
Humboldt R.
Humboldt L.
GREAT BASIN
UTAH
Wasatch Mts.
Green R.
Colorado R.
Gunnison R.
Rock Sprs.
ROCKY MT. NAT. PARK
Longs Pk.
Boulder
DENVER
Leadville
Pikes Pk.
Cripple Creek
COLORADO
Colorado Sprs.
Pueblo
Ouray
Silverton
Durango
MESA VERDE NAT. PARK
ZION NAT. PARK
Trinidad
Arkansas R.
Greeley
S. Platte R.
KANSAS
Berkeley
Oakland
San Francisco
San Jose
Stockton
YOSEMITE NAT. PARK
San Joaquin R.
Tonopah
Goldfield
Monterey
Fresno
GEN. GRANT NAT. PARK
Mt. Whitney
SEQUOIA NAT. PARK
CALIFORNIA
Pasadena
Los Angeles
Mohave Desert
Santa Barbara
SANTA BARBARA IS.
Redlands
Riverside
San Diego
Imperial Valley
Colorado R.
Grand Canyon
GRAND CANYON NAT. PARK
Flagstaff
PETRIFIED FOREST
Prescott
ARIZONA
PHŒNIX
Salt R.
Yuma
Gila R.
Tucson
Tombstone
Bisbee
Douglas
Raton
Las Vegas
SANTA FE
NEW MEXICO
Albuquerque
Roswell
Silver City
Las Cruces
Canadian R.
Pecos R.
Rio Grande
OKLA.
TEXAS
LOWER CALIFORNIA
Gulf of California
MEXICO
PACIFIC OCEAN
ROCKY MTS.
WESTERN STATES
SCALE OF MILES
0 100 200 300 400
122° Longitude 117° West from 112° Greenwich 107°

this surplus of water, great lakes were formed in the region. The largest of these was Lake Bonneville, the ancestor of Great Salt Lake.

This old Lake Bonneville was ten times as large and more than fifty times as deep as Great Salt Lake is now. Through long, long ages, it had been gradually increasing in size, but as the mountains to the west grew higher and shut out more and more of the moisture carried by the winds, the lake ceased to grow. After a long while, the amount of moisture which evaporated in the hot sunshine became greater than the rainfall. When this happened, old Lake Bonneville began to grow smaller. Its waters, which had been high enough to flow into the Snake River and thence to the ocean, gradually became too low to find an outlet. If you should go from Salt Lake City to Idaho, you might ride through the very valley in which once flowed the waters of the ancient lake.

Only pure water evaporates. All the salt and other mineral matter which streams bring to lakes and ponds remain in their waters unless other streams, flowing from them, carry it away. Thus, bodies of water which have no outlet gradually become more and more salty. When Lake Bonneville was connected with the Snake River, it was a fresh-water lake. When it became too low to have any outlet, it gradually changed to a saltwater lake. As more and more of its water has evaporated, the proportion of salt has grown greater, until today the lake is five or six times as salty as the ocean.

After reading this story, you do not need to be told that salt is one of the products of Utah. At Saltair, on the eastern shore of the lake, operations on a large scale are carried on. The water is pumped into shallow ponds, where it quickly evaporates in the hot sunshine. The salt which remains is loaded on cars and sent to the refineries for the final processes.

You will find it great fun to bathe in Great Salt Lake. Try as you will, you cannot sink, for the large amount of salt has made the water heavier than you are. When you finish your bath, you will enjoy a sponging off in fresh water, for your body feels sticky with salt.

In 1846, a company of travelers crossed the Great Plains, made their way with difficulty through the high passes in the Rocky Mountains, and finally came out on the high Western Plateaus. During the tiresome weeks of their journey, they lived in their canvas-covered wagons. The men walked many weary miles, driving the slow, patient oxen, while the women and children rode. As the company emerged from a canyon in the Wasatch Mountains and looked westward, they saw the waters of a large lake glittering in the sunshine. Between them and the lake was a valley, crossed by streams of pure mountain water. Here was the Land of Promise for which they were searching. Here they settled and made their homes.

These people were the Mormons, and the lake which they saw, as you have probably guessed, was the Great Salt Lake. Near the lake they selected the spot for their capital, which has

FIG 77. To the left is the Tabernacle in Salt Lake City. It is built in the shape of an ellipse and will seat nine thousand people. On the right is the beautiful granite Temple, one of the finest churches in the country. (Courtesy of the Keystone View Co.)

since grown into the beautiful Salt Lake City. The Mormons soon saw that their farms could never be very large, nor their colony very prosperous, unless they could obtain more water than Nature furnished in its rainfall, and they soon began to use the mountain water to irrigate their fields. They were the first people in the United States to recognize the benefits which might come from irrigation. By making use of water, they soon had flourishing settlements and prosperous farms of grain, fruits, and vegetables surrounded on all sides by the bare, brown desert. Today, their capital is a large city. Its streets are bordered by trees, under which trickle the irrigating streams that make their grateful shade possible.

While we are here, we must visit the Tabernacle, as the Mormon church is called. It is a queer-looking building made in the shape of an ellipse and so constructed that a whisper in one part of the great auditorium is easily heard in any other part, though the room is large enough to accommodate nine thousand people. The Mormon Temple, close at hand, covers more than an acre of land and is one of the finest buildings in the country.

Look at your map of Utah and find the Wasatch Mountains. It is in the central part of the state, near the base of these mountains, that the most water can be obtained for irrigation. Therefore, it is in this region that we shall find the best farms. In other parts of the state, where there is less water for irrigation, we shall find many ranches and thousands of cattle and sheep.

Locate on the map (Fig. 61) the Strawberry Valley Project. This irrigated area takes its name from the river which furnishes water to reclaim fifty thousand acres from the desert. Instead of worthless sagebrush and cactus, there are now growing here alfalfa, grain, sugar beets, and other vegetables, and delicious fruits. Can you find out for your arithmetic lesson how large an area in your locality fifty thousand acres would cover? How does the size of your city compare with it?

The streams which flow down the eastern slope of the Wasatch Mountains join the Colorado River and flow into the Gulf of California and the Pacific. The few streams on the western slopes never find the ocean but lose themselves in the sands of the Great Basin. The water of these rivers is very brackish and disagreeable to the taste. Indeed, it is doubtful if you found a river, even though one was represented on the map and its channel lay right before you. In this dry region, few rivers last throughout the year. When the snows melt in the mountains, the river channels are filled with rushing torrents, and even some lakes dot the landscape. But a few weeks or even days afterward, a dry hollow marks the place where the waters of the lakes shone, and gullied rock beds are all that is left of the rivers.

The Humboldt River is the largest inland stream in the Great Basin. It flows for three hundred and fifty miles through this uninviting country, its waters unpleasant to the taste and its banks unbordered by green trees and waving grass. Finally, it loses itself in Humboldt Lake, the largest of the deep depressions, or sinks, which are found scattered over the Basin.

This unattractive river and the salty sinks are in Nevada, the Sagebrush State. Nevada has fewer people and fewer farms than any other state in the country. In some places, irrigation is changing the desert into good farm lands, but there are many places within her borders where no water can be obtained. In Fig. 61, what irrigation project do you find in Nevada?

Though large areas in Nevada and other parts of the Great Basin are dreary and desolate in appearance, they are by no means valueless. Great mineral wealth lies below the surface. Every year, millions of dollars' worth of gold, silver, copper, iron, lead, salt, borax, and sulphur are taken from the mines there. There are also hills of granite, and sandstone and marble of good quality.

One of the driest, barest regions in the world is Death Valley, a part of the Mohave Desert in southern California. One can travel over this desert for long distances without seeing water or any green shrub or spear of grass. Parts of it are two hundred and fifty feet below the level of the sea. This is the lowest area on the continent. Death Valley received its name from a party of pioneers who lost their way in this terrible place. Many died in the desert, and only a few of the stronger members of the party finally reached a settlement.

The southern part of the Western Plateaus is occupied by the Colorado Plateau. The soil in the part of southern California known as the Imperial Valley is very fertile, but too dry for farming. Accordingly, a company was formed to tap the Colorado River and carry some of its water into the valley to irrigate the land.

Did you ever hear of a river's running away? This is what the Colorado did when the engineers tried to use its waters. The great dam and the gates which they were building to control the water were nearly completed, and all would have been well had it not happened that the autumn rains came earlier than usual. The water rose swiftly, and under the tremendous pressure, the gates gave way, and the whole river, instead of a small part of it, came pouring into the Imperial Valley. Of course, the bed in the lower course of the river was left dry. The Mexicans began to get excited because we had stolen their river, whose waters they had used for irrigation. We didn't want the river and would have been only too glad to give it back. It caused much damage and cost more than a million dollars before the engineers finally succeeded in capturing it and sending it back to its former channel. Since then, other attempts have been made to use the waters of the Colorado for irrigation. They have been successful, and splendid crops are now being raised in the Imperial Valley.

Have you ever heard of *mesas* and *buttes*? They are familiar names in the Southwest, and you will see many of them in your trip. Mesas are hills, but they are very different from the hills in other parts of the United States. They are flat-topped like tables, and the Spanish word *mesa* means a table. Some mesas are very large, rising hundreds of feet above the level of the plateau around. Ages and ages ago, this whole southwestern country was on a level with the mesa tops. The rains, the floods, and the streams of centuries have worn all the softer material down to the present level, leaving only the harder materials in the shape of vertical-sided, flat-topped hills rising above the rest

FIG 78. This is a mesa in New Mexico. Compare its shape with that of other hills which you have seen. Explain its formation. (Courtesy of the Department of the Interior)

of the country. Buttes are small mesas or parts of mesas. The city of Butte, Montana, of which you read in previous chapters, was named from a hill of this kind which stands close by.

The Enchanted Mesa in New Mexico has long been regarded by the Indian tribes around as sacred. The Mesa Verde, or green mesa, in Colorado is another famous one. The plateau on which it stands is a mile and a half above sea level, and the top of the mesa rises several hundred feet above this. Its flat top covers several square miles. The government has set apart this region as a national park. This has been done because of some ruins of ancient cliff-dwellers that have been discovered in the canyon of a little river beside the mesa. How should you like to live in a cave in the side of a canyon, as these ancient cliff-dwellers did? You would be protected alike from the blazing sun above and from enemies who might appear below. They could not climb up the wall except by a trail or ladder, which could be easily guarded. Neither could they climb down the vertical wall from the top.

These cave houses sometimes contain one or two hundred

FIG 79. This ancient cliff-dwelling in the Mesa Verde National Park is a part of what is known as the Spruce Tree House. It is two hundred feet long and contains one hundred and fourteen rooms. Where is this national park located? (Courtesy of the Denver and Rio Grande Railroad)

rooms and must have been the homes of whole clans or tribes. The rooms in which they lived, the stone tools which they used, the stone axes and spears with which they fought, the pottery necessary for their primitive housekeeping, and the skeletons of the people themselves have told us much about the lives and customs of this early race.

There are today between three and four hundred thousand Indians in the United States, most of whom live on reservations set apart for them. Some of them have farms and raise cattle and grain. The largest reservation is in Oklahoma, and about a third of the Indians live here.

The next largest Indian reservation is in the southern part of the high plateaus, chiefly in Arizona and New Mexico. Here you will find the Navajo and Hopi tribes. You would be much

FIG 80. Many Indians used to live in tents, called tepees. What has our government done to improve the condition of the Indians? (Courtesy of the Department of the Interior)

interested in some of their work, for they make fine lace, fashion beautiful baskets, and weave splendid blankets from the wool of their sheep.

The southwestern part of our country is often called Canyon Land. Many of these canyons are narrow with vertical sides hundreds of feet high. Through the long years the rivers have cut their channels deeper and deeper, but in this dry region there are no branch rivers to cut the cliffs from the sides and so broaden the valleys. How different are these rivers of the Southwest from those in other parts of the country? They have few or no branches and grow smaller rather than larger in their lower courses; they drain the land but do not water it; they are barriers rather than helps to communication. They are fed not by numerous side streams and frequent rains but by the mountain snows. In the spring, when the snows melt, the rivers are

FIG 81. Today more than forty thousand Indians in the United States live in neat houses similar to the one in the picture. (Courtesy of the Department of the Interior)

swollen to many times their usual size. Later, many of them rapidly evaporate in the hot sunshine and entirely disappear.

Of all the canyons in the Southwest, indeed of all those in the world, the Grand Canyon of the Colorado River is the most wonderful. The river flows through a series of self-dug gorges hundreds of miles long, a mile deep, and in some places more than ten miles wide. The rock has been carved by the water into many different shapes — pillars, towers, statues, and monuments. These are of marvelous colors — pink, gray, red, and yellow.

Into this great gorge one could easily put the Yosemite and Yellowstone canyons, the Pyramids of Egypt, and the city of Chicago and yet make but a very small beginning toward filling up the great gash which the river has made. It is hardly possible to believe that a river could accomplish any such stupendous carving, with its only cutting tool the soil carried along in its waters. What ages of time must have elapsed while this tremendous work was going on!

The air of the region is so clear and dry that distances are deceptive. As one stands on the rim, the opposite side of the canyon appears not far off. The width is really stupendous, vary-

FIG 82. The Colorado River has done a more wonderful work in canyon-cutting than any other river in the world. With what tools has the work been done? Notice the size of the person sitting on the cliff. (Courtesy of the Department of the Interior)

ing from ten to twenty miles. A bird apparently about the size of a swallow floats in the air far below us. A swallow at that distance would be invisible. The bird is really a large eagle. The Colorado River, a foaming, dashing torrent, looks from the edge of the canyon like a small silver thread. The actual vertical distance from the rim to the river is a mile, but to reach the stream one must travel on horseback several miles down a steep, zigzagging trail. The trip down and back takes a day, and a "tenderfoot" pays for the experiment in aching joints and lame muscles.

You remember Nature's cemetery of which you read in the last chapter. There is another one in Arizona. This also is a cemetery of giants, but of giant trees, not animals. It is called the Petrified Forest. You look about you in vain for any forest, for you see no growing trees whatever. The trees are lying about, scattered on the ground. See the tall trunks and smaller broken pieces. Pick up one of the sections. How heavy it is! You tug hard at a piece less than three feet long, and yet you cannot lift it. It is heavy as a stone. It is stone. This is a *petrified* forest, and petrified means changed to stone. Long, long ago an inland sea surrounded by forests occupied this region. Gradually the sea overspread the area, the trees died, and the streams brought down sand and gravel and covered them many feet deep. Buried there in the darkness, a wonderful change took place. Bit by bit the particles of wood disappeared, and their places were taken by particles of mineral matter held in the water. Centuries passed while this work was going on. Gradually the land was raised, the water retreated, and Nature's agents began wearing down the plateau. Thus the old forest was once more brought to light, but it was a forest of wood no longer. All that was left of the trees was beautifully colored stone.

We shall not wish to leave the Western Plateaus without learning a little more about the mining industry, which is of such great importance here. You will find copper mines in all the states of the high plateaus, and billions of pounds are produced here. Arizona and Montana produce more than half of all the copper mined in the country, while these two states, with Utah and Michigan, furnish half of that mined in the world.

Lead is another mineral in the plateau region. Some famous lead mines are at Cour d'Alene, in Idaho, and much is mined with the copper ores of Utah. The billion and more pounds of lead which we mine every year would not make as big a pile as the same amount of some other mineral, because lead is heavier. It is an enormous quantity, however, and is more than nine-tenths of the entire world product.

Zinc is used in galvanizing iron and steel sheets, wire, tubes, etc. What have you ever seen made of galvanized iron? It is used also in the making of brass and is rolled into thin sheets. Zinc is mined in nearly half of the states of the country. You remember that the states in the Interior Highlands and New Jersey in the Appalachian Highlands produce a great deal (see page 84). Here on the plateaus, much is obtained from the copper, silver, and other ores mined in several states. The saving of thousands of tons of the zinc dust which accumulates in the smelters is a good illustration of the value of waste material.

SUGGESTIONS FOR STUDY

I

1. Climate of the Western Plateaus.
2. The Columbia Plateau and the Columbia River.
3. The Great Basin.
4. Old Lake Bonneville and Great Salt Lake.
5. The Mormons in Utah.
6. The Humboldt River.
7. Nevada, the Sagebrush State.
8. The Mohave Desert and Death Valley.
9. The Colorado River and the Imperial Valley.
10. Mesas and buttes; Mesa Verde National Park.
11. Indians in the United States.
12. Canyon of the Colorado River.
13. The Petrified Forest.
14. Minerals in the Western Plateaus.

II

1. Name the states which lie wholly or partly between the Rocky Mountain Highland on the east and the Sierra Nevadas and Cascades on the west. Name the capital of each of these states.
2. Why did not the Mormons use the water of Great Salt Lake for irrigating their farms?
3. Why are there so few large cities on the Western Plateaus?
4. Name the state or states in which the following features occur: lava beds, big trees, a great salt lake, the greatest canyon on earth, a river which does not reach the ocean, the lowest part of the United States, ruins of ancient dwellings, Indians who weave fine blankets, trees turned to stone, important copper mines, famous lead mines.

III

Make a list of the places mentioned in this chapter. Arrange them by cities, mountains, rivers, etc. Be able to locate the places and tell what was said in the chapter about each one.

CHAPTER IX

THE PACIFIC MOUNTAINS
AND LOWLANDS

This western section of our country contains the loftiest mountains, the largest trees, the highest falls, and the greatest amount of water power to be found in the United States. You can stand among orange trees laden with fruit and look up toward white, snow-clad peaks gleaming against the blue sky. You can visit prosperous farms lovely with growing grain, fruits, and vegetables, while a few feet away stretches the bare, brown desert. You can see oil wells sunk through the ocean water to the rich deposits beneath. You can watch the gold dredges, great boats on land, plowing their path ahead of them as the huge shovels bite into the gold-bearing soil.

There are only three states included in this area of mountains and lowlands — California, Oregon, and Washington. Next to Texas, California is our largest state. Look at a map and you will see that it stretches northward about as far as Massachusetts and southward to the southern boundary of South Carolina. Into California you could put the New England States, New York, and Pennsylvania and have room left for two Delawares.

We have called this part of the United States the Pacific Mountains and Lowlands. Mountains stretch through it from north to south, while between the ranges are many valleys. On the east of this section and separated from it by high mountains are the Western Plateaus, while to the west stretches the broad Pacific.

The low Coast Ranges hug the shore. Between these mountains and the higher Sierra Nevadas and Cascades is a long, narrow valley. This is drained for the most part by rivers flowing northward and southward — the San Joaquin and Sacramento in California and the Willamette in Oregon. Farther north, the land has sunk so far that the valley floor is below the surface of the ocean and has been filled with its waters. We call this drowned valley Puget Sound. It is around Puget Sound and San Francisco Bay that the best harbors are found.

Farther north, the valley is still more deeply drowned, and only the tops of the mountains to the west appear as islands. The water inside the island chain, and protected by it from the winds and waves of the Pacific, is the "Inside Passage" to Alaska, noted for its beautiful scenery.

In all the length of the long valley, from the southern United States to Alaska, there is only one east and west passage. This is where the Columbia River, of which you read on page 137, has cut its way through the deep lava beds and the mountain wall.

About a hundred miles from the ocean, the Willamette River joins the Columbia. On the slopes rising from the river lies the city of Portland. The Willamette River opens up a route southward, while the Columbia connects the rich lands of the interior with the Pacific. The falls of the Willamette furnish electricity for manufacturing, for lighting, and for running the streetcars.

The climate of these Pacific states is very different from that of those on the Atlantic coast or in the interior of the country. The ocean is always cooler in summer and warmer in winter than the land is; therefore, the westerly winds which blow from the water to the land bring to these states the more even ocean temperature. Then, too, the Japan Current flows across the Pacific Ocean, and its branches, the Alaska and California currents, flow along our western shores. Coming originally from the equatorial regions, the water in these currents and the air above them are warmer than the water and air around. The westerly winds are thus warmed, and they carry this warmth to the land as they blow over it. Therefore, these Pacific states have no cold winters with zero temperatures, as do the regions farther east.

Around Puget Sound, the rainfall is much heavier than in the

FIG 83. This is the city of Portland, with Mt. Hood rising in the background. What river flows through the valley?

regions farther south. During the summer months, the westerly winds which bring in moisture from the ocean move so far north that they do not blow over southern California, and the season there is hot and dry. You will read later how important this dry weather is to the fruit industry of California.

You remember that it was the discovery of gold that first attracted people in large numbers to the West. Gold is found in many of our Western states, but ever since the days of the "Forty-niners," California has produced more than any other state in the country.

The method of mining depends on the condition in which the gold is found. The veins in deep mines contain the metal as it was originally deposited by the underground waters. In the wrinkling and folding and bending of the earth's crust which took place when the mountains were formed, these veins were sometimes brought nearer the surface. As the streams cut into the land and carried away the soil, the particles of gold were also washed out and deposited far from the "parent lode." When the metal is thus found loose in the soil, it is called placer gold.

The deep mines are reached through a shaft or an inclined tunnel, and the miners blast out the gold ore much as the workmen do in coal mines. The larger part of the gold product of California is obtained by such deep mining. In parts of California and other Western states, whole hillsides have been washed away by powerful streams of water in order to obtain the gold from the soil. This method of obtaining gold is known as hydraulic mining. Less gold is obtained today in California by hydraulic mining than by any other method.

Large quantities of gold are obtained by dredging. The gold dredge works in a shallow pond sometimes not much larger than itself. It is provided with large steel buckets, which are let down by machinery against the gold-bearing ground, from which they take great mouthfuls. They then swing high in the air and deposit their muddy loads into spouts which feed them onto a steel screen. The finer gold-bearing sands pass through the meshes onto the gold-tables beneath. These are shallow boxes with cleats placed across them to keep the gold from washing away in the water which is constantly supplied. Mercury, the fairy of which you have read, is used here also to collect the tiny particles of gold. Later in our travels, we shall see gold dredges working in the frozen fields of Alaska, where the ground sometimes has to be thawed out by steam before the buckets can be filled.

California is one of our most important petroleum-producing states. We think of gold as being a valuable product, but her output of petroleum is worth several times as much as her gold. Pipelines connect some of the oil fields with San Francisco Bay, where the oil is pumped into tank ships and sent to other lands.

It was not long before the people who were attracted to the West by the minerals found that greater wealth lay in the soil, the forests, and the fish in the ocean. More people in the Pacific states are engaged in agriculture than in any other occupation, and the products raised on the farms are of vastly greater value than the gold that is mined.

It may seem queer to some of you that the farm products of California are so valuable when such large areas are dry and when one of Nature's laws is that where there is little or no rainfall, there can be but little vegetation. This is one of the places in our country where man has conquered Nature and has beaten her at her own game of making things grow. All that was needed for successful farming was water. In the early days, a large proportion of the small farms growing fruits and vegetables were in the mountain regions near the gold mines and near mountain streams where water might be obtained at small expense. As the years went on, and agriculture increased, men located their farms in the fertile valleys and went into the mountains miles away, caught the water when it was running to waste, stored it in huge reservoirs, led it across valleys, through deserts, and even under mountains, and finally brought it to their fields. You have read in previous pages about the reclaiming of the Imperial Valley in southern California and of the fine crops of fruits, grains, cotton, and alfalfa which it now yields.

There are wonderful farms in this part of our country. In Washington, some of the wheat ranches are as large as, or larger than, any which we visited in the Central Plains. The apple orchards in the valleys of Washington and Oregon are beautiful either in the springtime when covered with dainty blossoms or in the autumn when hung with rosy-cheeked fruit. Perhaps you will enjoy even better than these the orange and lemon groves of central and southern California, where long rows of trees are covered with balls of yellow fruit. These orchards stretch for miles, and thousands of carloads of these fruits go every year to all parts of the country.

There are large olive orchards in California, and thousands of barrels of olive oil are made annually. We shall find there also orchards of fig trees and groves of walnut and almond trees from which millions of bushels of nuts are gathered each year.

Do you like prunes? Millions of pounds of both prunes and

apricots come from California orchards. Both of these fruits are dried in shallow trays in the sunshine. You can see hundreds of such trays in a single field. Raisins are dried grapes. Try to imagine the acres and acres of vineyards and the great numbers of bunches of grapes which must be picked to furnish the thousands of tons of raisins which are sent away from California every year. The fruit is put into shallow trays similar to those used for drying prunes and apricots and is left in the sunshine, where the plump, juicy grape soon changes into the sweet, brown raisin. There are many large vineyards also where grapes are raised for the table and for other uses.

Perhaps you wonder why most of our dried fruit comes from California. The lack of rainfall there, which makes irrigation necessary, also makes possible fruit-drying on a large scale. Little or no rain falls from May till late October. After harvesting, the prunes, apricots, grapes, and other fruits dry in the clear, hot sunshine without decaying.

Los Angeles is situated in the fruit-growing area. It is the largest city in California. A strip of land connects it with the coast, giving it the advantage of location on the water. Close by is Pasadena. These and other cities are situated on the fertile lowland with beautiful mountain views around. Because of the scenery and the delightful winter climate, thousands of people from other states spend the winter in southern California.

There are cattle and sheep ranches in these Pacific states, and among other large farms, we should find many, especially in California, where beets are raised. Not far away, we should see the factories where beet sugar is made. Not many years ago, California farmers began to experiment in raising rice on their irrigated lands. It proved to be very successful, and the amount which is produced increases each year. The raising of cotton is another industry which has moved westward, and cotton is now being produced in central and southern California and in the southern states of the Western Plateaus.

In most areas which border on the water, fishing is an important occupation. This is true in our Pacific coast states, in western

Canada, and in Alaska. Most of our canned salmon, as well as large quantities of other fish, comes from this region.

Salmon are an interesting fish. The young are hatched in the shallow water of some mountain stream or pond. When only a few inches long, they begin their journey to the ocean. They have numerous enemies, and many are eaten by other fish, but thousands more make their way safely to the Pacific. When fully grown, by some remarkable instinct, they find their way back to the very stream in which they were hatched. Death alone can prevent this journey. They swim through rapids and leap over falls from eight to ten feet high. Though plump and strong when they leave the ocean for the freshwater streams, they are weary and worn when they reach the desired spot. Here the eggs are laid, often several thousand in one nest, and the young fish are

FIG 84. This salmon is leaping up over these falls in order to get farther up the river. Where do salmon live most of their lives? When do they seek freshwater streams? (Courtesy of Dr. R. D. Harlan, George Washington University)

hatched and soon begin their journey to the ocean. The parent fish die here, far from the salt water.

It is when the full-grown fish, strong and vigorous, are starting on their migration up the rivers that they are obtained for canning. Many are caught in baskets attached to fish wheels which revolve in the swift current; others are taken in traps; and still others swim against nets placed in rivers and become entangled in the meshes.

If all the fish which came up the rivers were caught, there would soon be no salmon left. Therefore, laws have been made forbidding nets or any other obstacles to be placed entirely across the rivers. So many salmon are caught each year, however, that unless something were done, they would become less plentiful and therefore more expensive. To prevent this, our government has given valuable help in this industry, as it has in so many others. The Fish Commission has established hatcheries in Alaska and the Pacific states, where millions of fish are produced and later released in many waters. State governments have done a similar work. Because of this help, the price of salmon has been kept lower than that of many foods. The lobster and the oyster would also have become very scarce or perhaps have disappeared entirely had it not been for the help of the government. Its work in preserving the whitefish and other varieties in the Great Lakes has been equally important. When you are enjoying an oyster stew, a lobster salad, a fried trout, or some creamed salmon, just remember that without the aid of Uncle Sam's helpers, these and other sea foods would cost your father more than he has to pay at present, if, indeed, he could get them at all. In what other ways have the Federal or state governments helped the people of our country to work better, play better, and live better?

There are large salmon canneries in Astoria, Bellingham, and other places in the Northwest. In the large plants, everything is done by machinery. The salmon pass first into a machine of whirling knives, wheels, and shafts. In the twinkling of an eye, the fish are killed and cleaned, and the heads, tails, and fins cut off. Endless lines of trays holding the cleaned salmon are carried by machinery under sharp knives, which cut the fish into pieces of the right length for the cans. Next comes the filler, a wonderful machine, whose great arm plunges continually back and forth. Another arm places the empty can in position. The machine pushes the fish into the can, the can slides away, and another one comes to be filled. Like tin soldiers, the rows of cans move on to a machine which fastens on the tops. Then they travel on to the huge steam boilers where the fish is cooked. So rapidly does the work progress that in some of the establishments a can, packed, sealed, and labeled, drops every second from the last machine, ready for the trip to different parts of the country.

In the Far Western states, we shall see forests more wonderful than any we have yet visited. These Pacific slopes are a good illustration of the effect which climate has on vegetation and therefore on the occupations of people. The eastern slopes of the mountains, which receive little or no rain, are treeless, but on the western slopes of the Sierra Nevadas and Cascades grow the very largest trees in the whole world.

FIG 85. How much taller than your house are the trees which stand beside it? How many times taller than the cabin in the background are these "big trees" in California?

Some of the "big trees" of California (sequoias, if we call them by their right name) are three hundred feet tall and have a diameter of thirty feet. Some of their branches are as large as ordinary trees, and their bark is often from one to two feet thick. Compare the height of your school building with that of a giant sequoia. Measure your schoolroom and see if it could be placed on the flat surface where a tree had been sawed off.

These wonderful trees are not only the largest but the oldest living things in the world. When Columbus sailed to the New World, they were in the prime of life. Even when Christ was born in Bethlehem, they were strong and vigorous and larger than other full-grown trees. They are too precious to be cut for lumber, and therefore the government has included the areas where they grow in its national parks. In what national parks of California are some of the sequoias growing?

Lumbering is carried on in California among the redwood trees. Farther north, especially in Washington and Oregon, grow deep forests of pine, fir, cedar, and spruce. Some of these are tall and straight as a church spire. What splendid flag poles and

FIG 86. This is only one of the many busy sawmills and lumber yards in the Pacific states. Is this lumber soft or hard wood?

masts for ships they make! The Western lumberman dealing with such large, heavy trees has many problems unknown to woodsmen in other parts of the country. The trees must not break in the crashing fall, neither must they damage other valuable trees. Sometimes by a derrick and a block-and-tackle system provided with strong steel ropes, a tree is slowly lowered to the ground. Sometimes a man climbs to the required height, cuts a notch, inserts a charge of dynamite, lights the fuse, and quickly descends. As the flame reaches the explosive, the top of the tree is blown completely off. The tall, straight trunk is then felled.

Some of the trees are felled by hand. In other cases, a gasoline engine with cutting gear attached does the work. Sometimes an electrically heated wire is used.

These huge logs are cut into different lengths, varying with the uses to which they will be put. They are too heavy for horses to draw out of the woods, so "donkey engines" are used instead. Attached to these engines is a coil of steel wire which

FIG 87. The government forests are divided, and a man is appointed to guard each section. Forest rangers spend much of their time in the saddle. Can you see in the distance the fire which is attracting the attention of these men? (Courtesy of the Department of Agriculture)

FIG 88. This beautiful road takes us from Tacoma to Mt. Rainier National Park. Where is this park?

will reach half a mile or more. The coil is unwound and attached to a log. The signal is given, the "donkey" gets to work, and as the cable is wound up, the great log, ripping and tearing through the underbrush, is jerked toward the engine. This is usually placed near the railroad which has been built into the woods. The logs are loaded, often by steam derricks, on flat cars and are taken out to the lumber mill.

These Western forests are the largest and most valuable in the United States. If they are cut as carelessly and wastefully as other forest regions have been, our lumber supply will soon be exhausted.

Here again, a department of our government, the Forestry Bureau, has come to the help of our future citizens and is trying to preserve our forests for their use. This Bureau has for some years been educating the lumbermen in the right way of using a forest, in the necessity of saving the young trees, and in the value of planting new ones. In several of the Western states, large areas of forested land are now under government control. Whatever private owners may do with their property, here in the national forests, lumbering will be carried on in such a way that the woods will be of permanent value.

All this Western region is one of Nature's most interesting workshops; here she is building our greatest mountain systems. Here, as in all regions of young and growing mountains, cracks and fissures appear in the rocks. When a slipping occurs along one of these cracks, old Mother Nature is not alarmed, for such occurrences have been common in her life, but they are startling to people. We call such slippings earthquakes, and they often do great damage to life and property. Earthquakes often occur on the Pacific coast. Most of them are very gentle, however, and cause little damage. Even in 1906, when the great earthquake occurred in San Francisco, much greater damage was done to the city by the fire which followed than by the earthquake itself. In this disaster, parts of the city were entirely destroyed and thousands of people were made homeless.

Many of the mountain peaks in this Western region are volcanoes which were active long ages ago. Mt. Baker and Mt. Hood are two of the most noted. Mt. Shasta is one of the most beautiful. Its foot rests in the luxurious green of northern California, and its snow-capped head rises magnificently toward the blue sky above. Lassen Peak is today the only active volcano in the United States proper.

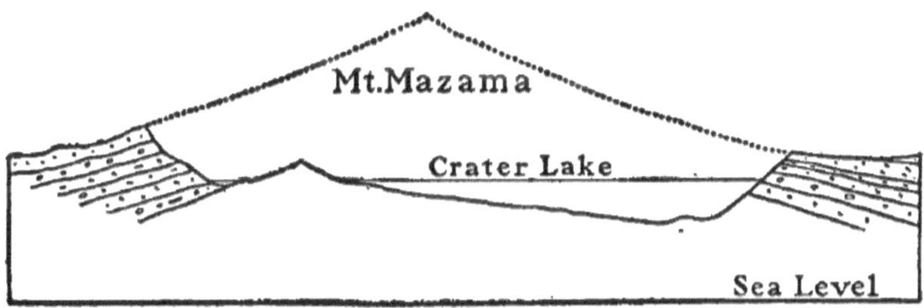

FIG 89. The dotted line shows the height of Mt. Mazama before it blew its head off in its great eruptions. Notice the level of the lake in its crater. Where is Crater Lake?

There is nothing lovelier in this or any other region than the sleeping volcano Mt. Rainier. Next to Mt. Whitney, it is the highest mountain peak in the country. Its crater, from which in ages past tremendous masses of lava have flowed, is a mile wide. The snows of centuries have filled it full to overflowing, and by their enormous weight have started frozen rivers down its sides. Nearly thirty ice-rivers, or glaciers, radiate from its summit. In some of these, the ice is more than a thousand feet thick. Slowly, very slowly, perhaps only a few inches a day, these glaciers move down toward the valleys, where they melt and form rivers. Mt. Rainier does not have a monopoly on our glaciers, for there are others in the United States, but this wonderful volcano does have the largest and most complete glacial system of any mountain in the country.

The most curious of the volcanoes of this region is in Oregon. In some awful eruption of the past, its head was blown off. Now the blue waters of Crater Lake fill the hole in the top of the mountain. The mountain, the lake, and the scenery around make the region so attractive that the government has made it a national park.

The Yosemite Valley in California is another example of Nature's handiwork. To preserve its beauties for everyone

FIG 90. This picture of Crater Lake shows you a portion of the crater wall within which it lies. How can you account for a lake in the crater of a volcano? (Courtesy of the Department of the Interior)

to enjoy, Congress has set apart an area of more than eleven hundred square miles, which is known as Yosemite National Park. The park receives its name from Yosemite Creek, a small stream flowing into the Merced River. The tributaries of the Merced River leap down over high cliffs in falls and rapids into the main stream. These falls are very lovely. The upper fall of Yosemite drops more than fourteen hundred feet, a distance equal to nine Niagaras, while the lower fall is more than three hundred feet high.

Our trip to the Pacific states would not be complete without a visit to San Francisco. This city is no longer the largest on our Western coast, for the reports of the census of 1920 give Los Angeles the first place. San Francisco is, however, the most important shipping center in the Far West. Study the map on this page, and you will see that it is located on a peninsula, which juts northward between the ocean and the drowned valley of San Francisco Bay. Ships from all over the world sail through the Golden Gate into the splendid harbor, bringing goods from many far-away countries — rice, tea, and silk from China and Japan, jute from India, sugar and pineapples from the Hawaiian Islands, coffee from Central and South America, and many, many other products. At her great docks, we should find vessels being loaded with lumber, petroleum, grain, cotton and cotton goods, and many kinds of canned and dried fruits and vegetables. Great shipyards border the water. Manufactories of many kinds, sugar refineries,

FIG 91. This map shows you the position of San Francisco on a peninsula, with a drowned valley forming the bay to the east of the city. Through what passage do ships sail to enter the bay? What is a drowned valley (see pages 11 and 54)?

stockyards, and meat-packing establishments are found in the city.

Around San Francisco Bay are other cities of importance — Oakland, Berkeley, and Alameda. The relations between these places and San Francisco are very close, making this the largest metropolitan region in the West.

Look closely at the map opposite page 134 and see how far Puget Sound extends into the state of Washington. The city of Tacoma is located near its southern end, and a little farther north is Seattle, the largest city of the state. Tacoma and Seattle are built on hills rising from the water. Because of the splendid forests around both cities, they have become important lumber centers. Large quantities are manufactured, and many great rafts and shiploads are exported. The swift streams that flow down the western slopes of the Cascade Mountains give to both Tacoma and Seattle abundant water power. Coal is mined not far away. Both cities, therefore, have advantages for manufacturing, and both, because of their location, are important commercial ports.

Seattle is often called the Gateway to Alaska. Most of the supplies and passengers bound for Alaska leave the United States from this port. Let us take passage here on the steamer waiting at the dock and start on our northward journey to this distant part of our country.

SUGGESTIONS FOR STUDY

I

1. Wonders of the Pacific states.
2. Surface of the region.
3. Gold-mining.
4. Irrigation and farming.
5. Fishing and canning.
6. Forests and lumbering.
7. Some famous volcanoes and national parks.
8. Some cities of the Pacific states.

II

1. Find in the appendix of your textbook in geography the names of the five highest mountain peaks of the United States. In what mountain system and what state is each one located? What are the three highest mountains of all North America?
2. Sketch a map of the three Pacific states. Show the following rivers - Columbia, Snake, Willamette, San Joaquin, Sacramento.
3. On the above map, show the highest mountain peak of the United States, the valley of California, and the mountain ranges that border it, the Imperial Valley, Puget Sound. Show also the chief seaports.
4. How would the commerce of the seaports be affected if the land along the Pacific coast should rise?
5. Large quantities of fruit are raised on the Atlantic Coastal Plain. Why is the fruit not dried there as it is in California? If conditions are different in the East, state why they are so.

III

Make a list of the places mentioned in this chapter. Arrange them by cities, mountains, rivers, etc. Be able to locate the places and tell what was said in the chapter about each one.

CHAPTER X

THE GREAT COUNTRY OF ALASKA

Alaska is a great country. When the United States bought it from Russia in 1867, nearly everybody thought it was a cold, barren land of more "square miles than square meals." Even the men who urged its purchase knew little or nothing of its gold and copper deposits and coal lands, its forests and fur-bearing animals, and its rivers and bays teeming with fish. Many thought that the United States was foolish to buy such a country.

In the fifty and more years since we bought Alaska from Russia, the minerals that have been obtained there have paid its purchase price many times over. The copper mined in Alaska in a single year is worth several times the amount of money that we paid for the country, while the value of the gold and the fish and fur products is enormous. Besides the copper, gold, fish, and fur, it is now known that Alaska contains vast beds of coal.

The great river of Alaska, the Yukon, is one of the largest rivers of North America. Its valley lies between the Coast Ranges on the south and the Rocky Mountains on the north. In our trip up the Yukon River, we shall sail as far as New York is from Salt Lake City. The highest mountain of North America, Mt. McKinley, is in Alaska, and some of the largest glaciers of the world cover the mountain slopes and fill the valleys.

Nome, the famous mining town in western Alaska, is as far west of San Francisco as Boston is east of that city.

It is farther from Skagway, in southeastern Alaska, to Attu — the most western of the Aleutian Islands — than it is from New Orleans to Hudson Bay.

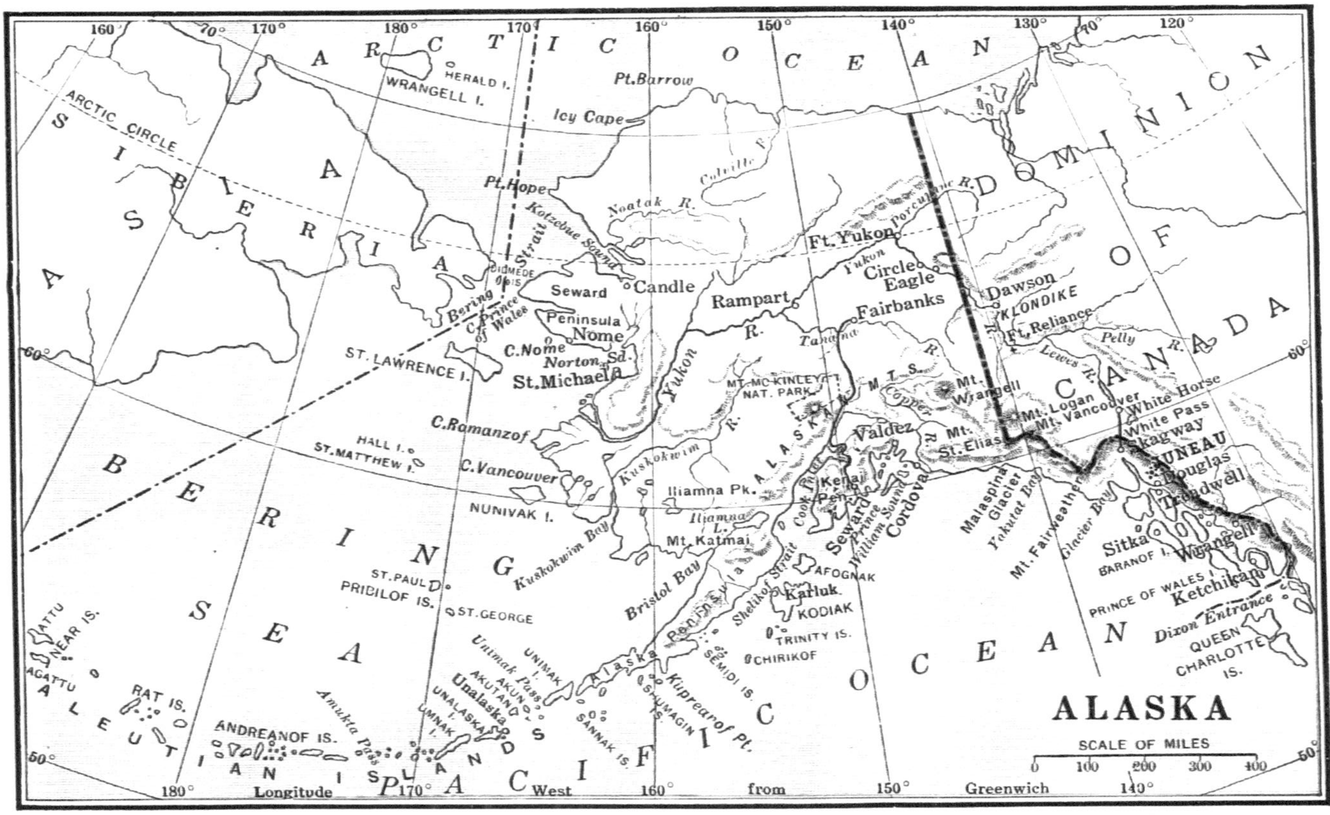

ALASKA
SCALE OF MILES
0 100 200 300 400
ARCTIC OCEAN
PACIFIC OCEAN
BERING SEA
SIBERIA
DOMINION OF CANADA
ALEUTIAN ISLANDS
Longitude West from Greenwich
50° 60° 70°
120° 130° 140° 150° 160° 170° 180°
HERALD I.
WRANGELL I.
Pt. Barrow
Icy Cape
ARCTIC CIRCLE
Pt. Hope
Colville R.
Noatak R.
Kotzebue Sound
Bering Strait
DIOMEDE IS.
Seward
Candle
Rampart
Ft. Yukon
Porcupine R.
Yukon R.
Circle
Eagle
Fairbanks
Dawson
KLONDIKE
Ft. Reliance
Pelly R.
Lewes R.
C. Prince of Wales
Peninsula
Nome
C. Nome
Norton Sd.
St. Michael
ST. LAWRENCE I.
Yukon R.
Tanana R.
MT. McKINLEY NAT. PARK
A L A S K A N M T S.
Copper R.
Mt. Wrangell
Mt. Logan
Mt. Vancouver
White Horse
White Pass
Skagway
JUNEAU
Douglas
Treadwell
Mt. St. Elias
Valdez
Kenai Pen.
Seward
Prince William Sound
Cordova
Malaspina Glacier
Yakutat Bay
Mt. Fairweather
Glacier Bay
Sitka
BARANOF I.
Wrangell
PRINCE OF WALES I.
Ketchikan
Dixon Entrance
QUEEN CHARLOTTE IS.
C. Romanzof
HALL I.
ST. MATTHEW I.
C. Vancouver
NUNIVAK I.
Kuskokwim R.
Iliamna Pk.
Iliamna L.
Mt. Katmai
Cook Inlet
Kuskokwim Bay
Bristol Bay
Alaska Peninsula
Shelikof Strait
Karluk
KODIAK
AFOGNAK
TRINITY IS.
CHIRIKOF
SEMIDI IS.
Kupreanof Pt.
SHUMAGIN IS.
SANNAK IS.
ST. PAUL
PRIBILOF IS.
ST. GEORGE
NEAR IS.
ATTU
AGATTU
RAT IS.
ANDREANOF IS.
Amukta Pass
UNIMAK I.
Unimak Pass
AKUN
AKUTAN
Unalaska
UNALASKA I.
UMNAK I.

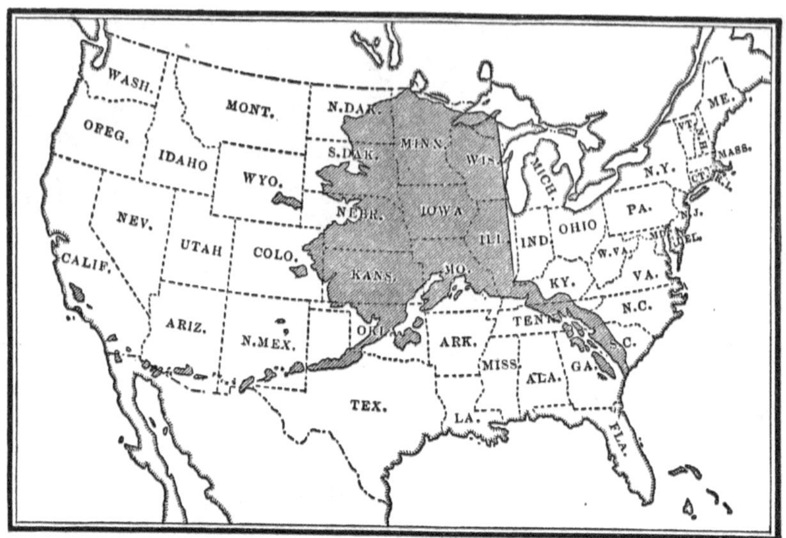

FIG 92. The shaded portion is a map of Alaska. How much of the United States do you think it covers? From the areas given in the appendix of your textbook in geography find out how nearly correct your estimate is southern Alaska.

Alaska lies nearly as far north as Greenland, but the two countries are as different from each other as California is different from Pennsylvania. The harbors in southern Alaska are never frozen, while those of both Greenland and Labrador are icebound for several months.

It is because of the westerly winds and the Alaskan branch of the warm Japan Current that Alaska is so much warmer than the countries equally far north on the eastern coast of North America. Along the eastern shores, the cold Labrador Current flows from the Arctic Ocean, between Greenland and the continent. This current chills the air around it and makes the contrast in climate between the Atlantic and the Pacific coasts all the greater.

The high mountains near the coast of Alaska shut out from the interior much of the warmth and rainfall which the winds bring to the shore lands. Consequently, interior Alaska is much colder, and a temperature of fifty or more degrees below zero is not uncommon in the winter.

Southern Alaska is about as far north as Scotland, where

FIG 93. This is Mt. McKinley, the highest mountain in all North America. Where is it?

the people raise cattle and sheep, and where there are good farms and flourishing cities. Norway and Sweden, in about the same latitude, are prosperous countries, with well-educated, industrious people, who live comfortably on their little farms and carry on lumbering, mining, manufacturing, and commerce with other countries. In the future, Alaska will doubtless become as prosperous as these European countries.

Our first stop is at Ketchikan, situated near the boundary between Alaska and Canada. It is one of the most important towns in Alaska. The business section is near the shore, and the better houses are on the hills behind. Some streets are so steep that cleats are fastened across them to keep people and horses from slipping.

The best time to visit Ketchikan is in the early summer. Then the swift little river that flows through the town is filled with salmon. The canning of salmon is one of the important industries of Alaska. The money received for one year's catch of this fish would pay the price of Alaska several times over. Other fish — halibut, cod, and herring — are caught in and around Alaska, but the catching and canning of salmon is a more important industry than all the rest put together.

FIG 94. Do you think that this picture was taken near the coast or in the interior of Alaska? Give the reason for your answer. Compare this picture with FIG 100. What seasons are represented in the two pictures?

Except in the summer, when the salmon are running, the many canneries along the Alaskan coast are deserted. In June, when the salmon begin their migration up the freshwater streams, all is bustle and excitement. Crowds of laborers — Chinese, Japanese, and white men — come in on the ships. Indians gather from the villages around. Tugs with huge nets put out from the shore and come in heavily laden. Many salmon are caught in traps, and boats with fish wheels capture thousands in their netted baskets. Indians spear the fish in the shallow streams. The harvest of the sea is rushed with all speed to the canneries, where work goes on day and night.

For about a month, the rush of canning continues. Then the catch of salmon grows less each day, until it ceases altogether. Then the Indians go back to their villages, and the other laborers return to their homes or enter other employments. The cans are loaded by thousands on the ships waiting in the harbors, and the salmon-canning industry is over for the year.

Salmon is an important food of the natives of Alaska. If you were to visit a village during the summer months, you would find large quantities of fish hanging on bars and drying in the sun. When thoroughly dry, it is packed in storehouses raised a few feet from the ground so that the contents may be out of reach of the dogs.

Leaving Ketchikan, we steam steadily northward. Our route leads through narrow channels lined with tall spruces and cedars. Steep mountain sides, hidden beneath green trees, rise from the water for hundreds of feet, and the slopes extend as far, or farther, down into the blue depths.

On the shore of a narrowing channel which goes glimmering on past the town lies Juneau, the capital and the largest town in Alaska. There are few level places in the town. Parallel with the beach are streets, each one higher than the one before it; while others, steep and crooked, climb the hills. The business part of the town lies near the water, and, above, the vine-draped cottages cling close to the mountainside.

Juneau has many modern conveniences — electric lights, a good water supply, a public library and hospital, churches, theaters, newspapers, and a chamber of commerce. We enjoy its crooked streets, its winding stairways, and the shops where souvenirs are sold. Perhaps you would like a beautiful basket, a

FIG 95. This is Juneau, the capital of Alaska. Read page 148 and account for the beautiful channel on which Juneau is situated. (Courtesy of the Alaska Department of the Seattle Chamber of Commerce)

silver bracelet, a spoon of hammered copper, warm moccasins fashioned by clever fingers in some Indian's hut, or little ornaments carved from a walrus tooth or a reindeer's horn. Juneau is not the bleak, dreary place which many people imagine these Alaskan towns to be. The winters are not so cold as those of Boston, and the long summer days are delightful. In this high latitude, during the warm months, the sun rises very early and sets very late. During June, it can hardly be said to set at all, so little does it dip at midnight below the horizon.

In the moist air and the long daylight hours, flowers, fruits, and vegetables grow quickly. Among the tall grasses in the fields, many wild flowers bloom. If we wander away from the towns, climb the mountain sides, or follow the rippling streams, we shall tread on them at every step.

Across the channel from Juneau is Douglas Island, where there are famous gold mines. All day long, the great stamps bang and pound and echo as they crush the ore. Some of the mines here have been flooded by an inrush of water from the channel, but others, separated by cement bulkheads, are still worked. We have permission to visit them, and the "cage" drops us swiftly through the deep shaft. At the bottom of the shaft, tunnels lead off in different directions to the pockets where the miners are working. We follow our guide through the long tunnels; we listen to the jarring noise of the drills eating their way into the hard rock; we jump at the noise of the explosions when a miner blasts out great fragments of the rocky wall; but when our guide tells us that we are standing under the deep waters of the channel which separates the island from the mainland, we decide hastily that it is time to go up to the surface.

In the early days of mining in Alaska, there were no deep mines with shafts and tunnels. The placer gold was taken from the sands and gravels near the surface, as it was in the days of the "forty-niners" in California. Hydraulic mining is now carried on in Alaska as it is in some of our Western states, and the huge streams of water, sent with the force of a cannonball, wash away whole hillsides. In many places, deep mines have been started to obtain the rock in which the gold is embedded. It is the loose

FIG 96. This is Sitka, the former capital of Alaska. What is the present capital?
Which place has the better location for trade?

surface gold, easily obtained by placer mining, that has started the excitements, the gold rushes, and the stampedes to parts of Alaska. The deep deposits, however, are the real sources of the yellow metal, and these will furnish a more lasting source of supply.

From Juneau to Sitka, the old capital of Alaska, the distance is about a hundred and fifty miles. Like Juneau, Sitka is beautifully situated, with a ring of snow-topped mountains behind it, and in front, a bay of sparkling water dotted with green islands. It is off the main line of travel, and with the moving of the capital to Juneau, it lost much of its importance.

One of the interesting sights at Sitka is the government Agricultural Experiment Station. The work done by the Department of Agriculture has been very helpful in teaching people that Alaska is not a cold, bleak, barren place filled with nothing but mountains and glaciers. Here, at Sitka, potatoes, cabbages, turnips, carrots, peas, celery, radishes, and lettuce grow well in

FIG 97. All aboard for Alaska via the famous Inside Passage. Why is the water in this passage smoother than in the open ocean?

the long, sunlit days. Berries of all kinds — strawberries, raspberries, currants, and salmonberries — are large and delicious.

The sail along the southern shore of Alaska is extremely beautiful. You can see from your map how close to the shore the mountains lie. Green at their bases, but silver-white at their summits, they seem to rise straight out of the sparkling blue water. For hundreds of miles, the chains extend, merging at the west into the volcanic ranges of the Aleutian Islands.

For many years, Mt. St. Elias, on the boundary between Canada and Alaska, was thought to be the highest mountain on the continent. It is known today that Mt. McKinley, situated nearer the center of Alaska, is higher than Mt. St. Elias.

Excepting Greenland and the little-known Antarctic continent, Alaska is the greatest glacier land of the world. In its bays and inlets, thousands of icebergs, children of the glaciers, are born. Many of the valleys between the mountains are filled with rivers of ice. The largest glacier in the world, covering an area greater than the state of Rhode Island, is in Alaska. It is fifty miles wide at the water's edge and extends back thirty miles to the mountains that feed it.

Would you like to sail into Glacier Bay, one of Nature's

FIG 98. You can understand from this picture why glaciers are sometimes called rivers of ice. How fast do glaciers move?

cold-storage houses? Put on your thick coat, for though the air is balmy in the open waters outside, in the bay itself it is crisp and chill, with the touch of Jack Frost in its breath. Our course must be slow, for icebergs are floating all around us, and new ones are constantly breaking off from the glaciers at the edge of the water.

> Icebergs to right of us,
> Icebergs to left of us,
> Icebergs in front of us,
>   Volley and thunder.

Around the bay and in its arms, there are dozens of glaciers. The most famous one is Muir Glacier, at the head of the bay. It is named for the noted scientist, John Muir, who explored and studied it. If the bay could be emptied of its water, we could see the face of the ice-sheet more than a thousand feet high, while a milk-white river, possibly half a mile wide, rushes out from beneath it.

At the mouth of Yakutat Bay, we pass an Indian village. In July, it is almost deserted. Most of the Indians are camping on an island in the bay in order to get their winter supply of sealskins and oil. These are obtained from the hair seal and not from the fur seal, whose coat is so valuable. The men hunt and kill the seals. The women and girls skin them and scrape off the hair from the skins and dry them. They boil out the fat from the flesh in large pots over smoldering fires on the beach. When this work is finished, they leave the little tents and bark huts, and camp near the mouth of some stream where they can catch and salt a supply of salmon for the winter. With plenty of oil for fire, with skins for clothing, and with fish to eat, they will live comfortably until the seal comes again to the shallow waters and the salmon flock up the rivers.

On our sail along the southern coast of Alaska, we come to the mouth of the Copper River and, a little farther on, to the Kenai Peninsula, with Prince William Sound on the east and Cook Inlet on the west. Among the mountains around Prince William Sound, in the Copper River valley, and farther north in the valley of the Tanana River, there are very rich copper deposits. When railroads from the southern ports to the interior open up the country, much larger quantities than are obtained at present will be mined, great smelters will be built, and

FIG 99. This girl is scraping off the hair from the skin of the seal. What will she do with the skin later?

copper in great amounts will be shipped to Seattle and other Western cities.

Rich beds of coal also lie in the mountains around. Yet in spite of these deposits, thousands of tons are imported every year at great expense. The United States government has built a railroad northward from Seward to Fairbanks, nearly five hundred miles away. As more roads and railroads open up the country near the coal beds, the importation of this useful mineral will not be necessary.

After leaving Seward in our westward journey, the shores of Alaska begin to look very different from the green, wooded country along which we have been sailing ever since we left Seattle. Rich grass is growing in the fields and meadows and on the slopes of the hills. We cannot help thinking what fine

FIG 100. Large areas in Alaska will make fine ranch land, and in the future many more cattle will feed on its rich grasses. To realize the beauty of this scene, try to put the colors into it. (Courtesy of the Alaska Department of the Seattle Chamber of Commerce)

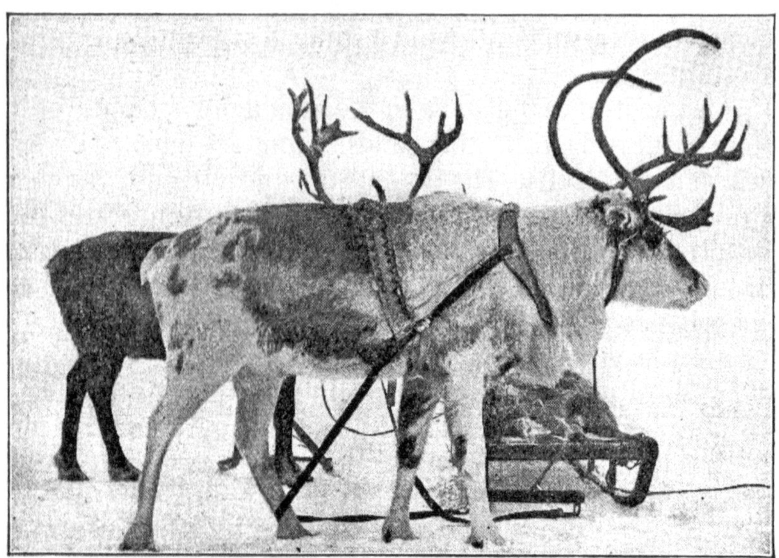

FIG 101. How has the introduction of reindeer into Alaska helped the Eskimos? Into what other parts of North America have they been introduced? (See Index)

ranch land this is, and we try to imagine the fields occupied by thousands of cattle or reindeer, ranch houses dotting the land, and boats sailing from the harbors of southern Alaska carrying meat and other ranch products to southern cities and towns.

There are many thousand reindeer in Alaska. The flesh of reindeer is as nourishing and appetizing as beef, and it is eaten not only in Alaska but in Seattle and other Western cities to which it is shipped in considerable quantities. Reindeer are very valuable to the people of Alaska. The flesh and milk are used for food, and the skin for clothing. The animals are trained to draw sledges and can travel faster than dogs can. When going on a long trip with dogs, a large part of the load that they carry must consist of their food. It is not necessary to carry food for the reindeer, as they feed on the thick moss which grows in nearly all parts of the country. When deep snow covers the ground, they dig down with their sharp hoofs until they come to the moss hidden under the drifts.

The Indians and Eskimos in many parts of Alaska used to live in what, to them, was a comfortable way. Game was plentiful, and whales, seals, otters, beavers, and various kinds of fish were more than enough to supply their simple needs. As more and more white men went to Alaska, animals became more scarce and the natives found it harder to get food. The game became so timid and was driven so far from the settlements that the natives in some villages were in danger of starvation.

Individuals have given money, Congress has appropriated larger sums, missionaries and the Bureau of Education have helped to carry out the plan of introducing reindeer from Siberia into Alaska, and today many natives who were in danger of starvation are living comfortably and caring intelligently for their increasing herds. The introduction of reindeer and the teaching of the natives to care for them is one of the best things that the United States has done for Alaska.

The Alaska Peninsula and the Aleutian Islands are a part of the great volcanic belt which stretches around the shores of the Pacific from Cape Horn, in the bleak Antarctic Ocean, through China and Japan. Some of the worst volcanic eruptions and earthquakes of the world have occurred on these coasts. You have read of the earthquake in San Francisco and of the lava fields of Washington and Oregon, and you have probably seen pictures of the low, frail houses which are commonly built in Japan because earthquake shocks are so frequent there.

Find on the map of Alaska the name of Mt. Katmai. This is today the largest active crater in the world, though there is no telling when a tremendous eruption in some other part of the earth may cause this statement to be no longer true. In 1912, Mt. Katmai had an awful eruption. It is estimated that the lava and ashes thrown out at that time amounted to forty times as much material as was moved in digging the Panama Canal.

After the eruption, some scientists went to Alaska to study the region and the effects of the explosion. In their explorations, they discovered a remarkable area, more wonderful even than the Yellowstone Park or the Grand Canyon. They called it the Valley of Ten Thousand Smokes. In this remarkable place, there are thousands, perhaps millions, of craters and fissures, or cracks, in the earth from which steam is constantly escaping.

The columns of smoke in some cases rise only a few feet, while in others they are tall enough to hide the hills around.

There are no geysers in the valley today. The region is too young and the escaping steam too hot. A geyser consists of hot water mixed with steam. The vents in this valley are so hot that no water can exist in them except in the form of steam. Sometime in the distant future, as the volcanic area grows older and the heat becomes less intense, there may be wonderful geysers here.

Have you ever heard of fox-farming? On more than fifty of the Aleutian Islands, this interesting industry is carried on. There are similar farms on which foxes are raised on the mainland of Alaska, in Canada, and in places in the northern part of the United States.

Caring for the foxes is interesting work. The animals are shy and usually afraid of strangers. See those sharp eyes peering out from behind the bushes? There go other frightened foxes darting swiftly away. That group gathered around the heap of bones makes us laugh at their fierce growls and sharp little barks. See the lines of fish drying on the poles near the shore? Salmon and other fish form one of the chief foods of the foxes. On the islands near where seals are found, the foxes eat seal meat and fat. They also like whale flesh or birds' eggs.

What a soft, thick fur the foxes have, and what a lovely color they are! It is a bluish Maltese. These are known as blue foxes. Many of this kind are raised because the fur is fashionable and therefore valuable. The next time you see in a store window a muff or a scarf made of the fluffy gray-blue fox fur, perhaps you will think of the fox-farmers and their interesting farms on the Aleutian Islands.

Bering Sea is a lonely place, and we shall meet but few vessels there. We may chance to see a ship from Seattle bound for St. Michael and the Yukon, a vessel on its way to the seal islands, which we shall visit later, or a whaling ship returning from its long voyage in the Arctic Ocean.

Whaling is an important industry in Northern waters. Some of the vessels from San Francisco and Seattle go on long voyages of many months. There is less of this deep-sea whaling done today than formerly. More vessels put out for short voyages from stations on the shore.

After killing a whale, the body is drawn near to the ship by winding up the line. The monster is kept afloat by air pumped into the body, and it is then towed to the station on the shore. There it is cut up and the fat meat cooked to get the oil. If the ship is one of the fleet which will remain out in the ocean for months and take as many whales as possible before putting into the harbor, the cooking is done on board.

There are several different kinds of whales, and each one is valuable for certain products. The fat meat of all whales yields large quantities of oil, but the best is obtained from the sperm whale, which lives in warmer waters. One of these whales will yield many barrels of oil.

Another kind is the beluga, or white whale. This is caught chiefly for its skin, from which a valuable leather is made. This is used in the manufacture of machinery belting, shoestrings, traveling bags, and other articles where a tough, strong leather is required.

The bowhead whale, which lives in Far Northern waters, furnishes us with whalebone. This whale is a huge creature, but it has a small throat and therefore lives on small fish. Hanging from the roof of its mouth is a fringed sheet of bony material which prevents the fish from escaping from the mouth after once entering it. The whale can then swallow its dinner at its leisure. This ragged sheet is what is known as whalebone. The whale's mouth is so large that the sheet of whalebone is several feet long and weighs half a ton or more.

The natives of Alaska eat whale meat. Whale steak is now considered a good food and is sold today in some of our large markets. Sometime in the future, canneries in Alaska may export canned whale as well as canned salmon. At present the flesh that remains after the oil has been cooked out is used in fertilizers.

Our next stop in Bering Sea will be at the Pribilof Islands, where the government of the United States carries on the largest sealing industry in the world.

In the early summer, the seals leave the deep waters of the

FIG 102. This is a breathing-hole which the seals have kept open in the thick ice. Why do seals have to come to the surface of the water to breathe?

Pacific Ocean and swim northward to their summer homes on the Pribilof Islands. Here the baby seals are born. They are helpless little creatures, with large, soft eyes and a cry much like that of a young baby. The male seals and the young animals remain on or near the islands all summer. The mothers often swim long distances from shore in search of food. If a seal is killed on one of these trips it really means two deaths, for without its mother, the little seal on the island is sure to starve to death.

For years there were so many seals that came to the islands that thousands and even hundreds of thousands were killed each season. Sealskin is one of the most beautiful and durable of furs, and seal fishing was a profitable industry. Some years ago it was found that the seal herds were fast decreasing in numbers and, if not protected, would soon disappear. The United States has now taken charge of the killing of the seals and is trying to protect the herds by treaty with England, Russia, and Japan — all of whom are interested in the seal industry — by arresting sailors who are breaking the laws, and by prohibiting the killing of any seals for long periods. The Eskimos who live on the Pribilof Islands depend to a great extent on seal flesh for food, and the government allows them to kill a certain number of seals each year.

We could not think of leaving Bering Sea for our trip up the Yukon without visiting the famous little boom town of Nome. In 1899 there was no settlement where Nome now stands. In less than two years, more than ten thousand people were living in tents and rough shanties, and hundreds of men were turning the long stretch of beach into miniature mountain ranges and valleys in an effort to get the gold that was hidden in the sands. The Nome of today is much smaller. It is only a little town on a wind-swept beach, but it is sure of its future, though it lies almost at the entrance of the Arctic Ocean. There is gold in the barren tundra behind, and gold in the deep rock of the mountains, of which the riches on the beach were only the washings. Where gold is, there men will flock.

For seven long months the dooryard of ice stretches westward from Nome toward Siberia, on the other side of the sea, and no ship can approach the shore. The snow gets deeper as the winter goes on, until sometimes the little houses are nearly buried in drifts. The people of Nome have many good times during the long winter. They go skiing and sleighing — in dog teams, of course, with the driver running alongside. One of the

FIG 103. This is a rookery on one of the Pribilof Islands. At what time of the year do the seals come here? Why has the government restricted the killing of seals?

most exciting events of the winter is the annual dog race from Nome to Candle and return, a distance of nearly four hundred and fifty miles. One of the rules of the race is that each driver shall return with the same set of dogs with which he set out. This insures good treatment of the dogs on the way.

Gold is still mined near Nome, but not in the same place or in the same way that it was in 1900. Most of it is mined today back of the town, instead of on the beach in front of it. We see men shoveling up the gravel and putting it into an inclined runway called a sluice box. One of them turns the water in at the upper end to wash away the coarse gravel. The gold, which is heavier, is caught on cleats fastened across the bottom of the box. It looks like hard work, and we hope that these miners may "strike it rich." Off to the right of us, standing in a small pond of water, is a gold-dredger at work. Dredging is a common method of mining here on the Seward Peninsula and in some other parts of Alaska where the gold is found near the surface of the ground.

A day's sail southward from Nome across Norton Sound brings us to St. Michael, a small town, but an important one

FIG 104. A winning dog team in the race from Nome to Candle. How should you like to drive such a team? (Courtesy of the Alaska Department of the Seattle Chamber of Commerce)

FIG 105. All ready for a prospecting trip. What minerals in Alaska have prospectors already discovered?

to the people of Alaska. Vessels going up and down the Yukon stop here, and supplies from the United States are left here to be distributed. St. Michael feeds and clothes the miners for hundreds of miles around and sends goods and supplies to all parts of the country. We will take a steamer here for a sail up the Yukon. Few people realize the size of this great waterway of Alaska. Only two rivers in North America are longer. What are they? At its most northerly point near Fort Yukon, where it makes a sharp bend in its course, the Yukon crosses the Arctic Circle. Lying so far north, it is open to traffic for only about four and a half months of the year, but during that time it is used by many barges and vessels.

At the mouth of the Tanana River we change to a smaller boat to go up the Tanana to Fairbanks. Like most other Alaskan towns, Fairbanks owes its life to gold, and all around it is a rich mining region. With its window boxes and pretty flower gardens, the town is an attractive place. The warehouses and the amount of freight that is being unloaded from our boat tell us that it is also an important center and that many of the smaller settlements and camps around depend on it for supplies of food and clothing, tools, and other necessities. The government railroad by which people can ride southward in a comfortable train from Fairbanks to Seward, and there connect with a steamer for Seattle, will cause a great gain in the growth of this Northern town.

FIG 106. This field of wheat is growing near the arctic circle. Why does the grain grow so rapidly during the short summer? (Courtesy of the Alaska Department of the Seattle Chamber of Commerce)

Mining in this part of Alaska is carried on with difficulty because of the frozen soil. Much of the ground of Alaska is frozen several hundred feet deep. In places during the summer, this thaws for a few feet. In order to do mining of any depth, the ground must be softened, and if Mother Nature will not do this for the miners, they must do it for themselves. By building fires, the miner can loosen a little of the surface soil. If he wishes to get deeper, he uses steam. Pipes heated by steam are forced into the frozen soil. These melt the frost around them, and the earth can then be more easily loosened. By the use of steam, miners have opened shafts and galleries many feet below the surface. The mining in the underground tunnels is not dangerous because the frozen earth makes a hard, safe roof.

Leaving Fairbanks, we make our way again up the river. It seems hardly possible that we are almost at the Arctic Circle, for looking off there to our right, we see a large field of wheat. There is also a patch of good-looking cabbages, and another

FIG 107. These men are shooting the Whitehorse Rapids. The current is so swift as the water is forced through the narrow passage that the foaming white-crested waves were thought to resemble the white mane of a horse. Hence the name.

of turnips, while close by we see potatoes, peas, carrots, and beets growing. The season is short, but the days are very long, and the crops grow almost continuously.

As we sail across the Arctic Circle, we almost expect to see a dotted black line, such as is shown on maps, stretched across the river to tell us that we are really in the frigid zone. Near Fort Yukon, which lies just north of the boundary between the temperate and frigid zones, the river bends southward again, and we cross the Arctic Circle for a second time and are back again in the temperate zone. Circle, our next mining town of importance, was named because of its nearness to the Arctic Circle, but it is farther away from it than Fort Yukon is.

Eagle is our last town in Alaska before crossing into Canadian territory, and Dawson is the first important town on the other side of the boundary. It has taken us about two weeks to cross the country of Alaska by river.

Leaving Dawson, our steamer continues its way for three hundred miles farther to Whitehorse, the head of navigation on the Yukon. The river has grown much narrower and shallower than the broad, deep stream which flows through central

FIG 108. The picture shows you the position of Skagway. Why has this town grown to be of some importance?

Alaska. Between Dawson and Whitehorse there are rapids and steep-walled canyons. The current is swift, and the journey is more exciting than in the lower river. At Whitehorse Rapids, above Whitehorse, many miners in the Klondike rush lost all their outfit and in many cases their lives. At the wharves of the town of Whitehorse, several vessels are moored, and freight is waiting to be taken down the river to the mining towns. The piles of supplies and the number of people are much smaller than they were in the rush of 1898, when in a few months between thirty and forty thousand people passed over this route to the gold fields. It took them several weeks of hard, exhausting labor and suffering, often in peril of their lives, to go from Skagway to Dawson. We have come from Dawson to Whitehorse in a comfortable steamer, and here we shall change to a modern train and ride at our ease, enjoying the wonderful scenery, over the once-dreaded White Pass down to Skagway, the gateway to this rich region.

The changes that have come to Alaska in the last fifty years are truly wonderful. The improvements in the next fifty years will be far more marvelous. In this hundred years, Alaska will have changed from an unknown, uninhabited waste to a prosperous land filled with people who depend on its rich resources for life and its comforts.

SUGGESTIONS FOR STUDY

I

1. Resources of Alaska.
2. Position and climate.
3. Ketchikan and salmon-canning.
4. Juneau, the capital, and Sitka.
5. Minerals of Alaska.
6. Glaciers and icebergs.
7. The reindeer industry.
8. Mt. Katmai and the Valley of Ten Thousand Smokes.
9. The Alaska Peninsula, the Aleutian Islands, and fox-farming.

10. Whaling and sealing.
11. Nome and St. Michael.
12. On the Yukon River.
13. Fairbanks and other Alaskan towns.
14. Homeward bound.

II

1. How has Alaska proved a good bargain for Uncle Sam?
2. On a map of the United States, draw Alaska as on page 166. Show the route followed in the chapter. Write the names of the places mentioned.
3. For what industries will Alaska be famous in the future?
4. How can you tell on a map that Nome is as far west of San Francisco as Boston is east of that city? What do you call the lines which help you to measure distance east and west?

III

Make a list of the places mentioned in this chapter. Arrange them by countries, cities, mountains, rivers, etc. Be able to locate the places and tell what was said in the chapter about each one.

CHAPTER XI

OUR NORTHERN NEIGHBORS, CANADA AND NEWFOUNDLAND

North of the United States stretches the great country of Canada. Its boundary line of thirty-nine hundred miles is more than twice as long as the border line between our country and Mexico. More than half of this boundary is water. On the land, it is marked at intervals of about two miles by monuments from three to five feet high made of aluminum bronze. There is no other boundary line in the world so long where there are no forts, no garrisons, and no armed soldiers patrolling the border.

Canada covers a vast area. It is as large as Europe, not including the country of France. What two countries cover a greater area? So much of it stretches into the frozen regions of the North, so much is mountainous, and so much is, as yet, little developed that the country is thinly peopled. Though nearly the size of Europe, Canada contains only about a fiftieth as many people.

In the far-northern part of Canada, there are many miles of frozen deserts. No vegetation grows here, and no people make their homes in this dreary waste. South of this desolate area is a deep forest belt where valuable fur-bearing animals make their homes. Still farther south, there are areas of fertile land like our own great plains. As in the United States, there are in the west mighty mountain ranges forever topped with snow. In the east are the older, lower highlands, which have been smoothed and rounded by Nature's workers—the rains, the snows, the frosts, the streams, and the great ice-sheets.

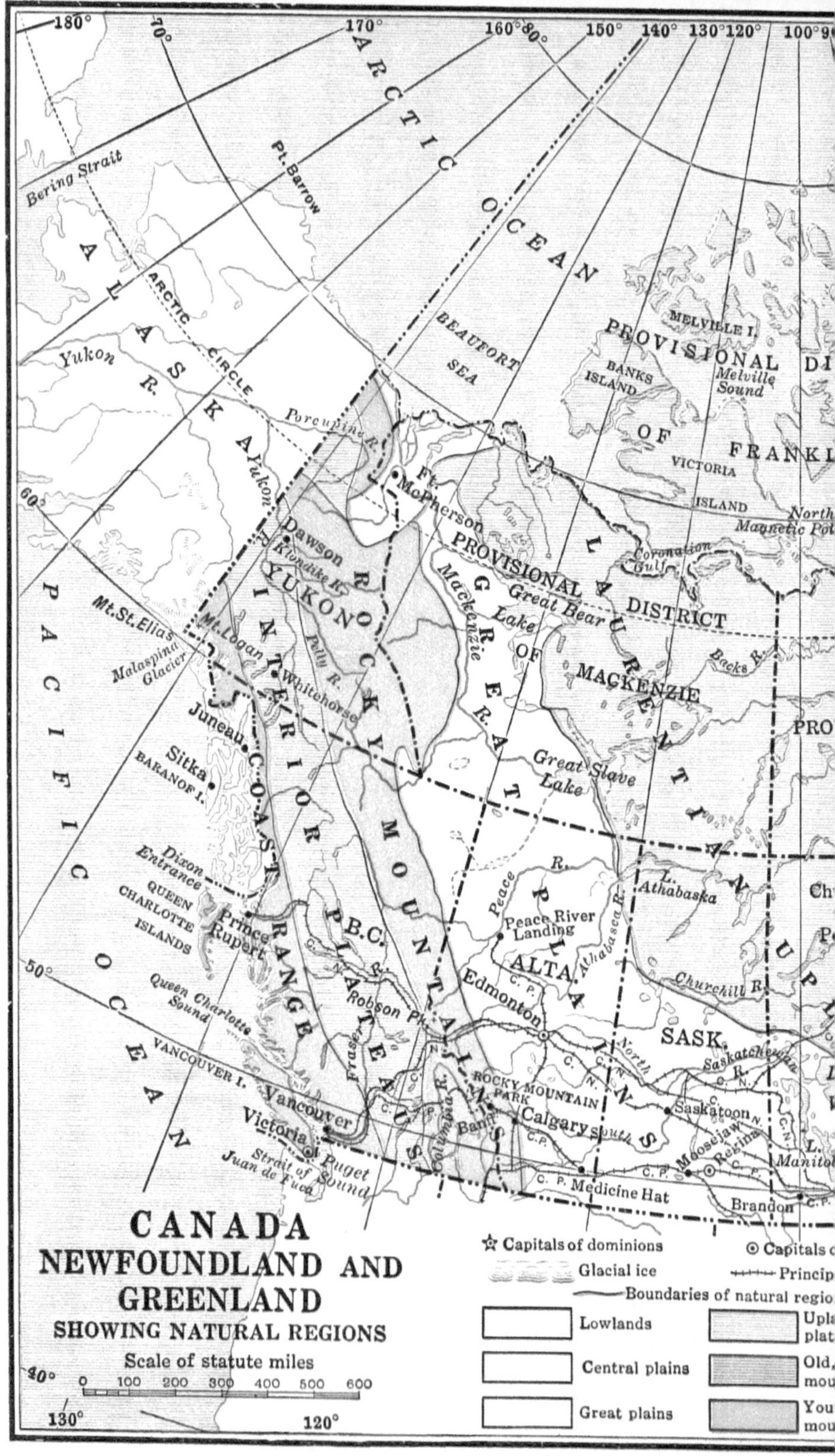

ARCTIC OCEAN
Bering Strait
Pt. Barrow
BEAUFORT SEA
PROVISIONAL DI
MELVILLE I.
Melville Sound
BANKS ISLAND
OF
FRANKL
VICTORIA ISLAND
North Magnetic Pol
Yukon
ALASKA
ARCTIC CIRCLE
Yukon R.
Porcupine R.
Ft. McPherson
PROVISIONAL
DISTRICT
OF
MACKENZIE
Coronation Gulf
Backs R.
60°
Dawson
Klondike R.
YUKON
INTERIOR
Mt. St. Elias
Malaspina Glacier
Mt. Logan
Pelly R.
Whitehorse
ROCKY
Mackenzie R.
Great Bear Lake
GREAT
PROVISIONAL
LAURENTIAN
PRO
Juneau
Sitka
BARANOF I.
COAST
MOUNTAINS
Great Slave Lake
PACIFIC
Dixon Entrance
QUEEN CHARLOTTE ISLANDS
RANGE
Peace R.
R.
L. Athabaska
Ch
50°
Prince Rupert
PLATEAUS
P. B. C.
Athabasca R.
P
Queen Charlotte Sound
Fraser R.
Robson Pk.
Peace River Landing
ALTA.
Churchill R.
OCEAN
VANCOUVER I.
Vancouver
Columbia R.
Edmonton
C. P.
SASK.
Saskatchewan R.
North
Victoria
Strait of Juan de Fuca
Puget Sound
Banff
ROCKY MOUNTAIN PARK
Calgary
C. P.
South
C. P.
C. N.
Saskatoon
C. N.
Moosejaw
Regina
L. Manito
Medicine Hat
C. P.
Brandon
C. P.
40°
130°
120°
CANADA
NEWFOUNDLAND AND
GREENLAND
SHOWING NATURAL REGIONS
Scale of statute miles
0   100   200   300   400   500   600
☆ Capitals of dominions
Glacial ice
Boundaries of natural regio
Lowlands
Central plains
Great plains
⊙ Capitals
Princip
Upla
plat
Old,
mou
You
mou

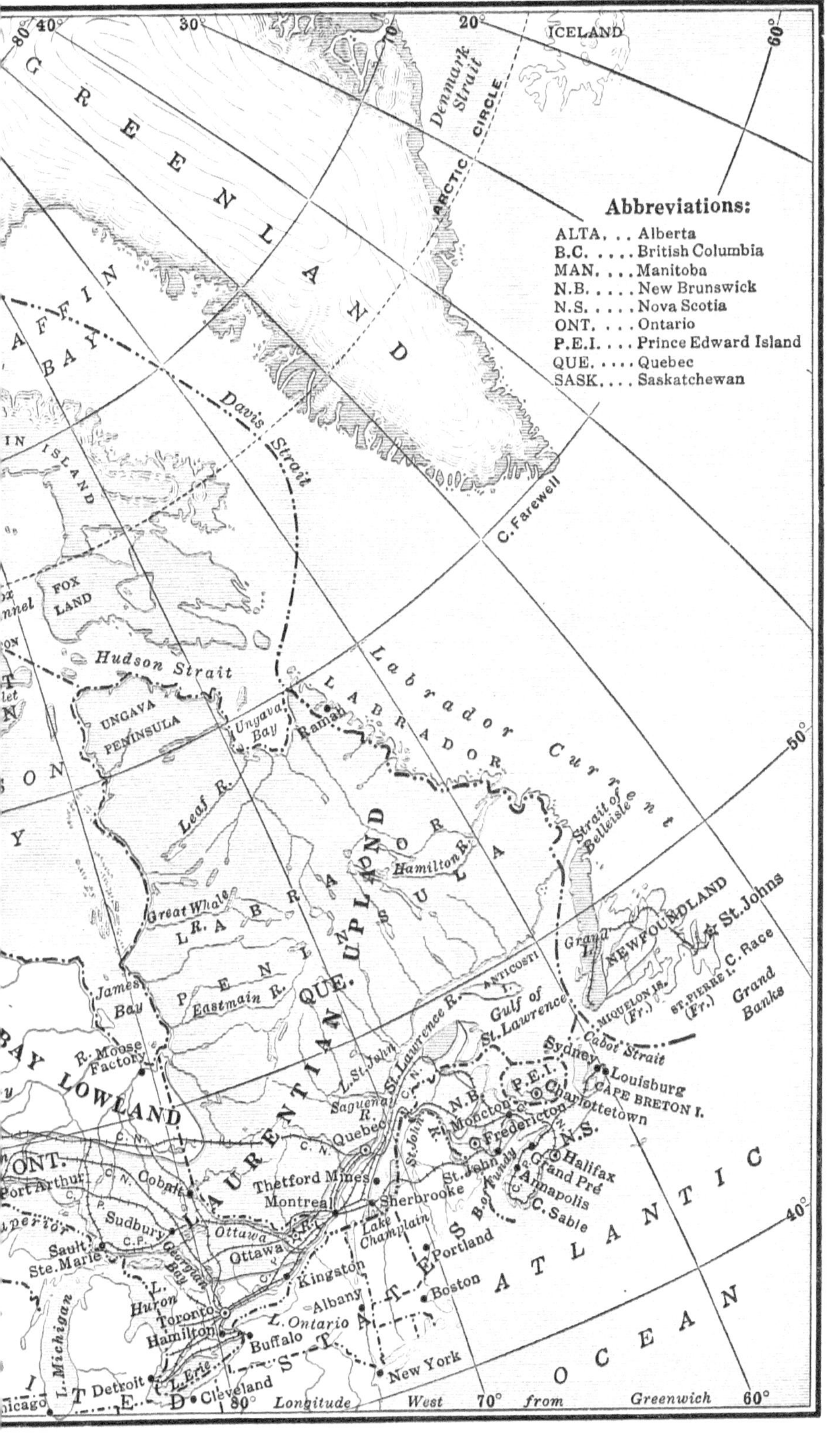

Abbreviations:
ALTA. . . . Alberta
B.C. . . . . British Columbia
MAN. . . . Manitoba
N.B. . . . . New Brunswick
N.S. . . . . Nova Scotia
ONT. . . . Ontario
P.E.I. . . . Prince Edward Island
QUE. . . . Quebec
SASK. . . . Saskatchewan
ICELAND
GREENLAND
Denmark Strait
ARCTIC CIRCLE
BAFFIN BAY
BAFFIN ISLAND
Davis Strait
FOX LAND
Hudson Strait
UNGAVA PENINSULA
Ungava Bay
Ramah
LABRADOR
Labrador Current
C. Farewell
Leaf R.
Hamilton R.
LABRADOR UPLAND
Great Whale L. R.
QUE.
Strait of Belleisle
NEWFOUNDLAND
St. Johns
Grand L.
Eastmain R.
James Bay
PENINSULA
ANTICOSTI I.
Gulf of St. Lawrence
MIQUELON IS. (Fr.)
ST. PIERRE I. (Fr.)
C. Race
Grand Banks
HUDSON BAY
R. Moose Factory
BAY LOWLAND
LAURENTIAN UPLAND
St. Lawrence R.
L. St. John
Saguenay R.
Sydney
Cabot Strait
Louisburg
CAPE BRETON I.
P.E.I.
Charlottetown
Quebec
Moncton
N.B.
Fredericton
N.S.
Halifax
ONT.
Port Arthur
Cobalt
Thetford Mines
St. John
Bay of Fundy
Grand Pré
Annapolis
Sudbury
Montreal
Sherbrooke
C. Sable
Sault Ste. Marie
Ottawa
Lake Champlain
Portland
Georgian Bay
Ottawa
Kingston
Albany
Boston
ATLANTIC OCEAN
L. Huron
Toronto
L. Ontario
UNITED STATES
L. Michigan
Hamilton
Buffalo
Chicago
Detroit
L. Erie
Cleveland
New York
80° Longitude   West   70°   from   Greenwich   60°

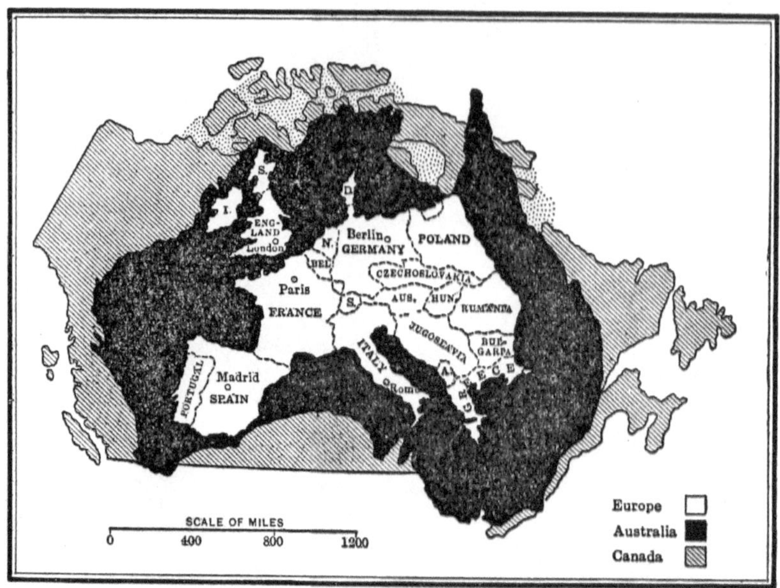

FIG 109. What continent and a part of what continent are shown on this map of Canada? What do you notice about their comparative size?

Our northern neighbor is not a republic like the United States. It is the largest dominion of the British Empire, whose possessions lie in every continent and every ocean. Although it is a part of the British Empire, Canada is free to manage her own affairs, to develop her industries, and to trade with all parts of the world, as independent nations do.

Newfoundland is not a part of Canada. It is another dominion of the British Empire. The ruler of Newfoundland is a governor appointed by the king of England. Labrador is under the administration of Newfoundland.

More people in Canada are engaged in farming than in any other occupation. Look in the supplement of your geography, where the areas and population of the different countries of the world are given, and you will find that in Canada there are on the average between two and three people living on each square mile. In the United States, there are more than thirty. In France, there are about two hundred. In England, there are more than six hundred people living on every square mile of its surface. You can

FIG 110. You will find beautiful scenery on your trip through western Canada. These twin mountains overlook the peninsula on which Vancouver is built. To what system do they belong?

easily see that in countries where the population is so dense, there is little room for big farms, many people are crowded into large cities, and manufacturing is the chief occupation. In countries like Canada and the United States, many people own large farms, where more grain, cattle, and other products are produced than are needed at home. Therefore, large quantities of these products are shipped away, and in return, manufactured goods and articles, which on account of the soil or the climate cannot be produced there, are brought into the country.

We shall find a visit to Canada most enjoyable. If you are interested in great farms, fruitful orchards, fields of grain, fine cattle and sheep, and splendid horses, you can see all these. If you like city life and cities, you can find them on river and lake and plain. If you are interested in Nature's gifts, you can visit mines where the workmen are mining coal, iron, copper, gold, silver, nickel, and asbestos, or drilling wells to obtain petroleum.

If you are fond of the great outdoors, you can climb snow-

FIG 111. In many parts of Canada we shall find deep forests. The shipping and manufacturing of lumber are important industries. Are the trees in the picture of hard or soft wood?

capped peaks or ride for many miles over grassy plains and through deep forests; you can watch the lumbermen felling and loading some of the largest trees you ever saw and visit the mills where great logs are ground into pulp. You can live with the trappers in the deep woods or go on a cruise with the whalers to Arctic waters, sail with the cod and mackerel fishermen to the Grand Banks, or visit the Pacific shores and watch the catching and canning of salmon. You can ride on some of the longest railroads, the mightiest rivers, and the largest lakes of the world. In the cold weather, you can join the crowds who are skating, coasting, skiing, and sleighing; you can watch the ice-boat races and the races where the sledges are drawn by dogs or reindeer. In the summer, you can enjoy long hours of balmy sunshine, read stories by daylight late in the evening, and, if you go far enough to the north, see the sun, a round red ball, shining at midnight on the southern horizon.

With all these and other interesting sights before us, let us start on our trip among our northern neighbors.

SUGGESTIONS FOR STUDY

I

1. Position of Canada.
2. Size of the country.
3. Surface of Canada.
4. Government of Canada.
5. Newfoundland and Labrador.
6. Population and occupations.

II

1. Bound Canada; Newfoundland.
2. Name some large rivers and lakes on which you might sail in a tour through Canada.
3. Use the scale of the map and find the distance across Canada from east to west. About how long do you think it would take you to travel across it in the train? Name some cities which you might visit in the east; in the central part; in the west.
4. Write to the Board of Trade in some of the large Canadian cities asking for pamphlets which describe their cities and industries for use in your school. Look up the names of some of the great Canadian railroads and write to them for material on the provinces through which they pass. The departments of government in the provinces, especially that of Agriculture and Immigration, also issue descriptive pamphlets. From these and similar sources you can build up a fine library on Canada for your school.

III

Make a list of the places mentioned in this chapter. Arrange them by countries, cities, mountains, rivers, etc. Be able to locate each place and tell what was said about it in the chapter.

CHAPTER XII

IN THE MARITIME PROVINCES

Our visit to Canada will take us first into the Maritime Provinces. The word "maritime" means bordering on or connected with the ocean. Nova Scotia with Cape Breton Island, New Brunswick, and Prince Edward Island are known as the Maritime Provinces.

The Appalachian Highlands, of which you read in Chapter III, extend northward into these three provinces. Like New England, this area is very old — so old that Nature's workers have had time to wear down the lofty peaks which once rose higher than those of the Rocky Mountain Highlands, fill up the valleys, and carry much of the soil into the sea. Here, therefore, we shall find low, rounded hills and mountains and broad valleys, making the scenery much like that which we saw in New England.

Boundaries between countries do not limit production areas. You remember reading in the chapter on New England of the forest regions which cover the northern part of Maine, New Hampshire, and Vermont. This forest area stretches northward into Canada, and lumbering is an important occupation there.

As you have already learned, most countries which lie on the water carry on fishing. These Maritime Provinces border on one of the best fishing grounds of the world, and many of the men spend the greater part of their lives on the water or in preparing fish for market.

NOVA SCOTIA AND CAPE BRETON ISLAND

Nova Scotia is a prominent peninsula on the eastern coast of North America. Look on the map and you will see that it is nearly surrounded by water. It is joined to New Brunswick by an isthmus about thirteen miles wide.

Can you tell why Nova Scotia is called the Gateway to Canada? Can you see what advantages it has because it is nearer than any other division of North America to Europe and its great markets, and at the same time not far from the rich Canadian lands where raw materials and manufactured products can be obtained?

Nature has given the peninsula many valuable gifts. It has great forests, rich beds of coal with iron deposits near, and a large amount of water power. Off its shores there is an abundance of fish. Its soil is fertile, and agriculture is its most important industry. All over the peninsula we shall find good farms. We shall see farmers tending their cattle, caring for their orchards, planting or harvesting their hay and grain and vegetables. Of all the fertile valleys, you would like best to visit that of the Annapolis River, which stretches along the western part of the province, not far from the Bay of Fundy. The valley is especially beautiful in early June, when the apple orchards are in bloom and the air is sweet with their fragrance. So many apples are raised here that the district has become famous for this crop.

This part of Nova Scotia is the land of Evangeline, the home of the Acadians, of whom Longfellow tells us in his poem. Some of the descendants of those French people whose homes were here when the province fell into English hands are still living and working on their little farms.

The old city of Annapolis, called Port Royal by the French, lies in the Annapolis Valley. It is the oldest town on the continent north of Florida. The old stone ramparts and the powder magazine, with the lilies of France stamped on the hinges of the door, are relics of the old French days. More important today to the people of Annapolis than fortifications and munitions of war are the fine farms in the valley and the fish in the waters around. Many of the fish brought to shore in the fishermen's boats are salted and dried, and large numbers are shipped away, especially to the United States and South American countries.

Halifax, on the eastern coast of Nova Scotia, is the larg-

FIG 112. This is apple-blossom time in the Annapolis Valley. To what country do you think most of the apples will be sent? From what harbor may they be shipped?

est city of the Maritime Provinces. It is also the chief British military and naval station in the Western Hemisphere and, of course, is therefore strongly fortified. The commerce of the city is very important. It lies nearer to England than any port on the mainland of Canada. Many vessels from all parts of the world enter and leave its splendid harbor annually. Commercial cities, however, need something more than a harbor; they must have the goods to ship away. From the sea around, from the peninsula itself, and from the great area stretching away to the west, Halifax receives large quantities of freight. Thousands of barrels of fine apples from the Annapolis Valley and other parts of Nova Scotia and Canada find their way to foreign markets through this port. Large quantities of fish from neighboring waters, fish oil, furs from the great interior, hides, skins, and wool from many ranches, lumber and lumber products from the deep forests, and grain and meat from prosperous farms are loaded onto the great ships waiting at the docks.

In northwestern France is the province of Brittany, inhabited

FIG 113. The picture shows a fine team of three horses drawing a potato digger. The wheel which you see on the rear of the machine revolves, sending the prongs one after another into the ground. They loosen the soil and throw out the potatoes.

by a people known as Bretons. Living near the sea, fishing has long been their most important occupation. They fished not only on the coast of France but made longer and longer voyages, until they finally crossed the wide ocean to Canadian shores, where the fish were very abundant.

The island at the end of the peninsula of Nova Scotia soon became an important fishing center which the Bretons named L'Isle Royale. The English called the part of the island where the Bretons had their fishing stations the Cape of the Bretons. When the region fell into English hands, they called the little island Cape Breton Island.

One of the places in Cape Breton Island which you will wish to visit is Louisburg. It is not so important today as it was in the middle of the eighteenth century, when England and France were at war with each other. Much of Canada at that time was in the hands of the French. In order to get into the country, it was

FIG 114. This schooner is just ready to be launched in a Nova Scotia shipyard. To what use do you think it may be put?

necessary for the English to sail up the St. Lawrence River and capture the stronghold of Quebec. If you look at the map opposite page 190, you will see that this was impossible while the strong fortress of Louisburg, guarding the mouth of the great river, was in the hands of the French. Therefore Louisburg must be taken first. After a siege of two months, the English captured the fort and garrison. Then they sailed up the St. Lawrence and lay siege to Quebec, which soon fell into their hands. Later, all the French possessions in Canada passed into English hands.

Two small islands, St. Pierre and Miquelon, near the coast of Newfoundland, are still owned by the French and are used as headquarters by their fishing vessels.

Perhaps you have read more stories of the fishing around these Maritime Provinces than you have of any other industry and think, therefore, that it is more important. The fisheries are exceedingly valuable and are the most extensive in Canada, but both farming and mining are of greater importance.

While in the Maritime Provinces, you will have a good oppor-

FIG 115. These fish, which have been caught on the Grand Banks, are drying in the sun. To what countries may they be carried?

tunity to visit some mining towns. The coal fields of Nova Scotia are the only ones in eastern Canada and the only coal deposits in all North America which lie directly on the sea. This is a great advantage in shipping. The mountain system in which the deposits lie is very ancient and has been worn down into low hills. This makes the mining less expensive. For these three reasons, the coal mines in Nova Scotia are extremely valuable.

The largest coal deposits are in Cape Breton Island, near the port of Sydney. There are coal beds also on the other side of that island, toward the Gulf of St. Lawrence, and still other rich veins on the northern side of Nova Scotia. During the months when the river and the gulf are not closed by ice, the shipping of coal from the mines to the inland cities of Canada is a very easy matter.

Sydney, the capital of Cape Breton Island, is an important industrial and commercial center. It is surrounded by the richest coal beds of eastern Canada, while iron can be brought easily from the mines of Newfoundland; it has a splendid landlocked harbor; it is nearer to Europe than any port in the United States; it is at the entrance of the Gulf of St. Lawrence and the great waterway leading into the heart of Canada. A good farming community around supplies the produce needed by the city workers who are employed in stores, mills, and factories.

NEW BRUNSWICK

Across the Bay of Fundy from Nova Scotia, and connected with it by a narrow strip of land, is New Brunswick. This province is nearly as large as the state of Maine, which it joins. It is a region of thick forests, green hills, lovely lakes, and swift rivers.

Covered with deep forests and with water touching it on all sides, you know that the chief occupations are lumbering and fishing and the industries connected with them. Most of the people have farms, but many spend a part of their time either on the ocean or in the woods. There is considerable mineral wealth in New Brunswick, but mining has not yet become an important occupation.

Most of the New Brunswick forests are spruce, but there are also

FIG 116. Here are the logs starting on their journey from the forest to the sawmill. The horses will draw them to the bank of the river. What season of the year is it?

hemlock, fir, and cedar trees, besides the harder woods — oak and birch. Lumbering is carried on here much as it is in Maine and Minnesota. In the spring, when the ice breaks up in the streams, the logs are floated down to the river ports, where great sawmills and pulp mills are situated. Every year enormous quantities of boards, sashes, doors, boxes, moldings, shooks, shingles, laths, and many more things than we could find time to mention, besides many tons of pulp for the making of paper, leave the harbors of St. John, Fredericton, and Moncton, the three most important cities of the province.

St. John is located at the mouth of the St. John River, where its waters leap into the Bay of Fundy. When it is low tide in the Bay of Fundy, the water falls from the river into the bay. When the tide rises, the bay is higher than the river, and the water flows north into the St. John. It is at this time that steamers can ascend the river. The tides in the Bay of Fundy are said to rise higher than anywhere else in the world. At the head of the bay, the water at high tide is fifty feet higher than it is at low tide. Here at St. John, it rises from twenty-five to thirty feet.

FIG 117. Here are the logs starting on their trip down the river. At what time of the year do they usually commence this journey?

The fine, deep, sheltered harbor of St. John is open all the year, while many Canadian ports are icebound during the cold weather. Halifax, on the southern coast of Nova Scotia, and St. John, on the southern coast of New Brunswick, are the two chief winter ports of Canada.

Fredericton, the capital of New Brunswick, is a beautiful city, overlooking the winding stream and encircled by green hills. Here, as in other cities of the province, we see the logs in the river, the sawmills close at hand, and the factories for making various articles of wood, while at the wharves are the ships waiting for their cargoes of lumber, wooden articles, and pulp.

PRINCE EDWARD ISLAND

Prince Edward Island is snuggled in close to the semi-circular shore of the Gulf of St. Lawrence. This smallest province of

FIG 118. In this picture the logs are in the log boom near the mouth of the river, waiting to be taken into the sawmill which you see farther down on the right. From what Canadian ports may lumber be shipped away?

Canada is only a little larger than Delaware. It is long and narrow, and all parts of it lie near the water.

Prince Edward Island is more densely populated than any other part of Canada. It is sometimes called the Garden Province. The scenery is lovely, the climate good, the soil fertile, and both land and ocean harvests are plentiful. Many of the people are farmers or fishermen. The farms look prosperous and the fields of vegetables, grain, and fruits flourishing. Most of the farmers have orchards of apples, plums, and pears, and many berries and small fruits are raised. In the pastures, we can see many cattle and sheep. In some of the towns, there are cooperative dairies to which the farmers for miles around bring their milk to be made into butter and cheese.

In the chapter on Alaska, you read of the farms where blue foxes live. Many silver foxes are raised here in Prince Edward Island. They are beautiful creatures with their thick coats of soft black fur and their white-tipped tails. Their fur is very expensive. A pair of foxes with perfect fur are worth several thousand dollars.

In other parts of Canada, we might find fox farms and also those where other fur-bearing animals are raised, such as the

FIG 119. Isn't this fox a beauty? Its name is Black Beauty, and it is worth several thousand dollars. What kind of fox is it? Of what other kind did you read on page 178?

otter, beaver, mink, muskrat, and skunk. As prices of furs rise and the fur-bearing animals grow scarcer, people are finding that it pays to raise them instead of depending for our supply on the wild animals.

Charlottetown, the capital of Prince Edward Island, is an old French city. The French sailors who first entered its harbor were so pleased with the surroundings that they named it Port la Joie, the "Port of Joy." When the province came into English hands, this name, like so many others in Canada, was changed in order to honor Queen Charlotte of England. The wide, leafy streets, the cordial, homelike atmosphere, the attractive grouping of the public buildings in the parklike heart of the city, the well-tilled fields, green pastures, and quiet streams around, make a stay in Charlottetown very restful and pleasant.

SUGGESTIONS FOR STUDY

I

1. The Maritime Provinces.
2. Surface and occupations.
3. Position and boundaries of Nova Scotia.
4. Climate and resources.
5. Farming in Nova Scotia.
6. Annapolis.
7. The port of Halifax.
8. The naming of Cape Breton Island.
9. The old stronghold of Louisburg.
10. Coal-mining.
11. Sydney.
12. Boundaries of New Brunswick.
13. Forests and lumbering.
14. St. John and the Bay of Fundy.
15. Fredericton.
16. The Garden Province of Prince Edward Island.
17. Fox-farming.
18. Charlottetown.

II

1. Name the Maritime Provinces and their capitals.
2. What ocean current warms the western coast of North America? What one chills its eastern coast?
3. Read the part of "Evangeline" that describes the Annapolis Valley. What occupations are mentioned as being carried on in those early days?
4. Name the places in eastern Canada whose names have been changed. Why was this done?
5. What is said about the fishing industry on pages 23 and 24?

III

Make a list of the places mentioned in this chapter. Arrange them by countries, cities, mountains, rivers, etc. Be able to locate each place and tell what was said about it in the chapter.

CHAPTER XIII

NEWFOUNDLAND AND LABRADOR

The Appalachian Highlands extend in a northeasterly direction through the United States, New Brunswick, and Nova Scotia. The mountains have been drowned in the Gulf of St. Lawrence, and only the tops of the highest appear as islands. The large island of Newfoundland lies at the tip end of the system, with its eastern coast well drowned by the sinking of the land. Notice on a map how irregular this coast is with its long peninsulas and deep inlets. Can you picture the high cliffs and black rocks worn and smoothed by the wild seas which dash against them?

Newfoundland is about the same size as Ohio, but it contains only about one twentieth as many people as that state, or not much more than half as many as live in the city of Cincinnati. The surface, soil, and climate have much to do with this scanty population. Newfoundland has many low mountains and hills covered with deep forests. Thousands of lakes are scattered over the country.

Land in the valleys is fertile, and parts of it are good for sheep-raising and cattle-raising — industries which may sometime be more important than they are at present. The towns are principally on the coasts, and there are few good roads or railroads leading far into the interior.

In the northern part, especially, there are deep pine forests, and large sawmills have been built here. Many fur-bearing animals live in the woods, and in the winter trappers on snowshoes make long trips to visit their traps.

Newfoundland is farther north than any part of the United

States. It lies in the path of the cold Labrador Current, which sweeps down from the Arctic Ocean west of Greenland and along the Labrador coast. This current makes the climate cold and disagreeable. It does more than this. Flowing northward from the Gulf of Mexico along the shores of the United States and swinging eastward across the Atlantic is the warm Gulf Stream. The air above it is full of moisture which has been evaporated from the ocean water. These two ocean rivers, one from the cold North and one from the warmer South, meet off Newfoundland. The air above the cold Labrador Current chills that over the warmer Gulf Stream. When chilled, the air can no longer hold all the moisture which it was carrying, and this partially condenses, thus forming thick fogs. The fogs spread over enormous areas. Sometimes they even stretch halfway across the Atlantic Ocean.

Often, huge icebergs, broken off from the great Greenland

FIG 120. This is the NC-3 leaving Trepassey Bay, Newfoundland, May 16, 1920, on the first seaplane race across the ocean. Why was the eastern coast of Newfoundland chosen as a starting point? (Courtesy of the United States Navy Department)

FIG 121. Icebergs are the children of glaciers. Why should so many icebergs float south with the Labrador Current? How much of the left-hand iceberg in the picture is below the surface of the water?

glaciers, come floating southward, hidden in the dense fog. Lookouts on vessels keep a sharp watch for these floating masses of ice, which are many times larger than a ship. Numerous accidents have been caused to fishing vessels and ocean liners by collisions with icebergs.

Though very dangerous to shipping, the icebergs serve a useful purpose. On them, in the spring, many seals rear their young. As the ice masses float southward, the Newfoundland sailors go out and kill the seals. These are the hair seals, not the kind which are caught in Bering Sea.

The Labrador Current brings southward in its waters another valuable product. This is the slime composed of small forms of sea life on which herring feed. The herring, with many other small fish, are eaten by the cod; hence, both these varieties swarm in great numbers in the waters around Newfoundland. So many people are engaged in fishing that it has become the chief occupation of the province.

Around Newfoundland and the Maritime Provinces, there is a submarine plain wider even than that along the coast of the United States. It is built of the soil which once topped the very ancient mountains of this region. Off the coast of Newfoundland, this shelf is called the Grand Banks. It is in the shallow waters of the Banks and the region in and around the Gulf of St. Lawrence that the cod and herring are caught in enormous quantities.

The codfish has been called the Bread of the Sea. It is very abundant and makes a nourishing food. The nations of the world have quarreled many times over the fishing grounds of the cod because the industry is so valuable. Millions of pounds are caught annually in the waters of eastern Canada. Dried, salted, and smoked, it is shipped away to Brazil, the West Indies, and countries of southern Europe. The refuse left after the fish are dressed is used in making glue, oil, and fertilizer.

Not only the ocean, but the lakes and rivers in Newfoundland and the eastern provinces of Canada abound in fish. The trout is the most valuable fish of these inland waters, and several million pounds are caught each year. Besides trout, the whitefish, pickerel, pike, and other freshwater fish are plentiful. Would you like to go on a fishing trip some summer to these northern lands? We shall not expect to see in Newfoundland, with its

FIG 122. This is Indian Harbor, one of the few ports on the Labrador coast. The boats are fishing craft.

scanty population, any very large cities. St. John's, the capital, is the only one of any size. As is often true on a drowned coast, its harbor is a splendid one — deep, landlocked, and entered by a narrow channel bordered with high cliffs.

We should enjoy a visit to St. John's in the spring, when the fishermen are preparing for their trip to the Grand Banks. It is a busy time around the wharves while the boats are being loaded with food, salt, nets, and all other needful supplies for the voyage. When the vessels return, the wharves have an even busier appearance. The cargoes must be unloaded and the fish prepared and packed for export. Then, it must be loaded on the ships which are waiting to carry it to far-distant countries. The ocean harvest of one part of the world helps to feed the people in lands far away. In return, the products of field, farm, forest, and factory of the people across the ocean are sent back to the fishing countries. Thus, each nation in the world helps and in turn is helped by other nations.

Go north from the island of Newfoundland, across the Strait of Belleisle, and you come to Labrador, which stretches north-

FIG 123. These are some of the people in the bleak land of Labrador. What do you think these people may do for a living?

ward to Hudson Strait. With its shores washed by the cold waters of the Labrador Current and its rocky, barren surface, Labrador is indeed an inhospitable land, with little to attract either visitor or settler. Its few inhabitants are mostly Eskimos and Indians who live hard lives with few comforts. Their chief occupation is fishing, and their chief food is fish. When, for any reason, the fish are scarce, or when an epidemic visits the region, there is great suffering among them.

You remember the great value which the reindeer are proving to be to the Eskimos of Alaska, who train them to draw their sledges and use the flesh and milk and skin for food and clothing. Reindeer have now been introduced into Labrador, and it is hoped that this animal may help to make the life of the people there more comfortable. The government at Ottawa has taken steps to supply reindeer also to the people around Hudson Bay. Like the Eskimos in Alaska, they will be taught to care for the animals and to train them for transportation purposes.

SUGGESTIONS FOR STUDY

I

1. Position, surface, and size of Newfoundland.
2. The Labrador Current and fogs and icebergs.
3. Fisheries of Newfoundland.
4. St. John's, the capital.
5. The bleak land of Labrador.

II

1. Sketch the St. Lawrence River, the Gulf of St. Lawrence, and Newfoundland. Show the Labrador Current, the Grand Banks, and the city of St. John's.
2. Show the routes into the Gulf by way of the Strait of Belleisle and Cabot Strait.
3. Can you tell why so much fish from Newfoundland goes to southern Europe rather than to its northern countries?

III

Make a list of the places mentioned in this chapter. Arrange them by countries, cities, mountains, rivers, etc. Be able to locate each place and tell what was said about it in the chapter.

CHAPTER XIV

ON THE UPLANDS AND LOWLANDS OF QUEBEC AND ONTARIO

Passing westward from the Maritime Province of Newfoundland into the mainland of Canada, we come to an area older even than the worn-down Appalachian Highlands, which we have just seen. This is the Laurentian Upland. This region is probably the oldest part of the continent, the first land to appear above the waters which once covered the area where North America now lies. Slowly, very slowly, only a few inches or at best a few feet in a century, the land rose, the higher parts first appearing as islands in the vast ocean. Very gradually, with the rising of the land, the islands were joined, until at last the part of North America was formed which stretches from the St. Lawrence River and the Great Lakes toward the Arctic Ocean. This was the beginning of our continent.

These ancient Laurentian Highlands have been worn down until, at present, they are for the most part only low hills between which are fertile plains, broad, open valleys, lakes and ponds, and many streams. The upland region occupies nearly all of the province of Quebec, the districts of Keewatin, Mackenzie, and Franklin, and parts of Ontario, Manitoba, and Saskatchewan. The part of the Laurentian Upland east of Hudson Bay is occupied by the Province of Quebec. Look at the map and you can see that Quebec is a great peninsula lying mostly between Hudson Bay and the St. Lawrence River and Gulf of St. Lawrence. Labrador lies like a strip of trimming along its eastern edge and separates it from the Atlantic Ocean.

Notice on the map how the crest of the Laurentian Upland divides the rivers, separating those which flow into Hudson Bay from the southward-flowing branches of the St. Lawrence. No coal deposits are found in this region, but the many streams which leap over the hard rock cliffs into the valley of the St. Lawrence furnish plenty of "white coal." As the years go by, this power will be used more and more to generate the electricity which will light cities, run cars, and move machinery in many factories.

There are many minerals found in the old Laurentian Upland. Iron, gold, silver, copper, nickel, asbestos, and others are mined. Most of the gold, silver, and nickel are obtained in the province of Ontario, of which you will read later. You are already acquainted with the mining of gold and silver and iron and copper, but perhaps you have never read about the mining of asbestos. Indeed, it is mined in very few places on the earth. Nearly all the asbestos used in the world comes from Thetford Mines, south of the St. Lawrence River, in the province of Quebec.

Have you ever seen steam pipes or hot-water pipes wrapped in asbestos cloth to keep in the heat? Perhaps your mother has an asbestos mat which she can place on the stove without danger of burning. The fiber used in these articles is a mineral that can be woven into cloth as vegetable and animal fibers are. Of course, such a mineral is very valuable not only on account of its fibrous structure but because it will not burn. It is such a poor conductor of heat that cloth made of it, when wrapped around steam pipes and boilers, prevents the heat from escaping. Sometimes, the walls of safes are packed with it as a precaution against fire getting at the contents. Shingles made of asbestos are a protection to roofs.

The rock containing asbestos is mined by blasting and is then crushed and screened. The fiber is separated from the rock by the use of vacuum fans and is graded according to length by means of screens over which it passes. It is then bagged and shipped away.

Do you realize that the province of Quebec is nearly a fourth as large as the United States? The northern part is a wilderness

FIG 124. Jacques Cartier did not see the cattle feeding in the green pastures or the neat little houses of the French settlers along the river. Describe the scene as he saw it. (Courtesy of the Keystone View Co.)

of deep forests, rocky hills and mountains, and swift-flowing streams. The forests will furnish lumber for many years. In them, fur-bearing animals live, and here also, valuable minerals have been found.

As you may imagine, the most important part of Quebec lies near the St. Lawrence River. Here are the chief cities and towns, and it is in this part of the province that most of the people live. To see something of their life, to visit their homes and their cities, and to learn more of their industries, we will take a trip up the St. Lawrence. From the island of Anticosti, which lies in its great drowned mouth, to Lake Ontario is more than a thousand miles. For nearly this entire distance, the province of Quebec lies on either side of the river. In its upper course, near Lake Ontario, the United States lies south of the river and the province of Ontario on the north.

As we make our way up the great river, let us shut our eyes for a moment and imagine that we are living four hundred

FIG 125. This is a street in old Quebec. In what ways does it differ from the streets in your home city?

years ago instead of in the twentieth century, that our craft is a small sailing vessel instead of a fine steamer, and that the man who commands it is not our genial English captain but Jacques Cartier, a Frenchman and the first white man to sail up the St. Lawrence. If we would see the picture that he saw along the banks, we must forget the little villages with their white cottages overtopped by the glittering church spire, the strips of tilled ground green with growing crops, and the pastures where cattle are feeding. Cartier saw only the wooded shores where, perhaps, an Indian, lurking in the shadows, gazed at the white-winged bird sailing over the blue waters. He heard only the splashing of the streams as they cascaded down the cliffs to join the great river.

For years thereafter, Canada was governed by France and inhabited largely by French people. After England gained control of the country, English people began to make their homes here, but many descendants of the early French settlers still inhabit the land. They live not in the large cities, for the most part, but in the smaller villages and hamlets, many of which are located on or near the river. Here they till their ground, care for their cattle, work in their orchards, and attend their merrymakings. In the winter, when there is less to do on the farms, many of them work in the lumber camps.

Perhaps no city in all North America is more interesting to

the visitor than Quebec. It is different from other cities. It is a French city and an English city, an old city and a modern city, a fortification, a tourist resort, and a river port. There is the Lower Town, with its old stone houses and its queer planked streets, some of which are too narrow and steep for vehicles. There is the Upper Town, built on the cliffs, with its splendid views of the river and its traffic and the green hills beyond.

In the olden days, all shipping up the St. Lawrence River had to stop at Quebec. With the improvement of the river beyond, ocean vessels now go on to Montreal, Canada's largest city. There are always good reasons for a city's growth, and we can find many for the growth of Montreal. Its harbor on the river is one of the best in the world and, though it is a thousand miles inland, large ocean vessels can come upstream to its wharves. The St. Lawrence River is a highway leading to the fertile West; and the Ottawa River, which enters the St. Lawrence River close by, opens up another route to the rich Western plains.

By means of a canal, the rapids in the St. Lawrence at Lachine are avoided and connection is made with the Great Lakes. The route through the valley of the Richelieu River and Lake Cham-

FIG 126. The Château Frontenac, a famous hotel on the cliffs, overlooks the river and the Lower Town of Quebec

plain links Montreal with the Hudson River and the great port of New York. Were it not that the water routes around Montreal are closed by ice during the winter, the city would be much more important than it is at present, for it is three hundred miles nearer to Liverpool than is New York City.

Montreal is a great railroad center, and the long steel highways tie it to the west, the east, the north, and the south. It is Canada's great gateway for incoming and outgoing trade. With all these and other advantages, no wonder it has grown to be the largest city of the Dominion.

You can easily think what must be some of the city's industries. Logs from the forests are floated down the Ottawa River and other streams and are manufactured into lumber, wooden articles, furniture, and pulp. These are shipped away to other parts of the world. From the west come quantities of grain to be exported and to be made into flour in the city's great mills. In one mill, the largest in the British Empire, thousands of barrels of flour are made every day. There are hundreds of factories and mills in the city. The making of boots and shoes, cloth and clothing, iron and steel, and machinery, and the refining of sugar are a few of its important industries.

Instead of continuing our trip on the St. Lawrence, we will go up the Ottawa River, making use of a canal to avoid its rapids, for a visit to Ottawa, the capital of Canada. It is a beautiful capital city, located on a cluster of hills, some of which are crowned by splendid government buildings. At its feet, the Ottawa River plunges over the beautiful Chaudière Falls and then sweeps on past the Parliament Buildings to join the St. Lawrence on its way to the sea. The Chaudière Falls and those of the Rideau River, to the south, not only make the city a beautiful one but they furnish a great amount of water power. This is used for lighting the capital, for running the car lines, and for moving the machinery in mills and factories.

As you look down from the hills upon the city, you can see near the river immense quantities of lumber. The piles are so long and so high that walking among them is like walking through narrow streets with buildings on either side. The saw-

FIG 127. These are the splendid Parliament Buildings in Ottawa. Why are they located in this city?

mills in Ottawa are the largest in the country. Their screaming saws are constantly adding to the piles of lumber, making new ones or replenishing the old.

The Ottawa River is the most important branch of the St. Lawrence and flows through one of the greatest pine forests in the world. It is the most important lumber stream of Canada and is filled with huge logs from trees felled, perhaps, many miles away.

From Ottawa, we can continue our trip by water still farther. Look at the map and you will find, near the eastern end of Lake Ontario, the city of Kingston. Between Ottawa and Kingston, there is a series of lovely lakes and winding streams. These have been connected by the Rideau Canal, and we will make our way to Lake Ontario through this very beautiful route.

A sail through Lake Ontario takes us to Toronto, next to Montreal the largest city of Canada. It is the capital of the province of Ontario and contains fine government buildings which add to its beauty. Its famous university is the largest in the country. Its streets bordered by fine old trees, its comfortable homes, its lovely lake views and trips, make Toronto a pleasant place in which to live.

It is not these things, however, which have caused the city to grow. It is situated near the iron deposits of Ontario and therefore contains many iron foundries. With a plentiful supply of this useful mineral, with the vast forests to the north, and with the lake traffic at its doors, it naturally carries on some shipbuilding. Can you tell why Toronto is an important railway center, and why there are in the city works where agricultural implements are manufactured and meat-packing establishments? Electric power for these and other industries is obtained from Niagara Falls.

This southern part of Ontario is often called the Lake Peninsula. Look at the map, and you will see that it is bounded on three sides by lakes. This area is not a part of the Laurentian Upland but is an extension of the Central Plains of the United States. Nine-tenths of the people of the province of Ontario live in this peninsula, and most of the larger cities and towns are located here. As in the plains in the United States, the soil is very fertile, and the more even climate of the surrounding water tempers that of the land. These two factors, the soil and the climate, make southern Ontario a rich farming area. Many crops are raised on the prosperous-looking farms, and

FIG 128. These people live in the famous fruit farms, and in the belt of the Lake Peninsula. What lakes bound this peninsula? (Courtesy of the Keystone View Co.)

in the pastures, there are fine-looking cattle and hogs. It is for its fruit, however, that the peninsula is especially famous. All around, we see orchards of apple and peach trees. We should enjoy a visit here in the spring, when the orchards are in bloom, making the whole country like a great garden. We should also enjoy an autumn visit, when the apples are being picked and the luscious grapes in the vineyards gathered. This famous fruit area extends not only through southern Ontario but stretches south of the lakes into New York and Ohio.

Just at the western point of Lake Ontario is the city of Hamilton. It almost seems as if the mountain at whose foot the city lies was placed just where it is to keep the waters of the lake from going farther westward. Down the mountain slopes comes a little river leaping and plunging into the lake. Its waters have been harnessed, and electric power from this source and from Niagara Falls is used in the plants, where steel, iron, cotton and woolen goods, agricultural machinery, electrical wires and cables, and many other articles are made. Situated in the heart of the fruit district, Hamilton ships away apples, peaches, and grapes, as well as the products of its factories.

If we were to continue our way westward through the Great Lakes, we should sail through the Welland Canal into Lake Erie. This canal was built to avoid the falls in the Niagara River. Were it not for the Welland Canal, no water communication on the Lakes could pass between Lake Erie and Lake Ontario. In such a case, Canada would lose the traffic which now passes from the Lakes to the St. Lawrence River, and the city of Buffalo in New York State would be even larger than it is at present. All ocean-bound lake freight from both Canada and the United States would have to be transferred at Buffalo to train or canal barge, taken across New York State, and down the Hudson River to the great port of New York.

The surface of Lake Ontario is more than three hundred feet lower than that of Lake Erie. The Niagara River covers one hundred and sixty-four feet of this difference in level in its one great leap over the cliff. We are fascinated by the swirling, greenish-blue waters of the river above the Falls, and we are almost terrified by the mighty plunge of the roaring waters. Dressed in rubber clothing to protect us from the flying spray, we venture in behind the Falls. We photograph them from the little steamer, from which we view the great sheet of water. We should like to study the industrial life which has grown up around the Falls and see how the falling water has been made to move machinery, light streets and buildings, and run cars not only near the Falls but also in cities miles away. If all the water power in Niagara was used, no water would be left to flow over the cliff. Therefore, our government and that of Canada have made an agreement never to use more than a fourth of Niagara's power. In this way, the beauty of the Falls will be preserved.

The sail through the Lakes is most interesting. Part of the time we can easily imagine that we are on the ocean itself, for no land is visible. Beyond the head of Lake Erie, the waters narrow into the Detroit and St. Clair Rivers and the little Lake St. Clair. At the northern end of Lake Huron, the waters narrow again, this time into St. Mary's River, the rapids of which are avoided by the Soo Canal, of which you have already read. Here

FIG 129. Bridges go jackknifing in the air at Sault Ste. Marie. Where is this city? What is the water shown in the picture? (Courtesy of the Canadian Pacific Railroad)

are the twin cities of Sault Ste. Marie, one in the United States and one on the Canadian side.

On the northern shore of Lake Superior are Fort William and Port Arthur, which someone has called "the coupling pins" between the hungry East and the plenteous West. The sights in these towns foretell what we shall see farther west. The huge grain elevators filled with wheat, oats, barley, and flax speak of the great farms out on the plains. The thousands of cans of salmon point us to the canneries on the Pacific shore, and the many barrels and boxes of fruit tell us of great orchards and the delightful climate which makes this crop a profitable one.

We wish that we had time for a trip into northern Ontario. In this part of the province, there are fewer people and fewer cities and towns than in the south, but the deep woods, blue lakes, and rippling streams, the fishing and hunting, make a vacation spent in central and northern Ontario very enjoyable. As we go northward, we pass over the crest of the divide which separates the rivers. Now we find that all the streams are flowing northward and northeastward into Hudson Bay

FIG 130. These great grain elevators in Fort William tell a wonderful story of the wheat fields of Canada. Why have Fort William and Port Arthur become important places? (Courtesy of the Canadian Pacific Railroad)

instead of southward into the St. Lawrence. This region is called the Hudson Bay Lowland. You can see from the map that it includes northern Ontario and a little of Manitoba. There are many lakes and rivers here, and the fish which they contain are an important resource. The forests will yield lumber for Canadian enterprises for many years. Some day, when the forests are partially cleared, the farmers will make use of the fertile soil, and agriculture will become important. But for years to come, the mineral deposits of northern Ontario will be its most important asset. Ontario has the largest mineral production of any division of Canada, and this production will be greater in the future than it is at present.

Before leaving Ontario, we must visit the district around Sudbury, where famous nickel mines are located. What have you seen that is made of nickel? It is one of the most useful of metals. If you have ever bought or sold anything "for a nickel," you know one great use of the metal. As an alloy with iron, it is known as nickel steel. This is used in machinery, armor plates for warships, bridges, motor cars, steel rails, and many smaller articles, such as knives, forks, wire, and harness mountings. Many cooking utensils and articles of kitchenware are made of nickel and nickel alloy. What is there made of nickel in your kitchen or bathroom?

There are few places where nickel is found; only two, in fact, where it is produced in large quantities. One of these places is in New

FIG 131. One can find no pleasanter way to spend a summer than camping, tramping, and fishing in northern Ontario. Why is this part of the province not so well developed as the south?

Caledonia, an island far away in the Pacific Ocean. The other place, where more than half of the world's supply is obtained, is in Canada.

Find on your map, north of Georgian Bay, the town of Sudbury. Nickel has been discovered in the Cobalt district and other parts of Canada, but here around Sudbury are the largest nickel mines in the world. The falls in a little river not far away furnish the power for developing electricity, and this power is brought on wires and is used for running the elevators and other machinery and for lighting the mines.

Nickel ore is usually found combined with iron, copper, and sulphur. It is mined much as coal and iron ore are. The miners break off great masses of the rock from the walls and load it on cars. These carry it to the shaft where it is hoisted to the surface. In some mines, the ore is found on or near the surface.

The ore is next taken to the smelter. Here it is fed into blast furnaces, where much of the iron and the rocky matter are separated from the nickel. The molten nickel, now known as matte, is run from the furnace into huge ladles. These are lifted and carried by electric traveling cranes to the converters — enormous receptacles twenty-five feet long and ten feet wide. While the matte is being heated, a blast of air is blown through the converters. This carries off much of the remaining iron, leaving the nickel and copper.

With a shower of sparks like fireworks, the melted metal is poured into ladles and run into molds. Here it cools and hardens and soon becomes solid again. This is afterward crushed, barreled, and shipped over Canadian railroads to Montreal, where it is loaded on vessels and taken to the refining works.

Much of the nickel from around Sudbury goes to refining plants near Swansea, in the country of Wales. Great coal deposits lie in this vicinity, and large quantities are needed in the refineries. Here the matte is first roasted and the sulphur driven off; then it is separated from the copper and is further refined by intricate chemical processes until the final result is pure nickel.

SUGGESTIONS FOR STUDY

I

1. The ancient Laurentian Upland.
2. "White coal" and minerals of the upland.
3. Asbestos, its mining and uses.
4. A trip up the St. Lawrence River.
5. Quebec and Montreal.
6. Ottawa and some other Canadian cities.
7. The Lake Peninsula.
8. Niagara Falls and the Welland Canal.
9. Sault Ste. Marie, Fort William, and Port Arthur.
10. Northern Ontario.
11. Nickel mines around Sudbury.

II

1. What city of the western United States is situated about as far north as the city of Quebec? Which of these places do you think has the milder climate? Give the reason for your answer.
2. Why is it that the most important parts of Quebec and Ontario lie on or near the St. Lawrence River and the Great Lakes?
3. Describe to the class some city, province, industry, or other feature of this section of Canada. Mention no names. See if the pupils can guess what you are describing. The one who guesses it first may describe something else.

III

Make a list of the places mentioned in this chapter. Arrange them by countries, cities, mountains, rivers, etc. Be able to locate each place and tell what was said about it in the chapter.

CHAPTER XV

OVER THE GREAT CANADIAN PLAINS

East of the Rocky Mountain Highland in Canada, as in the United States, lie the Great Plains, growing gradually higher and drier as we travel westward toward the mountains. These Great Plains cover parts of Manitoba, Saskatchewan, Alberta, and a little of British Columbia, and extend northward into the Provisional District of Mackenzie. Several railroads now stretch away over this vast area where, not so many years ago, not even roads existed. This is a young country, active and vigorous, and growing each year in strength and wealth.

Manitoba lies in the very heart of Canada. It is larger than Washington, Oregon, and Idaho. It has a healthful climate, a fertile soil, fine pasture lands, deep forests, rivers to furnish water power, lakes abounding in fish, and rich mineral deposits. It is the central province of Canada, and all railroads linking up the East and West must pass through it. The manufactures needed in the newly developed West and supplied by the manufacturing East are distributed in Manitoba. The products raised in the West and needed in the East are shipped through this province. All this makes Manitoba a most important part of Canada. It has also caused the remarkable growth of Winnipeg, the capital of Manitoba, into the third largest Canadian city. The railroads converging here bring from the Great Plains, which stretch for hundreds of miles in all directions, the produce of thousands of farms — cattle, sheep, horses, barley, rye, oats, flaxseed, and, much more important than all these, wheat.

Winnipeg is now the greatest grain center of the world and

the largest flour-milling center of the British Empire. There are more grain elevators here than in any other city of the world. Its stockyards are filled with sleek-looking cattle, thick-coated sheep, fat hogs, and fine horses. More than twenty-five railroads radiate from the city. Winnipeg is favored in its water connections as well as in its railroads. It is situated at the junction of the Red and Assiniboine Rivers and is connected by water with Lake Winnipeg. These waters not only make the city more beautiful but also favor its trade.

We shall find a visit to Winnipeg most interesting. The city has fine broad streets and avenues, bordered by magnificent residences and splendid business blocks, some of the latter real skyscrapers. It is not only the people of Winnipeg who have made the city what it is; it is the people in the country around—the farmers, the trappers, the ranchmen, the miners, and the emigrants who have come by thousands from eastern Canada, the United States, and European countries and who have settled in the wide plains to the north, east, west, and south.

We have not read a chapter in Mother Nature's storybook for some time. If we wish to understand more fully the prosperity and progress of Manitoba and the reason for the growth of its capital city, we must turn the pages until we find the story of this part of Canada as she tells it.

FIG 132. The men in this picture are plowing, harrowing, and seeding a farm on the rich plains of Manitoba. Does this scene differ from one in the country near your home? (Courtesy of the Department of Agriculture of the province of Manitoba)

FIG 133. This is a prosperous farm on the Canadian plains. Notice the fine-looking cattle and the comfortable barns. The tall round structures are silos. For what are they used? (Courtesy of the Department of Agriculture of the province of Manitoba)

Once upon a time an enormous lake, larger than the five Great Lakes, covered the central and southern parts of Manitoba and extended southward into Minnesota. You will find a part of this lake shown on the map on page 14. Here in Canada the great glacier did an important work. It blocked the outlet of this lake, which continually grew larger and larger. Many rivers and streams flowed into it from the surrounding country, each bringing in its muddy waters the fine soil from the hills. Finally, after long centuries, the ice gradually disappeared, and the waters of old Lake Agassiz, as scientists call it, began to find their way to the ocean by way of the Nelson River and Hudson Bay.

The present Lake Winnipeg, nearly the size of the state of New Hampshire, is only a small remnant of Lake Agassiz. The rich soil of the region once covered by the waters of the old lake is the result of the work of the rivers which, long centuries ago, brought their loaded waters to it. This soil makes possible today the abundant harvests of the Manitoba farmers.

Thousands of men from older lands in eastern Canada and the United States have sold their farms in these more developed regions, where land brings higher prices, and have settled in Manitoba and the provinces farther west. Yet there is room for thousands more. Saskatchewan is considerably larger than North Dakota, South Dakota, and Nebraska. The greater part of their area lies in the thinly populated portion of the United

States, yet the whole province of Saskatchewan contains only about a fourth as many people as live in these three large states.

Many of the towns are young and small and look new. They are growing rapidly and, in a comparatively few years, will be good-sized cities. We can ride hour after hour over the flat or rolling country, stopping at young, prosperous-looking towns along the way. For miles on either side we can see fields of wheat or other grain. There are thousands of acres of fine pasture land where the cattle and sheep stop their grazing to watch us pass, and the horses and colts kick up their heels as they scamper away to a safe post of observation.

Along every new railroad, towns spring up like magic. The Canadian Pacific Railroad was the pioneer of western Canada and was responsible for the opening up of vast agricultural areas. A railroad, first known as the Canadian Northern but now one of the Canadian National railways, lies farther north than any other which crosses the country and was the last to be built. With the building of this road, the wheat and cattle industries were extended farther northward, and farms were started all along the way. Were other railroad lines to be built still farther north, the same result would doubtless follow.

Hudson Bay is navigable for about four months of the year. On its west coast, there are two fine harbors, Port Nelson and Churchill. A railroad is now being built across central Canada to Churchill, and steamboat connection will be made for the voyage across the Atlantic to England. You can see how such a line will help in developing agriculture and in marketing the wheat crop of northern Manitoba and the provinces to the west. Wheat will be the chief product carried over this route, but lumber, furs, fish, and other articles will furnish large amounts of freight. Much of the land in central Canada is as fertile as that in the south, and these areas will soon be dotted with comfortable farmhouses, large wheat fields, and pastures filled with cattle, sheep, and horses.

Though so far north, the western part of these Great Plains is not so cold as one might expect. The warm west wind, called the chinook, blows in through the passes of the Rocky Mountains. On account of it, the snow in southern Alberta lasts only a comparatively short time, and in places, the cattle and horses can live outdoors all winter. There are some areas, especially in southwestern Alberta, where, on account of the mountain wall, there is but little rainfall. In parts of this region, however, there are good pasture lands, and there are other parts where, by scientific work in dry farming, good crops can be raised.

We must not think of these provinces, however, as valuable only for their agricultural possibilities. We have spoken before of the fish, furs, and water power. Many minerals are found here also. In Alberta especially, there are very large beds of both hard and soft coal, and millions of tons are mined here every year. Natural gas and rich petroleum deposits have also been found, and these will help in manufacturing. Gold has been mined for some years along the North Saskatchewan River, and iron is found in the province of Saskatchewan. The valuable clay beds, the building stone, and the forests are worth millions of dollars in the building up of the region.

Should you like to spend a summer in the forests, among the lakes and rivers of northern Manitoba, Saskatchewan, or Alberta? You could enjoy splendid fishing and take long tramps after deer, mountain lions, and smaller game. Your guide through

FIG 134. In a trip over the Great Plains we shall see at every station the great elevators in which the grain is stored until it is taken on the cars to the flour mills or the shipping ports. In what provinces of Canada might you see such a scene as is shown in this picture? (Courtesy of the Department of Agriculture of the province of Manitoba)

FIG 135. This part of Canada is a great ranch country in which you can see thousands of sheep and cattle. In what natural regions of the United States could you see similar sights? (Courtesy of the Department of Agriculture of the province of Manitoba)

these regions may be a trapper who collects the skins of the fur-bearing animals which make their home in the forests.

In a trip through the provinces of the Great Plains, we shall wish to stop at some of the cities. They all look new and up-to-date. The streets are wide, well laid out, and well lighted, and the buildings are modern, well built, and equipped. In all these cities, we see large grain elevators and stockyards, which tell us of the splendid farms in the surrounding country.

Regina is the capital of Saskatchewan. This city was formerly the headquarters of the Royal Canadian Mounted Police. Since their duties have extended over all Canada, the headquarters have been moved to Ottawa. That the frontier lands of Canada have been so free from lawlessness and crime is due largely to the work of these men. They are splendid horsemen, strong and fearless, and tireless in tracking down criminals. Many wonderful stories, which are every bit as thrilling as the tales of heroic deeds done by Canadian soldiers in the World War, are told of the brave acts which these men perform.

While in Saskatchewan, you might like to stop also at Moose-jaw or at Saskatoon, important centers for collecting the products of the surrounding country. In Alberta, we must visit Edmonton,

FIG 136. Baa! baa! I have lost my nice warm coat. Can you tell me what is going to be done with it? (Courtesy of the Department of Agriculture of the province of Manitoba)

the capital of the province, not only because it is a traffic center and an important depot for Northern fur traders but because of its beauty also. It is situated on a tableland above the North Saskatchewan River. The winding river, the green valley, and the vast plains beyond make a wonderful picture. The city itself is interesting as well. The Parliament buildings are models of their kind, and those of Alberta University are imposing.

Nearly south of Edmonton is Calgary, the trade center of a great ranch country in Alberta. Its wonderful growth started with the building of the Canadian Pacific Railroad, and it has kept on growing ever since. In the vicinity, there is found a fine brown sandstone, and many of the buildings are constructed of this material. Calgary is sometimes called the Gateway to

FIG 137. These are buffaloes which live in the Rocky Mountain Park. It is said to be the largest herd now existing. Many thousand buffaloes used to roam over the Great Plains of the United States and Canada.

the Canadian Rockies. Many summer tourists come here, and large modern hotels have been built to accommodate them.

The trip westward from Calgary through the Canadian Rockies is one never to be forgotten. The snow-crowned peaks, the ice rivers, the deep valleys, the forested slopes, and the mountain lakes make a series of wonderful pictures. At Banff, eighty miles west of Calgary, we are in the midst of the finest mountain scenery. Banff is the station for those tourists who are to spend some time in the Rocky Mountain Park. This is a government reservation which covers ten thousand square miles. How does this park compare in size with the state in which you live? In this area are the greatest glaciers, the most imposing peaks, and the bluest lakes. Have you ever seen a picture of Lake Louise, the gem of the park? When you look at it, try to put into it the wonderful coloring of the blue water, the silvery peaks, and the green slopes.

The people who live in the Provisional Districts of Keewatin, Mackenzie, and Franklin are mostly Indians. There are a few Eskimos on the cold islands to the north. Imagine how hard their lives must be! They can raise no crops on account of the cold. They build no permanent homes because they have to move from place to place in search of food and clothing. Much of their time is spent in fishing and in hunting the caribou and other animals. There are no towns in this region, only widely scattered trading posts where the Indians bring the furs which they collect during the winter months.

Look on the map and see how far north these Provisional Districts lie. The Arctic Circle passes through them, and north of this line, there is little but cold, frozen wastes. It is in these northern lands of North America and Asia that we find the greatest barren areas of the world. Do you suppose that with their scientific knowledge, men will ever be able to overcome this handicap, as they have that of the lack of water by means of irrigation? I wonder if any boy who reads this book has it in his mind to so fit himself by a splendid education that he can help in the working out of some of the great problems connected with feeding and clothing the constantly increasing number of people in the world.

SUGGESTIONS FOR STUDY

I

1. The Great Plains of Canada.
2. The growth and importance of Manitoba.
3. The city of Winnipeg.
4. Old Lake Agassiz and Lake Winnipeg.
5. New towns and the railroads.
6. The railroad to Hudson Bay.
7. Climate and agriculture.
8. Minerals of the central provinces.
9. Some cities of the plains.
10. The Canadian Rockies.
11. The Provisional Districts.

II

1. Why do new railroads cause an increase in population in fertile regions?
2. Write to the Canadian Pacific Railroad at Montreal for

descriptions and pictures of the Rocky Mountain Park and Lake Louise.

3. Name all the reasons you can for the growth of Winnipeg.

4. Of what other ancient lake and the present smaller remnant have you read in these chapters? Are these lakes fresh or salt? Why?

III

Make a list of the places mentioned in this chapter. Arrange them by countries, cities, mountains, rivers, etc. Be able to locate each place and tell what was said about it in the chapter.

CHAPTER XVI

MOUNTAINS AND VALLEYS OF WESTERN CANADA

Have you ever done any mountain climbing? There are plenty of chances for such exercise in the mountainous region of western Canada. These are real mountains, thousands of feet high, with rough, jagged slopes and snow-covered tops. They are very unlike the low, green mountains, with their rounded summits and broad valleys such as you saw in eastern Canada. These western giants are younger, and although Mother Nature long ago set her agents — the rain, wind, frost, snow, and ice — at work on them, they must continue their labors for hundreds and thousands of years before they can wear them down, build up the valleys, and fill up the sea near the coasts as they have done in the east.

There are two Canadian provinces in this Western region — British Columbia and Yukon. British Columbia is the larger and much the more important of the two.

There is much for us to see in British Columbia. Its wonderful scenery is unexcelled in magnificence anywhere in the world. The soaring peaks rise from green, wooded slopes into lofty summits of white and gray, which are changed into beautiful rosy tints in the rays of the rising or setting sun. We can look from our car window far up to these dizzy heights. We can also look far down between black vertical walls where mountain torrents, green and white, are rushing to the sea. We see blue lakes sparkling in the sunshine, we race through broad meadows where winding rivers flow between their green banks, and we

FIG 138. Tramping through the woods in the unsettled parts of British Columbia, you might chance upon some wild deer. The camera caught these in their first quick, startled glance. In an instant they were bounding away.

go slowly through deep, dark canyons. We could spend weeks in this province and still not tire of its beauties.

Perhaps you would like to follow the Fraser or some other river down to the sea and go out with the fishermen, who, with nets, traps, and fish wheels, catch enormous quantities of salmon as they start up the streams in the early summer. You might visit the huge canneries where the fish are cleaned, cut in pieces, packed, cooked, and sealed, all without being touched by human hands.

If you are a good sailor, you might like to take a cruise with the men who are engaged in the halibut, herring, and cod fisheries, or if you would not mind some discomforts, you might go on a whaling voyage. The harvests of the sea are very important, and thousands of men are engaged in gathering them. Many more are

FIG 139. These lumbermen are working in the spruce forests of Vancouver Island. Judging from the height of the man, how many feet in diameter do you think this log is?

busy drying, salting, canning, packing, and shipping the fish and preparing the oil, whalebone, fertilizer, and other by-products.

Some of you, perhaps, would prefer to stay on land and go into the deep forests with the lumbermen. Thousands of acres here are covered with splendid forests of fir, cedar, pine, spruce, oak, and maple. The Douglas fir is, at present, the principal commercial tree. What giants these trees are! Many of them are three hundred feet high and from eight to ten feet in diameter. If one of these trees stood beside your schoolhouse, how high would it be compared with the building? How many of you would it take to join hands around the trunk?

Of all the resources of British Columbia, the minerals are most important. The mining industry is not so well developed as in Ontario, but the mineral wealth in the mountains is enormous. Which kind of mine would you prefer to visit — gold, silver, copper, lead, coal, or iron? Quantities of all these minerals are mined every year, yet many vast beds, especially of coal, are yet scarcely touched.

Even though the country is so mountainous, there is splendid farming land in the valleys between the mountains, along the rivers, and on Vancouver Island. Here we can visit, as in the provinces farther east, farms where grain, sugar beets, and many other vegetables are raised. The stock farms, with their fine cattle, horses, and hogs, are interesting. We can walk through orchards of apple, apricot, peach, pear, plum, and cherry trees or watch the workers in the vineyards or on the farms where strawberries and other small fruits are raised. All these crops are very similar to those which are raised on the farms across the boundary line of the United States.

Vancouver is the largest city of British Columbia. You will know without being told that this shore city is a beautiful one. The lovely bay, the steep cliffs, the blue water of Puget Sound, and the green hills and lofty mountains of Vancouver Island rising beyond make a lovely picture. We could drive for hours in the deeply wooded parks, where fine avenues have been laid out under the great trees. Less beautiful but more important are the great wharves and the steamers waiting for their loads of lumber, fish, grain, and meat. Someone has said that behind Vancouver is the whole of Canada and in front is the highway to the crowded East. These facts make it sure that Vancouver will always be one of the great Pacific ports of North America. Large vessels bound for

FIG 140. This is a part of the water front at Vancouver. What do the buildings tell you about the city? What industry of Vancouver was illustrated in FIG 111?

FIG 141. This is a view of Victoria. See the beautiful Olympic Mountains in the distance. Notice the ships being built and the huge rafts of logs. What will be done with these?

the Hawaiian Islands, China, Japan, Australia, New Zealand, and for England and other European countries sail from her harbor, while smaller ones follow the coast waters to Alaska and Seattle and other ports closer at hand.

Across Puget Sound, on Vancouver Island, is Victoria, the capital of British Columbia. It is a beautiful city with a fine harbor, a background of hills, mountains, forests, and lakes, and a climate which, cool in summer and warm in winter, attracts people at all seasons of the year. Man has added lovely gardens, fine boulevards and parks, attractive residences, modern hotels, and government buildings that are examples of some of the finest architecture in America.

Down near the water, the sights are much like those in Vancouver. In the immense dry dock, a steamer is being repaired. A raft of huge logs is being towed out of the harbor by a tug so small in comparison that it reminds one of the story of the lion and the mouse. In the lumberyards, it looks as if there were material enough to build houses for everybody in the world who wanted them. The fishing vessels are bringing in herring, halibut, cod,

FIG 142. These Indians are spearing salmon in the rapids. The boys are holding up some fish for you to see. Do you think the salmon were headed up or down stream?

and salmon, which, in various forms — dried, salted, and canned — are being loaded on ships bound for all parts of the world.

Prince Rupert is situated more than five hundred miles north of Vancouver, on an island close to the shore. The town is the terminal of the most northern railroad of British Columbia. Though the railroad runs so far north, the climate there is warmer than that of the eastern provinces. This is due to the westerly winds, which have been blowing over the warm Japan Current. Many towns have sprung up along this railroad route. These towns furnish supplies to the farmers who have bought land nearby, while they, in turn, bring in large quantities of freight to be shipped to centers farther east.

Prince Rupert is an important fishing center. Those buildings down by the water are cold-storage plants and are filled with millions of pounds of fish. If you went through one of them, you would need to wear your winter coats, for the temperature in some of the rooms is below zero and the walls are covered with white frost. The fish in this cold-storage house is mostly halibut. Dozens of vessels and hundreds of men are engaged in catching halibut along the shores of southern Alaska and British Columbia. Perhaps the fish that you had for dinner came from these western waters, for large quantities — frozen, salted, and smoked — are sent to all parts of the United States. The supply on our Pacific shores seems endless, and the fishing industry of the future is sure to become increasingly important.

Not only halibut but great numbers of herring and codfish are caught along these western shores. Many of the herring are used for bait in the halibut fisheries, but some find their way into the markets of various cities. Some of the cold-storage plants in Prince Rupert are filled with salmon, and there are large canneries in the city.

The province of Yukon lies north of British Columbia. If you wish to visit this northern country, you will find it easier to go part of the way by water, for as yet no roads or railroads penetrate the mountains and forests of northern British Columbia

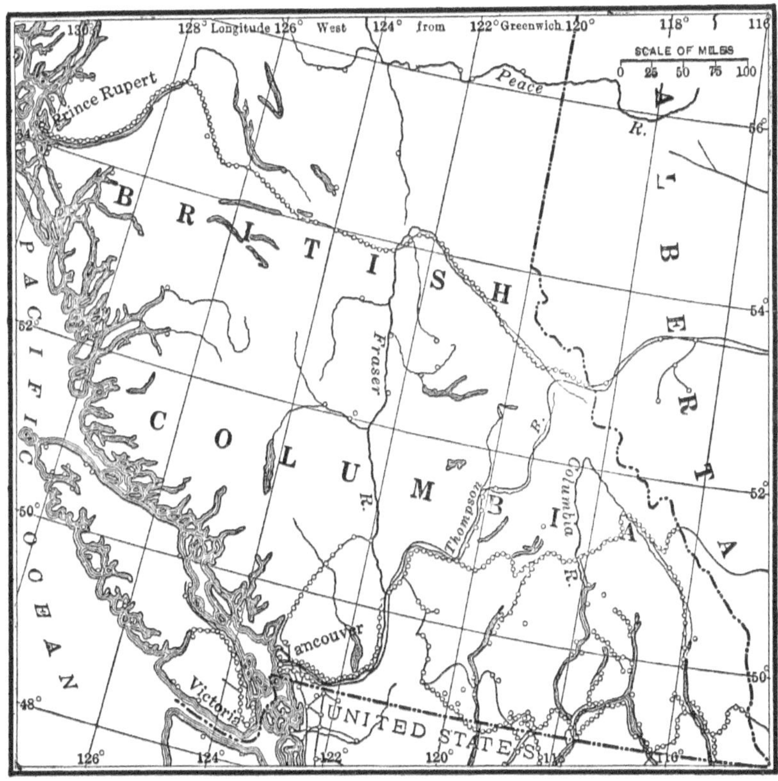

FIG 143. The little circles on this map represent settlements. Notice how thick they are along the railroads. Why should there be so many more near the railroad lines than anywhere else in the country?

and Yukon. The sail, however, through the Inside Passage is very beautiful, and the vessel twists and turns among the green islands which seem to block the way. The end of the route is at Skagway. From here, a train takes us in a few hours over the mountain passes into the Yukon valley. How different it all is from the trip of the early prospector, who, with his heavy pack, was weeks in making the same distance.

The train from Skagway carries many supplies for Dawson and the mining camps; when it makes its return trip, it will bring some of the gold that has been mined in the north. Coal is found in Yukon, not far from Dawson, and is used in the city and also in a power plant where electricity is generated. This is carried on wires to different mining centers and used in operating the mines.

Klondike is the name of a little branch of the Yukon River, which is partly in Canada and partly in Alaska. Dawson, the town which became famous during the gold rush, is situated in Canada, just below the point where Klondike Creek enters the Yukon. Its wharves seem larger than are necessary for the river traffic, and as we walk about, we notice that many of the houses are empty. In its boom days, when the rush to the gold fields was on, fifty thousand people were living here. Now its population is only about three thousand, and the place reminds us of a stout person grown too thin for his clothes.

The names of some of the creeks and claims in the region around Dawson tell us of the richness of the gold deposits there and of the hopes and disappointments of the miners. There is a Bonanza Creek, with a Poverty Bar near at hand; a Peril Strait and a Good News Bay, a Too-Much-Gold Brook, and a Lost Hope Harbor.

SUGGESTIONS FOR STUDY

I

1. Surface and scenery of western Canada.
2. Fisheries of the Pacific coast.

3. Lumbering in British Columbia.
4. Mineral wealth.
5. Western farms and their products.
6. Vancouver and Victoria.
7. Prince Rupert.
8. The province of Yukon.

II

1. Find in the appendix of your textbook the size of Vancouver. How does it compare with that of your home city?
2. Which is larger, Vancouver or Victoria?
3. Have a class debate on the question as to which will become the more important province, Quebec or British Columbia.
4. Into what does the Fraser River flow?
5. What materials do the railroads of Canada carry east? What fills the freight cars on the west-bound trips?
6. From the map on page 245, what do you think is an important effect of the building of railroads?

III

Make a list of the places mentioned in this chapter. Arrange them by countries, cities, mountains, rivers, etc. Be able to locate each place and tell what was said about it in the chapter.

CHAPTER XVII

THE COUNTRY OF MEXICO

Mexico lies at the meeting place of two zones — the temperate and the torrid. Its position, combined with its height, gives it a greater variety of soil, surface, and vegetation than is possessed by any equal area in the world. The country has treasures of gold, silver, and copper. Pearls are obtained from its western waters, and oil from its Gulf coast. The grasses in its pastures will feed millions of cattle, and deep forests of valuable hard woods grow in its low, hot lands. In no country of the world can you pass more quickly from the heat and jungles of tropical lands to the cold snows and barren areas of perpetual winter. Mexico is an old land. People lived in its humble villages, slaved for their rulers in its rich palaces, and worshiped in its great temples long before the Norsemen ever visited the eastern shores of North America. A century had passed after Cortes and his Spanish soldiers had robbed the Mexican temples of their rich treasures before the Pilgrims landed on Plymouth Rock.

Lower California is a peninsula about eight hundred miles long that extends southward from the boundary of California. It is mostly a mountainous desert region with few inhabitants and with as many contrasts as the mainland of Mexico itself possesses. Low, hot plains lie close to high, cold mountains, and plateaus of black lava enclose green valleys. This part of Mexico is rich in minerals and contains much fertile soil, but lack of water and means of transportation have prevented its development.

Before and during the Great World War (1914-1918), affairs in Mexico were in a very unsettled condition. Until 1911, General Porfirio Diaz had been president of Mexico for some thirty years. Since that time, several revolutions have occurred, and some of the presidents have held office only for a short time. Much of the capital invested in the Mexican railroads has come from the United States. Much of the mining property and the oil business is in the hands of United States corporations. The unsettled conditions put not only United States money but the lives of United States citizens in danger. Several times, war between the two countries seemed near, but the troubles have each time been peacefully adjusted.

These recent troubles are not the only difficulties which have occurred between Mexico and the United States. In 1845, a war began between the two countries which lasted about three years. Trouble over the boundary line of Texas, together with the desire of the United States to possess the territory of California, which then belonged to Mexico, brought on this war.

As a result of the war, we paid Mexico several million dollars and received from her the region including the states of Texas, California, New Mexico, and Arizona. The gaining of this area had a direct effect in bringing on our Civil War, which occurred a little more than a dozen years later, for the question whether or not slavery should be allowed in these territories was every-where heatedly discussed.

The land gained from Mexico gave the United States enor-mous mineral wealth and a long stretch of coastline on the Pacific Ocean. It brought China, Japan, and other Eastern coun-tries into closer relationship with us and stimulated our com-merce with those countries. The year after the close of the Mexican War, gold was discovered in California. In Ellis's *History of the United States,* the following description of the gold rush is given:

> "Then began such an emigration as was never before seen. The ships passing around Cape Horn and up the Pacific coast to San Francisco were crowded; a steady procession streamed over the mountains and prairies, caring nothing for snow, rain, hurricane, heat, cold, wild beasts, or the fiercer wild Indians. The emigrants came

from eastern states, from the countries across the Atlantic, and after a time even from distant Asia. Portions of California became a great mining camp; the few earlier settlers who had been living in San Francisco found in the course of a few months that they had twenty thousand neighbors. In two years the population of California increased to a hundred thousand people, and still the ships poured out their swarms upon the wharves and the processions streamed over the Sierras."

Many of the people of Mexico are of Spanish descent, and their cities and towns resemble those of old Spain. This is because Mexico was discovered and settled largely by Spaniards. In 1521, Hernando Cortes entered the country of Mexico and claimed it for Spain, at that time one of the most important nations on earth.

Cortes found Indians, called Aztecs, living in Mexico who were superior in civilization to any of the tribes in the more northern countries of North America. They spun and wove, tilled the soil, delved in the mines, and decorated their palaces and temples with skillfully wrought ornaments of gold and silver.

We think of Egypt as the land of ancient peoples, and thousands of tourists travel there every year to see the ruins of temples, tombs, and other buildings which were erected many centuries ago. In Greece and Rome, also, are wonderful ruins which tell us much concerning the conditions of life in ancient times. In the canyons and on the plateaus of Arizona and Colorado, in the jungles of Mexico and Central America, and south of the equator in Peru and Bolivia, there are many silent cities as wonderful as those in the Eastern Hemisphere. There are ruins of temples, fortresses, halls, palaces, and tombs where ancient peoples once lived, worked, worshiped, played, and died. The pottery which they used, the images and idols which they worshiped, and the weapons with which they fought are found in many localities.

Some of the most wonderful relics of early peoples are found in Yucatan. Here are relics of temples, pyramids, prisons, courts, stairways, and beautifully carved walls. Not far from the city of

FIG 144. This is one of the buildings in the ruins at Mitla. Can you see the carvings on the walls? What countries of the world contain ruins of ancient peoples? (Courtesy of the Pan-American Union)

Mexico, some wonderful pyramids have been recently discovered which, in size and age, rival those of Egypt. Other well-preserved ruins are in Mitla, an ancient city situated in a valley surrounded on three sides by mountains. The quarries from which the stone was obtained for the buildings are some miles away from the city and a thousand feet above it. Here hundreds of workmen labored with their stone tools, for they knew nothing of iron and steel. The heavy wooden beams in the ancient buildings were also hewn into shape with stone axes.

The people who live in Mexico today are of more interest to us than are the ancient inhabitants of the land. The country is about sixteen times the size of New York State, but it contains only about one and a half times the number of people. Two-thirds of these can neither read nor write. Someone has divided the people of Mexico into two classes — those who ride and those who walk; that is, the rich and the poor. The middle class, made up of skilled mechanics, clerks, and professional and commercial men, is much smaller in proportion to the population than in the United States. In countries of high civilization, it is this large, intelligent, industrious middle class which forms the strength of the nation.

The population of Mexico is more usually divided into three classes — the white inhabitants, the Mexicans, and the Indians. Some of the white people are refined and cultured. Their children are educated in European universities, their homes are beautiful, and they appreciate the best of the world's art, literature, and music. The true Mexicans, who make up more than a third of the people, are of mixed Spanish and Indian blood. Nearly half of the population of Mexico are Indians, descendants of the many tribes who once spread from Alaska to Panama. There are today in Mexico ten times as many Indians as ever lived at any one time in the United States. These descendants of the ancient rulers of the country are now its laborers. They work in the mines, toil on the ranches and farms, and sweat in the tropical jungles.

The great mountain system which extends from Cape Horn, at the southern point of South America, to Alaska divides in southern Mexico into two ranges. The higher of these follows

FIG 145. These are some of our neighbors in Mexico. Notice the wide hat and the shawls which these Indians are wearing. They are selling onions in a corner near the market (Courtesy of the Brown Bros.)

FIG 146. This happy-looking girl who is feeding her chickens lives on the Isthmus of Te-huan-te-pec. In what part of Mexico is it? (Courtesy of Underwood & Underwood)

the Pacific coast, and the lower one stretches along the eastern border, while between the ranges is a vast, high plateau. This cool tableland, in places more than a mile and a half high, makes up a large part of the country. This arrangement of the surface of Mexico results in three distinct varieties of climate. The low coast plains are hot. Except where they have been cleared, they are covered with dense tropical forests of hardwoods, among which are mahogany and ebony trees, and others not so well known. Tall and graceful palm trees grow everywhere. Giant vines hang from the trees like ropes or coil around them like great serpents. The huge trees, the clambering vines, the tall ferns, the creeping plants, the spreading roots — all unite to make the forests impenetrable, and the native makes his way through it all only by the use of his machete, a long knife with which he cuts a path through the woods or defends himself if danger arises. Comparatively few people except Indians live on the coastlands. Their villages are made up of little bamboo huts thatched with palm leaves, around which half-naked children play in the sunshine, while the men and women take life easy in the usual manner of dwellers in tropic lands.

Here and there in cleared areas are groves of banana trees, each bearing a huge bunch of fruit. Sugar, coffee, and rubber plantations are numerous. On some of the farms, long rows of pineapples stretch as far as the eye can see. On the eastern slopes, and especially in Yucatan, the valuable fiber known as henequen is raised. This industry is so important that you will read more about it in another chapter. It is on this Gulf Coastal Plain also that the petroleum deposits are found.

The climate of the high plateau of Mexico is that of the temperate zone, cool and pleasant. On either side of the plateau, mountain ranges raise their heads toward the sky, and snow-capped giants gleam white in the sunlight. Three of these volcanic peaks are among the highest mountains of North America.

FIG 147. This is Mt. Popocatepetl, a famous volcano in Mexico. What other volcanoes can you name which lie in the volcanic belt along the western coast of the Western Hemisphere? (Courtesy of the Brown Bros.)

The names of two of them, Popocatepetl and Iztaccihuatl, are long and hard. Mt. Orizaba is the highest of the three.

The high mountain ranges shut off most of the rain from the Central Plateau, and parts of it are too dry for agriculture. There are millions of acres in highland Mexico and the peninsula of California which are covered with nothing but cactus and sagebrush. Mineral treasures are, however, found here in abundance. The easterly trade winds prevail in Mexico, and consequently, the heavier rainfall is on the eastern slopes of the mountains.

Many people coming to the city of Mexico by water land at Vera Cruz and make their way inland from this port. Four hundred years ago, Cortes, the conqueror of Mexico, entered the harbor of Vera Cruz. When his Spanish soldiers were fighting against Montezuma and his Indian warriors, they had their base of supplies here, and it was from this ancient seaport that the Spanish galleons sailed for Spain heavily laden with gold and silver torn from the Aztec temples and dug from the rich mines by the slave labor of the Indians. Ever since that time, the city of Vera Cruz has been the chief port of the country.

Vera Cruz is an odd combination of the old and the new. Splendid modern buildings stand side by side with little negro cabins. The old walls, the quaint courts, the low, one-story adobe houses painted in all the

FIG 148. It looks almost as if these bunches of bananas were walking away on their own legs, doesn't it? In what part of Mexico might you see such a sight as this?

colors of the rainbow tell us of the old Spanish life, while the busy wharves, the fine breakwater, the railroad station, and the trains climbing the slopes to the western plateau tell their story of industry, of progress, and of new life and aims in the ancient seaport.

The city of Mexico, which is two or three hundred miles away, is connected by rail with Vera Cruz, and the day's ride between the capital and its port is delightful. The tropical jungle near the coast is nowhere more beautiful. As we climb, we see villages of thatched huts or of low, red-tiled houses and palm-shaded streets. We run between fields of tall corn, waving cane, trim, glossy coffee trees, cotton plants full of fluffy white balls, and acres of rubber trees. Farther up the slopes, the country looks like one big plantation of century plants, or maguey plants, if we call them by their right names.

All the way from Vera Cruz, we have caught glimpses of Mt. Orizaba, the highest peak of Mexico, towering into the air for seventeen thousand feet. Now we leave the train for a short visit at the town of the same name, which is situated between the hot lands and the cool plateau.

The delightful climate, the quaint, shady park with flowers and blossoming trees, and the wonderful view of snow-topped Orizaba make the city a pleasant resort. The great cotton mills, among the largest in the country, indicate the progress of Mexico and point to a future when many of its products will be manufactured at home.

Leaving Orizaba, we enter the wildest part of the route to the capital. Deep, narrow ravines and yawning chasms, dizzy heights and snow-capped peaks, dark tunnels, and cobwebby bridges make the trip one long to be remembered. Bananas, coffee, sugar cane, and all tropical vegetation are left behind. At last, more than eight thousand feet above the level of the ocean, we make our way through a pass in the mountain chain to the Mexican Plateau. Descending nearly a thousand feet into the beautiful Valley of Mexico, we catch our first glimpse of the capital. We see the broad, flat roofs, the towers and domes, the gleaming lakes in the distance, and, still farther away, the wall of blue mountains with snowy-white peaks against the bluer sky.

The valley in which Mexico is situated is a great bowl surrounded by a rim of hills and mountains. Once, long ages ago, the basin was occupied by an inland sea, the remnants of which may be seen today in the shallow lakes which lie in the valley. For three hundred years, the question of draining the basin has been a problem for the people and has many times been unsuccessfully attempted. The rim of mountains has been finally pierced by a tunnel more than six miles long. This tunnel and a deep canal carry away the surplus water and city sewage under the mountain rim to the slopes beyond.

The location of the capital in a high, protected valley gives it a delightful climate, neither too hot nor too cold to be enjoyable. The city is nearly three hundred miles south of the Tropic of Cancer, the boundary line of the torrid zone, but it is about a mile and a half above the level of the sea. The nights and mornings are always cool, and the sun at midday is always hot. The

FIG 149. This is a part of the market in Durango. Few of the Indians buy much in the modern stores. They like better the open markets which are found in every Mexican city. (Courtesy of the Pan-American Union)

people, however, choose this time to stay indoors. They close the heavy shutters and doors to keep out the heat and rest or sleep. During the hot hours, many of the stores are closed, and the streets are nearly deserted. Later, when the blazing sun is lower, the crowds reappear, and the evenings are given up to pleasure and the enjoyment of the cooler air.

As in other countries settled by the Spaniards, the Mexicans, as one writer says, have their front yards in the middle of their houses. These patios, or central courts, are used in common by all the dwellers in the block. In many cases, the rooms have no doors or windows except those leading into the patio. In the single houses of the better class, the patios are pleasant places, with fountains and flowers, which may be enjoyed by the family unseen by the people in the streets. The windows in the front rooms open onto iron-grated balconies. These are favorite seats

FIG 150. This is another scene in a market. This is a pottery market, where all kinds of earthen jars are sold. What do you suppose they are, used for? Describe the costume of the Indians in the picture. (Courtesy of the Brown Bros)

for the women. The women of Mexico lead a more secluded life and go about in public much less freely than is the custom in our country. Therefore, the balconies, where they can watch the throngs in the streets, are very popular.

There are other interesting contrasts to be seen in Mexican streets. Side by side with a modern trolley car is an Indian carrying a heavy load on his shoulders. In the dust of a passing automobile trudges a copper-colored resident with a load of charcoal on his back. Coming through the boulevard, we see some horseback riders, their saddles and bridles glittering with silver trimmings, while close at hand plods a descendant of the Aztecs with a little papoose fast asleep in the blanket on her back.

In San Francisco Street, there are brilliantly lighted shops, carriages, automobiles, and beautiful ladies in Parisian toilets. Not more than a mile away, one can find quiet roads lined with little adobe huts where the Indians live in much the same way that they did when Cortes landed on the Mexican shores. The patient burro, heavily loaded with fruit, vegetables, wood, or charcoal, plods slowly toward the city markets; many children play in the grass; and Indian women, with their babies tied safely on their backs, pound away at the stone kneading board, spending hours in grinding the corn for the tortillas, which are the bread and meat of many of the people of Mexico.

The corn from which the tortillas are made is soaked for a long time. This is necessary in order to remove the husks and soften the grain. Then the Indian woman, on her knees, beats, kneads, and rolls the corn for some hours. This is done on a stone kneading board with a smooth stone for a rolling pin. She then takes a small piece of the dough, works it in her hands, tosses and pats it into shape, and flattens it out until it is not much thicker than a knife blade. After making several of these little cakes, she cooks them over her charcoal fire on a flat stone or an iron griddle. Tortillas, with frijoles, the Indian name for beans, are eaten universally throughout Mexico.

The central square of the capital is known as the Plaza Mayor.

Here stands the great cathedral, one of the largest and oldest in the Western Hemisphere. This ancient building is more than four hundred feet long and two hundred feet wide. Compare this building with the church that you attend or with your school building and decide how much larger a space it covers.

Though parts of the city remind one of the past rather than of the present, much of it is modern in every respect. Its paved streets, its electric cars and lights, its beautiful public buildings, its fine shops, and its railroads, which radiate in every direction from the capital, all speak in no uncertain tone of the future and foretell a development of progress and industry greater than as yet has ever been known within the borders of this southern republic.

The drive on the beautiful boulevard known as the Paseo takes us to the foot of the famous rock hill and castle of Chapultepec. This is the finest public park in the country. Here Montezuma, ruler of the Aztecs, had his summer palace; and here, on the summit of the hill, surrounded by ancient cypress trees, is the old

FIG 151. This picture shows you what a beautiful city the capital of Mexico is. The broad avenue is the Paseo. If you ride for about three miles down the Paseo, you will come to Chapultepec. (Courtesy of the Brown Bros.)

castle built by the Spanish viceroys in the early days of the conquest. Today, this old castle is the summer residence of the president of Mexico. From its high terrace, one gets a wonderful view unsurpassed anywhere in the world. As you look out over the broad valley, can you imagine some of the stirring scenes which have taken place here in the past? Indian tribes have made war on one another, with the chieftain Montezuma or some earlier Aztec ruler watching the fierce fighting from the castle heights. Across the smiling plateau, cruel Spaniards have marched with their Indian captives. French soldiers have rested beneath the dark cypresses, and blue-coated Americans have sought their grateful shade. Today, the old castle, still looking down on the sunny plain, sees more peaceful scenes. The beautiful city, the smiling fields, the rich crops, and the busy people are painting a picture of future success and development for this country, so rich in natural resources, at which the world may gaze and rejoice.

FIG 152. This is the old castle of Chapultepec. From what you have read in the text try to describe some of the scenes which have taken place in the valley which it overlooks. Tell what you think people riding in aeroplanes over the valley in the future may see. (Courtesy of the Pan-American Union)

There are several routes by which one can enter Mexico from the United States, some by way of the coast and others over the plateau. The railroad from Laredo, Texas, which runs through the city of Monterey, follows an ancient Indian trail by which probably the early races found their way into the country. It was along this route that the United States forces invaded Mexico in 1845.

Monterey is an important railroad center, with lines reaching down to the coast cities, southward to the capital, and westward to the center of the country. The wide plateau, brown and bare, with its desert growth of prickly pear, cactus, and mesquite, with here and there a few "feather-duster" palms, stretches away to the distant hills and mountains. At the stations and along the route, we catch interesting glimpses of Indian life on the plateau — barefooted women, brown-skinned children, blanketed men, heavily laden burros, and clumsy wooden carts drawn perhaps by several yokes of oxen with their yokes lashed to their horns by strips of rawhide.

From Monterey, the railroad twists and turns and climbs until it has risen nearly seven thousand feet. Here, it enters the great plateau region. A little more than two hundred miles south of Monterey, the railroad crosses the Tropic of Cancer, the location of which is marked by a stone pyramid. We are now on the boundary of the torrid zone, but the climate is not uncomfortably warm, for we are higher than the top of Mt. Washington in the White Mountains of New Hampshire.

On these vast, high plains, there are many haciendas, large estates worked by hundreds of Indian laborers known as peons, who in many cases are but little better off than if they were slaves. Some of these haciendas are very old and are still in the hands of the same families to whom the land was granted by the Spanish rulers nearly four hundred years ago. Many of the haciendas are immense. There are some that cover areas as large as our smallest states. Each one is a small town in itself. The house of the owner is large and comfortable, while most of the peons and their families live in little adobe huts. There is often a school on the estates for the children of the peons, sometimes there is a resident doctor, and always a church with its priest.

The work carried on at a hacienda depends on the part of the country in which it is situated. Mining, stock-raising, and farming are the principal industries of the cool plateau. Coffee, rubber, fiber, sugar, liquor from the maguey plant, and fruit are some of the products raised on the haciendas in the warm parts of the country.

The lack of development in Mexico and South American countries is partly due to the fact that most of the land is in the hands of a few people. If the large estates could be divided, the system of peonage given up, and the Indians taught to cultivate farms of their own, their interest and ambition would be much greater than it is now, and the country would soon benefit by the change.

About halfway between Monterey and the city of Mexico lies San Luis Potosi. Like other cities on the Mexican Plateau, San Luis Potosi is very old, and long before the *Mayflower* landed in Plymouth Harbor, the Indians were furnishing their Spanish conquerors with silver from rich mines. These mines are still worked and are producing large quantities of silver.

There is much in San Luis Potosi to remind one of early days — the low houses built in the Spanish style around a patio, the huts of the Indians, and the central square such as is found in every old Spanish city. But there is also much to tell us of the present and the future — in the mines and their modern equipment, the smelters and reduction plants, the irrigated farms, the mills and factories, the fine buildings which can be seen in the city, the telephone and telegraph systems, the electric lights, the banks, and the railroads.

The old city of Queretaro lies on our southward route. In the region around there are fields of cotton, and in the city, there are factories for its manufacture. One of these mills employs two thousand hands. The grounds are beautifully laid out, and the workmen live in neat homes.

Another route leading from the United States into Mexico is by way of El Paso. The importance of this city dates back to the time of the gold rush to California in 1849, when the prairie schooners of the emigrants were familiar sights in its streets. West of El Paso there is no natural boundary between Mexico and the United States. Near the city, the Rio Grande breaks through the mountains and forms the boundary between the two countries as it flows on its eastward course to the Gulf.

The route from El Paso into Mexico takes us through the state of Chihuahua, twice the size of Ohio and the largest of the twenty-seven states which make up the republic. This is the great cattle state of Mexico. The soil is too dry for agriculture but not too dry for the growth of grasses which make splendid pasture land. Here and there we pass the buildings of a hacienda and notice in the distance large numbers of cattle feeding on the brown slopes. From time to time we catch glimpses also of flocks of sheep and goats. Numbers of burros, mules, and horses also feed in the pastures.

Chihuahua, like other Mexican states, is rich in minerals. Some mines are worked today, and the output in the future will be greatly increased. It contains vast forests which will furnish lumber and other forest products for years to come. Some day, when irrigation is practiced, this state will be an important farming region and rich crops of grains, vegetables, and fruits will be raised here.

Farther south, where the railroad branches to Monterey, is the chief cotton region of Mexico. More cotton is raised here than in all the rest of the republic. Mills for pressing out the oil from the seeds and factories for making soap are located here. Notice the railroad which runs down to Tampico. Cotton is a very important article of freight on this railroad, and large quantities are shipped to the United States and to foreign markets.

As we continue our way southward, the cotton fields alternate with acres of corn, another important product of Mexico. Much of the corn land is irrigated. The narrow irrigation ditches are filled with water saved from the floods of the rainy season. We see also large areas covered with guayule, that formerly worthless shrub which has made a part of the desert region of Mexico a veritable gold mine. You will read more of this industry, as well as of the others, in the next chapter.

Guanajuato — a long, hard Spanish name; consult the vocabulary and find out how to pronounce it. This state is a treasure house of minerals, and the city of Guanajuato is one of the

FIG 153. This is the city of Guanajuato. Describe its situation. For what is it famous? (Courtesy of Underwood & Underwood)

famous mining centers not only of Mexico but of the world. It is on a branch of the railroad which runs between El Paso and the city of Mexico. In the next chapter, you will read about the mines here and see something of the methods of mining.

Before finishing our trip on the Mexican railways, we will visit one more interesting city. Taking the road leading west from Guanajuato, we reach Guadalajara, a place named for the old Moorish city of Guadalajara in Spain. Next to the capital, it is the largest city in Mexico. It is also cleaner and healthier than any other in the republic. The fertility of the soil in the valleys and the mineral wealth in the mountains have given the city its wealth and furnished the means for its progress, while mountain and valley, wide-stretching cornfields, and orange groves yellow with fruit have contributed to its beauty.

Not far distant is mount-encircled Lake Chapala, the largest lake in Mexico and, next to the Andean lake, Titicaca, and its connecting waters, the highest lake of the Western Hemisphere. Lake Chapala is a hundred miles long. It is larger than and fully as beautiful as the lakes of northern Italy, which annually attract thousands of tourists. Good railroad connections, comfortable hotels, and proper advertising will some day make Lake Chapala famous as a resort.

On our way south through Mexico, we have seen on every side and in nearly every city evidences of mining, ranching, and farming industries. In the low, hot valleys there are other important occupations. In the future, our relations with Mexico and other southern countries of the Western Hemisphere will be closer than ever before. Therefore, it is important that we should learn about these different industries and know more about the resources and occupations of these southern neighbors of ours.

SUGGESTIONS FOR STUDY

I

1. Mexico, land of contrasts.
2. Size, surface, and climate.
3. The peninsula of Lower California.
4. Conditions in Mexico.
5. The war of 1845 and its results.
6. Present and former people of Mexico.
7. Ruins of Mexico.
8. Vera Cruz and city of Mexico.
9. A stop-off at Orizaba.
10. Routes from the United States to Mexico.
11. Haciendas and peons.
12. Cities and occupations on the plateau.
13. Minerals in Mexico.

II

1. What countries of the world besides Mexico does the Tropic of Cancer cross?
2. Make a list of the ports of Mexico situated on the Gulf of Mexico; on the Pacific Ocean.

3. Be able to make a diagram at the blackboard to illustrate the surface of Mexico as you would travel across it from east to west.
4. Which is a more valuable boundary between countries, a range of mountains or a river? You might have a class debate on this topic.
5. Why does the east coast of Mexico have a greater rainfall than the west coast?
6. Find Buena Vista on the map. Read the poem entitled "The Angels of Buena Vista," written by Whittier. Explain how the poem came to be written.

III

Make a list of the places mentioned in this chapter. Arrange them by countries, cities, mountains, rivers, etc. Be able to locate each place and tell what was said of it in the chapter.

CHAPTER XVIII

SOME MEXICAN INDUSTRIES

What part of Mexico shall we visit first? Shall we go to the haciendas on the plateau and see the cattle, horses, goats, sheep, mules, and burros feeding in the high pastures? Shall we visit the mines, which have been worked for centuries, or shall we go out into the barren areas and watch the Indians pulling guayule, that shrub which has proved itself of so much value in the rubber industry? Perhaps you would rather visit the plantations on which is grown the henequen plant, whose leaves are so important in the manufacture of twine. If you prefer, we can go to the low, hot Gulf coast and learn something of the oil industry there. In this same tropical region, we can visit farms of many kinds, stroll down a shady "banana walk," watch the laborers cutting the tall sugar cane, see some young rubber plantations, or pick the ripe, red coffee berries from the glossy green trees.

We can follow the native workmen and watch them as they fell the big mahogany trees, gather vanilla beans from the vines, or dig the sarsaparilla roots. We may chance to see an Indian collecting cochineal. Certain kinds of leaves are often thickly covered with the bodies of these tiny insects. The natives rub them off, dry them, and ship them to other countries, where they are made into a valuable dye. Before we knew how to make dyes from coal tar, cochineal was a more important product than it is today. We can, if you like, visit great mills and factories in some of the Mexican cities, although at the present time, manufacturing is not nearly so important as some other industries.

All these and scores of other interesting sights are awaiting us, and we must hasten to continue our travels.

FIG 154. These are the looms for weaving cloth in one of the great cotton mills in Orizaba. What are you told about these mills on page 256? (Courtesy of the Keystone View Co.)

Mexico has been called the treasure house of the world. Most of its states and territories possess mines. There are more than twenty thousand mines in the country. Some of them have been worked for centuries, and enormous quantities of precious metals have been taken from them, but they are still seemingly inexhaustible. Mexico and Peru furnished for years the enormous wealth that enabled Spain to build up her great empire.

For years Mexico was the greatest silver producer of the world, and today it is surpassed only by the United States. Its gold output is large. It contains more than a thousand copper mines, in which people from the United States have invested millions of dollars. In the state of Durango, there is a hill of nearly pure iron ore, one of the largest solid masses in the world. The petroleum deposits along the Gulf shore have been worked only a comparatively few years, yet in that time, the production has increased by leaps and bounds. There are rich deposits also in other sections. Lead is mined; coal has been found, and considerable is mined, but not nearly enough to supply the needs of the country, and large quantities are imported from the United States. The difficulty and expense of getting coal to some of the more remote regions are already causing manufacturers to consider harnessing the swift mountain rivers and using their power in the mills and factories.

Mother Nature scattered her gems in Mexico as freely as she did her more useful gifts. Beautiful onyx, sky-blue turquoise, fire opals, yellow topaz, emeralds, garnets, agates, amethysts, and many crystals of exquisite beauty are found in various parts of the country.

More than any other nation, the people of the United States are interested in the mineral wealth of Mexico. Most of the money invested in her mines has come from our country. Railroads must be built in the mining regions, tools and machinery imported, and more manufacturing plants established. Many new mines will be opened, and new regions will be settled. In all of this work, the United States will take an active part, for, excepting Canada, Mexico is our only near neighbor. We need her minerals and her vegetable products, many of which do not grow in the United States. She needs our money, tools, machinery, and manufactures of many kinds, and our skilled workmen to help in developing her riches.

The great mineral area of Mexico extends along the highland region for nearly the entire distance from the United States border to the Isthmus of Tehuantepec. Of all the mining cities, Guanajuato is the most important. It is a queer old city founded by the Spaniards before ever the Pilgrims set foot on Plymouth Rock. After the coming of the Spaniards, the city grew rapidly and was soon recognized as one of the greatest silver-producing centers of the New World. Mine after mine, some of them producing more wealth than Aladdin ever dreamed of securing with his wonderful lamp, was opened in the vicinity.

As we enter Guanajuato through the narrow canyon made by the Guanajuato River, the city seems a wonderful place to us. It is situated in the torrid zone, yet the air is cool and delightful. This is because the city is more than a mile above the level of the sea. The low coast cities in the same latitude are very hot, but the weather here on the plateau is like a June day in the northern United States, with the crispness of an October night.

The streets in Guanajuato are the steepest that we have ever seen. The houses climb one behind the other up the slopes, and the roofs of those in front are on a level with the ground floor of those behind. On some of the steepest grades, stone steps take the place of streets. In parts of the city, the streets are both too narrow and too steep for vehicles, and goods are carried on the backs of donkeys and Indians. On the ridges and plateaus above the city, there are many cornfields, each enclosed by its cactus fence.

There are mines all around the city and even under it. From the windows of the train, as we climbed up to the plateau, we could see the openings of mines, the ore heaps, and the reduction works. As we stand in the central plaza, we know that far beneath us, deep in the bowels of the earth, are miles of tunnels and shafts and thousands of workmen. Most of the mines are modern in every respect, equipped with electric lights and up-to-date machinery. The electric power is developed from falls a hundred miles away and is brought on wires through valleys and over hills to help man obtain the treasures hidden in the earth. Scattered through the hills, there are great ore heaps from which the silver has been extracted in such a crude way that the waste still contains much valuable material. Part of this has been worked over and, by use of modern methods, enough silver has been obtained to pay for the work.

It is a great change to go from the cool, dry plateau of Mexico to the low, hot coast lands, yet it is in this part of the country that the petroleum industry is carried on. This industry is one of the most important in Mexico. If you have obtained a pamphlet on petroleum from the United States Geological Survey at Washington, find out how Mexico ranks in its production.

The world is depending more and more on petroleum for fuel. Our automobiles and trucks, which are increasing in numbers every year, are propelled by gasoline, a product of petroleum. The airships, which are every year becoming more and more numerous, also use gasoline. Many manufacturing plants are using oil for fuel, and many ocean vessels are saving time, labor, and space on board ship by using oil instead of coal in their engines.

All the way along the Gulf Coast, experts find signs of oil. The shipping of petroleum has greatly increased the importance of Tampico. This is a city of oil. It can be seen on the waters of the Gulf around and on the surface of the little river on which the port is situated. Tank ships lie at the wharves waiting to be filled. Large pipes carry the oil from the wells to Tampico, where it is pumped into the holds of these great tankers. Other products are shipped from Tampico, but the petroleum is of much greater value than all the other exports put together.

Most people think of Mexico as a mining country, and it is true that its mineral riches are enormous and that mining is one of the chief occupations. The wealth, however, which is contained in its soil, little developed as it is, is greater than its mineral treasures. Though Mexico is one of the important gold-producing countries of the world and has produced more silver than any other country on earth, her corn products exceed in value either one of these precious metals. This is true in spite of the fact that large areas in the country are as yet uncultivated, undrained, unwatered, and unsettled. The natives carry on farming in a very primitive way, and the yield per acre is very small. If the farms of Mexico were developed so that the amount of corn produced on each acre would equal that of Argentina, France, or the United States, the Mexican product would be enormously increased.

The poor showing of Mexico is due chiefly to ignorance and lack of ambition on the part of the people to increase their crops. Most of the corn is used at home, and as long as the peon has enough for his tortillas, he is not anxious to exert himself to raise more. When the large estates are broken up so that the peons may cultivate their own land, take an interest in new ways of working, receive some education, and gain some ambition to improve their lot, we shall see a tremendous increase not only in corn but in all the agricultural products of Mexico. What a

FIG 155. These men are tying up into bales the guayule which they have gathered. For what is guayule used? (Courtesy of the Pan-American Union)

splendid thing it would be if the boys of Mexico could have some land on which to experiment in raising corn, and to compete for prizes awarded to the greatest producer, as so many boys in our country are doing. Some such stimulus is needed to make the Mexicans understand the great possibilities of their country and the value of introducing new methods into their work.

One of the products of Mexico and one which will doubtless be of greater importance in the future than it is at present is rubber. Most of the product comes at present from southern and southeastern Asia and the East Indies. This is all "plantation rubber"; that is, the product of trees that have been planted on large farms. In Brazil, once the greatest rubber-producing country of the world, the rubber is obtained chiefly from the trees that grow wild in the tropical forests.

In Mexico there is a rubber-producing plant very different from the trees on the plantations or in the Brazilian forests. This is guayule. Enormous areas, especially in the northern part of the country, are covered with this plant, which grows from one to three feet high. The workers pull the shrubs, knock off the dirt, and load them on burros until the little animals are nearly hidden. Let us follow the burros from the field to the station in the desert. Here the guayule is unloaded and pressed into bales. The station is far from a railroad, and the bales are loaded on a heavy cart drawn by several mules. They will haul the guayule over the dusty plateau to the nearest railroad station, whence it is taken by train to the factory where the rubber is extracted. Large sums of money have been invested in the industry, factories have been built near the guayule fields, and towns where the operatives and field laborers live have grown up in the vicinity.

Chewing-gum is made from chicle, the sap of a tree that grows in the tropical countries of Mexico, Central America, and northern South America. If you were to see the chicle gatherers at work in the Mexican forests, you might perhaps think that they were gathering maple syrup, for the methods are somewhat similar. The sap, which looks something like milk, trickles slowly through the cutting made in the bark into a dish placed near the base of the tree. It is collected by Indian workmen and carried to the boiling sheds. Here it is boiled in huge kettles until the water is evaporated and only the pure gum remains. This is shaped into uneven loaves, packed in bags, and hauled by mules or oxen to the nearest railroad station. Millions of pounds of chicle are shipped into the United States every year. The habit of chewing gum has spread into other lands until today our exports of gum are valued at hundreds of thousands of dollars.

FIG 156. This is a load of the guayule bales on the way from the field to the nearest railroad. How has this shrub affected that part of Mexico where it grows? How will the building of good roads help the guayule industry? (Courtesy of the Pan-American Union)

Did you ever stop to think of the enormous quantities of string, cord, and rope used in the different countries of the world? Think of all the stores, factories, and homes in every city, town, and village where cordage of some variety is used. Think of the miles of rope and cable which are needed on ships and of the enormous quantity of twine which is used all over the earth to tie up the bundles of grain in the grain fields. It seems almost impossible to believe that each year at harvest time enough twine is used to reach to the moon and back more than a hundred times.

Much hemp and manila fiber are used in the making of cordage, but most of the binder twine used in the grain fields is made of the henequen fiber of Mexico.

No country of the world has a greater variety of fiber-producing plants than Mexico. Many of them belong to the agave family. The common century plant, which you have seen in gardens and conservatories, is one of the many varieties

FIG 157. These men are boiling the chicle which they have gathered, to evaporate the water. You can see from the way it clings together as the workman holds it up that it is already of a gummy consistency. (Courtesy of the Pan-American Union)

of this family. All the relatives of the century plant resemble it somewhat in appearance, though some of them grow to a much larger size.

The different members of the agave family have for centuries been of great use to the Indians of Mexico. The thorns have proved useful for pins and needles or for a tool with which to pierce the tongue or the ears for punishment or ornament. A drink is made from the sap. The tall flower stalks furnish rafters for the native huts or fences for the farms. For centuries the fiber has been used in making ropes and cloth. The large leaves are laid on the roofs for thatch, or when dried are burned for fuel. From them a paper tough as parchment has been made on which the ancient Indians in their picture-writing recorded historical events. The Indian women make a substance somewhat like soap from certain varieties of the plant. The tender

FIG 158. This is a field of henequen. Have you ever seen a plant which looks somewhat like the henequen?

parts of other varieties are eaten. No one at present can tell the many useful ways in which the fiber-producing agave family, as well as many other plants and trees of the torrid zone, will serve the world in the future.

Of all the members of the agave family, the henequen is the most important. The henequen and sisal plants are similar, and the fiber from the leaves of both is often called sisal. The Indians of Mexico have for a long time made hammocks, ropes, baskets, bags, and other articles from both sisal and henequen as well as from other fibers.

To see something of the henequen industry, we will go to Yucatan, for fiber production is the chief occupation in that peninsula. Yucatan was once the poorest part of Mexico. Today, owing to the production of fiber, it is one of the richest states of the country. The Indians are the laborers on the plantations, most of which are owned by people of the white race and by Mexicans.

FIG 159. The man at the left is cutting off the long leaves of the henequen plant. The man at the right is cutting the thorns from the leaves.

FIG 160. Notice the railroad tracks on which the loads of leaves are drawn from the field to the mills. Most of the large sisal plantations have such tracks as these.

Perhaps you have never heard of the town of Progreso, on the northern shore of Yucatan. Yet from this little port of only a few thousand people comes much of the fiber which binds up the grain crops of the world. As we land at Progreso, we notice the big warehouses in which the fiber is stored and the

FIG 161. The leaves have been put through the processes in the mill, and the fiber is now hung out to dry in the sun. What is made from this fiber?

FIG 162. This is a maguey plant. To what family do both the maguey and henequen belong? How tall should you think the plant in the picture is? For what is it used? (Courtesy of the Pan-American Union)

bales piled high on the wharves. There are bags of chicle also and piles of hides, but the fiber is by far the most important.

As we go inland, henequen plantations stretch away on every side. For miles along the low, flat country, once covered with a tropical jungle, are the long rows of stiff, thick-leaved plants. See the Indians cutting the full-grown leaves. They remove the thorns and then tie the leaves in bundles. Each leaf weighs two pounds or more, and fifty of them make a heavy load for an Indian to carry on his back. On some of the larger plantations, there are railroad tracks and small cars to carry the bundles of leaves to the cleaning plant. Here the leaves are run between heavy rollers which press out the juice and break up the woody part, leaving only the greenish-yellow fiber. This is dried, pressed into bales, and sent to Progreso to be shipped away to the twine factories.

The future of Mexico seems rich with promise. No nation on earth has greater advantages for commerce with other countries. Her coast line on the Pacific Ocean is twice as long as ours, while that on the Atlantic would stretch from Maine to Georgia. They lie, moreover, near the great world routes of trade. With this long coast line, the splendid crops of which the country is capable, and her productions of mine and forest, Mexico has great advantages among commercial nations. With her variety of climate, her lowlands and uplands, she can produce everything required for the life of man. Her mineral wealth is enormous. At present, mining is better organized than any other industry, yet even this is still in its infancy, and the millions of dollars' worth of gold, lead, copper, and petroleum which she is now producing are only a small part of what we may expect from her in the future.

SUGGESTIONS FOR STUDY

I

1. Some Mexican industries.
2. Mineral wealth of Mexico.
3. Guanajuato and its mines.
4. The petroleum industry.
5. The corn crop of Mexico.
6. Rubber plantations and guayule.
7. Chewing-gum and chicle.
8. The fiber industry and Yucatan.
9. The future of Mexico.

II

1. Which do you think is of greater importance to the railroads which run between the United States and Mexico, the freight which is carried or the passenger traffic?
2. What freight is carried by southbound trains? By those returning to the United States?
3. Which do you think is of greater importance to Mexico, its coast lands or its plateaus? Why not have a class debate on the question?
4. Of what interest is it to us whether or not Mexico is a peaceful, prosperous country? Have we any responsibility in the matter?

III

Make a list of the places mentioned in this chapter. Arrange them by countries, cities, mountains, rivers, etc. Be able to locate each place and tell what was said about it in the chapter.

CHAPTER XIX

THE SEVEN LITTLE COUNTRIES OF CENTRAL AMERICA

The seven countries of Central America form a series of stepping-stones from Mexico into South America. They are all situated in the torrid zone. Since none of the United States is tropical, we are interested in these little countries, for we need their products, and they, in their development, need our money, our manufactures, and our skilled workmen, engineers, surveyors, road builders, bridge builders, and others.

The great Western Highland, which begins near the Arctic Ocean, extends, as you know, through North America, Central America, and to the very southern tip of South America. The high plateau, with its higher ranges on either side, which is found in the United States, Mexico, and some countries of South America, runs also through the republics of Central America. The climate on the cool highland is delightful, but the low coast cities are hot. The prevailing trade winds coming from the east bring much moisture to that coast, and the heavy rainfall, with the heat, makes an unpleasant combination which few white people enjoy.

The Central American countries are alike in that each has a chain of highlands in the interior and low, hot coastlands with deep tropical forests and tangled jungles. All of them have volcanoes, more or less threatening. Being so similar in surface and climate, the same products are raised in all of them. The low, tiled adobe houses are common throughout the highland region, and the palm-thatched bamboo huts are found in the villages scattered along the coast.

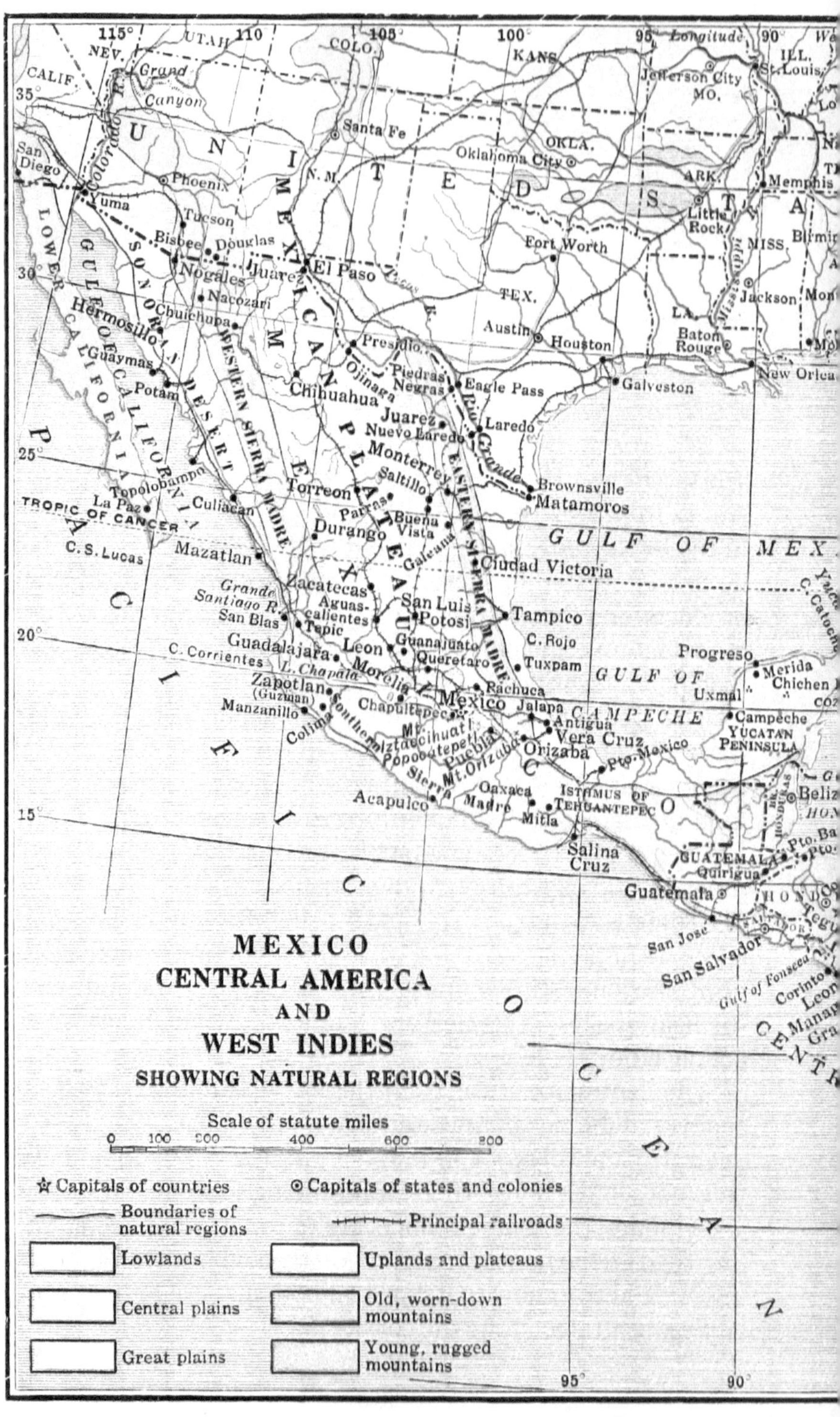

MEXICO
CENTRAL AMERICA
AND
WEST INDIES
SHOWING NATURAL REGIONS
Scale of statute miles
0 100 200 400 600 800
Capitals of countries
Capitals of states and colonies
Boundaries of natural regions
Principal railroads
Lowlands
Uplands and plateaus
Central plains
Old, worn-down mountains
Great plains
Young, rugged mountains

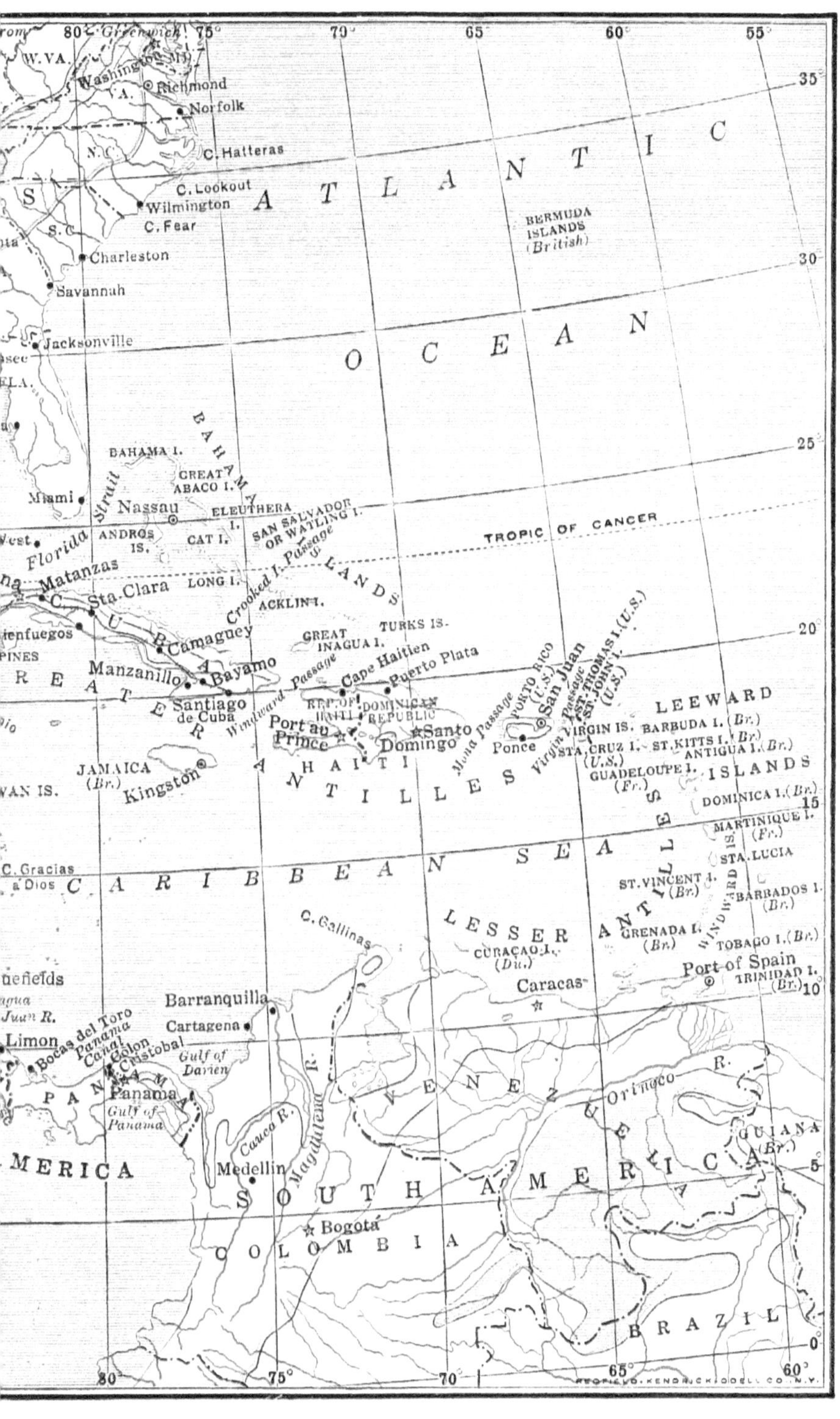

W.VA.
Washington (D.C.)
Richmond
Norfolk
C. Hatteras
C. Lookout
Wilmington
C. Fear
Charleston
Savannah
Jacksonville
Miami
ATLANTIC
OCEAN
BERMUDA ISLANDS (British)
BAHAMA I.
GREAT ABACO I.
BAHAMA ISLANDS
Nassau
ELEUTHERA I.
SAN SALVADOR OR WATLING I.
CAT I.
ANDROS IS.
Florida Strait
West
Matanzas
Sta. Clara
LONG I.
Crooked I. Passage
ACKLIN I.
TROPIC OF CANCER
Cienfuegos
Camaguey
CUBA
GREAT INAGUA I.
TURKS IS.
Manzanillo
Bayamo
Windward Passage
Cape Haitien
Puerto Plata
GREATER ANTILLES
Santiago de Cuba
REP. OF HAITI
DOMINICAN REPUBLIC
Port au Prince
Santo Domingo
PORTO RICO (U.S.)
San Juan
Ponce
Mona Passage
ST. THOMAS I. (U.S.)
ST. JOHN I. (U.S.)
Virgin Passage
VIRGIN IS. (U.S.)
LEEWARD
BARBUDA I. (Br.)
STA. CRUZ I. (U.S.)
ST. KITTS I. (Br.)
ANTIGUA I. (Br.)
GUADELOUPE I. (Fr.)
ISLANDS
JAMAICA (Br.)
Kingston
ANTILLES
HAITI
DOMINICA I. (Br.)
MARTINIQUE I. (Fr.)
STA. LUCIA
C. Gracias a Dios
CARIBBEAN SEA
WINDWARD
ST. VINCENT I. (Br.)
BARBADOS I. (Br.)
LESSER
C. Gallinas
ANTILLES
GRENADA I. (Br.)
CURAÇAO I. (Du.)
TOBAGO I. (Br.)
Port of Spain
TRINIDAD I. (Br.)
Caracas
Bluefields
Barranquilla
Juan R.
Bocas del Toro
Cartagena
Limon
Panama Canal
Colon
Cristobal
Gulf of Darien
VENEZUELA
Orinoco R.
PANAMA
Panama
Gulf of Panama
Cauca R.
Magdalena R.
GUIANA (Br.)
AMERICA
Medellin
SOUTH AMERICA
Bogotá
COLOMBIA
BRAZIL

Our impressions of this southern land will depend very much on which part of the country we visit, for there are two Central Americas — one of the cool highland and the other of the hot coastland. Most of the people live on the plateau, and the larger cities are located there. In this part of Central America, the Spanish language is spoken, and the houses, the life, and the customs are like those of old Spain. There were several reasons why the Spaniards settled in this part of the country. On the plateau, the climate is much pleasanter than on the hot coastal plain. It was also much more healthful. The people living there were much safer than they would have been near the coast, subject as it was in those days to raids and attacks from pirates.

The highland regions of Central America are nearer the Pacific coast than that of the Atlantic, thus making the low plain on the Caribbean wider than the one on the western side. Many Negroes live in the thatched huts of the eastern lowlands. English is spoken, and the trade with England and America has brought closer relations between those countries and this part of Central America than exists anywhere else in the peninsula.

The plateau regions in Central America, as in Mexico, are rich in minerals. Mines were worked by the Indians long before the coming of the white man. During the years when the Spaniards ruled the land, the Indians worked some of these mines for their conquerors. Gold and silver are exported today from Central America, and there are rich deposits yet untouched. As the countries develop and modern methods and modern machinery are more commonly used, not only gold and silver but other minerals which exist there will be mined in larger quantities.

Agriculture, however, is and probably always will be the most important occupation. Everything that can be raised in the temperate and torrid zones can be produced somewhere in Central America. In the rainy season, Nature fertilizes the land every year with the soil which the streams bring from the mountains. In the future, irrigation will be practiced much more than at present and will help the farmers who live in the drier regions of the plateau.

Some of the seaports of Central America are nearer to New

Orleans than New Orleans is to New York. Many of the products raised in Central America are such as cannot be grown in the United States, so that we need to import them. Fiber plants grow here, as in Mexico, and rubber, cotton, and sugar do well. The drier grasslands make excellent pastures, and the export of hides and skins has increased in the past few years.

In every country, from Mexico in the north to Argentina in southern South America, corn is an important product. It is today, as it has been for hundreds of years, the chief food of the people. Every Indian has his patch of corn and beans, and every Indian woman spends a large part of her time in preparing the beans and grinding the corn for the tortillas.

The forests of Central America are very valuable and will, in the future, yield many products now unknown. There are trees from which drugs, dyes, oils, gums, and nuts may be obtained. The medicines which may be made from the plants of the jungles and forests would be sufficient, one would think, to cure all the ills of mankind.

Coffee is one of the most valuable crops of Central America, and thousands of the people work on the coffee plantations. There is no prettier scene than the long rows of neatly pruned trees with their glossy green leaves and red cherrylike fruit. Harvesting time is the busiest season on the

FIG 163. These women are sorting coffee berries. Can you tell all the processes through which the fruit of the coffee tree goes before we use it in our kitchens? (Courtesy of the Keystone View Co.)

plantation. At the first hint of daylight, a great bell calls the Indians to work, and men, women, and children start for the fields, where all day their fingers fly, picking the red berries. Sometimes they have races to find out who is the fastest picker.

These red berries look very different from the brown coffee beans which the grocer grinds for us. The fruit is first crushed to mash the pulp. This sticky mass is next washed off from the seeds, which are then spread out to dry. After drying and sorting, the berries are shipped away to other countries. Here, they are roasted until they are brown.

The banana has been more important than any other thing in the development of life, the building of cities and towns, and the improvement of seaports on the eastern coast of Central America.

When you see the bunches of bananas hanging in the fruit store or notice a load of the fruit passing through the streets, do you ever wonder where they all come from? At the end of the last century, we were eating five million bunches a year. Today we average more than a dozen times as many. Other countries of the world also use millions. What a wonderful thing it is that this delicate fruit can be brought from tropical countries on journeys thousands of miles long and delivered in good shape not only at the seaports of Europe and America but at cities and towns hundreds of miles inland! Big plantations, railroads on which the fruit may be quickly carried to the shipping port, and refrigerator ships are the three chief reasons why, wherever you may live, you are able to have good bananas to eat.

All the way along the low, hot eastern coast of Central America, as far south as Brazil, and on many of the islands around the Caribbean Sea, large banana plantations may be found. Get out your thin clothing, prepare for a hot trip, and we will make a visit to Limón, the chief seaport of Central America, for in this region we shall find a good example of what the banana industry has done for the country.

Not so many years ago, the coast regions of Central America were practically uninhabited. Most of the population of these countries lived in the higher interior. They were shut off from the rest of the world not only by many miles of ocean but by miles of hot, insect-ridden, unhealthful coastlands. The ruins in these countries tell us that centuries and even thousands of years ago, great cities with fine temples and splendid palaces existed in these fertile valleys, but for many years, the only settlements on the coast were little villages of squalid huts and fever-racked populations. The ports were avoided by all travelers. Today, however, ships from all over the world anchor in their harbors and land their passengers at cities as healthy as many in our own country.

A great fruit company has done more than any other agency to make the banana a common world food. By means of the banana industry, this company has developed more land, built more towns, and contributed more to the welfare and prosperity of the eastern coastland of Central America than have any other persons inside the peninsula or out. Limón, but little more than fifty years ago, an unsettled swamp and jungle, is now a

FIG 164. Here is the home of some of the workers on a banana plantation. In what parts of Central America does the banana tree grow? (Courtesy of the Keystone View Co.)

FIG 165. This man is carrying bananas from the plantation to the railroad. See the long leaves of the banana trees in the background. (Courtesy of the Publishers' Photo Service)

city of thirty-five thousand people. It is the leading banana export city of the world. A "banana railroad" takes us from the port out into the country. We ride for a short distance through a tropical jungle where all along the track are trees, ferns, shrubs, vines, and roots, making a dense mass impenetrable by anyone without the use of a hatchet. Blossoms of brilliant reds, purples, and yellows decorate the greenery, and the great trees are masses of color.

A short distance inland, all this changes, and for miles, we run through a green avenue where the huge, drooping leaves of the banana trees meet over our heads. You would know from the names of some of the banana plantations that the industry was in the hands of people from the United States. One is called the "Boston," another the "Chicago," and a third the "New York."

Many of the workers on the plantation are Negroes from Jamaica. They are paid good wages, are accustomed to the hot

FIG 166. These bananas are being loaded on the train which has been sent up from the coast to collect them. (Courtesy of the Publishers' Photo Service)

climate, and live comfortably and contentedly in their little cabins surrounded by garden patches of vegetables and corn.

Earlier in the day, word was sent to the plantations that a ship would dock at Limón at night and that bananas were wanted for her cargo. It was necessary to send word also that the cargo was intended for New York City. If it were destined for New Orleans or for some interior city, such as Chicago or St. Louis, or if it were going to London or Paris, a different degree of ripeness in the fruit would be required.

See that workman cutting the bunches of bananas from the tree with his machete. He loads his pile of fruit on the tram-cars drawn by mules, and it is taken to the railroad, where it is unloaded on a long platform. An inspector keeps watch of the bunches as they are unloaded and rejects any which look to him too ripe or which have any other defect that may prevent them from reaching their destination in good condition. The fruit is covered with leaves to protect it from the sun. Later in the day, it is loaded on the train which runs down to Limón, stopping at the plantations along the route.

At Limón and at some of the other important ports, the

fruit company has installed loading machines. These have an endless-chain arrangement with canvas pockets on which the bunches are placed and carried to the ship. Workmen at the other end of the conveyor take the bunches from it and pass them from hand to hand down into the hold of the ship. Here they are carefully packed. All night long the work goes on. The dusky, barefooted laborers enliven the hours with songs and jokes. Before the dawn breaks over the blue sea, hundreds of tired workers are curled up on and around the wharves, sleeping as soundly as if they were on a soft bed.

During the voyage, a refrigerating plant lowers the temperature of the compartments where the fruit is stored to about fifty degrees. This prevents the fruit from ripening but is not cold enough to chill it.

Some of the fruit company's finer ships are arranged to carry passengers as well as freight. These are fitted with every convenience for comfort; some have a contrivance by which the cooled air may be used in the staterooms when they are uncomfortably warm.

There is a great future for the banana industry in tropical America as well as in other parts of the world, for people are beginning to realize the food value of the fruit. For the poorer inhabitants of Central America and other tropical countries, it is a daily food.

GUATEMALA

One of the most important countries of Central America is Guatemala. This country is larger and contains more people than Louisiana. Most of them live on the plateau, where the climate is cooler and pleasanter than on the low coastlands. Many of the inhabitants are Indians, whose life is very different from our own.

Guatemala is a land of contrasts, not only in its surface of high mountains and deep lakes, cool uplands and hot lowlands, level plains and towering peaks, but in its people and their homes. We shall see the Indian woman in her quaint

FIG 167. This is a farm scene in Guatemala. Describe the scenery of the country.
(Courtesy of the Pan-American Union)

costume and the white beauty in her Parisian clothes. We shall find little adobe huts and, not far away, the modern homes of wealthy people. We can bargain with the native sellers in the markets, who squat behind their piles of produce, or we can patronize the shops with their imported goods. In the country regions, we can watch the Indian tending his cattle or gathering wild honey from the trees. We can buy from some Indian woman a piece of the rich embroidery on which she has spent hours of labor, or perhaps a beautiful basket woven from the fiber of some native plant and dyed with the juice of some tropical shrub. Perhaps we shall have an invitation to dinner, when we can share their tortillas and frijoles cooked on the hot stones in an outdoor kitchen.

On the narrow trails which serve as roads in parts of the country, we may chance to see some Indians carrying heavy burdens on their backs. Their strength and endurance are wonderful. Going at a "jog trot" of about six miles an hour, an Indian will carry for many miles a load of from one hundred to two hundred pounds. In some of the towns and cities, these

FIG 168. This is one of the monuments among the ruins in Quirigua. Do you not wish that you could read this picture-writing and learn what events are recorded here? (Courtesy of the Pan-American Union)

burden bearers are so hidden by their loads that it looks almost as if the piles of pottery, fruits and vegetables, trunks, and boxes were hurrying through the streets on their own brown legs.

Guatemala, the capital of the country, is the largest city of Central America. Situated on the plateau, nearly five thousand feet above the level of the coast cities, it has a delightful climate. In the summer, the thermometer seldom goes above eighty-five degrees, and in the winter, it seldom sinks below sixty-five degrees. All around are green hills, and beyond them, higher mountains rise against the blue sky. The view of the city from the hills is interesting. Its long, straight streets cross one another at right angles like the lines on a checkerboard. The grand old cathedral in the central plaza towers over the low, one-story houses. The Spanish who built their cities on the interior plateau were doubtless more safe and comfortable there than they would have been on the coast, but the location was not favorable for commerce. For many years, all goods had to be carried over steep, narrow trails on the backs of mules and Indians. Today, railroads from both the Pacific coast and the Gulf of Honduras, on the east, run to the capital.

In this part of North America, we shall be continually reminded that we are in earthquake land. The sun-dried brick walls of the houses in Guatemala and other Central American cities are often several feet thick. The low houses, with such heavy walls, are not easily shaken. In spite of all precautions, however, a terrible earthquake occurred in Guatemala in 1919 which caused great destruction and loss of life. In this terrible disaster, as in all times of suffering, the members of the American Red Cross were promptly on the spot, caring for the injured and burying the dead. Antigua, the old capital of Guatemala, has been more than once destroyed. Its broken arches, pillars, and walls are green with vines and moss; the bells in the ruined churches are silent; and the images of the saints in their carved niches look down no longer on the busy life of a large city.

Other and older ruins in Guatemala represent the life of Indian tribes who were working and worshiping in their ancient cities centuries before the Spanish explorers came to America. Among these, the ruins of Quirigua are the most remarkable. Near them is an Indian village, but the people in it have no knowledge concerning the tribes who once lived here. Would it not be interesting to know what people carved these stones and built these temples and palaces, and to understand the uses to which they were put? Perhaps if the Spaniards had not destroyed so many documents, we might know more about these ancient people of Mexico and Central America.

BRITISH HONDURAS

To the east of Guatemala is the little colony of British Honduras, nearly as large as Massachusetts. Belize, the capital and seaport, contains a third of all the people who live in the colony.

Approaching from the sea, the steamer winds its way among little coral reefs scattered along the shore. Soon the white buildings in their setting of green come into sight. The little chimneyless houses nestling under the palms are raised on strong mahogany posts above the low, swampy land in which the city lies. Mountains rising in the hazy distance and the blue waters of the harbor, dotted with green islands and enlivened by craft of different kinds, make a pleasant setting for the little capital.

As soon as we set foot on shore, we should know that we were not in a Spanish colony, for the flowers are in the front yard instead of being hidden from sight in the patio. The houses of two or three stories are separated from the streets by neat white fences, and in the streets, we see negroes rather than Indians.

For many years, the coast of British Honduras was frequented by pirates, and many are the legends which are told of wild sea fights in the Caribbean and buried treasures on the islands and mainland. Perhaps you would like to hunt for some of this hidden wealth, but I am afraid you would fare no better than have the hundreds of searchers who have looked in vain for the hidden riches of gold and silver.

The old pirates finally grew tired of the hard, dangerous life and decided that, instead of robbing vessels and killing the crews, there was a better living as well as a safer one in selling the valuable woods of the tropical forest. Logwood was one of these important trees. From the wood in the heart of the tree, valuable dyes are made. Before the days of our cheaper, mineral dyes, these were in great demand. They are still shipped in considerable quantities from Belize. Mahogany wood also is an important product. It is obtained near the shores and also along the banks of the Belize River, which leads into the interior. Thousands of logs are floated down the river to the coast, where they are shipped away.

The Belize River is a small stream, but it is a useful one, for it offers means of transportation into the interior of the colony for two hundred miles. How far would a trip of this length take you from your home town?

In the forests of Belize, you might see workmen gathering chicle, digging sarsaparilla roots, and collecting coconuts. Some of the natives work on coffee and banana plantations. The names of some of the places in British Honduras are suggestive of the sights in and around them. Where would you rather go, to Orange Walk, All Pines, or have a sail down Monkey River?

HONDURAS

Extending eastward from Guatemala is another Central American country. This is Honduras. It is about as large as the state of Mississippi, with between a half and a third of its number of people. There are fewer white people than in Guatemala and more negroes.

Nature has been generous to Honduras in her gifts of soil, climate, and other resources necessary for the support of human life, but as yet they have been little developed, and at present, Honduras is one of the most backward of the Central American countries. The natives are but little interested in the development of their country. Why should they work hard in the hot sunshine to earn money when yams, as nourishing as potatoes, grow without labor, when coconuts are plentiful and yield not only meat but drink, when sugar cane grows with very little care, and when all that is needed to build a house can be obtained in the forest close at hand? A few cows, which find food on the rich grasslands, furnish milk and

FIG 169. This is a street in Tegucigalpa, the capital of Honduras. Can you tell what products may be in these carts which have come from the farms in the country? (Courtesy of the Brown Bros.)

cheese. A little patch of maize supplies the corn for the tortillas, and the beans from the little garden furnish the appetizing frijoles.

One of the resources of Honduras, in common with other Central American countries, lies in the rich tropical forests. Not only lumber in great quantity and of the finest quality will in the future be shipped from the forests of Central and South America, but also tanning extracts, dyes, drugs, oils, gums, resins, balsams, nuts, fruits, fibers, and many products as yet unknown. Today, the mahogany tree is the King of the Tropics, but it may sometime yield its throne to a greater monarch. Mahogany trees do not grow in groups by themselves, but are widely scattered through the forest. They are taller than most other trees and have conspicuous yellowish-red leaves. The lumberman often locates one by climbing to a high limb of some giant tree, which affords him a wide view of the green forest roof. After the tree is felled, the heavy logs are hauled to the riverside by oxen. This must be done in the dry season, when the ground is firm and hard. They are floated down the river and shipped to London or to some port in the United States. What articles made of mahogany have you ever seen?

Puerto Cortés is the most important seaport on the Gulf of Honduras and one of the best on the Caribbean Sea. This is the seaport at which Cortés landed, and therefore it is named in his honor. The great explorer was not very favorably impressed with the country, for in his report to the king of Spain, he speaks of the deep mud which he encountered and in which his horses sank nearly up to their bodies. This was evidently in the wet season, when the rains come down in sheets, the rivers rise into torrents, and parts of the lowlands are flooded.

The principal and almost the sole industry around Puerto Cortés is the growing and exporting of bananas to the United States, and the fruit vessels take annually millions of bunches from this port. This is only an example of what enormous crops may be produced in these Central American countries when other industries are as well organized as is the banana trade.

Like the capitals of the other Central American republics,

FIG 170. This is a view of Tegucigalpa. What differences would you find between this city and Puerto Cortés on the coast? Describe the surface of interior Honduras. (Courtesy of the Pan-American Union)

Tegucigalpa, the capital of Honduras, is situated on the interior highland, with green hills growing into higher mountains rising around it. Like them, also, Tegucigalpa has its plazas, its great cathedral, and its low, thick-walled, brightly colored houses built around a central patio. As we read of these southern cities, we must remember that they are much older than those in the United States. When San Francisco was yet undreamed of, when St. Louis was only an Indian camp, when New York and Boston were only small towns, Tegucigalpa, Guatemala, and other places in Mexico and Central America were large, busy cities.

Honduras is a country with which, in the future, we shall doubtless have much closer relations. Her ports are nearer to New Orleans than New Orleans is to Chicago. She has rich mineral deposits and many thousand acres of fertile land where all kinds of tropical fruits and vegetables which we cannot produce in our cooler country may be grown. Her pasture lands will supply thousands of cattle, and her coffee can be grown and imported into the United States cheaper than we can obtain it from Brazil.

It is wise for us to encourage a better understanding not only among Central American countries themselves but between them and the United States. Then we shall see many vessels plying between these Caribbean countries and our ports, bringing to us their products and carrying to them our manufactured goods.

SALVADOR

Little Salvador, the smallest republic in the Western Hemisphere, is not as large as Massachusetts. Excepting the little colony of British Honduras, Salvador is the only country in North America which does not border on two oceans. It is more progressive than some of its larger neighbors and is more densely peopled than any other country in North or South America. More than half of the people who live there are Indians.

Revolutions have not been uncommon in Central American countries, and Salvador has had difficulties with her more backward neighbors. Few troubles at home have hindered her progress, for many of her people are contented, prosperous farmers, tilling their own little farms, and such citizens have little time or inclination for making war.

This little republic shows her progress in her good roads and bridges. In her capital, San Salvador, there are more automobiles than in any other Central American city. We shall

FIG 171. These women in Salvador are making tortillas. Read the description given on page 259, and tell how they are made. (Courtesy of the Keystone View Co.)

find here beautifully shaded parks with fine monuments and gardens, a splendid National Palace, a National University, and a large cathedral. More than any other Central American capital, San Salvador is like a European city in its shops and stores and its broad streets. The government is a progressive one and is interested in the education of its people. It is encouraging evening schools and other forms of education, and is trying to introduce and foster modern methods of agriculture.

Near the western coast of Salvador grows the balsam tree, one of the most beautiful and useful of the forest trees of the tropics. The balsam which comes from it has been used for centuries by the natives of Salvador and is valuable today in medicine and surgery. Natives who live near the forest tap the trees and fasten small pieces of cloth below the cuts which they make. The sticky sap soon saturates the cloths. They are then removed and new ones put in their places. The saturated cloths are put into a kettle of boiling water, the impurities which collect on the surface are skimmed off, and the cloths are squeezed to press out the balsam. This is separated from the water and further purified, after which it is shipped away in tins of about fifty pounds' weight.

Coffee is Salvador's chief crop, but it has many other industries which, with the help of the government, are proving successful. Among her chief products are sugar, cotton, cocoa, rubber, grains, vegetables, indigo, tobacco, and cattle. There are rich mines in the country, and gold and silver are two important exports.

NICARAGUA

Nicaragua is the largest of the Central American countries, but it has had many revolutions and consequently has not made great progress, though it is wonderfully blessed by Nature's gifts. There is no country where sugar, coffee, cotton, and other products will grow better; no land where there are finer pastures for cattle, finer forests of valuable hardwoods, and richer deposits of minerals; no valleys and lowlands more suited to tropical and semitropical fruits.

In the other Central American countries, one ascends from the low, hot coast until, a mile or so above sea level, one emerges on the cool Central Plateau, where are the chief cities and the old Spanish capitals. Nicaragua is quite different. In the center of this republic, between the two mountain ranges, is an interior basin, part of which is occupied by Lake Nicaragua, which lies only about a hundred feet above sea level.

Nicaragua is almost divided by water, for Lake Nicaragua is one hundred miles long and nearly as wide at its widest point. From its eastern side, the San Juan River flows into the Caribbean Sea, while its western border is less than twenty miles from the Pacific Ocean. When the building of a canal to connect the Atlantic and Pacific Oceans was talked of, there were many who wished it to run through Nicaragua. The distance was longer

FIG 172. This man is getting water from Lake Nicaragua, which he will later sell in the streets of some town. Describe the cart. (Courtesy of the Keystone View Co.)

than through Panama, but Lake Nicaragua and the river would furnish a natural route for many miles.

Sometime in the future, the commerce of the world will be even greater than it is today. The many millions of people across the Pacific in Asia will produce more articles for export and will need more imports from other countries; then perhaps other canals will be needed to join the waters of the two great oceans. The United States is looking forward to this time and intends that no other nation shall build or control a canal so near to her lands and to the Panama Canal. So we have made with Nicaragua a treaty which gives us the exclusive right to build and maintain a canal across that country and to control the land on both the eastern and western coasts near where such a canal might end.

Where Lake Nicaragua lies was once a great plain with many volcanoes rising from its surface. Now the peaks form islands in the lake. Some of them rise nearly a mile above its surface, and there are mountains in the country which are much higher. The blue water, the mountains, and the luxuriant vegetation which covers their slopes make this part of Nicaragua very beautiful.

Corinto is the chief port of Nicaragua on the Pacific Ocean. The town is an interesting place to the stranger. Green islands dot the harbor, and tall, graceful palm trees line the shores. What

FIG 173. This picture shows a street in a small town in Nicaragua. Describe the houses. Of what are the roofs made? (Courtesy of the Brown Bros.)

a crowd there is to greet the boat! What will you buy from the eager vendors — a parrot, a monkey, some luscious fruit, some beautiful flowers, a Panama hat, or a comfortable hammock?

As in the neighboring republics, we shall find most of the people of Nicaragua living in the interior. This is the pleasantest part of the country to visit. Here are the capital and the chief cities, with their old Spanish customs and traditions. Here are the real Nicaraguans — hospitable, courteous, and charming.

León, the old capital and today the largest city of Nicaragua, is thirty-five miles up the slopes from the seaport, Corinto. On the way from the coast to the interior we see on each side of the railroad many sugar and cocoa plantations and thousands of glossy-green coffee trees. Many cattle are raised on the plateaus, but the grassy pastures would furnish food for many more.

Managua, the present capital of Nicaragua, is not so attractive as some other cities. Granada, named for the old Moorish city of Spain, is much more beautiful and is more like the ancient Spanish cities across the water. Bluefields is the most important port on the Caribbean coast and, like the other seaports there, is fast becoming a center for the banana industry. As commerce between Nicaragua and the United States increases, we shall find that many vessels will sail from Bluefields to New Orleans and other ports, bringing us many products from this little country.

We need her sugar, cocoa, rubber, fruit, coffee, gold, hides and skins, cabinet woods, and other products. We shall send back in increasing quantities to Nicaragua and her neighbors cotton goods, breadstuffs, chemicals, dyes, medicines, leather goods, tools, and manufactures of iron and steel for her railroads, bridges, buildings, and mines.

COSTA RICA

There are more white people in Costa Rica in proportion to its population than in any other country in Central America. Perhaps this may be the reason why it is more progressive and has had fewer revolutions than some of its neighbors. Costa

FIG 174. These are some of our neighbors in San José. From their appearance, what should you judge of their education and culture? (Courtesy of the Publishers' Photo Service)

Rica was not settled by holders of large estates who held Indian tenants as their slaves, but by hard-working men and their families. They tilled their own farms and reaped the rewards for their industry, and it is to these industrious farmers that this little country owes her prosperity.

Though only a small country, Costa Rica is rich in its resources. It has more than a dozen small navigable rivers which afford means of transportation. Its climate is so varied and its soil is so rich that many products can be grown, chief among them coffee, bananas, tobacco, cocoa, sugar, indigo, rice, and coconuts. Gold and silver are mined, and other minerals are widely distributed. Rubber trees and valuable hardwoods grow in its forests. Other trees also yield materials for dyes and drugs and for tanning hides.

Though all of the resources named are valuable, two products alone — coffee and bananas — have really made Costa Rica. Bananas built the railroad from Limón to San José, and coffee built the road which leads from the capital down to the Pacific Ocean.

You remember reading on page 287 something of the growth of the city of Limón and of the wonderful development of the banana industry of Central America. Let us take a trip by rail from Limón up to San José, the capital. In a distance of

FIG 175. These coffee piles are sometimes called Costa Rica's gold mines. Can you tell why? (Courtesy of the Keystone View Co.)

a hundred miles, we ride through a jungle of tropical vegetation, through miles of banana plantations, and through hardwood forests graybearded with moss. We cross high bridges spanning deep ravines and follow foaming streams which rush down the slopes. We catch glimpses of pleasant homes surrounded by groves of cocoa trees or orchards of oranges and grapefruit, and, climbing higher, we ride by long rows of coffee trees. When nearly four thousand feet higher than the Caribbean, we catch our first sight of San José, nestling in its high valley, with green hills rising around. In the coastal lowlands, there is always summer, but here at this height, the climate is like a perpetual springtime. San José is one of the most progressive cities of Central America. We enjoy its clean streets and fine public buildings, and its general air of content and well-being. Its splendid cathedral, its national library, its hospital, and its opera house all testify to the goodness of heart and the refinement of mind of its people.

Besides being taught to use books, the children in the schools of Costa Rica are taught also to use their hands and to make useful articles from the products of their country. They work with leather and wood and become skillful in making rope, baskets, hammocks, and other things from the fiber plants which grow in the country. The little schoolhouses are found everywhere in Costa Rica, and they have had a great influence on the prosperity

FIG 176. Does this beautiful opera house in San José tell you anything about the people of the city? (Courtesy of the Newman and B. & D.)

of the country. The boys and girls of today, you know, are the men and women of tomorrow, and the welfare of any country depends on the education which its children receive and the kind of citizens they make.

PANAMA AND THE CANAL

Panama is the most important country of Central America, not on account of its size or industries or products but because of its position and the canal which runs through it. This country, considerably smaller than the state of Indiana, is a long S-shaped isthmus connecting the continents of North and South America. This narrow strip of land has long been a barrier to trade between the Atlantic and Pacific Oceans. The building of the Panama Canal has removed this barrier and has had a great effect on the trade routes of the world.

Through the center of Panama, from northwest to southeast, runs a strip of land ten miles wide which belongs to the United States. We paid the government of Panama ten mil-

FIG 177. This is a girl from Panama and her pet parrakeet. Find out what you can about the bird. (Courtesy of the Newman and B. & D.)

lion dollars for it. The name of this land is the Panama Canal Zone. In the center of the zone, five miles on either side from its border, lies the Panama Canal. Let us take a trip through the Canal. It is only about fifty miles long, but it will take us from six to ten hours to pass through it from end to end. This may seem rather a long time to go such a short distance, but we must remember that we may be delayed in getting through the several locks and that Gatun Lake is the only part of the Canal where we can put on steam and sail at full speed.

At the Atlantic end of the Canal are Colon and Cristobal. Of these two towns, Colon is the older. It lies outside the Canal Zone and belongs to the Republic of Panama. The younger town, Cristobal, lies within the border of the Canal Zone and belongs to the United States. The cities together are called Cristobal-Colon, which means Christopher Columbus. Such a name seems thoroughly appropriate, because on one of his voyages, Columbus sailed into Limón Bay, the water on which these cities are situated. The beach was just as smooth and as white, the sea as blue, and the palms fringing the shore as graceful then as now. In those days, however, no breakwater ran out into the Caribbean Sea to protect the harbor from the fierce "northers," no ships with the British jack, the French tricolor, or the Stars and Stripes lay in

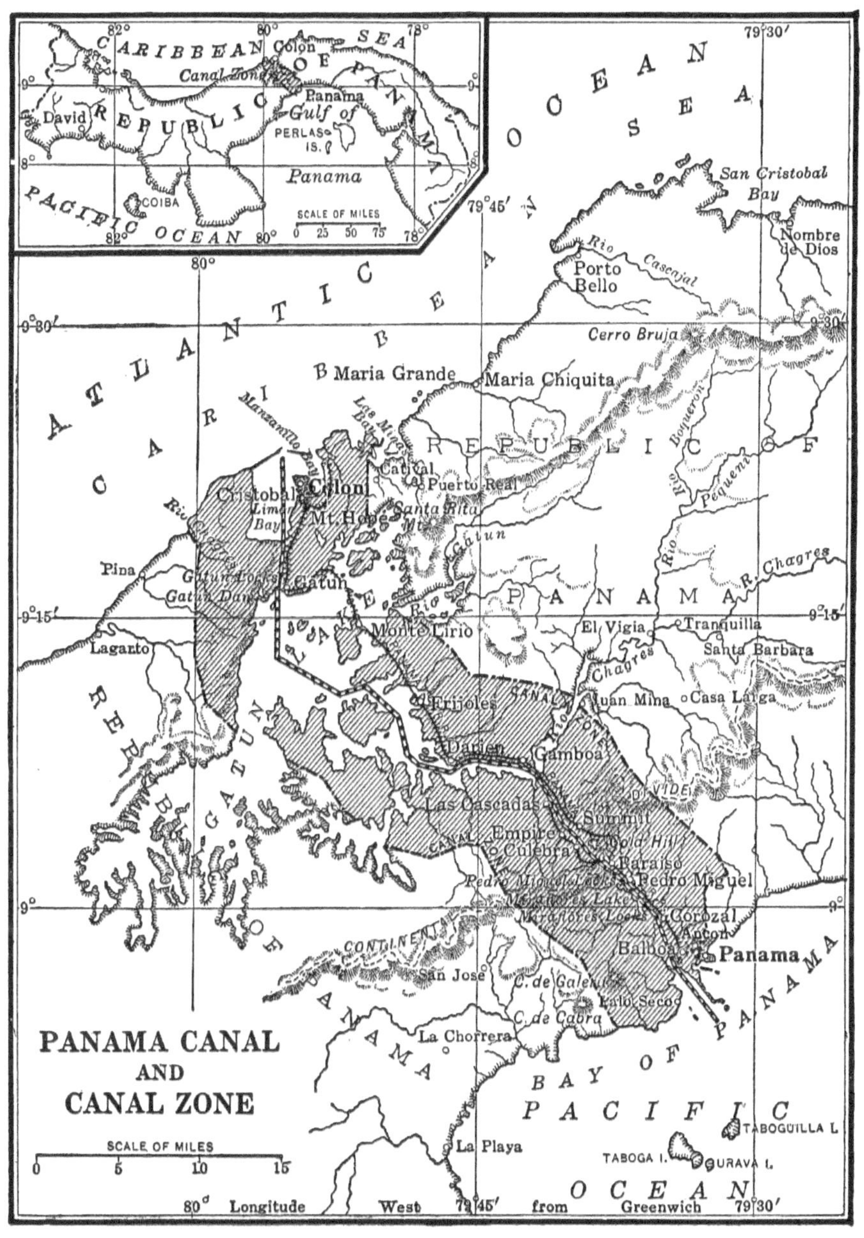

Find on the map the places along the Canal which are mentioned in the text.
Colon on the Atlantic Ocean lies farther west than Panama on the Pacific.
How do you account for this fact?

the bay, and no town with its low houses and red roofs gleamed beneath the waving palms.

Before "Uncle Sam" began his work on the Canal, Colon, like Panama on the Pacific coast, was a dirty, unhealthful place, a hotbed of malaria and yellow fever. The sewage was thrown into the streets, the water supply was from unscreened rainwater barrels and water carts, and the undrained land around was the breeding place of swarms of mosquitoes, which carried the germs of disease. The health crusaders from the United States, under the direction of the late General Gorgas, cleaned up the city and installed modern conveniences. They sprinkled oil on the ponds and stagnant water. This formed a scum on the surface and killed the young mosquitoes breeding in the water by preventing them from getting to the air. Vermin-infested quarters in the town were torn down and houses were carefully screened. These and other improvements have made the cities at either end of the Canal very different places from what they were in former years. The work of the United States officials in driving disease out of the Canal Zone, and the labor of the United Fruit Company in banishing tropical diseases from the settlements on the eastern coast of Central America, have shown the world that with proper care tropical lands may be healthful, pleasant places in which to live.

Seven miles from Colon we come to the Gatun Locks and Dam. The dam, built to control the waters of the Chagres River, is the largest in the world. It is about a mile and a half long, nearly a half mile thick at its base, more than a hundred feet high, and a hundred feet across the top. It looks now more like a real hill than an artificial embankment, for Nature has covered it with a thick green carpet.

The Chagres River rises in the hills to the east and cuts across the path of the Canal. This river was one of the greatest problems to the engineers who planned the Canal. In the dry season it was a harmless little stream, while during the heavy rains of the wet months it became a torrent. In twenty-four hours its waters have been known to rise from thirty to forty feet. The engineers finally decided to build a dam at Gatun high enough and strong enough to allow the waters of the river to spread out behind it

FIG 178. This vessel is passing through the Gaillard Cut. A slide has just occurred on the right bank and a steam shovel is at work removing the earth. Describe the digging of this cut.

into a lake so large that even the floods poured into it during the rainy season would cause no damage. In the middle of the dam is a spillway through which surplus water is allowed to escape. The lake thus formed, Gatun Lake, is the largest artificial lake in the world and covers an area of one hundred and sixty-four square miles.

Near either end of the Canal are locks by means of which vessels are lifted from the level of the ocean to that of the lake and lowered from the lake down to ocean level. We are lifted to the lake level in the Gatun Locks, and we steam at full speed through the lake until we come to Gaillard Cut, formerly called Culebra Cut. Here the hills of the Isthmus are the highest, and consequently, the cutting was the deepest. The cut is about eight miles long, and in places the hills were dug away to a depth of more than three hundred feet. The slopes of the hills on either side are now clothed with green, and as our vessel glides along, we can scarcely realize that we are sailing through a man-made channel and not on a natural river.

Beyond the cut, we come to Pedro Miguel Locks, where we

are lowered thirty feet to the level of Miraflores Lake. Passing through the lake, the Miraflores Locks lower us fifty-five feet more to the level of the Pacific Ocean.

What a wonderful invention are these locks, which enable vessels to go up and down stairs. A lock is a huge concrete box with gates at either end. The locks in the Panama Canal are each more than a thousand feet long, and the gates weigh from four hundred to eight hundred tons each. Measure one thousand feet from your schoolhouse and see how far one of these locks would extend.

As we enter the Miraflores Locks, the invisible giant, electricity, closes the huge gates behind us. It also sets in operation the valves which connect with great tunnels in the walls of the lock. The water slowly leaves the lock through the tunnels, and as it lowers, our vessel lowers with it. When we are on a level with that of the Canal beyond, the huge gates before us slowly swing open. No vessel goes through a lock under its own steam. Four electric locomotives run on tracks on the top of the lock walls. Two, one on either side, are attached by strong cables to the front end of the vessel, and two, one on either side, are attached to the stern. These keep us in the middle of the channel and pull us out of the lock.

A run of about three miles from the last locks brings us to the American town of Balboa, the Pacific terminus of the Canal. Balboa is built at the foot of Ancon Hill. On the other side of the hill, two miles away, is the city of Panama, the capital of the Panama Republic. It was built in 1673 after an older city had been destroyed by pirates. The ruins of this old Panama, draped with moss and hung with vines, can still be seen on the seashore five miles east of the present city.

The Panama Canal has a great influence on the trade routes of the world and the development of different countries. Before the building of the Canal, vessels sailing between the eastern and western coasts of the United States were obliged to go entirely around South America, making a journey nearly fourteen thousand miles long. By way of the Canal, New York is only a little more than five thousand miles from San Francisco. How many miles are saved in sailing between the two cities by way of the Canal instead of going around South America?

Perhaps of all foreign countries, those of western South America will profit most by the Canal. You will realize the reason for this when you notice on a map how far to the east South America lies. Its most western point is farther east than Detroit, Michigan. Through the Canal, the route from New York to western South America is nearly directly south. Find Valparaiso, the chief seaport of Chile, on your map. From New York to Valparaiso by way of the Atlantic Ocean and around southern South America is more than eight thousand miles. By way of the Canal, it is but a little more than half that distance. By the old route, it is about ten thousand miles from New York to Ecuador. Today it is less than a third of that distance. Voyages from England to the western United States, western South America, and the Pacific Islands are shortened in proportion.

As you think of the wonderful things that have been accomplished thus far in the twentieth century, remember that one of them is the building of the Panama Canal. It has separated two continents, joined two oceans, and cut in two the distance between many ports.

SUGGESTIONS FOR STUDY

I

1. Position and surface of the Central American countries.
2. Climate and life on the plateau; on the coastal plains.
3. Mineral wealth and agriculture.
4. Forests of Central America.
5. A coffee plantation.
6. The banana industry and the port of Limón.
7. Size, surface, and scenery of Guatemala.
8. Life in Guatemala.
9. The capital city, Guatemala.
10. Ruins of ancient cities.
11. Belize, the capital of British Honduras.

12. Industries in British Honduras.
13. Conditions and resources in Honduras.
14. Tropical forests and their value.
15. Puerto Cortés and Tegucigalpa.
16. Size and prosperity of Salvador.
17. San Salvador, the capital.
18. The balsam tree and other products.
19. Conditions and resources in Nicaragua.
20. Surface of Nicaragua and the Canal route.
21. Some cities and seaports.
22. People and resources of Costa Rica.
23. Limón and San José.
24. Importance of Panama.
25. The Canal Zone and the Canal.
26. Colon and Cristobal.
27. Our sanitary work in the Canal Zone.
28. A trip through the Canal.
29. The city of Panama.
30. Influence of the Panama Canal.

II

1. Name the seven countries of Central America. Which is the largest? The smallest? The most northern? The most southern? The most eastern? The most western?
2. Which Central American country is not a republic? In which one is the United States most interested?
3. Draw a diagram of the Canal. Mark on it the names of the places mentioned.
4. What products shall we probably import in large quantities from Central America in the future? Why must we depend on other countries for such products?

III

Make a list of the places mentioned in this chapter. Arrange them by countries, cities, mountains, rivers, etc. Be able to locate each place and tell what was said about it in the chapter.

CHAPTER XX

SOME ISLANDS AROUND NORTH AMERICA

GREENLAND

No man knows more of this bleak northern land than did the late Rear Admiral Peary, that brave Arctic explorer whose courage and perseverance finally won for him immortal fame as the discoverer of the North Pole.

Rear Admiral Peary described Greenland as follows[1]:

"All that there is of land, as we understand the term, in Greenland is simply a ribbon 5 to 25 (and in one or two places 60 to 80) miles in width, made up of mountains and valleys and deep branching fiords; a ribbon surrounded by the Arctic Sea, playground of the iceberg and the pack ice, and itself in turn surrounding and supporting, like a Titan dam, the great white ice cap beneath which the interior of the country is buried."

The interior of Greenland today is simply an elevated unbroken plateau of snow lifted from 5000 to 8000 and even 10,000 feet above the level of the sea; it is an Arctic Sahara, in comparison with which the African Sahara is insignificant. For on this frozen Sahara of inner Greenland occurs no form of life, animal or vegetable; no fragment of rock, no grain of sand, is visible. The traveler across its frozen wastes, traveling as I have week after week, sees outside of himself and his own party but

---

1   By permission of the Royal Geographical Society.

three things in all the world, namely, the infinite expanse of the frozen plain, the infinite dome of the cold blue sky, and the cold white sun, nothing but these. The traveler, too, across this frozen desert knows that at no time during his journey are the highest rocks of the mountain summits below him nearer than from 1000 to 5000 feet down through the mighty blanket of snow. Such is the interior of northern Greenland.

On the ribbon of land around the coast of Greenland, some Eskimos live, most of them on the southwest shores. Their time is spent in fishing and hunting. These Eskimos have been friendly to the white men who have visited there, and their help has been of great value to the brave explorers who have ventured farther and farther north until at last they have stood on the "top of the earth."

FIG 179. These are two happy little girls from the southwest coast of Greenland. Tell the class how they live, what they eat, etc. (Courtesy of the Brown Bros.)

ICELAND

Little Iceland belongs properly with the continent of Europe rather than with North America. It is nearer to Europe than to our continent, and it is a continuation of the sunken mountain system which extends through Great Britain and northwesterly across the northern Atlantic.

Iceland is not a bleak desolate region covered with ice as Greenland is. Within its borders, in an area about the size of the state of Ohio, nearly a hundred thousand people live. Most of these make their

FIG 180. This is the main street in Reykjavik, the capital of Iceland. Would
you find a street like this in Greenland?

homes on the lowlands in the southwestern part of the island.
They raise cattle, sheep, and ponies, gather the soft down from
the nests of the eider duck, and fish along the coasts.

Iceland is a beautiful country. No area on earth of equal size
contains such glaciers, such deep, narrow cliff-bordered inlets,
such mineral springs and geysers, and so many volcanoes. Here,
as nowhere else in the world, it is possible for one to see some
of Nature's agents at work building up the surface of the earth.

For four hundred years Iceland was independent, ruled by the
descendants of the early Norse settlers. Then for more than a
century it was governed by Norway, and after that by the Danes.
In 1919 it was freed from Denmark and is again independent.

Reykjavik, the capital of Iceland, is in about the same latitude
as Nome, Alaska. The winters in the Iceland city, however, are

milder than in some cities of the United States. Can you tell why this is so?

THE BERMUDA ISLANDS

We shall find the islands which lie farther toward the south much more enjoyable than those in the Far North which are situated on or near the Arctic Circle. In February or March, when the snow lies deep on the ground in the northern United States and the temperature is below zero, perhaps you would like to take a trip to the Bermuda Islands. You would have plenty of company on such an excursion, for thousands of tourists visit them at this time of the year as well as during other months. They lie far out in the Atlantic Ocean, east of the state of Georgia. There are more than three hundred of these tiny coral islands,

FIG 181. This picture shows you a field of onions in Bermuda. The men are packing them for export. Why is Bermuda warm enough to raise onions when it is too cold to do so in the United States in the same latitude? (Courtesy of the Brown Bros.)

but all of them together cover an area of less than twenty square miles. How does this area compare with that of your town or city? Could you place all of these islands within its boundaries?

The Bermudas are surrounded by ocean waters and are situated near the path of the warm Gulf Stream. Therefore, the climate of the islands is mild and balmy. It is because of the absence of frosts that valuable crops can be raised in the early spring, when they bring high prices in the markets of New York City. You have probably seen Bermuda onions for sale in stores. Potatoes, tomatoes, and other vegetables are also raised in considerable quantities. There are some farms where large fields are entirely covered with long rows of beautiful Easter lilies, and the air all around is sweet with their fragrance.

The Bermuda Islands are a part of the British Empire. If you will look on the map of North America, you will see that they are located on the ocean route between England or Canada and the British possessions in the West Indies. Therefore, the Bermudas are an important station for British vessels.

SUGGESTIONS FOR STUDY

I

1. Coast of Greenland.
2. Interior of Greenland.
3. Position and surface of Iceland.
4. People and occupations.
5. Wonders of Iceland.
6. Government of Iceland.
7. Number and area of the Bermuda Islands.
8. Products of the Bermudas.
9. Government of the Bermudas.

II

1. Can you find out when Rear Admiral Peary discovered the North Pole? By whom and when was the South Pole discovered?
2. Name three regions in the world where there are wonderful geysers.
3. For what is eiderdown used?
4. Using the scale of the map, find out how far the Bermuda Islands are from New York. How long do you think it would take you to sail there from New York?

III

Make a list of the places mentioned in this chapter. Arrange them by countries, cities, mountains, rivers, etc. Be able to locate each place and tell what was said about it in the chapter.

CHAPTER XXI

A TRIP TO THE WEST INDIES

Christopher Columbus made a mistake when he named the islands southeast of North America the West Indies. He thought that he could reach India by sailing around the world westward from Spain. His theory was right, but North America and the islands near it lay in his way. When he saw land, he supposed that he had reached the coast of India; therefore, he named the islands on which he landed the West Indies.

If you look at the map opposite page 282, you will see that the West Indies extend from between Florida and Yucatan to the coast of South America, inclosing between them and the mainland the Gulf of Mexico and the Caribbean Sea. You have read of the ancient Laurentian Upland in Canada, of the worn-down Appalachians in the eastern United States, and of the more youthful, lofty mountains in the western part of North America. The mountain ridge of which the West Indies are composed is younger than any of these, so young, indeed, that the ocean waters still cover many of the valleys between the peaks, thus making islands instead of a continuous mountain chain.

The West Indies are of much more importance now than in former years and will become increasingly so in the future. With the growth of ocean traffic, the building of the Panama Canal, and the development of the countries of northern South America, the passages between the islands are being used more and more as important routes of commerce. With our growing knowledge of life in tropical regions and of methods of protection against diseases common to such lands, and with the constantly increasing call of the world for food, clothing, and other useful products, these southern islands are being rapidly

FIG 182. Sisal fiber is produced in the Bahama Islands. This man and woman are taking the leaves to the mill in Nassau. Where is this city?

developed, and larger and larger quantities of raw materials are being exported each year to many countries, chief among them the United States and Great Britain. These two nations own most of the West Indies and are more interested than any others in their products. They also send to the islands more manufactured goods than do any other countries.

THE BAHAMA ISLANDS

North of the main island chain is a group of smaller islands. These are the Bahamas, belonging to Great Britain. In the building of these islands, Nature is employing her little coral workers instead of heat, steam, pressure, and other agents which are working on the islands to the south.

Can you find on the map the little island of San Salvador? This is the land on which Columbus first set foot after his long voyage across the Atlantic Ocean in 1492. There are between six hundred and seven hundred islands in the Bahama group, some of them very tiny indeed, and some large enough for farms and villages. Here we shall find orange and pineapple plantations and those where sisal fiber is produced. On the wharves at Nassau, the chief city of the Bahamas, we shall see not only these products but many sponges, and enormous turtles turned on their backs to prevent them from escaping.

THE GREATER ANTILLES

The most important islands of the West Indies are Cuba, Jamaica, Haiti, and Porto Rico. They are called the Greater Antilles. The group of smaller islands, which stretch from Porto Rico to the mainland of South America, are known as the Lesser Antilles. Cuba and Haiti are independent, Jamaica belongs to the British, and Porto Rico to the United States.

FIG 183. These men are loading sugar cane onto cars to be taken to the mill. Notice how much faster the work can be done by machinery than if the men had to do it by hand. (Courtesy of the Pan-American Union)

FIG 184. This is a field of young tobacco in Cuba. Notice how the tobacco is shaded by taller plants. (Courtesy of the Brown Bros.)

Cuba is the most important island of the West Indies. It covers about the same area as Pennsylvania, but it is of a very different shape. If a map of Cuba were laid on a map of the United States made on the same scale, it would reach from New York City through the states of Pennsylvania, Ohio, and Indiana to Chicago on Lake Michigan. Nowhere would it be wide enough to touch both the northern and southern borders of any one of these states.

Christopher Columbus called Cuba the fairest land that he had ever seen. Its deep, landlocked bays form some of the finest harbors in the world. Its mountains and valleys and swift streams make the scenery beautiful. Its fertile valleys, its splendid farms, and its fine cities with their palm-shaded avenues tell of peace and prosperity.

Until 1898, Cuba was a Spanish colony. At the end of the war between the United States and Spain, that country surrendered her control over Cuba, and the United States took possession of this rich island. We helped to improve the schools, build roads, develop industries, and establish a good government. As soon as we thought that Cuba was fitted to govern itself, we withdrew our soldiers from the island, and it became an independent republic.

While in Cuba, you can visit plantations where many different products are raised. Among these are rice, cocoa, coffee, and fruit and vegetables of many kinds. You can see the lumbermen in the hardwood forests felling the mahogany, cedar, and logwood trees. You can go, if you wish, into copper, manganese, and iron mines or watch the workmen getting out and loading asphalt, which may later be used in improving the roads on the island or even in the city or town where you live. You cannot travel far on the island, however, without seeing something of the two most important products — sugar and tobacco.

Cuba is today the greatest sugar-producing country of the world. This island and India have been rivals in recent years in the production of sugar. Some years India has led, but since the great sugar shortage during the World War, when the price increased so tremendously, Cuba's product has excelled that of any other country. One authority declares that if her great crop of millions of tons were piled up in a wall as high as an ordinary dwelling house and thick enough for four men to walk side by side on the top of it, such a wall would extend entirely around Cuba's two thousand miles of coastline. Most of the sugar is raised in the eastern part of the island, and the larger part of the tobacco in the west. Whether you visit the fields where the big-leaved plants hide the ground from sight, the curing barns where the long leaves are dried, or the cigar factories in Habana where hundreds of workmen roll cigars and fashion cigarettes, you will see what an important part this industry plays in the life of the Cuban people. There are many other industries which might be profitable in Cuba and, as the years go by, larger and larger quantities of other products will be raised. But today tobacco is king, and sugar is queen of the products of this Gem of the Antilles.

Of course, before leaving Cuba, you will stop at Habana. A seventh of all the people of the island live in this city, which is nearly the size of New Orleans. Many wealthy owners of sugar and tobacco plantations have fine residences in the capital, where they live part of the time. You would enjoy riding through the palm-bordered avenues, mingling with the crowds, shopping in the fine stores, visiting the great cigar factories, looking out over the magnificent harbor, or watching the vessels at the wharves being loaded with sugar, tobacco, and cigars. And you would appreciate as never before the importance of this great city, which is the center of commerce not only of the island of Cuba but also of the West Indies.

Nearly a hundred miles south of Cuba is Jamaica. It has fine harbors, fertile plains, and a healthful climate. These facts, together with its position, make this island an important one.

In a visit to Jamaica, you would land at Kingston, the chief city. It is located on a fine harbor on the southeastern coast, the most important part of the island.

On the plains around Kingston and running back into the hill country are large farms where bananas and coconuts are produced. Other fruits — pineapples, oranges, and lemons — are grown to some extent. There are plantations also where sugar cane, coffee, and cocoa are raised. In the forested regions of

FIG 185. From the appearance of this avenue, the Prado, what can you say of the beauty of the city of Habana? (Courtesy of the Brown Bros.)

the interior, the logwood tree grows. Salt is obtained along the coasts, and some million bushels are exported.

There are three independent republics among the West Indies — Cuba, Haiti, and Santo Domingo. Haiti and the Republic of Santo Domingo are on the same island — Haiti in the west, and the larger republic in the east. In Haiti, which is a former colony of France, most of the people speak French. In the Dominican Republic, settled largely by the Spaniards, the Spanish language is spoken. Most of the people in Haiti are negroes, while those in the eastern republic are chiefly mixed races — descendants of the natives, the early Spanish inhabitants, and negroes.

There are many mineral deposits on the island which will someday be mined. At present, most of the people are farmers. You would be surprised at the number of coffee trees, especially in Haiti, and at the millions of pounds of coffee which are shipped away. People in Haiti are beginning to find out also that cotton-raising is profitable and are planting it each

FIG 186. These women of Jamaica are having a pleasant time chatting together as they carry the products of their little farms to market. What do you suppose is in the baskets? (Courtesy of the Brown Bros.)

year in increasing amounts. In both Haiti and the Dominican Republic, much tobacco is raised, and cigars and cigarettes are made. While staying on this pleasant island, we can visit sugar and cocoa plantations. We can go out with the lumbermen into the deep tropical forests and watch them fell the big mahogany and logwood trees. All these products help in supplying the world with needful materials, and as years go on, many more will come from these tropical islands.

The capital of the Dominican Republic is Santo Domingo. Bartholomew Columbus, brother of Christopher, the great discoverer, founded a city here in 1496. It was destroyed by a hurricane a little more than half a century later, and the present capital was started a short distance away.

Port au Prince, which you will find on the map, situated on a splendid harbor on the western coast of Haiti, is the capital of that republic. It is a city of more than a hundred thousand people, much larger than the capital of the Dominican

FIG 187. Do you wish to buy a Panama hat? These men of San Juan, Porto Rico, have a good supply for sale. How long has Porto Rico belonged to the United States?

Republic. How does it compare in size with the city or town in which you live?

The United States has many island possessions, most of them situated in the Pacific Ocean. Porto Rico is the most important one in the Atlantic Ocean. It was ceded to us by Spain in 1898. It is smaller than Connecticut but, like that state, is thickly populated, for it averages more than three hundred people on each square mile.

Like Cuba, Haiti, and Jamaica, the other three islands of the Greater Antilles, Porto Rico is a beautiful place, with its deeply wooded mountains, fertile plains, and rich tropical vegetation. As in other islands of the West Indies, you might find the climate on the lowlands a little too warm for comfort. Also, like the other islands of the region, there is a good deal of rain on the eastern side, for the northeast trade winds, which blow most of the year, bring much moisture from the Atlantic Ocean.

Porto Rico is one of the West Indies in which the production of sugar has increased rapidly. The sugar exports today are worth more than all the others put together. The people raise tobacco and make many cigars and cigarettes. Coffee and cotton, fruits, and vegetables are produced. The fruits and vegetables can be raised during the winter, and we are glad to get them in our city markets at a time of the year when farmers in most of our states cannot raise such products.

Our government has done many things to help Porto Rico since it came into our possession. Good schools help to make good citizens, so one of the first things we did was to build schoolhouses and hire good teachers to go there. We helped the people also to build roads and railroads.

The capital of Porto Rico, San Juan, is situated on the north side of the island, and Ponce, the largest city, is on the south. A railroad running around the western shore of the island now connects these two places.

THE LESSER ANTILLES

This group of the West Indies is a chain of small islands, like stepping-stones, extending from Porto Rico to South America. Most of them belong to the British, though the French and the Dutch own a few.

Near the northern end of the group are the Virgin Islands. We are more interested in these than in any other of the Lesser Antilles. In 1916, we bought from Denmark three of the Virgin group — St. Croix, St. Thomas, and St. John. We paid Denmark twenty-five million dollars for these three little islands, which, like so many others in the West Indies, are the tops of mountains rising above the water. On the coastal lowlands made from the soil from the hills, there are many farms where good crops of sugar and cotton are raised.

The Virgin Islands have long been famous for the production of bay rum. The finest quality and the greatest quantity made in any country came from these little islands. Thousands of gallons were made each year from the shining leaves of the bay tree and shipped to the United States, Great Britain, and other countries.

FIG 188. This is the beautiful harbor of St. Thomas on St. Thomas Island, one of the Virgin Islands. Why is the possession of such a harbor in this locality of great value to the United States? (Courtesy of the Brown Bros.)

It was not their beautiful scenery, the bay rum, or any other product which induced the United States to buy these islands. It was rather because of their position. St. Thomas, the southernmost island, has one of the finest harbors in all tropical America, and more important than this is the fact that it lies on the route from Europe to the Panama Canal. Having built this Canal, it was necessary that we have somewhere, not too far away from it, a place from which it might be defended in case we should be at war with any nation. At St. Thomas, we have a fine harbor where our vessels may remain in safety and where we may accumulate coal and other supplies.

Let us hope, however, that there may be no more wars. War tears down, destroys, ruins industries, despoils homes, and lays waste forests and farms. In times of peace, nations can improve their schools, develop their industries, increase their trade, get acquainted with one another, and thus become firmer friends and better neighbors. As we are one of the strongest nations in the world, our attitude toward all the great problems which the world is facing will greatly influence weaker nations. It rests with you boys and girls what kind of an influence ours shall be. Will you try to make it a helpful one?

SUGGESTIONS FOR STUDY

I

1. Position and formation of the Bahamas.
2. Products of the Bahamas.
3. San Salvador and Nassau.
4. The Greater Antilles.
5. Importance and size of Cuba.
6. Cuba under Spain and the United States.
7. Products of Cuba.
8. The great city of Habana.
9. Jamaica and its chief city, Kingston.
10. The Republic of Haiti and Port au Prince.
11. The Dominican Republic and its capital city.

12. Porto Rico.
13. San Juan and Ponce.
14. Position and ownership of the Lesser Antilles.
15. The Virgin Islands.

II

1. Look up manganese and find its uses. Where is it produced?
2. Why do you think that the railroad in Porto Rico from Ponce to San Juan was built around the western shore of the island instead of across the interior?
3. Vasco da Gama, a Portuguese, expected to reach India from Europe by sailing eastward around the world. Columbus, with the same object in view, sailed to the west. Which theory do you think was the more correct? Trace the routes of each of these explorers.
4. Why has the building of the Panama Canal increased the importance of the West Indies?
5. What possessions has the United States in the Pacific Ocean?

III

Make a list of the places mentioned in this chapter. Arrange them by countries, cities, mountains, rivers, etc. Be able to locate each place and tell what was said about it in the chapter.

GENERAL REVIEW

1. Find in the appendix of your textbook the names of the ten highest mountain peaks of North America. How many of these are in Alaska? In Canada? In Mexico? In the United States? On an outline map of North America show the system in which each is located and the position of the peak.
2. Find the eight longest rivers in North America. In which country is the longest one? Sketch a map of each river, showing the direction in which it flows, the water into which it discharges, and the chief cities located on it.
3. Name the largest city of each country of North America. Find the names of the twenty largest cities of North America. How many of these are located in some country other than the United States? Name a feature for which each city is famous.
4. Write or be able to name the states in each natural region of the United States. Name their capitals. Do the same with the provinces of Canada.
5. Sketch a map of the Great Lakes. Show on it the chief lake ports in the United States and Canada.
6. Name all the bodies of water on which you would sail in going from Duluth, Minnesota, to New York City.
7. What countries in North America are republics? Describe the government of the others.
8. What parts of the British Commonwealth lie in or around North America? What possessions of the United States? What other nations have possessions in the New World?
9. On an outline map of North America, write the names of the following products in the areas most noted for them:

Asbestos	Cotton	Lumber	Sugar
Cattle	Dried fruits	Nickel	Tobacco
Coal	Furs	Petroleum	Turpentine
Codfish	Gold	Salmon	Wheat
Copper	Iron	Sheep	Wool
Corn	Lead	Silver	Zinc